CRITICAL ACCLAIM FOR ROBIN LEE HATCHER— WINNER OF THE *ROMANTIC TIMES* STORYTELLER OF THE YEAR AWARD!

"*Midnight Rose* is a thrilling tale of high adventure....If you like passion mixed with intrigue, humor, and danger, you'll love *Midnight Rose!*"

—*Affaire de Coeur*

"With *Devlin's Promise,* Robin Lee Hatcher fulfills her promise to deliver great romance to her legion of fans!"

—*Romantic Times*

"Tenderness and passion are Ms. Hatcher's hallmarks!"

—*Romantic Times*

"*Promised Sunrise* is a wonderful tribute to the brave men and women who had the courage to travel West...filled with compassion, realism, and love!"

—*Romantic Times*

"Robin Lee Hatcher writes a fast-paced story with much intrigue, romance and adventure. She draws her characters so well, the reader hates to say good-bye to them!"

—*Affaire de Coeur*

BELOVED BETRAYER

"Damian...what's wrong?"

"What's wrong?" he echoed Cassandra. "Isn't it obvious what's wrong?" He glanced over his shoulder. "I never meant to let this happen, Cassandra."

Clutching the sheet against her naked breasts, she slid toward him, reaching out with one hand to take hold of his arm. "I wanted it as much as you."

He laughed sharply. "You couldn't have known what you wanted. You were a virgin."

"Damian? Look at me."

He turned his head.

"Damian, I...." She swallowed the lump in her throat, then moistened her dry lips with the tip of her tongue. "I love you."

"When I've told you the truth, Cassandra Jamison, you'll forget that you ever spoke those words to me."

The Magic

Robin Lee Hatcher

LEISURE BOOKS ■ **NEW YORK CITY**

A LEISURE BOOK®

April 1993

Published by

Dorchester Publishing Co., Inc.
276 Fifth Avenue
New York, NY 10001

Copyright © 1993 by Robin Lee Hatcher

Printed in the United States of America.

To Darlene, Libby,
Judith, and Stella

★

You know why.
Thanks.

The Magic

Prologue

London, 1696

The boy heard the sniffles and sobs coming from other rooms in the dark, boarded-up building. He'd been listening to the sounds for about four days, and as he'd done more than once during the endless hours, he wished he could cry, too. Not so much for himself, but for his father. He couldn't imagine the great sea captain closed up in a place like this, shut away from fresh winds and billowing sails.

But no matter how bad things became, no matter how dark and hopeless things might look, his father would never approve of his twelve-year-old son giving in to tears, and so the boy didn't cry. Someday, when both he and his father were free, he would tell the story of

11

these days of captivity, and his father would slap him on the back and tell him how proud he was. Someday . . .

He felt something brush against his leg. He scrambled to his feet and kicked sharply.

Rats! How he hated the bloody creatures. They were always sneaking up on him in the dark, trying to bite him, slapping his bare feet with their skinny tails.

Well, they could bloody well find something else to chew on. He wasn't about to be their supper.

The sudden movement left him feeling lightheaded. He'd had nothing to eat except some stale bread and brackish water since being brought to this place. Just thinking about food made his mouth water and his stomach growl.

A door creaked open behind him, spilling a stream of yellow lamplight across the straw-covered floor. He turned around, shielding his eyes against the unaccustomed brightness.

"Is that 'im, m'lord?" the one holding the lantern asked.

"Yes. That's him. See that he's taken aboard the *Seadog* tonight."

Rage blinded the boy as he recognized the hated voice. He lunged toward the doorway. "You bloody bastard! I'll kill you for what you did to my father."

A wicked blow to the side of his head knocked him back into the filthy straw.

"Behave yourself, boy, or you'll find yourself keeping your father company in Newgate." The man rubbed his hands together, as if wiping them clean. "I'm surprised he didn't teach you better manners. A boy should know how to speak to his betters."

The boy shook his head, trying to rid his ears of the dull ringing sound. He blinked as he braced himself on his elbows and glared up toward the black silhouette in the doorway. "You're not my better. You're a liar and a thief. When I get free, I'll prove my father's innocence and then you'll—"

Sharp laughter cut into his angry tirade. "You're a bigger fool than your father, boy. It would take a miracle to prove he's not a traitor." Again the low chuckle. "And it would take a magician to escape the place I'm sending you." The man backed out of the doorway, his laughter lingering in the stale air of the room.

"I'm not wrong!" the boy shouted as the door slammed shut. "I'll be back. I swear by my father's honor, I'll be back!"

Chapter One

Atlantic Ocean, April 1714

Cassandra Jamison leaned against the rail and
turned her face into the fine, salty mist that
flew up the ship's sides as the merchantman
cut through the rolling Atlantic. She smiled,
relishing the feel of the deck beneath her feet,
the sun and spray on her face. Despite her
trepidations over what awaited her at the end
of the voyage, Cassandra couldn't help enjoying the journey itself. The first three weeks had
flown by beneath mostly cloudless skies, with
good winds and steady seas. Not once had she
been seasick. In truth, she'd never felt better in
her life.

"Ah, there's my sweet little sailor."

She turned as her uncle walked toward her

across the forecastle deck.

A tall, still handsome man in his early fifties, Farley Dunworthy, Baron Kettering, wore a full-bottomed wig over what Cassandra knew was a mostly bald scalp. His blue eyes—lighter than her own, more like her mother's—watched her with an affectionate gleam. He was fashionably attired in a long coat and waistcoat and wore scarlet silk stockings drawn over his knees and gartered below. Diamond rings adorned three of the fingers on his left hand, two on his right.

One would never guess that the family coffers have been in peril, she thought as she rose on tiptoe to kiss his cheek. But she didn't begrudge him his rich attire. Her uncle was an important man, a peer of the realm. The Baron Kettering couldn't be expected to appear as a pauper just because the family was experiencing some difficult times. And now, with the marriage settlement collected from Aldin Abernathy, those times would soon be behind them.

But she didn't want to think about Mr. Abernathy. The day was too beautiful to be spoiled.

"Good day, Uncle Far." She motioned toward the water. "Isn't it splendid? I should have insisted that you take me sailing long ago. I've never felt so wonderful in all my life. If only I'd known."

" 'Tis splendid, indeed, my dear. You know, before my brother Gregory died and I inherited his title, I used to captain the *Peacock* myself. I was rather successful in trade, I might add. I grew fond of sailing to foreign ports." He chuckled as he gazed affectionately at his niece. "I've never seen a girl as taken with the ocean as you are. If you'd been born a boy, I would have made you a captain of one of my ships when you were older."

"I'm one and twenty. Isn't that old enough? Perhaps you should teach me to captain a ship despite my being female."

Farley chuckled. " 'Tis not likely there's a man aboard who would follow your orders, Cassandra. They'd all be too busy trying to steal a kiss from you. You're far too pretty to think about doing a man's job." He turned his gaze out across the water. "No, 'tis better you marry well and provide some male heirs to inherit Tate Shipping when I'm gone. 'Tis bad enough there'll be no one to inherit my title."

Cassandra frowned. She'd been trying her best *not* to think of marriage or heirs. She would be forced to think of all that when they reached America. They were only a few weeks away from the Carolinas, where her betrothed, Aldin Abernathy, awaited her arrival in Charleston.

She saw Farley's eyes narrow and followed the direction of his gaze. At first, all she could see was the blue of the sky touching the green-black curve of the sea. She was about to ask what was wrong when he spoke.

"Do you see her?"

She squinted her eyes as he had done. "No."

"There." He pointed.

At first, she shook her head. And then she did

think she saw something. It was a mere dot in the distance. "What is it?" she asked.

"Another ship. I thought I saw her yesterday, but I couldn't be sure. She's closer today. I think she may be following us."

"Is it an English ship?"

"I don't know. She's too far out to tell."

Cassandra peered harder, as if that would bring the ship into focus.

Farley turned away from the rail. "I think I'd best talk to the captain. Perhaps you should return to your cabin."

"But why?" She glanced at her uncle, surprised. " 'Tis so far away. What possible danger could it be to us?"

"I don't want to alarm you, my dear, but she could be a pirate vessel."

"A pirate vessel?" Cassandra looked back across the ocean, her pulse quickening slightly. "But surely they wouldn't bother a ship sailing under the English flag?"

"Pirates respect no flags, and they have no loyalties," Farley responded, his voice grave. He paused a moment longer, then walked toward the stern.

Despite her uncle's warning, Cassandra didn't return to her cabin. Instead, the wind blowing wisps of pale blond hair around her face, she made her way back to the quarterdeck, keeping her gaze all the while upon the small dot near the horizon.

Cassandra had never been a girl given to the vapors. Perhaps it was because she'd seen her mother use the ploy too often through the years. Regina Dunworthy Jamison was famous for taking to her bed whenever life became too difficult. Cassandra had sworn never to do the same. She had little patience for such silly theatrics. She'd always thought it made much more sense to face one's fears head on.

Even so, she felt a strange tremor as she considered the possibility that her uncle's ship might be overtaken by pirates. Never once in her sheltered life had she imagined that she might come so close to danger as this. It was just a bit frightening—and exhilarating at the same time.

" 'Tis not who the master thinks it is, milady."

Cassandra gasped as she whirled toward the voice. The one-eyed sailor known as Mouse grinned, revealing the wide spot where several teeth should have been.

She tried to still her racing heart. "And how would you know who my uncle thinks it is?" she asked, surprise making her tone uncharacteristically haughty.

"I been wi' Master Dunworthy fer nigh on eighteen years. Ever since 'e took over Tate Shipping. I sailed under 'im in the early years when 'e captained the *Peacock*, before 'e become a lord 'n' all." His grin disappeared, and his voice lowered a notch. "I've come t'know 'ow yer uncle thinks. Better than ye, I reckon."

Cassandra frowned at the little man, uncertain how to respond. It wasn't that he was a stranger to her. She couldn't remember a time when he hadn't been coming and going from Kettering Hall, doing her uncle's bidding. She knew he was more than just a sailor, though why Uncle Far would turn the rough-looking, one-eyed man into a sort of secretary, she didn't know. Judging by his poor speech, she was certain he could neither read nor write. She couldn't begin to guess what possible help he could be to Tate Shipping.

Now, as he stood before her, watching her with a knowing glint in his lone eye, he made her feel . . . well, as if he could read her mind. She didn't like it. She didn't like it by half.

As the curtain of night fell over the Atlantic, Damian stood near the bow and stared toward the west. He heard the sucking of the wash around the hull, the whipping of great clouds of canvas overhead, the creaking of the blocks. Below, the bow wash piled high, then swept past in a blur of eddies and green waves that crashed together before shattering into a frothy wake. The *Magic* seemed as set upon her course as he was. It was almost as if the ship were a part of him. Perhaps she was.

He could still see the silhouette of the *Peacock* on the horizon, outlined by the last golden rays of day. How deceptively far away she looked.

But not far enough to save her.

Damian had given orders to his men just an hour ago. They would proceed through the night under full sail. The *Magic* was one of the fastest three-masted square-riggers to traverse the seas, and her crew was a seasoned one. They knew how to coax extra speed out of her unfurled sails. They would have no trouble catching up with a merchant ship with a belly filled with cargo.

And what a cargo. Tea. Oriental silks. Spices. Porcelains. Such merchandise would bring a high price from the colonists in America. It would bring great wealth to the men who delivered such wares to the buyers.

And the loss of such a fortune in freight would bring great hardship to the one who lost it.

He smiled grimly. Aye, they would have no problem overtaking the *Peacock*. Damian planned to surprise her at dawn.

He turned, sensing a movement behind him. Oliver, his lieutenant, was crossing the deck with quick strides.

"Is everything ready?" Damian asked as the other man drew near.

"Aye. 'Tis ready." Oliver's brows drew together to form a single line of worry. "Sink me, but I ain't sure 'tis such a good plan, Damian. About the young lady, I mean."

"I didn't ask for your opinion."

"No, sir. That you didn't."

Damian glared at his lieutenant, waiting for him to continue. Oliver had never been one to keep his thoughts to himself. Damian knew better than to expect his friend to start now.

" 'Twould seem to me that the *Peacock*'s cargo should be enough. Dunworthy's never risked so much on one voyage. He's stripped his ship of all but fifteen of her cannon. She's manned by fewer than a hundred, and them not of much worth. And 'tis not *us* they'll be expecting. We ain't never yet had such an easy task set before us."

Damian raised an eyebrow. "And?"

"Ain't it enough that Dunworthy'll bear the loss? Must we take Miss Jamison, too?"

"Yes." There was a warning in the hard tone of Damian's voice.

"She's a hardly more than a green girl. She's naught to do with Tate Shipping, and you can't hold her accountable for what Dunworthy's done." He paused, then added, "From what I've heard, she's an innocent lass."

Damian's jaw tensed, but in no other way did he reveal his surge of anger. "And which of his victims *wasn't* innocent? Wasn't Mouse innocent when Dunworthy cost him his eye? What about Professor? And what of you, Oliver? What of your innocence?" His harsh gaze flicked to the ragged scar that stretched the length of Oliver's face. "Do you remember what he did to you?" He turned toward the horizon once again. "She'll come to no harm. We'll be doing no more than her own uncle had planned for her. Most likely, she'll be better cared for by us than she would have been by the crew of the *Guinevere*. Once we've received the ransom, she can be returned to her intended, none the worse for wear."

The lieutenant was silent for a long time before replying. "As you say, captain." Oliver was only marginally successful at disguising his disapproval. Finally, when the ship's master remained silent, Oliver turned and walked away.

Damian listened as his lieutenant's departing footsteps faded into the sounds of the sea, all thoughts of Farley Dunworthy's niece fading with them. He refused to think of anything except the sweet taste of revenge. Already he was savoring the look of surprise on Farley's face when the pirate captain of the *Magic* boarded the merchant ship tomorrow at dawn.

Farley leaned back in his chair and lifted the glass of port to his lips. He sipped it slowly, enjoying the rich flavor as he rolled the liquid over his tongue before allowing it to trickle down his throat. As he did so, the tension began to ease from him.

The *Guinevere* was to have arrived two days before. He'd begun to fear that the disreputable captain of that questionable vessel had absconded with his funds. He'd worried that his plans were going awry. While Abernathy's marriage settlement had gone a long way toward clearing his debts, Farley needed a great deal more to completely overcome his recent losses.

His fingers tightened around the glass as he thought of the constant reports of pirates that had plagued Tate Shipping in the past three years. Time and again, his ships had returned to England, their holds empty, their captains telling tales of a swift vessel called the *Magic* that struck from out of nowhere and the buccaneer chieftain who bade them give his regards to Farley Dunworthy even as his men plundered the ships of everything of value.

Thank heaven Abernathy's proposal had arrived when it did. And thank heaven his niece was such a level-headed girl. When he'd explained to her how close to ruin they were and that her father and mother would end up penniless and homeless, she'd seen that there was little else for her to do but accept Abernathy's offer of marriage.

He sipped more port, then shook his head a bit sadly.

He would miss Cassandra. She was as close to a child of his own as he would ever know, and she'd always shown him great affection. True, he didn't think too highly of Abernathy. He suspected the man had a rather nasty temper and was given to over-indulgence in strong drink. But he was rich and he wanted Cassandra enough to pay dearly for her. Those were his two most important qualities. The only ones that mattered to Farley.

He hadn't hesitated in accepting Abernathy's offer. As far as he was concerned, the end always justified the means.

*   *   *

Cassandra tossed restlessly in her bed, her dreams haunted by visions of weddings and pirate ships. One dream melded into another, neither of them making sense. She was grateful when she awakened abruptly.

She sat up, drawing her knees close to her chest as she wrapped her arms around her shins. She tried to forget her dreams but was unsuccessful. Mr. Abernathy seemed determined to invade her thoughts, whether waking or sleeping.

She didn't want to marry this virtual stranger, a man twenty years her senior whom she'd met only once, a man who lived across a vast ocean, away from her parents, her home, and everything she loved. But what else could she have done once Uncle Far explained things to her? She couldn't let her parents be thrown into debtors prison, could she? Was it so terrible a sacrifice? Perhaps she would learn to love Mr. Abernathy. Perhaps . . .

"But you don't love him, Cassandra." Her mother's voice drifted to her from the past.

"I'll learn to love him."

Regina's faded blue eyes reflected great pain. "You should love the man you marry. You should feel a grand passion for him."

"Your marriage was arranged, Mama, and it turned out well."

"Yes," her mother replied, her voice as soft as a sigh. *"My marriage was arranged."*

Remembering the wistful look that had

crossed Regina's face threatened to bring tears to Cassandra's eyes now, just as it had then.

A grand passion. It was what she'd always wanted, always dreamed of. It was why she'd turned down earlier offers of marriage. She'd been waiting to fall desperately in love. She'd wanted to marry according to her heart. She hadn't wanted to *learn* to love, to be merely content. She'd wanted more. Much more.

She swallowed the hot lump in her throat. It did no good to think of such things. She had her duty to her family to think about. Uncle Far wouldn't have asked this of her if there'd been any other way. Her parents and her uncle had always given her everything her heart desired. They had never failed her. She owed them too much to fail them now.

Slipping out of her bunk, she padded across the room on bare feet to the porthole and stared out into the night. Moonlight danced across the surface of an ink-black ocean, sparkling across the crests of the waves as they rolled toward the horizon.

Then she remembered her other dream, the one about the pirate ship. She recalled the vile captain of her dreams. He was fat and dirty, as all pirates were, no doubt. He wore a brace of pistols on his hips and had a bloody sword stuck through his belt. He swaggered and used foul language and threatened to use her in some unspeakable fashion.

She shivered, wondering if the ship her uncle

had seen was truly a pirate ship. Then she scurried back to her bunk and snuggled beneath the blankets, seeking warmth and security and more pleasant dreams.

Chapter Two

At dawn, the *Magic* slid smoothly into position alongside the *Peacock*'s starboard beam without a single alarm being sounded.

"Now," Damian said in a calm voice.

The British ensign fluttered down from the mast. The *Magic*'s distinctive standard rose in its place, the black flag snapping smartly in the crisp morning wind.

Damian heard shouts from the other ship, and he knew they'd only just discovered it was not the *Guinevere* that had joined them. Pandemonium broke out aboard the *Peacock* as her officers and crewmen realized they had been fooled and their lives could be forfeit because of it. But it was too late for them now, and they knew it.

Muskets were fired into the air—a precautionary warning—as the crew of the *Magic* began to board its prey. The men of the *Peacock* surrendered with only minor resistance. Within a matter of minutes, the merchant ship and everything on it belonged to Damian and his crew.

Damian waited aboard his ship until all weapons had been confiscated and Farley Dunworthy had been brought on deck. Then he grabbed a rope and swung across the gap between the two ships, landing just a few feet from the owner of Tate Shipping.

Damian removed his tricornered hat and swept a deep bow toward the man he hated beyond anyone or anything else. "Baron Kettering, 'tis a pleasure to see you, my lord. I was beginning to despair that we should ever meet."

Farley, his wig askew and his lace cravat untied, glared at him with a show of bravado. "What do you want? Why have you boarded my ship?" His glance darted out to sea, scanning the water with a look of desperation.

"If you look for the *Guinevere*, you're wasting your time, sir. The ship developed . . . problems, shall we say, and had to turn back to England for repairs."

The baron turned a sickly shade of white.

"You *were* expecting her, weren't you? A shame you told your crew not to fire on us, but how were you to know we would replace the *Guinevere*? Ships can look so much alike, can they not?"

"Just who are you?"

"I'm the captain of the *Magic*."

"The *Magic* . . ." Farley whispered the name with a note of dread.

Damian laughed—a cold, mirthless sound—enjoying this toying with the enemy. "Ah, so you *have* heard of me. I was hoping your captains had given you my greetings, but one can never be sure when trusting messages to others."

"Heard of you?" Farley exclaimed. "You've bloody well near ruined me!"

Damian clucked his tongue. "Ruined you? My, my. Surely that cannot be true. Tate Shipping has been sailing the seas for nearly three decades. How could my men and I make such a difference in so little time?" He stepped closer to the baron and looked down at him. "Surely I couldn't ruin you in only three years. It would take all the sport out of it."

Farley's face went from pale to scarlet.

"So . . . you're beginning to understand at last. Aye, my lord, 'tis only *your* ships—and yours alone—which I seek. 'Tis why so many in London are beginning to think you mad. They *do* think you mad, don't they, my lord? Or is it simply that they think you've made stupid mistakes and are lying to protect yourself?" Damian smiled slowly. "Either way, things are becoming difficult for you in England, are they not?"

"You cannot get away with this . . ." the baron began.

"Cannot?" Damian raised an eyebrow. "It

seems to me that I *have* gotten away with it."

"Beggin' your pardon, sir." Oliver appeared at Damian's side. He wore an odd expression on his face, part amused, part perplexed. "If I might have a word with you."

Damian glanced back at the owner of the *Peacock*, his smile disappearing. "Put the baron with the rest of his crew," he said briskly to the two men holding Farley's arms. After watching them disappear through the hatch, he turned toward his lieutenant. "What is it, Oliver?"

" 'Tis the lady. Seems she don't welcome our company. Sink me if she ain't locked her cabin door to keep us out."

"Locked the door against a band of pirates?" Damian's grin returned. "How resourceful of her."

Cassandra listened to the sound of pillaging as it filtered through her door.

She had just begun her morning toilet when the musketfire had alerted her to trouble. She'd known without being told that they were about to be boarded by pirates. It was as if her dreams were coming true. She hadn't wasted any time in locking the door to her cabin. Then, just to be certain, she'd barred it with a chair— the only thing in her cabin that wasn't nailed down—tilting it up on its back legs and pressing it against the door beneath the latch.

The barricade seemed to be working, too. Several times, someone had tried to open the door, then moved on when they'd found it locked.

"What's t'become of us, Miss Cassandra?" her lady's maid asked plaintively.

"The shiftless bounders want only what is easily taken," she answered, hoping her words would help to bolster her own courage as well as to reassure the nervous girl cowering nearby.

It worked, too. She did feel better. So much so that she tried to think of a few more insults about the rabble outside her cabin door. With each passing minute, she felt more confident that they would escape either discovery or harm. She only hoped her uncle and the crew were faring as well as she and her abigail.

With a sudden crash and the sound of splintering wood, her cabin door burst open. Pieces of the chair slid across the floor, one of them landing near her foot.

Cassandra squealed as she flattened herself against the wall behind her. The back of her right hand covered her mouth to stifle any further sound. Her courage shattered, she waited for the pirate who had invaded her dreams the night before.

The intruder had to bend his head forward to be able to step through the fractured doorway. At first she was only aware of his black hair, thick and shiny and tied back with a ribbon at the nape. Then, as he straightened, she was overwhelmed by the sheer size of him. Well above six feet, his loose-fitting white shirt and snug black breeches revealed the great breadth of his shoulders and the bulging muscles of his arms and thighs.

He wasn't fat or dirty. He wore neither a brace of pistols or a bloody sword, nor had he swaggered and threatened her with foul language as the corsair of her nightmares had done—yet!

But when she looked at his face, she found him far more frightening than anything she'd imagined. His jaw and chin were covered with a black beard, hiding his features as effectively as a mask would have done. But it didn't hide his eyes.

They were the black eyes of a demon, and his look stole what was left of her breath away. As dark as his hair, his eyes seemed to bore through her, icy cold and without feeling.

"Miss Jamison, I presume." He swept the floor with his tricornered hat as he offered a bow. "A pleasure to meet you."

Never had she heard words that rang less true. She felt certain he was mocking her.

"I am Captain Damian of the *Magic*."

Her mouth and throat went dry as she continued to stare wordlessly at him.

"I'd be obliged if you would accompany me above deck." His gaze flicked toward Cassandra's maid, who had pressed herself into one corner of the cabin. "You may remain here, miss."

Cassandra swallowed. "What do you want with me?" she asked in a raspy voice.

He bowed slightly once again as he motioned with his arm toward the door. "After you."

"Where . . . where is . . ." She swallowed. "Where is my uncle?"

"*Please*, Miss Jamison." Although the words themselves were courteous, there was no mistaking the command in his tone of voice.

The last shreds of her courage disappeared. Glancing down at the floor, Cassandra crossed the cabin with hurried steps, making a wide arc around him as she moved into the passageway. He followed close behind her, so close she would have sworn she could feel the heat of his body.

Everything came to an abrupt halt on the main deck as the brigands ceased their looting. Voices were silenced. Even the breeze seemed to fall silent. Cassandra could feel the men staring at her; it was almost like a physical touch. She refused to meet any of their eyes. Instead, she set her gaze on a distant spot on the horizon, her chin lifted defiantly, her hands folded before her.

"Now there's a fine filly if ever I seen one," someone muttered nearby. "I wouldn't mind a tumble with the likes o' her."

"Mr. Binns!"

The sharp command caused her to stop and turn. If the captain's eyes had seemed cold before, they were ten times so now.

A young man, not much older than Cassandra, stepped forward. He swept his knitted cap from his head. "Beggin' your pardon, miss," he mumbled. "I meant no disrespect."

She didn't know how to reply. She was surrounded by outlaws and cutthroats, at the mercy of a demon captain, and yet there one of the pirates stood, as red-faced as a schoolboy, apologizing to her. Nervously, she glanced toward Captain Damian, only to find him looking elsewhere. She followed his gaze down the length of the ship.

A slender man, clad in blue breeches and a striped shirt, was walking toward them. Cassandra flinched as he drew closer, unable to look away from the hideous scar that ran along the right side of his face. His brown eyes met hers briefly, then returned to the captain.

"The captives are secured, captain."

"Good. See Miss Jamison onto the *Magic*."

Cassandra gasped. "You don't mean to take me off this ship?"

The captain turned to face her. He stared at her with his harsh gaze for several breathless heartbeats, and then, incredibly, he smiled. "I assure you, Miss Jamison. That is exactly what I intend to do."

Damian watched the blood drain from her face, and he wondered if she were going to faint. She seemed to stagger slightly; he reached forward to help balance her, but she jerked away from him the instant his fingers touched her elbow.

"What have you done with my uncle?" she demanded, forcing new strength into her voice.

"He's unharmed."

"I want to see him."

Damian shook his head. "That would be impossible. Oliver, show her to her cabin."

"I won't go." She whirled away, and her intent was obvious.

Damian grabbed her arm before she could take more than two quick steps away from him, spinning her to face him. He scowled, his voice low with warning. "I suggest you not try to do that again, Miss Jamison. I tolerate no mutiny on my ships."

Her dark blue eyes widened. Her heart-shaped mouth formed a small "O" as she stared up at him. Despite himself, he felt a stab of guilt as he returned her gaze. She truly looked the innocent pawn Oliver had said she was.

As quickly as the thought came to him, he pushed it aside, anger replacing it. This girl was Farley Dunworthy's niece. That was enough to justify what he intended to do.

"Come with me." His grasp on her arm tightened.

She braced herself, refusing to budge. "What do you intend to do with me?"

What *did* he intend to do?

An answer eluded him as he realized Binns was right. She was a fine filly if ever he'd seen one. Her silvery-blond hair, still tossed and tumbled from her night's sleep, fell like a cloud around the shoulders of her pale pink dressing gown. The features of her face were delicately formed, her nose tip-tilted, her mouth a soft shade of rose, her complexion like fresh cream. And there was spirit in the depths of her indigo eyes. This was no missish female who would swoon at the slightest confrontation. He'd like to taste her lips and see if they were as sweet as they promised. He'd like to . . .

She kicked him in the shin.

Caught by surprise, he roared in pain. "God's blood, woman!"

She pulled free of him and was off and running, her skirts lifted almost to her knees, headed toward her uncle's cabin. As if she could escape him on board a ship. The little fool!

Damian swore loudly, his black gaze sweeping the deck. His men turned away from his glare, busying themselves with gathering their booty and pretending they were both deaf and blind to what had transpired between the lady and their captain. Surprisingly, he heard no chuckles, but he knew they were laughing all the same. He wasn't enjoying the joke.

Still muttering curses, he set out after his rebellious captive.

"Uncle Far! Help me, Uncle Far!"

Cassandra jerked the door to her uncle's cabin open, but it was empty. She'd known it would be, but still she'd hoped.

Her gaze swept the room. It had been stripped bare of all valuables. Papers were strewn across the floor. The bedding had been peeled from the bunk and the mattress slit open. Violence seemed to pervade the cabin.

"Uncle Far," she whispered helplessly.

Hide! her mind screamed at her. *Find someplace to hide before it's too late!*

Her heart hammering loudly in her ears, she turned to obey her instincts, but it was already too late. Her way was blocked.

The captain's massive frame filled the small doorway. "He's in the hold, Miss Jamison, and unless you want the same fate aboard the *Magic*, I suggest you cooperate." The cold anger in his voice smote her like a physical blow.

She had heard the whispered tales of indignities forced upon women captured by pirates. She wasn't about to become one of them without some sort of fight.

"Stay away from me," she warned.

He stepped into the room, seeming to fill it completely, taking away any avenue of escape.

In a panic, she kicked at him again, but this time she missed.

"By thunder, woman!" he shouted. "I've had enough!"

With a quick sweep of his arm, he picked her up and tossed her over his shoulder, her head hanging against his back. Long strides carried them back to the deck.

"Put me down!" she demanded. She pounded her fists against his back and kicked her feet. "Put me down, I say!"

"Silence or I'll have you gagged."

She fell still, not doubting for a moment that he would do exactly as he threatened.

Laughter, loud and raucous, erupted all

around her. She raised her head, but she couldn't see through the thick veil of hair that tumbled over her face. To tell the truth, she was glad she couldn't see them. She would prefer to think this was all just a terrible nightmare.

When she glanced down again, she saw that her captor was standing on the railing of the ship. Her breath caught in her throat as they suddenly flew out over the ocean, then the air escaped her lungs in a rush when his feet once more touched the deck of a ship.

A pirate ship. She was on board a pirate ship. She was the prisoner of the devil himself. She was helpless to defend herself against him. With his bare hands, he could break her in two. God help her, what was she to do?

She heard a door crash open. A moment later, she was dropped ignobly onto a bunk. She scrambled to her knees as she swept her hair back from her face.

He stood before her, his legs braced apart, glaring down at her as if she were a cockroach he was about to crush beneath his boot.

"You needn't have any fear of me, Miss Jamison," he said in a voice filled with disdain. "You have nothing I want."

With those words, he turned and left the cabin. She heard a key turn in the lock, then listened to his fading footsteps as he walked away. Finally, there was nothing left to hear but the muffled sounds of the pirates as they completed the ransacking of the *Peacock*.

For the first time in her life, Cassandra was

completely and utterly alone with no one else to turn to for help.

She glanced around the tiny, windowless cabin, the walls so close there seemed no room left for enough air to breathe. How long did he mean to keep her locked in here?

You needn't have any fear of me, Miss Jamison. You have nothing I want.

She wondered if what he'd said were true. And if not, how would she save herself from him?

Fear thick in her throat, she sat back and waited for whatever would happen next.

Chapter Three

Cassandra jumped at the sound of a key turning in the lock. She had been waiting for hours for the captain's return. She'd imagined him doing a hundred different horrible and unspeakable things. She'd wondered if he would kill her when he was finished with her or leave her alive to suffer further indignities.

Now he was here, and the time for wondering was past. She rose from the bed and pushed her hair back behind her shoulders, holding her head high. She wasn't about to let this buccaneer see that she was afraid of him. She would stare him in the eye and refuse to crumble. He might ravish her body, but he would not break her. Cassandra Jamison was made of sterner stuff.

The door opened, but it wasn't the captain who waited on the other side. Instead, a slight fellow—not much taller than she was—with a thatch of yellow hair and round glasses perched on his beak-like nose stepped into her cabin. He was dressed in a long, black coat and maroon knee breeches. In his hands, he carried a tray. Delicious odors wafted from beneath the cloth that covered it. The smells made her stomach pinch, and she realized that she hadn't eaten since supper the night before.

"We thought you might be hungry, Miss Jamison," the fellow said as he set the tray on the table near the door. Turning around, he said, "Allow me to introduce myself. My name is Thomas Woodrow, but I'm called Professor by the crew of this vessel. I hope you will do the same." He glanced about the cabin. "Is there something else you need? I'll try to get it for you."

"I need off this ship. I need to return to my uncle."

He smiled apologetically, shaking his head. "I'm afraid that's the one thing I can't do for you." He shrugged. "Besides, we left the *Peacock* behind hours ago."

She'd long since guessed that was the case. She'd felt the movements of the ship and had known they were under full sail.

"Just who is this Captain Damian? Where is he taking me?" she asked.

"I'm not at liberty to say, but I can promise you'll come to no harm aboard the *Magic*. You

41

needn't be afraid. The captain is an honorable man. He'll tolerate nothing less from his crew."

"Honorable? He's a pirate. He's nothing but a common thief."

Professor shook his head. "You're wrong about him, Miss Jamison. It's not so simple as all that." He motioned toward the table. "Come and sit down. Our cook prepared something special just for you."

He pulled the bench out for her, and it was then that she noticed that three fingers were missing from his right hand. Only his thumb and little finger remained. He saw the direction of her gaze.

"The sea can be a harsh place," he said, as if in explanation, "and so can the men who sail it."

His words made her think of the dark and dangerous captain of the *Magic*. She wondered again what fate he had in store for her. Feeling her courage faltering, she stiffened her spine. She would not show fear.

Professor motioned toward the table. "Come and eat something, Miss Jamison, I beg of you. It will serve no purpose for you to go hungry."

Cassandra didn't know what to think of this man. He spoke with the voice and words of a gentleman. His clothes were clean and tidy. He certainly didn't resemble her idea of a plundering corsair. What was a man like him doing aboard a pirate vessel?

"When you've eaten, I have orders to take you up on deck for a stroll. As long as you cause no trouble, the captain has declared you may take the air three times a day."

Relief swelled in her chest, but she wasn't about to let Professor see it. "How very generous of the captain." Contempt dripped from her words.

" 'Tis what I thought. Very generous, indeed." He lifted an eyebrow. "Do I have your word that you'll do as you're told?"

She wanted to refuse the offer, but she was already suffering from the closeness of the cabin. She'd always hated being confined, and this small room with no windows was like one of her worst nightmares. If she didn't see a bit of blue sky and take in a breath of fresh air soon, she swore she would go mad.

"I'll cause you no trouble," she responded reluctantly, detesting her own weakness. She had capitulated so easily. She should have more pride, she told herself. She should fight harder.

"Good." He smiled, then headed for the door. "I'll return for you shortly."

Listening to the sound of the key turning in the lock once again, Cassandra swore that she would not succumb so easily next time.

"Damian?"

He looked up from his log book as Professor entered the captain's office that adjoined the great cabin.

"I'm sorry to trouble you, but I've come about Miss Jamison."

"What is it? Did she kick you, too?"

43

Professor grinned. "No. I think 'tis only you she wishes to harm physically."

"I doubt it not." Damian leaned back in his chair, waiting for his friend to continue.

"You seem to have forgotten something, Damian. You can't expect Miss Jamison to keep living in her nightrail. She needs her clothes and her hair brush and whatever other things a woman finds necessary to make her life civilized."

"Her trunk should be with the other booty. See that it's found and taken to her."

"And her cabin. Surely you could have put her elsewhere. There's hardly enough room for her to turn around in there."

"Would you have me put her in *my* quarters, Professor?"

Professor shrugged his shoulders. "Perhaps. I hadn't thought of that." He turned slowly, glancing through the doorway at the bed-chamber, letting his gaze take in every wall and corner of the great cabin. " 'Tis bigger, certainly, and more comfortable." His eyes returned to his captain. "Yes, I think she would do well in here."

Damian felt a jolt of anger. He pushed his chair away from the desk, rose, and walked to the gallery windows. Hands clasped behind his back, he stared down at the frothy trail left behind the ship, fighting all the while to control his rage.

"You forget that she's Dunworthy's niece," he said finally.

"But she isn't Dunworthy."

"He's treated her like she was his own daughter. How different can she be from the man who helped raise her?"

Professor stepped up beside him. "Perhaps we should find out," he answered gently.

"I have no wish to know anything more about Miss Jamison than I already do."

Even as he spoke the words, her image intruded in his head. Her silvery hair, like moonlight on the ocean. The gentle curves beneath the pink fabric of her dressing gown. The fear in her indigo eyes when she looked at him—and the enmity, too.

He set his jaw stubbornly. "She stays where she is."

"As you wish, captain," Professor responded.

A moment later, Damian heard his cabin door close. He let out a long sigh as he ran the fingers of one hand over his hair. What the devil was the matter with everyone? Had they all forgotten their plans? After what Farley had done to them, was a little inconvenience for that piece of muslin so terrible? She wasn't going to come to any harm. She wasn't going to die aboard this ship. As soon as they'd collected the ransom from Abernathy, they would send her to him. It was all very simple.

He turned away from the window, a scowl drawing his brows together as a vision in pink returned to haunt him.

Bloody hell! He wasn't doing anything her uncle hadn't planned to do. Farley was the one who had arranged to have his niece kidnapped by the motley crew of the *Guinevere*. Farley, driven by greed as usual, was the one who'd wanted to collect a ransom on top of the marriage settlement. Farley hadn't been concerned that his niece might come to any physical harm.

And if her own flesh and blood wasn't concerned, why should *he* be worrying about it?

With a sound of disgust, Damian stormed out of his cabin. Long, determined strides carried him quickly up to the poop deck. One glance at the captain's face, and the sailor at the helm quickly stepped aside.

Damian always found comfort in the feel of the wheel in his hands. He enjoyed the challenge of guiding a ship across the seas, whether the wind was at his back or fighting him every inch of the way. Above all, he valued the knowledge that it was *his* decision where to go. There was no one telling him what he must do. He was the captain of this ship. He was the captain of his own life.

The feel of the wind and sun on his face had just begun to sooth his foul mood when he saw Professor appear on the deck, Cassandra Jamison—still in her pink dressing gown—on his arm.

Cassandra drew in several deep breaths of fresh air. For just a moment, she forgot she was the captive of pirates and cutthroats. She only knew she was grateful for being allowed out of the tiny prison to which she'd been consigned.

Unable to help herself, she actually smiled at Professor.

" 'Tis the same way I feel about it," he said, as if they shared a secret.

She glanced away, not wanting to encourage a feeling of friendship between them. After all, he was as certainly her enemy as the captain of this vessel.

The captain . . .

She saw him at the helm. If not for his size, she wouldn't have recognized him. The full beard was gone, and for the first time she looked upon his surprisingly handsome features. He had a strong jawline with a square chin. His skin had been bronzed by the wind and sun. Heavy, dark brows capped his deep-set eyes.

His eyes . . .

Their gazes met across the length of the deck, and even from so far away, she could feel the power of his scrutiny. It was a look that kept her rooted to her spot.

What does he want from me? she wanted to ask, but her voice failed her.

"In a few weeks, your ordeal will be over," Professor said, answering her silent question. "We'll see that you're taken to your fiance in the Carolinas."

Cassandra gasped as she turned toward him. "How do you know of Mr. Abernathy?"

"He's to be contacted for your ransom, of course. We presumed, since you were on your way to marry him, that he would want it so."

Ransom? So that was why she'd been taken. They planned to collect a ransom. The answer satisfied her only briefly and then was followed by more questions.

What if Mr. Abernathy refused to pay a ransom? They weren't, after all, married. What if he decided she wasn't worth the cost? Surely there were other young women in Charleston whom he could marry with much less trouble and far less expense. What would these brigands do with her should Mr. Abernathy refuse to pay for her return?

She tried to ignore the sick knot that formed in the pit of her stomach, quickly offering arguments to her own questions. Of course Mr. Abernathy would pay the ransom. He had deemed her good enough to marry and of high enough worth to offer a substantial marriage settlement. Naturally, he would see to it that her ransom was paid and she was taken to him. He was not a heartless man who would cast her aside.

Was he?

No! He wasn't. Of course, he wasn't. Mr. Abernathy was . . . he was . . . Just what kind of man was her fiance?

But she had no answer. Only the same question.

What would Mr. Abernathy do about her ransom?

Nothing seemed quite so certain to her anymore. Just a few weeks ago, her life had been so orderly, so constant. Her world had revolved around the daily comings and goings of those closest to her—her father, her mother, and her uncle. She had known what to expect every morning when she'd awakened. If her life had lacked excitement, it had also lacked danger and fear. She had been content—or at least, *mostly* content.

But all certainty seemed to have been stripped away from the fabric of her life. She was surrounded by things heretofore unfamiliar to her. She'd never known men such as these. Nor did she know the man her uncle had arranged for her to wed. She didn't know what to expect from any of them.

Suddenly, it was all too much for her to bear.

"I think I should like to return to my cabin," she said softly, already fighting tears.

She turned and hurried down the steps before Professor could protest. Then, lifting her skirts to her ankles, she ran down the passageway until she reached her small cabin. Once inside, she dropped onto the bunk, buried her face in the pillow, and burst into tears.

Damian paused outside the cabin door and listened. He heard only silence, yet he knew Cassandra had spent much of the evening weeping. He knew because first Oliver and then Professor had told him.

It shouldn't matter to him. It was what any woman would do in the same circumstances. Her tears would be forgotten soon enough when she reached the colonies. She would only be his prisoner for a few more weeks. Her delicate sensibilities would not suffer any lasting effects. In fact, she would no doubt embellish her accounts and make an exciting tale of her weeks aboard the *Magic*.

Let her weep, he told himself as he turned to walk on by.

But something pulled him back. He turned the key in the lock and lifted the latch, then paused a moment.

What purpose would it serve for him to see her, to talk to her? None at all.

He pushed the door open before him.

She was lying on her side in her bunk, her pillow crushed against her chest, her knees pulled toward her body. Her silky hair fanned across the sheets. Her pink dressing gown had fallen open, revealing a length of white nightrail.

He stepped into the room as his gaze moved to her face.

It was easy to tell she'd been crying. Her eyes were puffy, her cheeks stained by tears. She looked considerably younger and more helpless than the defiant young woman who had kicked his leg only that morning.

With a quick glance, he took in the sparse surroundings of her cabin. Before becoming the captain of his own ship, he'd slept in smaller rooms than this. In fact, he'd felt lucky when he'd earned a cabin of his own. He'd spent many a month in the crew's quarters beneath the forecastle deck, crowded in with scores of other men.

He heard a startled gasp and turned once again toward the bunk.

Cassandra was upright on the bed, her feet tucked beneath her, the pillow still clutched to her chest. "What do you want?" she demanded hoarsely, eyes wide and frightened.

For a moment, he could only stare at her. It occurred to him that he'd never seen anyone as lovely before, despite the puffiness of her eyes and her disheveled hair. As he'd done that morning, he thought of kissing her mouth—a most inviting mouth, to be sure.

"If you harm me, you shall pay with your life," she warned, her brave chin thrust up. "My uncle is an important man in England. He shall see that you are taken and hanged from the nearest yardarm."

Damian's gentler thoughts dissolved, cold anger replacing them. "I know your uncle, Miss Jamison. Believe me, he would be able to think of much worse for me than a mere hanging." His hands tightened into fists at his sides. "I have learned much from him."

She shrank back, as if she feared he would prove what he'd learned. Her apprehension stoked his fury. It galled Damian that she should be terrified of him when it was her uncle who was so adroit at administering pain and death.

"I give you my word, Miss Jamison. No one shall be happier than I to see you off my ship."

Chapter Four

Cassandra didn't allow herself to fall into self-pity or tears again. Instead, she strengthened her resolve. She would not let the pirate chieftain see that she was afraid.

There was little opportunity for him to see either her fear or her resolve. In the following days, Damian didn't return to her cabin. Only on her walks above deck did she catch a glimpse of him. On those occasions, when she saw him standing behind the wheel of the great ship, he seemed totally unaware of her presence. Never once did their eyes meet.

Not that she cared. She had nothing to say to the man. In fact, should he ever speak to her, she was prepared to tell him what a fiend, what a cad he was. She struggled to find more vulgar words to describe what a low creature she found him and was frustrated that her vocabulary was so sadly lacking in adequate expressions.

Cassandra's only source of comfort as the ship continued on its westward course was Professor. He was the one who brought all of her things—her trunk filled with clothes, her hair brush and mirror, even her few precious books—to her cabin the second day she was on board the *Magic*. It was Professor who brought meals to her three times each day and stayed to talk with her, asking questions about Jamison Manor and her parents, about her likes and dislikes, helping her to think of other things besides her captivity. And it was Professor who took her walking on deck, letting her escape the confines of her tiny room for at least a short while every day. Always he treated her with respect, offering a friendly smile now and then, along with a word or two of encouragement.

She'd tried not to like him. After all, he was one of the brigands who had kidnapped her. Surely all pirates were wicked men with black souls, just like the captain of the *Magic*. But she'd found Professor's small kindnesses too difficult to resist. Besides, she was desperately in need of a friend.

And so, little by little, she began to believe him when he told her that she would come to no harm. And, little by little, with so much time on her hands, she began to wonder what a man like Professor was doing aboard a pirate ship and just how a friendship had been formed between him and Captain Damian.

Cassandra held on to the rail with both hands, relishing the wind on her face, knowing that it wouldn't be long before Professor would tell her it was time to go below.

"There'll be a storm by nightfall," the man at her side said.

"How can you tell?" she asked, gazing up at the dark blue canopy of sky, speckled with cottony clouds.

Professor shrugged. "See the grayish tint of the sky?"

She nodded.

"And look there, at the halo around the sun. It foretells foul weather ahead." He adjusted his glasses on the bridge of his nose, his gaze still on the ocean, his expression pensive. "I'm not fond of sailing, but I've learned a few things during past crossings."

"If you don't like it, why are you here?"

"Because . . ." He turned his back to the rail, his eyes moving toward the stern. " . . . I owe my life to Damian."

She followed his gaze until she, too, was staring at the captain.

Damian stood with his legs braced apart, his hands on the wheel, his white shirt billowing in the wind. Watching him, she felt neither fear nor loathing, only the very rightness of the sight before her. Never could she imagine a man who belonged more at the helm of a ship.

He was . . . magnificent.

She turned her back on the captain, angered that she had allowed such a thought to form.

"I was a teacher back in England," Professor continued, unaware of her inner turmoil. "I met my Sarah when her brothers became my pupils. Sarah and I fell in love and wanted to be married, but her parents objected. Sarah was very beautiful, and they thought she could do better than a poor schoolteacher." He smiled sadly. "They were right."

Cassandra's gaze moved to the man beside her. He was still staring over the water, but she realized now that what he was truly looking at was the past. She doubted he even remembered she was with him.

"We decided to run away, to leave England and begin a new life in the colonies. We signed papers of indenture to pay for our passage to America. We had no idea what was ahead of us." His voice lowered. "They crowded four hundred of us aboard a vessel meant to carry half that many. Many were diseased. We'd only been at sea two weeks when Sarah became ill."

Professor fell silent, and Cassandra hadn't the heart to ask him to continue. She was afraid she already knew the outcome of the story.

"I thought for a time that she would get well." His voice was so low she had to strain to hear him. "But she needed better food. I was certain the crew wasn't eating the slop they were feeding us. I went to ask the captain. He sent me to the ship's owner."

His face clouded. His hazel eyes flashed with an anger she'd never seen before.

"He refused to help. He said if she died, it would mean more food for the rest of us. It didn't matter to him what happened to Sarah."

Cassandra reached forward to lay her hand on his arm. He didn't seem to notice.

"I tried to steal some bread from the galley for her. I was caught." He lifted his right hand. "This was my punishment."

She gasped. "They cut off your fingers for taking *bread*?"

"I've seen worse punishments for smaller crimes." He glanced at her. "Sarah died a few days later. I wanted to die myself. I would have if not for Damian." He let his voice drift off into silence.

"What about Damian?" she prompted.

Professor glanced up at the sky. "I think the wind is rising. We'd better get you below before the storm hits."

"What about Damian?" Cassandra asked again, her gaze straying for the second time to the helm.

Professor took hold of her arm. "Perhaps the captain can tell you about it someday."

Reluctantly, she went with him. She would press him for more details when he brought her supper. Professor was always talkative then. Somehow, she would get the story out of him. She certainly didn't have any intention of asking Damian to tell her.

She glanced toward the helm one last time. *Magnificent . . .*

*   *   *

The storm blasted the ship in the last hour of daylight. It came out of the north, forcing high waves before strong winds. The fluffy white clouds of afternoon had darkened into thunderous heavens, and before long, the sky let loose its torrent of rain.

Covered in his oilskin jacket, Damian stood on the poop, lashed to the helm to prevent being washed overboard by the building waves that towered over the stern. He shouted orders to his men but doubted any could hear him above the shrieking of the wind. It mattered little. This crew had been with him for three years now. Some had been with him even longer. They knew their tasks and performed them well.

The *Magic* rode the worst of the swells, her mighty masts, canvas furled, swinging in great arcs and creaking beneath the wind's assault. Sea water drenched the decks and washed downward to soak everything below deck as well. It seemed for a time that the sea would swallow up the ship, like a giant cat swallowing a mouse.

The battle continued for hours, wave after wave smashing into the hull, rocking the vessel first to one side and then to the other.

And Damian fought back, determined not to lose. He was in his element now, relishing the test of wills. The sea was both his best friend and his worst enemy. It pushed him to fight harder and harder still. As always, he recog nized that this was a test of survival. Damian would prove once again that he would not be destroyed. He'd always refused to be destroyed.

It was nearly midnight when the rain abruptly stopped. The wind ceased to whistle amid the rigging. Giant waves soothed to a steady, familiar roll. Black clouds were replaced by stars overhead. It was almost as if the storm had never been.

Shedding his oilskin as he walked, Oliver crossed the main deck, followed by another sailor. "She was blowing like scissors and thumbscrews, eh, Damian?" Oliver shouted as he took the steps up to the poop deck two at a time. "There was a time or two when we was between wind and water, and well we all knew it."

"How did we fare?" Damian asked as his lieutenant helped free him from the helm.

"Right enough. The cargo's secure, if a bit damp."

During the storm, Damian hadn't given thought to anything beyond preserving his ship, but now that it was over, he recalled his unwilling passenger. "And what of Miss Jamison?"

"I've not checked on her yet."

Damian ran his hands over his hair, squeezing the water from it until it ran down his back in a steady stream. "I'll look in on her on the way to my quarters." He glanced toward the other sailor as the man took his place behind the helm. "Send for me if the wind picks up again."

"Aye, captain."

"Take over, Oliver."

"Aye, captain."

Cassandra gripped the sides of her bunk, afraid she might suddenly be flung across the room as had happened more than once during the storm. When not trying to keep from being beaten to death against the walls, she'd done her best to avoid drowning. Water had sloshed across the floor, convincing her that they were sinking.

And then it had stilled, as abruptly as it had begun.

Cassandra hated the calm almost as much as she'd hated the squall of the storm. Trapped in the darkness of her cabin, she was helpless to try to escape. What if the ship were going down and she'd been left behind, silenced forever in a watery grave?

Never was there a sound so sweet to her ears as that of a key turning in the lock. She jumped off the bunk, ready to feast her eyes on Professor, to let him assure her that the danger was over.

But it was Damian who stepped through the doorway, a lantern held high in one hand. His wet shirt clung to him, molding the fabric to his dark skin, defining the muscles of his chest, shoulders, and arms. His black hair was plastered against his head. She knew he must have spent the past hours out in the storm, and yet he didn't appear tired. There was a vitality about him that seemed to fill her cabin, making the very air pulsate.

"Oh . . ." The word came out of her on a whisper of air. "I thought you were Professor."

He grinned. "No one has ever mistaken me for *him* before."

She thought of her friend—not much over five feet tall with his thick yellow hair and watery hazel eyes behind round glasses—being confused with the dark visage before her. She couldn't help returning Damian's smile. "No, it isn't likely anyone would confuse you two."

How was it possible for a woman to look pretty with wet hair hanging in strings about her face and her gown sopping wet? Damian wondered as he gazed down at Cassandra. "I came to see how you weathered the storm."

As he spoke, he moved forward and lit her lantern from his own.

"I feel a bit battered, but I think there's no real damage done." In a self-deprecating motion, she rubbed her derriere with the palm of one hand. "Except perhaps to my pride."

She had her share of courage, this one. Reluctant though he might be, he couldn't help but admire that in her.

He took a step back toward the passageway but felt a reluctance to leave just yet.

"Is everyone else all right? No one was hurt or lost in the storm, were they?" she asked. "What about Professor? Is he all right?"

Was it possible that she was really thinking of others before herself, that Farley's niece was behaving so unselfishly? Although he found it difficult to believe, it appeared to be true.

"Captain?" Cassandra said, her voice rising with alarm. "Professor wasn't . . . he isn't . . . ?"

"He's most likely lying in his bed, thanking God for a reprieve. 'Tis what he usually does at the end of a storm, once the sickness has passed."

Her expression was an odd combination of grimace and smile. "He said he wasn't a very good sailor." She spoke more to herself than to him. Then she glanced up, and their eyes met again. "To tell you the truth, I was terrified. I thought we should all perish."

He'd never seen eyes quite that color before. Such a deep blue. So clear and open. It was as if he could see straight to the goodness of her heart. And then there was her mouth, pink and sweet and . . .

"My uncle told me of such storms, but I'd never been through one before."

Her uncle. Farley Dunworthy.

Damian felt a sudden coldness. "I'm glad you fared well, Miss Jamison," he said abruptly as he turned to leave. "I'll have one of my crew see if there's any dry bedding, but you'll probably have to make do like the rest of us. If we're lucky, we aren't in for a series of storms."

"Captain?" Her voice stopped him as he stepped through the doorway.

He turned, glancing back at her.

"Thank you for asking about me."

He made no reply. Silently, he closed and

locked her door behind him.

Cassandra clasped her arms in front of her, trying to warm herself. The chill had come upon her quickly, unexpectedly, just before Damian left her cabin.

She sank onto the bench beside the table, still clutching her arms in front of her chest while mulling over the captain's visit. She supposed he had only come to check on her as he would check on any of his valuable cargo. A dead captive wouldn't bring a very good ransom.

And yet, there had been a moment, when he'd smiled and she'd looked into his ebony eyes . . .

Good heavens! What was she thinking? That a scoundrel such as the captain of this ship of thieves might have a human heart after all?

Not likely.

Surely not.

Only . . .

I owe my life to Damian . . .

She wondered what Professor hadn't told her. She wanted to know the truth about the captain. For some reason, she *had* to know the truth.

Chapter Five

Cassandra waited impatiently for Professor to bring her breakfast tray. Not that she was hungry. What she wanted was to be above deck. She desperately needed to see the sunlight and feel its warming rays. Even though the clothes in her trunk had remained dry, she still felt the dampness all around her. She wanted to be up where the wind could pull through her hair and whip the hem of her skirt.

But when the key turned in the lock and her door opened, it wasn't Professor who stood on the other side. It was the man with the scarred face, the one she'd heard called Oliver, Damian's lieutenant.

"Miss Jamison." He nodded. "I fear last night's snorter has made today's breakfast a bit spare. Duffy's still tryin' to put the galley in order." He set a plate on the table near the door. "There's nought but a bit of salt beef, dry as a captain's Sunday sermon."

Cassandra glanced at the meat on the plate. She knew without tasting that it would be as hard and tough as harness leather. The *Magic*'s cook was a creative soul, and she'd eaten quite well up to now. In fact, her fare on the pirate vessel had been better than what had been served to her aboard the *Peacock*, though she hated to admit it. But the chunk of dried beef on the plate did nothing to increase her already absent appetite.

Her gaze returned to the lieutenant. "Thank you, Mr. Oliver. It was kind of you to bring my meal to me. But tell me, where is Professor?"

"Sink me, but he ain't feelin' himself this mornin'."

"Is it seasickness?"

"Aye, I fear so, miss. Professor does suffer from it more'n any man I e'er seen before. He hides it well enough in fair seas, but when the weather turns . . ." He shook his head.

She forgot all about her own need to go above, her only concern now for her sick friend. "Perhaps there is something I can do for him? Would I be allowed to see him?"

"I'll have t'ask the captain." When Oliver smiled, the hideous scar along the side of his face twisted the corner of his mouth into more of a grimace. "But I think all Professor needs is calm seas and t'be left alone with—beggin' your pardon, miss—with his bucket."

She caught his meaning and, despite herself, smiled sympathetically in return. "I suppose I should want the same if it were me." She sobered quickly. "But if there *is* anything I can do, please allow it. Professor has been so kind to me and . . ."

She stopped herself. Her words were no doubt wasted on this pirate. What would he understand of her gratefulness toward Professor?

"We all feel the same about him, Miss Jamison," Oliver said, as if he'd read her thoughts. "He'll be happier once we get him settled at Sorcery Bay."

"Sorcery Bay?"

The friendly twinkle left his brown eyes. "I'd be glad t'see you above deck for your walk, Miss Jamison, if you'd care to accompany me."

"Where is Sorcery Bay, Mr. Oliver? I thought we were going to Charleston. I thought I was to be ransomed."

"You are, miss."

"But—"

"Ain't my place t'say, miss. If you've got questions, you'd best be askin' the captain for answers." He held out his hand in invitation. "I'm not sure when I'll be free to see t'your walk again, Miss Jamison. You'd best go with me now."

She knew when she was being put off, and she didn't like it. Pressing her lips together, she stepped forward, holding her skirts aside as she moved past him. She walked with quick, determined strides, not once looking behind her to acknowledge Oliver's presence.

Her temper increased with every step. Enough was enough. She'd been a captive on this vessel for more than a week. She'd been manhandled by the captain, thrown over his shoulder like a sack of potatoes. She'd been frightened half-witless by the *Magic*'s scurvy crew when she was kidnapped. She'd been shut up in a windowless, airless cabin, with no one to talk to and nothing to do. She'd been tossed about in a storm that came close to drowning her. She'd suffered all sorts of indignities and all she'd asked for in return was an honest reply to a simple question.

The moment she stepped onto the main deck, her gaze swept the length of the ship in search of Damian. He was leaning against the starboard railing on the forecastle deck, his eyes scanning the sea.

For a moment, she simply stared at his handsome profile. His was a strong face. Each feature seemed to have been chiseled from granite. The blue-black shadow of a beard darkened his jaw and chin, but she found it surprisingly attractive. He wore his hair unfashionably long, and as usual, it was secured with a thong at the nape.

Despite herself, she thought he looked magnificent.

She shook her head to rid the idea from her mind.

He was a blackguard. A mongrel. A bloody rakeshame. He was a . . . a . . .

Oh, how she wished she knew the appropriately vile words to describe just what she thought of Captain Damian!

She hurried toward him, climbing the steps to the forecastle deck without hesitation.

"Captain Damian!" she shouted as she approached.

He turned. One eyebrow lifted, the only indication that he was surprised to see her standing there.

"Captain Damian, I demand to know what you intend to do with me. Just where is this Sorcery Bay? Why are we not bound for Carolina?"

Damian's jet-black gaze darted behind her. She saw the hint of a frown and knew that he was communicating his displeasure to his lieutenant. She thought of the scar on Oliver's face and the missing fingers on Professor's hand. Would she be the cause of some ghastly punishment to befall one or both of these men? What might this demon-captain do if he were truly angered? A shiver shot up her spine.

When Damian turned his eyes on her once more, the look of annoyance was gone. In its place was a gentle smile. "And good morrow to you, Miss Jamison. I'm pleased to see that you're none the worse for last night's unpleasant weather."

"I'm well enough." She braced her feet against the roll of the ship as it cut through heavy seas. "But that's not why I'm here."

Damian had known many beautiful women in his life. There was nothing so unusually pretty about this one.

True, her blond hair was silvery-pale. It glinted in the sunlight, promising to feel velvety-soft to the touch. True, her blue eyes made him think of warm seas at sunset, revealing her emotions like a signpost. True, her mouth was heart-shaped and moist, and her skin looked as smooth as silk. It was also true that her figure swelled and narrowed in all the most inviting places, and she always smelled of lilacs.

There was nothing so unusually pretty about Cassandra Jamison.

And yet, every time he was with her, he seemed to forget why he'd brought her on board the *Magic* in the first place. He seemed to forget that her uncle was his sworn enemy, that revenge against Farley was all that mattered to him, was all that had mattered to him for a very long time. He seemed to forget everything except how beautiful she was.

But he needed to remember everything *except* her beauty. It would be dangerous to do otherwise.

"Tell me, Miss Jamison," he said as he leaned back, his elbows bent and his forearms resting on the railing. "How did you feel about leaving England?"

"How did I—" She stopped in mid-sentence, then drew herself up and leveled a stormy blue gaze in his direction. "That is *not* at issue here, sir."

"Are you in love with this Mr. Abernathy? Were you eager to leave England for a marriage in the colonies?"

He saw the uncertainty flit across the fine features of her face. So, it was not a love match. Surprisingly, he felt a twinge of pity for her.

He turned to face the sea. "I didn't choose to leave England either."

He didn't look at her when she stepped up beside him, yet he was keenly aware of her nearness. Despite the wind, he would have sworn he detected the softest scent of lilacs drifting to his nostrils.

"Captain?"

When he let a few moments pass and still she didn't continue, he turned his head toward her.

The moment their eyes met, she completely forgot what she'd intended to ask him. Her breath caught in her throat, and her mouth went dry, but not from fear.

Cassandra wasn't certain how long they stood there, staring into each other's eyes. It felt like a fraction of a second. It felt like an eternity. She couldn't think, couldn't move. She could only stand there and look at him.

In a flash, an invisible wall slammed down behind the ebony gaze. She pulled back, as if the invisible cord that held them together had suddenly been severed.

In a cool, clipped tone, Damian said, "Sorcery Bay is my home. We go there to await Mr. Abernathy's response to the ransom request. When he has replied, you'll be sent to him."

He pushed away from the railing, walking toward the steps leading to the main deck.

"Captain?" she cried, feeling suddenly alone and afraid.

He stopped, but didn't turn.

She took a step forward. "What will you do if Mr. Abernathy refuses to pay the ransom?"

Damian swung his head around to look at her. She felt the icy coldness of his gaze.

"I don't know, Miss Jamison," he answered at length. "We shall think upon that problem if it arises."

Before he could turn away, she took another step forward. "Captain?"

His voice hardened. "What is it, Miss Jamison?"

"May I look in on Professor, just to see if he needs anything?"

Again, one eyebrow lifted, his look not so cold now as curious.

"I give you my word. I'll cause no trouble."

He spun away without answering her, but she heard him speak as he passed Oliver. "She may see Professor."

"Thank you," she whispered softly, her words snatched away in the wind. "Thank you, captain."

* * *

Damian ate his supper without tasting it. Throughout the meal, he'd been thinking of Cassandra. Thinking of her was becoming a habit, a habit that displeased him greatly.

He rose from the table and crossed to the windows that lined his quarters at the ship's stern. His view to the east showed a darkening sky. The first stars of evening were already visible.

Starlight, like the glitter in Cassandra's eyes.

He cursed. What was the matter with him? One would think he'd been without a woman for months, even years. In truth, Damian had never had to go begging for female companionship. Even before he'd earned his fortune as a privateer, he'd been sought after by beauties on both sides of the Atlantic. He'd bedded ladies of quality and those of more common birth. He knew well enough how to take and give pleasure.

But he'd also always known how to put thoughts of women from his mind during the weeks and months at sea. It had been an easy enough task. For eighteen years, he'd had one goal that was more important than any other, and that goal had left no room in his life, in his mind, or in his heart for anything or anyone else.

The moon rose in the east, casting its silvery glow over the ocean waves.

Silvery, like Cassandra's hair. Soft and silvery and inviting.

"Bloody hell," he muttered, turning his back on the sea beyond the windows. "Damn and bloody hell."

Cassandra held the cup of water to Professor's lips. He took several small sips, then leaned back against his pillows.

"Thank you, dear girl," he whispered.

Her friend's coloring was decidedly green but somewhat improved from this morning when she'd first seen him.

"Are you certain there is nothing more I can do for you?" she asked anxiously.

"I assure you, there is not. I would wish that we could be becalmed, but it would only lengthen the voyage, and I confess, I much prefer to be in my own bed." Professor made a half-hearted attempt at a smile. "Go on now with Oliver and take the air. It grows late. Besides, I know how you detest the smallness of these cabins."

Cassandra stepped away from the bunk. "If you'd like, I shall bring a book with me tomorrow and read to you."

"Aye." Professor closed his eyes with a sigh. "I should like that."

Oliver held the cabin door open for Cassandra, then followed her up to the main deck.

Stopping at the top of the steps, she glanced back at the lieutenant. "Professor said that the captain saved his life and that's why he's with him. But if he's so miserable at sea, why doesn't he stay on land? Surely there's something he could do there to repay Damian for whatever aid he gave."

"There is, an' he does it," Oliver answered.

She waited for him to continue.

"Professor's the overseer for Damian's sugar-cane plantation."

"Sorcery Bay?"

He nodded. "He was only on this voyage 'cause he was settlin' accounts on the last shipment with the captain's new London broker. He came over with the cane but decided to return on the *Magic* when he found we was in Plymouth."

"*You* were in England? You and the captain?"

He laughed at her surprised tone. "Aye, we go there when needs be. An' we walk about where folks can see us, too."

By the light of the moon, Cassandra studied the man who stood before her. She guessed him to be not yet thirty despite the weathered look of his skin. He was of average height, lean but strong. Though it was apparent that he was a commoner by birth and uneducated, there was intelligence in his brown eyes. She supposed he'd been handsome enough before his face was scarred. She wondered how it had happened, but asked something else instead. "What about you, Mr. Oliver? Have you always been a pirate?"

"The name's just Oliver, miss, and I ain't *never* been a pirate."

Her eyes widened at his bald-faced denial.

" 'Tis true. I'm an honest seaman, an' so're all the crew aboard the *Magic*."

"How can you say that? I saw you pillage my uncle's ship with mine own eyes."

"Aye. I suppose that's what you thought you saw."

"What I *thought* I saw?" Cassandra twirled away from him, irritated by the apparent riddles he spoke. "As if I didn't know what I saw!"

She began walking, pacing the deck as a wild animal paces its cage. She made three complete turns around the main deck before she stopped to stand before Oliver once again.

"What did you mean, what I *thought* I saw?"

The lieutenant shrugged. "Just what I said, miss. Things ain't always as they appear. Sink me, but a man can't steal what already belongs to him by rights."

"I am not some stupid chit without brains, *Mr.* Oliver." She spoke the words in anger and frustration. "Men who hoist a black flag and plunder other ships are pirates. And the captain who allows it is the worst of the lot."

Oliver's only response was to shrug his shoulders.

With a squeal of futility in her throat, Cassandra turned toward the hatch, intending to return to her cabin rather than continue this ridiculous conversation.

Oliver's voice reached her as her hand touched the handrail by the stairs. "You'll not find a man on this ship who thinks ill of the captain, Miss Jamison. But perhaps 'tis yourself you're tryin' to convince."

She glanced over her shoulder, her chin thrust in the air. "That's a lot of bilge water, Mr. Oliver."

She heard his laughter all the way to her cabin, wishing the whole while that what he'd said weren't true.

Chapter Six

I didn't choose to leave England either . . . I didn't choose to leave England either . . .

Cassandra awakened in the middle of the night, the echo of the captain's voice flitting through her mind. She wondered why she'd been dreaming about him, why the recalling of his words made her feel so bereft. She'd been angry with Oliver for suggesting that she cared one way or the other about Captain Damian. And now the blackguard was haunting her dreams.

I didn't choose to leave England either . . .

As she remembered it now, his voice had been both bitter and sad. She'd wanted to make things right somehow, to make whatever had caused him pain to be forgotten.

What a silly reaction, she thought as she

hugged her arms over her chest. As if that demon-captain needed to be comforted.

Demon-captain . . .

Why did that description no longer ring true? He was still a pirate. He was still her kidnapper. He was still all the terrible things she'd ever suspected him to be.

And yet . . .

Cassandra tossed aside the blankets, sat up, and reached for her dressing gown. With nimble fingers, she fastened the buttons down the front of the robe, wondering as she did so why she bothered to get out of bed. She couldn't take more than a few steps across her room before having to turn around. But that didn't matter right now. She felt too restless to lie in her bunk.

She wondered what time it was. How long before dawn? How long before Oliver came with her breakfast? She thought about trying to light the lantern but then realized she hadn't the means to light it. Up until the storm, she'd carefully kept the candle burning, trimming the wick, replacing the candle when it burned low, guarding it so she wouldn't be trapped by darkness. But last night she'd forgotten to check it, and while she'd slept, the taper had burnt itself out.

After pacing the few steps back and forth across her cabin three times, she paused by the door. She ran her fingers lightly over the wood until she touched the latch.

How she hated being locked in this minus-

cule place. How she hated the total isolation.
There never seemed to be enough air. Sometimes, she felt as if she couldn't breathe.

She pulled on the latch, more out of frustration than a belief that it would do any good. It
lifted with ease.

She caught her breath in wonder. No one
had come to lock her door last night after she'd
left Oliver up on deck. Had he forgotten? If
this were discovered, would he be punished?
What would the captain do to him for another
indiscretion?

She pushed aside those questions. For the
moment, they didn't matter. For the moment,
she cared only that she wasn't incarcerated in
this box of a room any longer. She had the
option to move about. And so she did.

Inching her way along the corridor, she
moved toward the hatch. Her heart beat rapidly. She knew she might come face to face
with one of the *Magic*'s crew members at any
moment. She was keenly aware that her brief
bid for freedom might be taken from her before
she'd had a chance to enjoy it.

She mounted the steps slowly, her eyes
watchful. If she stayed close to the main-
mast, the sailor at the helm wouldn't be able
to see her from the poop deck. She hoped there
wouldn't be anyone else above deck to discover
her. With luck, only a skeleton crew was awake
at this time of night, since the wind and seas
were moderate.

A spider web of shadows fell across the

planks of the deck, cast there by the moonlight filtering through the rigging, sails, and masts. The breeze off the ocean was cool but not uncomfortably so.

Clinging to the shadows, Cassandra made her way to the ship's railing, then eased herself down, sitting with her back against the wall of the poop deck, her knees pulled up to her chest beneath the wide skirt of her dressing gown. She closed her eyes, a smile curving her mouth. Never had anything felt so good to her as this. Never.

She took a deep breath of the fresh sea air, savoring it as one would savor a fine claret. Then she slowly exhaled. It was good to be free.

Free . . .

Oh, Cassandra, you must be ever so happy. Think of the adventure you'll be having, sailing to America, getting married, starting your own family.

Cassandra couldn't help smiling as she recalled Melissa Overstreet's words. Her good friend had no idea just how much of an adventure she was having on her voyage to the colonies.

I wish it were happening to me, Melissa had continued. *It must be sheer heaven to fall in love and get married.*

"Sheer heaven," she whispered on a sigh, wishing she'd been allowed to fall in love with the man she would marry. If only . . .

You should love the man you marry. You

should feel a grand passion for him . . .

Oh, Mama, why did things turn out this way? I don't want to marry Mr. Abernathy, no matter how wealthy he is. I want to feel that grand passion you spoke of. I want . . .

"Does sleep elude you, Miss Jamison?"

Her eyes flew open at the sound of the captain's voice. Her heart raced so hard she feared he would hear it.

Damian stood not more than five feet from her. Shadows fell across his face, obscuring it from view, but moonlight bathed the fluttering fabric of his white shirt, giving him a ghostlike appearance. Still, his presence was so powerful it was almost as if she could see him clearly.

Magnificent . . .

Why was that always the word that came to mind?

He stepped forward. A shiver of awareness shot through her as he drew near.

His voice was soft and low. "The night is cool. You could take a chill."

"I'm not cold." In truth, she felt strangely overheated.

"No," he said as she started to rise. "Don't get up." He stepped forward. "Allow me to join you."

Before she could react, he had lowered himself onto the deck beside her.

" 'Tis nights like this when a man remembers why he loves the sea."

Her stomach seemed tied in knots. Her skin tingled. "I know," she whispered.

"Have you ever been to the Caribbean, Miss Jamison?"

She felt him looking at her, but didn't turn her head. She was afraid she would be able to see his eyes. She was afraid of the way seeing him might make her feel, afraid of the way he already made her feel.

Sheer heaven . . . A grand passion . . .

He didn't wait for a reply. When he spoke, his voice was gentle, almost wistful. " 'Tis warm year 'round there. The sun beats down on the islands, sometimes so harshly it can burn a man's flesh off his back. The water is warm and clear. Every island is different. Some are large, many are small. Some are lush and green, filled with waterfalls and crystal streams. Others are rocky. My favorite time of year is now, in the early spring, when the trade winds blow in from the east."

"Have you lived there for many years?"

His voice deepened, and she heard that same bitter-sadness that had disturbed her dreams. "Many years."

She wished she could quiet her heart. Although not so rapid, it still seemed to be pounding inordinately hard.

"We'll arrive in Sorcery Bay in a few days. We'll await word there from Charleston."

Awaiting word from Charleston. It sounded so dreadful.

Damian rose to his feet, then offered her his hand and pulled her up from the deck. "You should return to your cabin, Miss Jamison. A ship's deck can be hazardous at night."

She looked up at him—an oak of a man. Tall, strong, powerful . . . *Magnificent* . . .

She felt a strange weakness in her knees. Instinctively, she reached out, placing her hands on his chest for support.

"Cassandra . . ." His whisper was like a caress.

What was wrong with her? What was she doing, standing here in her nightrail with this buccaneer, this outlaw of the seas? This was madness. She should return to her cabin. She should run from his touch. So why didn't she?

Damian didn't know what strange force had drawn him from his bed in the dark of night. He didn't know what sixth sense had told him he would find her there.

He did know he should order her back to her cabin. He knew it was better that she despise and fear, even hate him. He shouldn't whisper her name. He shouldn't allow himself to embrace her, to feel the nearness of her body to his.

Had he forgotten who she was? Hadn't he told her he would be glad to be rid of her when the time came? What was this terrible fascination he had for her?

But he didn't want to search for answers. Tonight he wanted to feel something he'd never allowed himself to feel before. He couldn't put a name to the emotion. He only knew he wanted to feel it a little while longer.

Her heart skipped as he spoke her name once more.

"Cassandra . . ."

His kiss brushed against her lips like the faint flutter of butterfly wings, yet the emotions it stirred were not so gentle. The kiss heated her blood, at the same time causing gooseflesh to rise on her arms. Her hands slid upward until her fingers closed over his shoulders.

His second kiss lingered, yet asked no more of her than she was willing to give. But she was too confused to *know* what she was willing to give. It was wrong of her to allow him to kiss her. A gentleman would never have presumed to do so. But Damian was no gentleman. He was a pirate, a thief, a marauder.

Sheer heaven . . . A grand passion . . .

No, she was mistaken. Damian could not be the man who would make her feel such things. He couldn't be.

She let go of his shoulders and stepped backward, her movement stopped by the railing. He didn't try to hold her, to keep her his prisoner. He didn't speak or explain or protest. He simply stood there, staring down at her in the moonlight, his face hidden in shadows.

A tiny sound escaped her throat. Her fingers flew to her hot cheeks. Then, without a word, she ran to the hatch and down to her cabin.

Damian cursed himself. Then he cursed Cassandra. He would not allow all his carefully laid plans to be ruined. He *couldn't* allow it.

It shouldn't have mattered to him that Cassandra was locked into that minuscule cabin. It *hadn't* mattered to him just ten days before.

If those same quarters were good enough for members of his crew—men who were his friends, his trusted officers—they should have been good enough for Farley Dunworthy's niece.

It shouldn't have mattered to him whether or not Cassandra was miserable behind that locked door. But for some reason, it had begun to matter to him a great deal.

For several days, he'd thought about those weeks he'd lived in that stinking hold aboard the ship that had carried him to Barbados, weeks without ever seeing the sun except when he'd carried another boy—a lad no older than himself at the time—up to the deck to be buried at sea. He'd thought about the years of servitude to William Spotswood, years when, by law, he was owned by another man, never allowed to go anywhere without Spotswood's permission.

He'd tried to tell himself it wasn't the same. Cassandra was being fed the best of their provisions. She was frequently allowed to exercise in the fresh air. She hadn't been harmed by a single man aboard the *Magic*. Her captivity would be brief, and she knew it. No, it wasn't the same thing at all.

Nonetheless, it had begun to matter to him, and against all reason, he'd known he could no longer keep her a prisoner in her cabin. And so, just yesterday, he'd told Oliver not to lock Cassandra's door after her evening walk.

And because of that decision, he'd found her sitting on the deck in the middle of the night.

Because of that decision, he'd taken her in his arms and tasted her sweet kisses.

He cursed softly again.

Perhaps taking her off the *Peacock* hadn't been such a good idea after all. When Mouse had sent word of Farley's plans for his niece, it had made sense for Damian to step in and keep her uncle from collecting the ransom. The plan had gone exactly as he'd intended. No one had been killed. Cassandra had come aboard his ship unharmed.

A wry grin turned the corners of his mouth. Unharmed but mad as a hornet. He thought of the way her eyes could flash with anger, remembered the way she'd kicked him in the shin. His smile faded, replaced by the memory of her kisses. She'd been hesitant at first. There'd been an unmistakable innocence in the way her lips had pressed against his. And yet, there'd been a willingness, a yearning in them, too. Even now the memory made his blood run hot with desire.

She's Farley Dunworthy's niece, he reminded himself. That was enough of a reason to steer clear of her.

At least it *had* been at one time.

He wasn't so certain any more.

Haunted by the strange feelings Damian's kisses had stirred to life and restless after a sleepless night, Cassandra gave little heed to Oliver when he brought her breakfast of porridge and biscuits with jam. She scarcely heard his apology for leaving her in the dark for so long nor his promise that it wouldn't happen again. She was only half-aware that she heard no turning of a key in the lock when he left her cabin.

Listlessly, she picked at the food on the tray before pushing it aside. In her mind, she saw Damian standing before her. Once again, she felt his hands upon her arms, tasted his lips . . .

"No!" she cried, trying desperately to erase the memory.

She needed something to do. She needed something to keep herself from remembering what had happened on the deck last night. She wanted something to make her forget this unconscionable attraction to a barbarous pirate.

Hastily, Cassandra rose from her bunk, went to her trunk, and pulled out a clean dress. Then she washed herself, changed out of her nightrail and dressing robe, and slipped into the willow-green gown of fine lawn. She brushed her long hair and caught it back at the sides with combs, letting the pale tresses hang in a smooth cascade down her back. In an attempt to lift her spirits, she dabbed some of her favorite lilac cologne behind her ears.

When she had completed her morning toilet, she picked up one of her precious books and opened the door to her cabin. Drawing in a deep breath, she turned away from the hatch and walked toward Professor's cabin. Once there, she knocked briskly.

"Yes?"

" 'Tis Cassandra, Professor. May I come in?"

"Yes, my dear girl. Please do."

She opened the door.

Professor was sitting up in his bunk, several pillows at his back. His face, though still pale, was a more human color this morning.

"Are you feeling better?" she asked, even though she could see that he was.

"I am, indeed. But I wasn't expecting Oliver to bring you to see me this early."

"He didn't bring me. I came on my own." She shrugged her shoulders. "He forgot to lock my door."

Professor motioned her to sit beside him. "Oliver doesn't forget anything. If your door was unlocked, it was because the captain said it could be."

"Damian?" She spoke the name softly, evoking images she'd been trying to forget.

Her friend didn't answer. She wasn't expecting him to. In truth, she didn't realize she'd said the captain's name aloud.

"I see you've brought a book with you," Professor said, drawing her attention back to him. "Are you going to share it with me?"

She nodded, took her place on the bench beside his bed, and opened the book. But even as she began to read aloud, her thoughts wandered once again to the captain.

Why had he told Oliver to leave her door unlocked? Why had he spoken to her so tenderly? And why had he kissed her?

*　　*　　*

Damian left the great cabin, intent on speaking with his sailing master. He stopped as soft words drifted to him down the passageway. There was something very pleasant about Cassandra's voice, he thought as he listened. He found it almost musical—sweet and feminine and soothing.

He wasn't really surprised that she had come to Professor's cabin rather than taking her morning stroll. It didn't surprise him that she had thought of her friend before herself. It seemed natural, somehow. Perhaps he'd even been expecting it.

He moved forward on quiet feet, stopping once he reached the doorway. Professor glanced up and saw him. Damian motioned with a finger to his lips for the other man to be silent.

Cassandra held the bound book with both hands. A frown cut a vertical crease between her brows as she concentrated on the words. With her head bent slightly forward, her hair had fallen over her shoulders, a silvery contrast to the pale green of her dress.

I wonder who taught her to read?

He wondered many things about her. What were her favorite colors? Was she fond of riding horses, perhaps of hunting foxes with the hounds? Had her childhood been a happy one? Why had she agreed to marry this man in the colonies?

He wondered . . .

He wondered too much about her.

She glanced up. The words of the story died in her throat. Her eyes widened as she stared at him. There was a flicker of doubt, perhaps still a shred of fear, in the deep blue gaze that watched him. And then it was gone, replaced by a smile that curved her pink lips and brought a twinkle to her eyes.

"Good morrow, captain."

God's blood! If he didn't get hold of himself, he'd be giving her his quarters before long, just as Professor had suggested.

He nodded. "Good morrow, Miss Jamison," he replied curtly.

Then he moved on, before he could get trapped again in pools of indigo and a smile as sweet as heaven's own breath.

Chapter Seven

Several days later, Professor stared at the northernmost point of the coral island of Barbados, basking in the early morning sunshine, as the *Magic* sailed past it. Normally, he would have felt great relief at the sight. It meant they would arrive at their destination in eight hours or less. It meant he was nearly home.

But this morning his thoughts were on his friend the captain and the pretty captive in her cabin below deck. Professor wasn't blind to what was happening between those two people. There had been an undeniable attraction between them almost from the very first time they laid eyes on each other, fight it though they might. Professor was willing to admit that it was an unlikely match. There was no reason for them to feel drawn to each other and dozens of reasons why they shouldn't be. Still, he had lived long enough to know that sometimes fate had other plans.

He heard Damian's voice as the captain spoke to one of the sailors on deck. He turned his head, watching as his friend climbed onto the forecastle deck and walked toward him.

"We'll be home before nightfall, Professor." Damian laid a hand on the other man's shoulder. "You'll be able to enjoy your food again. And just in time, too. You're almost as thin as a stalk of sugar cane."

"But not as tall." Professor smiled. It was an old joke between them. "It will be good to be home."

"Aye."

Professor thought of the way Damian and Cassandra had been carefully avoiding each other for the past five days. He knew something had happened between them that neither was ready or able to deal with. Damian had been unusually gruff, not just with the girl but with every man on the ship. Cassandra had been behaving as nervously as she had when she first came aboard.

Someone had to do something.

"Damian, you need to give up your life at sea." Seeing the captain's annoyed expression, he rushed on. "Settle down at Sorcery Bay. Find a wife and sire some children. Give up this wandering. It'll only bring you grief in the end if you don't."

"I can't, and you know it."

Professor sighed. "Yes, I know, but I keep hoping I can find the words that will change your mind. 'Vengeance is Mine,' sayeth the Lord. Maybe 'tis time we heeded the Good Book."

Damian's jaw tightened. "I haven't time to wait for God's vengeance."

He turned his back on Professor and drew in a deep breath of the ocean breeze, trying to cool the sudden anger he'd felt at his friend's words.

Professor was wrong. Vengeance wasn't the Lord's. It was his. He wanted it. He needed it. And he would have it. Every time he took back from Farley a small portion of what had been stolen from him, Damian tasted the sweet joy of knowing he'd struck another blow of revenge. He would never be entirely satisfied, of course. He could never take back enough to repay what could never be returned to him. He could never have his childhood back. He could never have his father with him again.

But he could have his revenge. And only when Farley Dunworthy was a broken man—scorned by his peers, rejected by his contemporaries, financially ruined—would Damian's revenge be complete.

The promise of that revenge was what had kept him alive for too many years. Years when it would have been easier to give up and die.

From the corner of his eye he saw a flutter of blue silk, and he knew that Cassandra had joined them above deck. He tried not to turn and look at her, but the temptation was too strong.

Her pale hair swirled about the shoulders of her blue gown, a dress much the same color as her eyes. The squared neckline of the bodice revealed just a hint of cleavage and set off the small sapphire necklace that lay in the hollow of her throat.

Her quiet elegance was well-suited for a wealthy man like Aldin Abernathy. She was made for a life of ease and pleasure. She had been born to wear luxurious silks and satins with sparkling jewels gracing her lovely, slender neck.

But as she stood there on the deck of the *Magic*, her hair flying in the wind, her hands clinging to the railing as she leaned forward, catching a spray off the ocean, her eyes flashing with pleasure, it seemed that she belonged there more than anywhere else.

A warmth spread through him, a foreign sense of tenderness wrapping gentle tentacles around his heart. He didn't want to feel it. There was no place in his heart, no place in his life, for the feelings this woman stirred within him.

If only he could stay away from her completely, he would be better off. Too often she made him almost forget what was most important to him. She gave him brief glimpses of a kinder side of life, a life he'd once known but one to which he could never return. That life had been taken from him by her uncle.

She turned her head and caught him staring at her. Her look of pleasure vanished, replaced by an expression he couldn't quite read. Then she looked away, her gaze once again set upon the island of Barbados.

"Don't take your foul mood out on the girl," Professor counseled from behind him. " 'Tis not her fault."

"Fault or not, I'll be glad to be rid of her when the time comes."

But even as he stalked away, he feared that he had lied to Professor. He feared he would *not* be glad to be rid of her when the time came.

Cassandra stared at the island. It was the first land she had seen in many weeks, and this small isle baking beneath a tropical sun was far different from England.

"We'll be at Sorcery Bay by afternoon," Professor said as he descended the steps from the forecastle deck.

"And then word will be sent to Charleston," she replied softly.

Professor was silent for a moment, then pointed toward the island that was already slipping from view. "That's Barbados. 'Tis where Damian and I first met. We were both working for Jedidiah Benjamin on his sugarcane plantation back then."

Cassandra knew Professor had come to the new world as an indentured servant. She wondered if that was also how Damian had come to the Caribbean. And if so, was it this Jedidiah who had held his indenture papers?

She turned to look toward the helm, her gaze finding the captain. He was talking with his lieutenant and occasionally pointing to the west. She watched the movement of his mouth, noticed the way the sea breeze was blowing strands of black hair free from the leather tie at his nape. She noted how white his teeth looked against the sun-bronzed color of his skin.

The harsh expression of a barbarous pirate chieftain that he'd shown to her ever since the night he'd kissed her had momentarily disappeared. Everything about him seemed more relaxed at this moment. If possible, he was even more handsome than usual.

He had avoided her as much as possible over the past five days, but she'd often felt him watching her whenever they were on deck at the same time. She refused to admit to herself that she missed hearing his voice, that she had hoped he might smile at her occasionally and share a brief glimpse of the man she sensed he truly was. It would be pointless to admit it. It would change nothing between them.

"Fate sometimes surprises us," Professor said obliquely.

She glanced at him in question, but he merely smiled and looked back out to sea.

The *Magic* slipped into the palm-fringed cove in the waning hours of afternoon. From his place on the forecastle deck, Damian could see the low white buildings of Sorcery Bay Plantation nestled amidst blue-green foliage. A warm breeze carried familiar scents out to the ship— the smell of ripening sugarcane mixed with the fragrance of blossoming tropical flowers.

It was good to be home.

While he waited for Abernathy's response, Damian would order the *Magic* to be careened. On the north side of the island was an inlet with a generous, sandy shore, a cove shielded from the view of passing ships, the perfect place to clean the hull of a vessel, scraping away the marine growth which could slow her in the water, and repair any sheathing that had fallen victim to the teredo worm.

The inlet was one of the reasons Damian had selected the small, once-deserted island for his plantation home. Another was its solitary placement among the islands of the Caribbean. Few ships ever passed this way; fewer still knew of its existence.

Another reason—but one he would be disinclined to admit, even to himself—was the pristine beauty of the place. The island boasted mountains that rose abruptly toward the sky, their peaks often shrouded in a silvery mist. Waterfalls and streams were abundant. Flowers grew in profusion like a parade of brightly dressed young women, coloring the land a hundred different shades and hues.

Yes, it was good to be home. Here he could allow himself to relax for a time. Here he could forget, if only temporarily, the driving force that kept him and the crew of the *Magic* at sea for months at a time.

The anchor was dropped into the turquoise-colored bay, and Damian ordered the skiff dropped over the side, then turned toward the main deck.

Cassandra was standing beside Professor, her gaze sweeping over the island. He had avoided her for days, doing his best not to think about the kiss they'd shared on the deck of the *Magic*, and yet thinking about it almost constantly. He didn't want to consider what it might mean, how that kiss could complicate things for them both. It had been a foolish thing for him to do, no matter how attractive he found her. It was better to remind himself once again that she was the niece of Farley Dunworthy and, therefore, his enemy. If only he could remember that she was his adversary, the next few weeks would be much simpler.

Yes, his adversary, his prisoner, his captive. She was nothing more to him than that.

Quick strides carried him toward her. When he arrived at her side, she glanced at him, then back at the island. " 'Tis beautiful. More beautiful than anything I'd imagined."

"Aye." He was looking at her as he spoke. "Beautiful."

"Is there a village on the other side of the island?"

"There's no village. Everyone on the island works and lives on Sorcery Bay."

Her eyes widened a fraction. "The island is yours?"

He shrugged. "If a man can own an island, then I suppose 'tis mine. There was nothing here until I came to build Sorcery Bay."

She studied him now as she'd studied the island moments before. He could see that she longed to ask him more questions but was trying not to show her interest.

But she couldn't keep silent. "Sorcery Bay is an unusual name. Why did you call it that, captain?"

His jaw tensed as he thought of the inspiration for the name; he forced himself to relax. "I suppose because I'd hoped to find something magical here."

"The *Magic* . . ." she whispered, as if she'd just made a discovery. She looked him full in the face. "What sort of magic do you seek, Captain Damian?"

Chapter Eight

The kind I could find in your arms, he thought, even as he resisted the temptation to pull her against him and take another of her kisses.

He forced himself to think about what she'd asked him.

He'd named the island and his ship for reasons of hate and revenge, not because of the look he could see in this woman's eyes. He hardened his heart against the gentle entreaty he saw there. He didn't understand the power she had over him, and he didn't want to understand it. Time and again, he had turned and walked away from her, and time and again, he had returned to be tempted once more.

Magic? Perhaps that was exactly what it was. There was no other explanation for the things she'd caused him to do and say from almost the first moment he'd laid eyes on her. Why, of all women, was she the one who intrigued him this way?

"Captain?"

He realized she was still waiting for an answer to her question, and as he did so often with Cassandra, he replied with a gruff tone. "You would never understand, Miss Jamison."

That said, he walked to the side of the ship where the sailors had lowered the skiff just moments before.

Cassandra followed him with her eyes, feeling a terrible loneliness wash over her.

"Look," Professor said in an obvious attempt to divert her.

She followed the direction of his arm.

"That's Big Joe," Professor told her, pointing to a man on shore. "He's the mill foreman at Sorcery Bay."

"I've never seen a slave before," she replied softly, unable to stop staring at the man whose skin was nearly as black as Damian's hair.

"Big Joe's a freedman. You'll find no slaves on this island, nor indentured servants either."

Professor's embittered tone caused her to turn and look at him in surprise. Had she said something wrong?

"Every man, woman, and child on this island is free to come and go as they please, thanks to Damian," he continued, his voice more gentle this time.

She glanced once again at the captain, once again wondering about this pirate whom others held in such high esteem. Was he nothing that he appeared to be?

"Come with me, Cassandra. The skiff is waiting for us. By heaven,'tis good to be back. I swear by all that's true, I'll not soon willingly put myself aboard another ship."

Cassandra nodded, even as she realized that she would miss the sea, at least a little. She looked toward the helm, and for just a moment, she envisioned Damian standing there, his white shirt and black hair whipped by a mighty wind, his muscular legs braced, his hands gripping the wheel. It was almost as if she could feel the salty spray against her cheeks and hear the crackle and snap of rigging and sails overhead.

In a matter of weeks, she would be sent to Mr. Abernathy in Carolina. And after that, she might never again feel the roll of a ship beneath her feet, might never again see the majesty of a ship in full sail. In a matter of weeks, this would all be lost to her.

Lord help her, she didn't understand the sadness that overwhelmed her. She was a prisoner here. These men were barbarians, pirates, thieves. She couldn't possibly miss them. No well-bred woman would miss such rabble.

Only, when she looked at Professor, it was difficult to believe he was a thief. Even Oliver, with his grotesquely scarred face, no longer seemed a barbarian. And Damian? He was no demon-captain. She was sure of it.

So who were they really, she wondered, these

Robin Lee Hatcher

men of the *Magic* and Sorcery Bay?

Before she could contemplate her silent question, Professor took hold of her arm and hurried her along the deck to where a rope ladder had been dropped over the railing. She glanced over the side to see the skiff bobbing up and down in the water. Two sailors held on to ropes to keep the boat from floating away on the current.

It seemed a terribly long way down to Cassandra. Although she had fallen in love with sailing and the sea, she wasn't particularly fond of the idea of being pitched into the water, especially since she was unable to swim.

"Are you frightened, Miss Jamison?"

Cassandra glanced sideways at the captain as he stepped up beside her through the crowd of sailors. She'd been wishing to see him smile again—just as he was doing now—but she didn't relish his making fun of her. "Of course not," she lied, irritated that he'd guessed her thoughts.

"Good." Damian motioned to Professor. "Lead the way, my friend."

Professor didn't hesitate to obey. With a nimbleness Cassandra would never have guessed him capable of, he lifted himself over the railing, grasped hold of the ladder, and quickly descended toward the skiff.

Cassandra tried to ignore the lump of fear that formed in her throat as she stared after him. The distance seemed to have doubled since the first time she'd looked down at the rowboat.

" 'Tis quite easy," Damian said. "But don't worry. I'll be along to see that you don't fall."

"I have no need of your help." Her brave words were belied by the quiver in her voice.

He let himself over the side, then waited on the ladder. "Oliver, help Miss Jamison over the railing."

She felt the lieutenant's hands close around her waist.

"You needn't fear, miss," Oliver said softly near her ear. "The captain won't let you fall."

"I don't need his help," she repeated, trying valiantly to believe it. "I am fully capable of descending a ladder."

"Aye, I'm sure you are." Oliver chuckled. "But sink me if it ain't a bit different when a ship is rocking with the tide."

The lieutenant lifted her onto the railing, then held on tightly as he helped her turn and place her feet on the rope rungs. Her fingers gripped the thick hemp so hard her knuckles turned white. Then she was aware of Damian moving up until his feet were only one step below her own. His arms encircled her as he held on to the rope on either side of her, providing a barrier between her and the sea below.

She looked up into Oliver's scarred face and saw his grin of encouragement. He winked. "You'll do fine, miss."

The strange thing was, she wasn't afraid of falling into the water any longer. She was scarcely aware of the rocking of the ship, of the tiny boat bobbing in the surf, of the flimsy ladder upon which she stood. She was only aware of the warmth of Damian's chest so close to her back. She was only aware of the whipcord strength of the arms that shielded her, keeping her safe.

"Now." Damian's voice was low, his mouth near her ear. She could feel his breath on the back of her neck. "We'll take one rung at a time. Slowly now."

Wisps of silvery hair curled like miniature fishhooks along her nape. But Damian knew he would find nothing sharp to poke him should he rub his lips along the delicate flesh of her neck. The shape of her pearl-pink ears was like that of a seashell, only infinitely more kissable than anything that lived beneath the ocean's surface. Her long, thick braid swung back and forth across her back, swaying like the rope ladder across the side of the ship. But there was nothing coarse about the pale tresses. He knew her hair would feel more like silk than hemp should he choose to run his fingers through it.

Damian moved slowly, taking each step with far more caution than it required. He was in no hurry to feel her move away from him. He liked it when her arm brushed against his or when her back touched his chest. Liked it far more than was wise.

Stepping into the boat, he placed his hands around Cassandra's waist and lifted her the rest of the way, setting her feet down in the center of the skiff. She turned to face him before he drew his hands away. The look in her wide blue eyes was one of confusion and wonder. A touch of color brightened the apples of her cheeks.

"Thank you, captain," she whispered.

Her voice touched a long-forgotten corner of his heart. For a moment, he allowed himself to enjoy the feeling. But only for a moment. He knew better than to be seduced by a pretty face or gentle voice. There was no place in his life for feelings such as she stirred in him. And never would there be a place for someone who loved Farley Dunworthy as she apparently did.

"Sit down, Miss Jamison." He motioned toward a thwart in the middle of the row boat. " 'Tis time we were ashore."

She looked a bit startled by his abrupt words and the gruff tone of his voice, but he chose to turn his back on her as she took her seat, instead watching as more sailors scurried down the rope ladder until the skiff was full. Ten pairs of calloused hands grasped hold of ten wooden oars, five on each side of the boat. One of the men pushed the craft away from the pirate ship, and then the rowers bent to their task.

The single-story buildings of the plantation were large, open, and airy, designed to catch the slightest of breezes to cool the interiors. A tall, lanky, mulatto woman—Ruth, Professor had called her—showed Cassandra to a room that faced the bay. She didn't speak, nor did she look Cassandra directly in the eye. She simply offered a quick curtsy, her gaze still averted, then slipped out of the spacious bedchamber.

Cassandra pondered the woman's shy behavior only a moment before turning to view her surroundings. The furnishings were sparse but well-made. The white-washed walls glowed in the late afternoon sunlight that spilled through wide windows. Though not as pleasant as her bedchamber at Jamison Manor, the room was certainly far better than the tiny cabin that had been her abode for the past two weeks at sea. And it was more than adequate for the short time she would be here.

In three weeks we shall hear from Mr. Abernathy. She should have felt comforted by that thought, but she didn't.

A light rapping sounded at her door, announcing the return of Ruth. The maid entered the bedchamber with quick, graceful steps. In her arms, she carried some brightly colored garments. She laid them out across the white coverlet on the bed.

Cassandra stepped forward to look at them. The yellow blouse was full, with short sleeves and a scooped neckline. The cotton skirt of parsley green was simply cut and gathered at the waist. There were no hoops or panniers, no laced corset, only a shift of white cotton to wear beneath the skirt and blouse.

"Too hot," Ruth said, pointing to Cassandra's velvet dress. "Can't breathe." She smiled as she held up the blouse. "You like?"

"It's quite lovely."

"You change. Ruth help you."

"No, I . . . I don't need your help. I . . ."

The woman's gaze dropped quickly to the floor. "You don't like."

Cassandra eyed the scanty attire—at least, it seemed scanty to her. Still, it would be heavenly not to wear this heavy gown in the heat of the tropics. Would it be so terrible if she wore this more comfortable garb for just a few weeks? No one need ever know. Certainly there was no one on this island whom she would ever see again.

"You're wrong, Ruth. I do like. I like them very much." She stepped toward the woman. "Please help me out of these things. I've had a devil of a time dressing myself ever since"—She thought of the morning Damian had broken through the door of her cabin, the chair she'd shoved against it splintering beneath the force of his strength—"Ever since I've been without my maid. None of my gowns have fit properly without someone to help with my corset."

Ruth smiled. "You breathe better without. You see. You like much better."

Within minutes, the servant had helped remove the heavy dress, multiple petticoats, and stiff corset. And even more quickly, she helped Cassandra into the shift, blouse, and skirt. After tying the simple ribbon closing at the base of Cassandra's neck, Ruth turned her toward the mirror.

"See? Much better."

Cassandra stared at her reflection. At least, she *thought* it was her reflection. The young woman in the mirror had a wild, wind-blown, carefree look. All her natural curves were clearly displayed beneath the light fabric. Her ankles showed beneath the hem of her skirt which would have sent Cassandra's mother into a dither. There even seemed to be an inordinate amount of skin showing above the neckline of her blouse, even though she knew she'd worn gowns cut much more severely than this.

"Much better," Ruth repeated. "You see. Captain Damian, he will like, too."

Cassandra's right hand moved to her belly, as if to still the sudden tumbling sensation she felt at the mention of the captain's preference for her attire. She saw her cheeks pinken, and her lips tingled, as if they had just been kissed. She wasn't even aware that Ruth had moved away until she heard the door close behind her.

Still, she couldn't take her eyes from the woman in the looking glass. Would Damian truly like what he saw?

With a stubborn thrust of her chin, determined to deny the sensation such thoughts brought with them, she muttered, "And why should it matter to me if he does? What do I care what the captain thinks?"

For a moment, she almost believed she didn't care.

Chapter Nine

The same day he arrived at Sorcery Bay,
Damian ordered one of his ships to sail to
Charleston with the ransom demand. After
that, he immersed himself in the workings of
Sorcery Bay Plantation, reacquainting himself
with the land, with the mill and refinery, with
the people who lived and worked on the island.
He learned that Big Joe had married Ruth while
he was away, and that Freddie Hastings' wife—
Damian's housekeeper—had presented her husband with twin sons. He saw that new fields
had been cleared and more cane planted and
that this year's crop was a good one. He saw
the many new houses that had been constructed in his absence and knew that the men and
women who lived there were prospering along
with him.

Sorcery Bay was growing and thriving. Professor had brought about many changes during Damian's absence—all of them for the better. Professor's careful attention to the day-to-day workings of the plantation and his concern for the people who lived on the island showed in many different ways.

And Professor wasn't the only one whom Damian could thank for the success of his sugar cane plantation. Big Joe had chosen and trained the mill hands well. Many of them were freed slaves. Some were sailors who were glad to be able to return to the land, if they were allowed to do so as free men, not beggars and paupers with no say in their future. They worked hard because they were working for themselves and their families.

During those first days back on the island, it was easy to avoid thinking about Cassandra Jamison. Damian ate early, then left the house, not to return until after nightfall. But eventually—once he'd studied the ledgers and records, once he'd surveyed his lands and crops, once he'd visited the mill and refinery—he had plenty of free time, and that was when his thoughts turned to Cassandra.

And once he began thinking of her, he longed to see her.

Early in the morning, over a week after their arrival at Sorcery Bay, Cassandra left the house and strolled down to the water's edge. Barefooted, she walked along the shore, enjoying the feel of the cool sand squishing up between her toes and the sea water splashing over her feet as the tide surged upon the beach. The air was filled with a delightful cacophony of sounds—exotic birds welcoming the dawn, the braying of a mule, the mooing of cows waiting to be milked.

She stopped at the sound of a dog barking. Turning, she watched as a small brown terrier raced toward her. She didn't know to whom the dog belonged, only that she had joined Cassandra the first time she ventured onto the beach for a walk and had never failed to show up whenever Cassandra walked there again.

"Hello, girl," she said, ruffling the dog's ears. "You're up early this morning."

The dog barked once, as if to return the greeting, and when Cassandra resumed her stroll, the terrier fell in at her side.

For a long time, Cassandra walked in contented silence, simply enjoying the beauty of the island. It was strange how at home she felt here in this tropical paradise. She should have been longing for the rocky slopes and rolling greens that surrounded Jamison Manor. She should have been missing the stone house that had been her family home for many generations. She had thought of little else during those first weeks aboard the *Peacock*. She'd longed to return to the familiarity of Northumberland.

But she felt no such longing now. She felt at peace.

111

Robin Lee Hatcher

Well, mostly at peace, she thought as her gaze strayed to the cove. The *Magic* wasn't there.

She wished she knew where the ship had gone and if Damian had gone with it. She hadn't seen him even once in the past week, and she couldn't help wondering if he'd left without even saying good-bye. She knew she could have sought out Professor and asked him, but she hadn't wanted him to think she was concerned about the captain's whereabouts.

She wasn't, after all. She was merely curious.

Suddenly, the terrier darted away from her side, racing along the stretch of beach at breakneck speed. Cassandra looked up and saw the horse and rider approaching her. She knew instantly that the man sitting so straight in the saddle was Damian.

He slowed the dappled gray stallion to a trot, then stopped him. The dog maintained her speed, gathering herself at the last possible moment and then hurling herself toward the rider. Damian caught the terrier in midair and pulled the dog against his chest. He laughed as she tried to lick his face.

"Enough, Circe. Enough." He stroked the terrier's coat several times, then leaned down from the saddle and dropped the dog the remaining distance to the ground. When he straightened, his gaze moved immediately to Cassandra. "Good morrow."

"Good morrow, captain."

He dismounted, his eyes sweeping over her once again, this time pausing upon her bare

112

feet. A smile curved the corners of his mouth as his gaze returned lazily to her face.

She felt scandalously lacking in clothes beneath his perusal. It was almost as if she were standing naked before him. Her skin tingled, and she felt an odd warmth in her loins.

"You've found the island to your liking?" he asked as he started toward her, leading the gray stallion behind him. Circe scampered back to Cassandra, and Damian's smile broadened. "And you've made a friend of Circe, I see."

"Is she your dog?"

Damian chuckled. "Circe doesn't belong to anyone. She's a true vagabond. She makes her home with those who have the choicest scraps and moves on when she finds the pickings unsuitable."

As he drew near, she felt the impact of his presence. It was almost like a physical blow, leaving her wishing she could reach out and steady herself on his chest, just as she'd done the night he kissed her.

"Have you explored beyond the bay?"

Cassandra shook her head, left mute by his nearness.

"Would you like to see it?"

"See what?"

"The island." He looked bemused by her question.

She nodded, forcing herself to attend to the present.

"Then allow me to show it to you. Merlin can carry us both." He swung up into the saddle,

113

then leaned over and lifted her off the ground, his hands around her waist.

It was as if she was flying. She felt that odd, recurring tumbling sensation again and quickly locked her fingers behind his neck as he settled her sideways onto the saddle in front of him.

"The island is small. I can ride around it in a day if I don't tarry."

She'd never sat in a man's lap before, never been held in a man's arms on horseback. She was pressed so closely to him, thigh against thigh, her side against his chest, her temple close to his lips. It was impossible to move away, impossible even to shift or change position. And so she remained rigidly still, scarcely daring to draw a breath.

He nudged the stallion into an easy lope. They rode in silence for several minutes before he spoke.

"I found the island eight years ago. At first, I thought I would live here alone, but then Professor joined me. Later, there were others who took refuge here."

She had trouble finding her voice. "You've accomplished much."

"I can take little credit for what's been done. I've rarely been here. I served as a privateer during the war with Spain. When peace came, I bought my own ships."

"The *Magic* isn't your only ship?"

"No. The *Magic* has a special purpose, but she's only one of several vessels in my fleet. My ships sail from the Americas to England to the Orient."

She heard him chuckle and glanced up.

"Sorcery Bay Shipping is legitimate, Miss Jamison. Not a pirate ship in the entire lot. In truth, I'm considered quite fair and honest. Men vie to serve on my ships because my crews are well-paid for their hard work."

She scarcely heard what he said. She knew he was telling her he wasn't the pirate she thought him, but it didn't matter at the moment if it were the truth or not. For now, she was only aware that he had a wonderful mouth, a marvelous smile. Had she ever seen the like of his smile before? She thought not.

His arm tightened about her waist. Her pulse jumped in response as she continued to stare up into his eyes. His smile slowly vanished. She felt her skin grow warm. It became difficult to breathe.

"I . . . I think I should like to walk," she managed to whisper.

She wondered if he'd heard her. He made no reply, nor did he slow the horse's gait. Flushing beneath his intense gaze, she turned her head forward and watched as the gray stallion carried them along the stretch of beach, the green island to their right, the turquoise sea to their left.

Damian fought the rising tide of desire. He should have stopped the horse and put her down. He never should have lifted her onto the saddle in the first place. But now that she was in his arms, he didn't want to let her go.

Perhaps he was the scurrilous pirate she thought him, for there was nothing he wanted more than to carry her into the shade of a tall palm and make love to her. He wanted to see her delicate white flesh naked in the sunlight. He longed to run his fingers through her hair and to breath in the gentle fragrance of her. He wanted to taste her, to kiss her mouth, to suckle on her breasts, to feel her passions rising to match his. He wanted to feel her fingers running over his skin, to hear her rapid breathing, to see passion's flush in her cheeks. He wanted . . .

Bloody hell!

He jerked back on Merlin's reins so suddenly that the stallion reared up on his hind legs. Cassandra squealed in fright and her arms tightened around Damian's neck. Her gaze flew back to his face.

As soon as the horse had settled, Damian lowered Cassandra to the ground, then dismounted himself. "We'll walk awhile," he said, his voice clipped.

He didn't look at her again. He couldn't. Not until he brought himself under control. Not until the desire to hold her and kiss her and make love to her had passed. If they'd been nearer to the plantation house, he would have left her and let her make her own way back. It would have been safer for them both.

Cassandra should have been frightened by what she'd seen in his stormy black gaze, but she wasn't. She should have been terrified of her own reaction to him, but she wasn't.

They continued on in silence for what seemed a long time. She knew when his mood changed; his pace slowed, making it easier for her to keep up with him. Finally, he stopped and turned in her direction.

"I'm sorry it was necessary to take you from your uncle's ship, Cassandra, but I had my reasons. Good ones, I think. I know you were frightened. I hope you'll believe me when I tell you that I never meant you any harm."

"I'm not frightened any longer, captain," she whispered, her voice trembling.

She thought he might take her in his arms. She thought he might bend low and kiss her once again. As terrible as it was to admit, she wished he would.

But he didn't. Without a word, he reached out to take hold of her elbow, then turned and guided her away from the beach and along a narrow track cutting through the tropical jungle.

Five minutes later, the underbrush gave way to another sandy shore. And there, lying on its side on the beach, was the *Magic*.

"What happened?" Cassandra cried. "Who did this terrible thing?"

Grinning, Damian answered, "We're cleaning her hull. It's called careening."

She felt an enormous sense of relief. When she'd seen the great merchant ship lying there like a beached whale, she'd thought it was destroyed.

Robin Lee Hatcher

"Come on. I'll show you." Damian dropped the stallion's reins, then guided Cassandra closer to the *Magic*. "These warm waters cause a ship's hull to become quickly fouled with barnacles. It checks a ship's speed, and speed is important for a man in my trade."

His trade. Piracy. She felt a twinge of despair.

"We emptied her of all her cargo and heavy cannons before running her up on the beach and pulling her over on her side. Look. You can see where the men have been scraping the hull. We've repaired some of the sheathing, too." He pointed to a spot where the double timbers had been replaced. "Today, they'll smear her with a paste of tar, tallow, and sulfur. It will keep away the teredo worms and marine growth for a time, and it adds speed."

She glanced at him, repeating softly, "And speed is important for a man in your trade."

He turned toward her, his hands closing around her arms. "Would it do any good if I told you I wasn't a pirate?"

"Lies never serve a purpose, captain," she answered softly.

At first, he said nothing. Then he nodded. "I suppose you're right." He turned again, drawing her with him. "Come on. I'll take you back to the house."

118

Chapter Ten

Damian made his decision in the middle of the night. He wouldn't wait to hear from Abernathy. He would sail for the Carolinas as soon as the *Magic* was seaworthy. He couldn't risk keeping Cassandra here with him any longer. If he did, he would be unable to keep his word that no harm would come to her.

No, it would be better to take her to her fiance now, and when Damian was rid of her, he would seek out a comely wench at the nearest tavern and find his release from the hot desire that gnawed at his vitals. Once that was done, he would be able to turn his thoughts back where they belonged. He would be able to concentrate once more on the methodical and total destruction of Farley Dunworthy.

He was standing on the veranda the next morning when Cassandra entered the dining room. For a moment, he allowed himself to peruse her without his presence being known.

He liked the way she looked in the simple blue cotton blouse and skirt. He liked the way she looked without petticoats and corsets forcing her body into an artificial shape. Her natural form was much more attractive. She had a narrow waist and high, firm breasts. Her hips were gently rounded, pleasing to his eyes.

Since arriving at Sorcery Bay, she'd become careless about protecting herself from the sun, and her skin had turned a golden brown. Her silver-blond hair, once again captured in a single braid, had been bleached another shade lighter.

He must have unconsciously made a sound. She turned toward him, her gaze darting to meet his. Her deep-blue eyes widened, revealing her thoughts as easily to him as if she were an open book. She was confused by her feelings toward him. She was disturbed that she was drawn to a man of his low character. Her gentle breeding would never allow her to feel anything for a pirate but disdain.

But was he any less confused by his feelings for her? Never before had one woman enthralled and enticed him as she did. Never before had a woman captured his thoughts and imagination so completely, at times even making him forget his single most important goal.

But there was no room in his life for her or the alien emotions she stirred in his chest. He knew it, and there was nothing he could do to change it.

He frowned as he stepped into the dining room. "Have Ruth pack your trunk. We sail for Charleston tomorrow."

"You've heard from Mr. Abernathy so soon?" Her cheeks grew pale.

"No. We've not heard, and we won't wait to hear. If we take you now, we can respond that much quicker when he pays the ransom."

Her voice dropped to a whisper. "And if he doesn't?"

God's teeth! Had she no idea what she did to a man? Abernathy would be a fool if he didn't pay the ransom. Any man with blood still flowing in his veins would gladly pay a king's ransom to hold this woman in his arms for even one night, let alone for the chance to make her his bride.

"If he doesn't, I'll take you back to England. I'll return you to your father."

"You would do that?"

He stifled the urge to tell her he would do whatever she wished him to do, instead saying, "What else *would* I do with you, Cassandra? Do you think I would keep you my unwilling captive forever?" His tone grew unnecessarily harsh. "I have no use for you beyond the ransom you'll bring."

His words stung more deeply than she cared to admit. "Why do you need the money?" she shot back, anger heating her chest. "Your plantation appears prosperous. Your shipping concern does well if I'm to believe what you told me yesterday."

"I *don't* need the money." His black eyes revealed a sudden fury. "But your uncle does, and I mean to see that he doesn't get it."

Her anger dissipated amidst confusion. "My uncle? But what has he to do with this? The ransom comes to you, not him."

He ignored her questions. "See that your trunk is packed. We sail as soon as possible." He strode past her, disappearing into the hall beyond the dining room doorway.

She stared after him, wondering why he had grown so angry with her, wondering what he'd meant about her uncle needing the money but not getting it. Mr. Abernathy had sent the marriage settlement to her uncle months ago, so ransom or no, Uncle Far had nothing more to receive. And why would Damian be determined to prevent her uncle from receiving money from Mr. Abernathy, even if he had reason to send it to Uncle Far?

She sat down on a chair beside the dark, burnished table, worrying the inside of her lower lip with her teeth as she pondered the many unanswered questions.

Could it be that Damian's shipping company was suffering because of Tate Shipping's past successes? But her uncle was an honest man. He would do nothing but what the fair rules of trade allowed. Surely Damian could understand this. He couldn't fault her uncle if Tate Shipping was successful.

But if that wasn't the reason for his anger, what was? His enigmatic words made no sense.

She glanced toward the empty doorway. If only she could learn the truth, perhaps she could better understand Damian. And despite her better judgment, she did want to understand him.

Cassandra rose from the chair. She would find Professor. He knew about Damian's past. Perhaps he would tell her what she needed to know.

What he couldn't tell her, of course, was *why* she needed to know.

A short time later, Cassandra located Professor in his spacious but cluttered office in a building that adjoined the main house. His desk was covered with papers and ledgers, and he was leaning forward, his elbows braced on the desk top, his brows drawn together in a thoughtful frown.

She rapped lightly on the doorjamb. "Professor?"

As he glanced up, he removed the spectacles which had been perched near the tip of his nose. "So, you have found my office, my dear. I wondered when you might start exploring the house. I've seen you walking the grounds."

"Am I disturbing you? I can come back another time."

"No, no. Please come in. My eyes grow tired of all these figures." He stood and motioned with his arm toward a chair opposite him. "Come and sit and let me look at your pretty face."

She moved obediently forward.

Professor's frown returned to crease his brow. "What's troubling you, Cassandra?"

"Damian has told me to prepare to leave Sorcery Bay. He's taking me to Charleston at once."

He raised an eyebrow but didn't comment.

"Professor . . ." She sat on the chair, then waited for him to take his seat again before she continued. "Would you tell me about Damian? Can you help me understand him?"

"And why is it you wish to understand him, my dear? Would it not be better to go to the colonies, marry Mr. Abernathy, and forget Damian?"

She glanced at her hands, now clenched in her lap. "I'm not sure I *shall* be able to forget him, Professor," she replied softly. She was surprised to feel the sting of tears in her eyes. She brought them under control before looking up again. "Please tell me about him."

He stared at her in thoughtful silence. She had nearly given up hope that he would answer her when he nodded.

"All right, Cassandra, I'll tell you what I feel at liberty to share about Damian. But there are some things only he can tell you."

She bobbed her head in agreement.

There was another lengthy pause while Professor decided where to begin. When he spoke, it was in a low but steady voice. "Damian was still a young boy, no more than twelve, when he came to Barbados as an indentured servant. His first master was a cruel man. Spotswood treated his animals better than he treated his servants and slaves. Damian came to know the feel of the lash on his back all too well during those early years, but there was no way for him to escape."

Cassandra bit her lower lip to stifle a groan of distress.

Professor rose from his desk and stepped over to the window. He stared for a time at the fields of cane. "Damian was filled with hate and bitterness, not just for the man who sent him to Barbados and not just for how he was treated by his master, but because of what he saw done to others with him. When he saw another servant mistreated, he always tried to help. It only earned him more severe punishment."

Cassandra envisioned the story Professor was telling. She could imagine the tall young man speaking out to protect the weaker, the less fortunate. It didn't surprise her, even though she knew it should, that he'd behaved so honorably.

Professor shook his head, adding softly, "His papers were sold to Jedidiah Benjamin when Damian was seventeen. Damian expected no better than what he'd experienced with Spotswood, but he found instead the first kind and gentle touch he'd known in years. I think, if his papers hadn't been sold to Jedidiah, that Damian would never have lived to see his twenty-first year."

Silence filled the room. Cassandra could feel in her heart the angry youth Damian must have been. She imagined the beatings he'd suffered, and she felt as if she were suffering them with him. She didn't know why his papers had been sold to Jedidiah Benjamin, but she silently thanked God that they had been.

When it seemed that Professor wouldn't continue without her encouragement, she said, "You mentioned once that Damian saved your life."

"Aye. He did."

"How?"

"I had no will to go on after Sarah died. I cared little what happened to me. I wanted only to die, too. Damian gave me the will to live. We discovered that we shared a common goal. He gave me a reason to go on."

Cassandra wondered what sort of goal the two men—two very different men—might have in common. She would have asked, but Professor didn't give her the opportunity.

"After Damian's indenture was completed, he returned to England, but he found there was nothing left for him there. He had no living family members, no property. The only people he knew were the Benjamins and the men and women he'd worked with in the cane fields of Barbados. He came back, found this island, and began building his own plantation. He refused from the very beginning to use slaves or indentured servants. Only free men labor in these fields."

"Damian told me he served as a privateer during the war with Spain."

Professor nodded as he turned away from the window, once again meeting her eyes.

"But why did he do it? Why go to sea to fight after starting Sorcery Bay?"

"Because he knew it was the only way he could ever raise the money to build or buy his own ships."

"Was that what turned him to piracy?"

He answered her question with one of his own. "Is a pirate all you see when you look at him, Cassandra?"

She didn't know what to say. She considered the different Damians she'd seen. She recalled all the things he made her feel. She thought of the terrifying scowl of a demon-captain. She thought of the way he looked at the helm, so tall and strong and sure. She thought of the surprising kindness she could hear in his voice at the most unexpected times. She thought of his confusing bursts of anger. She thought of his mouth upon hers, of the wonderful taste of his lips and the way he made her stomach tumble with just a glance.

"I think I've said enough, my dear. Whatever else you wish to know should come from Damian himself."

She rose from her chair, glad to escape the office, longing for a breeze of fresh air to help clear the confusion in her head.

"Cassandra . . ." His voice stopped her before she could take her first step.

She met Professor's hazel gaze.

"Damian bears more scars than those put on his back by Spotswood. The ones on his soul will be more difficult to heal. It will take more than Jedidiah's kindness to soothe Damian's desire for revenge."

Cassandra felt another wave of sadness wash over her. Professor had revealed only brief glimpses of Damian's life. Even while shedding some light on the man, his answers had brought only more questions. She felt she knew Damian less now than she had before. What she *did* know made her want to weep.

Were her threatening tears for a young boy mistreated by an evil master, she wondered, or because she would not be the one to help heal the wounds of his heart?

"Thank you, Professor," she whispered as she turned, head bowed, and left the office. She didn't hear his parting words.

"God willing, I will see you again, Cassandra Jamison."

Chapter Eleven

The *Magic* sliced through rough seas on her way up the coast toward the Carolinas. Gray clouds loomed on the eastern horizon, promising a storm before nightfall, but Damian planned to drop anchor in Charleston's harbor before the winds and rains were loosed upon them.

By morning, he would be rid of Cassandra. He would be glad when this business was behind him. He'd neglected his real duties too long. He'd let himself be diverted from what he knew had to be done. Damian had taken Cassandra to help quicken her uncle's financial ruin. Now it was time Damian was back in the shipping lanes, making sure that Farley had no opportunity to gather strength, not even temporarily. The baron was in serious trouble. This was no time for Damian to back away from his persistent attacks on Tate Shipping.

Standing on the poop deck, Damian gave a few instructions to the sailor at the helm before walking swiftly toward the hatch and going below. He wanted to make a few notations in his log, then he needed to make plans for the *Magic*'s next venture. With the taking of the *Peacock*'s cargo and Damian's interference in Farley's plans to ransom his niece, Tate Shipping's condition had to be even more tenuous than before. Damian needed to know what the baron planned to do now. For that, he would need to return to England.

He hesitated outside the door to Cassandra's cabin. He hadn't spoken to her since the morning he'd told her to prepare to leave Sorcery Bay. Any contact they'd shared had been done through Oliver. She'd rarely come up on deck during their journey north. When Cassandra had seen fit to leave her cabin—dressed once again in her tight stays and voluminous skirts—Damian had been careful to keep a generous distance between them. He was all too aware of the desire he felt whenever she was near. He could also sense her unhappiness, and his response to that unhappiness was an unwelcome one. He had no time to worry about Farley's niece. He needed no further complications. It would be better for all concerned if he kept things as they were.

And yet, try as he might, his thoughts were never far from the silver-haired beauty with her tanned cheeks, her wide blue eyes, her curving woman's figure clad in free-flowing island attire.

Swearing silently, Damian moved on down the passageway, a scowl darkening his chiseled features.

Cassandra let out her breath as the footsteps moved away from her door. She'd known it was Damian. She always recognized the determined, sure sound of his walk. She'd thought for just a moment that he might knock at her door, that he might speak to her again.

But, of course, he hadn't. In her heart, she'd known he wouldn't. He'd made it clear enough that he wanted nothing more to do with her. She'd tried dozens of times during their voyage to the Carolinas to tell herself that she felt exactly the same. Only she knew she was lying. She *did* want more to do with him. Much more.

She had fallen in love with the pirate captain of the *Magic*.

Cassandra closed her eyes and pressed her fingertips against her eyelids. Her skin felt feverish. Was she ill? Were her feelings for the captain no more than the irrational thoughts of a sick mind?

She felt a pang in her chest.

No, it wasn't her imagination. She had lost her heart to a man who would never be accepted by her parents, her uncle, or polite society— a man who would most likely die with a noose around his neck or from being run through with a saber.

It was a hopeless love, not just because of who Damian was but because he cared naught for her. Even now he was taking her to another man, a man who would soon be her husband, a man she didn't love and could never love. At one time, she had hoped she could grow to care for Aldin Abernathy, but such a thing could never happen now. Not now that Damian had stolen her heart.

Stolen her heart. What an appropriate choice of words, she thought as she straightened in her chair and dropped her hands away from her eyes. He'd stolen her heart as surely as he and his men had looted the *Peacock*, absconding with everything of value. But somehow this theft seemed much worse. Silks, satins and jewels, porcelains and spices could be replaced. Her heart could not.

Perhaps he was a demon-captain after all.

One thing was certain. She would never let him know how she felt. She would go to Mr. Abernathy with her pride intact. She would not let Damian see how unhappy she was. That was why she had spent the better part of this voyage in her cabin. As much as she longed to be above deck, she couldn't bear to look at him and be unable to speak to him. And she knew, if she did speak to him, that she would betray herself.

She drew another deep breath, fortifying herself for what lay before her. When the time came, she would take leave of Damian and the other men of this ship with her head held high. A Jamison knew how to do her duty. She would go to Mr. Abernathy and she would marry him and she would make him a good wife. She would do this for her parents and her uncle, and she would make herself forget Captain Damian.

Somehow, she would make herself forget him.

Damian had been watching for the *Sea Hag* as they'd sailed for Charleston. He'd feared they had passed each other in the night and so was surprised that evening to see the vessel at anchor in the harbor. Mick Brussels— the captain of Damian's ship, the *Sea Hag*— had sailed with the ransom note nearly two weeks before Damian left Sorcery Bay. He should have been on his way back with the ransom by this time.

A skiff was lowered into the water and sent over to the *Sea Hag.* It wasn't long before Oliver returned with Mick Brussels. Damian met with them in his cabin.

"I'm surprised to find you still here, Mick," Damian said as the other captain took a seat across from him.

"Aye. No more surprised than I am, sir. We had a devil of a time finding Mr. Abernathy. His plantation is a fair piece from Charleston, and when we finally found it, we learned that he was away and not expected to return soon.

We left a message for him. We only just today received his answer."

"And?" Damian prompted.

Mick glanced at Oliver, then returned his gaze to Damian. "He states he already paid a ransom and that he'll not be dunned for more."

"Already paid? But that's—" Damian stopped abruptly. His hands tightened into fists and he slammed one of them down on top of the desk. "God's blood! Farley requested the ransom without even having the girl!"

Neither Mick nor Oliver replied.

The fury in Damian's chest rendered him momentarily speechless. He had underestimated Farley's temerity. He should have realized that taking Cassandra wouldn't stop her uncle. What cared the bloody baron whether or not Cassandra was actually ever delivered to her groom? As long as Farley had the money, he would be satisfied. After all, no one would ever suspect that Baron Kettering had been involved in any way. He'd always been so devoted to his niece.

"What do we do with her now?" Oliver ventured.

Damian shook his head as he turned to stare out the windows. He doubted that Farley had given his niece more than a passing thought since she'd been carried off the *Peacock*. He doubted that Farley had even tried to learn what her fate had been. And now that the baron had collected the ransom, Damian doubted her uncle would try to find her.

Oliver cleared his throat. "Captain?"

he was a pirate, that he took from others to line his own pockets, that he didn't see what he did was wrong, didn't even consider himself a pirate. She wished she could have met Damian in some other way. She wished . . .

She pulled her cloak more tightly about her, trying to ignore the hollow feeling in her chest.

It did no good to wish that things were different than they were. Wishing changed nothing. Tomorrow she would be taken into Charleston. She would meet her groom, and before long they would be wed. That was her destiny.

She touched her lips with her fingertips and tried to recall the sweetness of Damian's mouth upon hers. If only she could have had one more kiss from him . . .

Her own tears mixed with raindrops on her cheeks. The lights along the shore were blurred by the mist in her eyes.

Lord, the pain in her heart was nearly unbearable. Why hadn't her mother warned her that grand passions were only grand if they were shared? Why hadn't someone warned her that love was only sheer heaven if it was returned?

Go to him. Tell him you can't marry Mr. Abernathy. Tell Damian you love him.

Cassandra choked back a sob.

If only she *could* go to him. But she'd been raised to believe that right was right and wrong was wrong. The lines of her world had always been so clearly drawn. There was good and there was evil. There was black and there was white. One did one's duty to one's family. One followed the rules of society. One's conduct must always be moral and upright.

Her parents and her uncle had instilled these values in her from the cradle. How could she go against them now? How could she become the mistress of a pirate? It would break her parents' hearts—and her uncle's, too. Mr. Abernathy would no doubt demand that his marriage settlement be repaid. It might ruin her entire family.

No, there was no running away from what had to be done. She could make a thousand wishes, but it didn't change what tomorrow would bring. When she lay for the first time with a man, it would be with a stranger. It could never be with the man she loved.

Chapter Twelve

Beneath a pewter-gray morning sky, Damian moved with stiff resolve across the main deck, steeling himself against the resigned, futile look in Cassandra's eyes. Her gaze didn't waver from his. He was the first to look away.

He saw that she was wearing a velvet gown of soft rose, a color that normally echoed a touch of pink in her cheeks. The tight stays of her corset pushed her breasts up toward the scooped neckline of the bodice, accentuating their fullness. He thought of Abernathy feasting his gaze upon them and felt a rush of anger.

"Miss Jamison," he said as he stopped before her.

She lifted her head slightly. "Captain Damian."

"Well, you've arrived safely in Carolina, just as I promised you would."

"Yes, you did promise that."

He saw the quiver in her slightly pointed chin. He pushed away the desire to touch it, still it. He pushed it away as resolutely as he had subdued the anger he'd felt at the thought of another man holding her, kissing her, making love with her.

Oliver came toward him. "We're ready to go, captain."

He nodded, his eyes not leaving Cassandra's face. "I suppose it would be useless to ask you to forgive me for taking you from the *Peacock*. I still believe it was better for you that we did."

Tears sparkled in her eyes. "I've forgiven you already, captain," she whispered.

His response was totally unexpected, especially to him.

There was nothing gentle about the way he grabbed hold of her, pulling her into his embrace. There was nothing tentative about the way his mouth pressed against hers, searching, probing, demanding. He drank her in, like a man marooned on a spit of sand who has just tasted his first drink of fresh water in many weeks.

As his hands slipped up her throat to cradle her face, he felt her rapid pulse, like the fluttering wings of a captured bird. He heard the tiny sounds she made, half-pleasure, half-protest. He caught them in his mouth and savored them as he savored her.

He ached with desire. He realized he was only a breath away from giving into madness, to picking her up and carrying her below deck, to telling his men to set sail for Sorcery Bay and to hell with Abernathy and Dunworthy and the whole damn world.

Dunworthy. The name cut through the haze of his passion like a sharp blade, and he knew that he couldn't say to hell with the man who had sent his father to his death.

Only a breath. But it had been just enough to stop him from doing what he knew he mustn't.

With a tight grip on Cassandra's upper arms, Damian set her back from him. "It seems I must apologize for one more thing, Miss Jamison. Please forgive me." He turned toward Oliver but refrained from meeting his lieutenant's gaze. "See that she reaches her betrothed safely. We'll set sail upon your return."

"Aye, captain."

Although he tried not to, he couldn't stop himself from glancing one last time at Cassandra. Her cheeks were flushed. Her eyes were wide and had a feverish appearance. She wore a stricken expression, and he knew that it was his fault. But he hardened himself against the temptation to offer comfort.

Without another word, he turned on his heel and strode away from her.

Cassandra was gripped with a blessed numbness throughout the journey to the Abernathy plantation. She was grateful that Oliver didn't expect her to carry on a conversation. She couldn't have done so, even if she'd tried. And she didn't want to try.

She had no idea how much time elapsed before the carriage turned off the main road, but when she looked up, she found a two-story manse at the end of a long drive, bathed in the sunlight of mid-day. What had happened to the clouds that had covered the sky when she'd left the *Magic*? Had she truly been in this carriage as long as that?

"We're here, miss," Oliver said.

Her only reply was to nod. What was there to say? That she was happy to be here? She wasn't.

The driver stopped the horses before the steps leading to the front entrance of the mansion. Oliver opened the carriage door and stepped to the ground, then turned and offered her his hand. She hesitated a moment, her eyes glancing toward the house, then back to Damian's lieutenant.

She saw something flicker in his brown eyes. Was it pity? Had he guessed she'd fallen in love with Damian?

"Miss Jamison . . ." he began.

Summoning her courage, she took hold of his hand and stepped out of the carriage. She lifted her chin proudly and held her shoulders erect as she faced the house that would soon be her home.

At that moment, the doors opened. Two black-skinned boys clad in red livery came out first, each stepping to the opposite side of the doorway. A moment later, their master appeared.

Aldin Abernathy was dressed in the fashion of the day, from his gold buckled shoes to his long coat and waistcoat to his white cravat, so carefully tied, to his full-bottomed wig. Of medium height, his figure was full but not portly. There was nothing remarkable about his face, but neither were his features disagreeable.

Abernathy paused at the edge of the portico, his gray eyes slowly perusing her. She felt uneasy beneath his gaze. There was an odd turn to his mouth that made her think he was sneering at her. "So, they have seen fit to send you to me at last, Miss Jamison." Suddenly, he turned his head and shouted, "Roman!"

A giant of a black man appeared quickly.

"Take these men and put them in the barn. We'll hold them for the constable." His gaze returned to Oliver. "We'll teach this rabble a lesson. You'll both hang for your part in this."

"Wait!" Impulsively, Cassandra stepped in front of Oliver before Roman reached him. "Mr. Abernathy, these man are innocent of any wrongdoing. They were hired only to bring me to you. They are not the pirates who took me from my uncle's ship." She glanced at the massive black man beside her, then at his master. "Please, sir," she continued more softly, "these men have shown only kindness toward me. Don't repay them this way. They might have left me on the docks in Charleston and let me find my own way here."

Abernathy's eyes narrowed, but finally, he nodded. "Very well. Roman, take them to the kitchens and see that they receive food and drink for their trouble." He held out his hand toward Cassandra. "My dear, come with me. There is much we must talk about."

She wished she could say more to Oliver. She wished she could tell him—tell him what? That he was her friend? That she would miss him? No, she couldn't have said those things, even if Abernathy weren't standing so nearby.

She glanced over her shoulder. "Thank you, sir, for bringing me here. You have been most kind."

" 'Twas my pleasure, miss."

This time when he smiled, she didn't even notice the scar along his jaw. She only saw the familiar face of a man who had treated her with nothing but gentleness the entire time she'd known him. She did, indeed, see a friend, and she knew she would miss him.

"I pray you'll be happy, Miss Jamison," Oliver added.

"Thank you, sir," she whispered, her throat too tight to speak more loudly.

Turning straight ahead, Cassandra stepped forward and accepted Abernathy's proffered hand. She noticed that his hand was small, his touch almost clammy. So different from . . .

But no, she couldn't think of *him*. She couldn't compare Abernathy to the captain, else she would never find any peace, any comfort in the life before her.

He led her into a small study at the rear of the house. The walls were lined with oak bookshelves. The furniture was dark and heavy. Brocade curtains framed the two windows. The room smelled of leather and pipe tobacco.

"Sit down, Cassandra," Abernathy said, motioning to a chair. After she'd done so, he moved to a sofa opposite her, standing behind it, his hands on the upholstered back. His gray eyes once again perused her, pausing for a lengthy stay on the cleavage revealed above the neckline of her gown. "I see you have been exposed to a good deal of sun. You shouldn't be so careless."

She didn't know how to reply and so didn't.

His gaze returned to meet hers. "I would like an accounting of these past weeks. I wish to know what happened to you."

"I'm not sure I know what you mean, sir." She sat a bit straighter in her chair, disliking his manner.

"You know quite well what I mean, Cassandra. I want to know how you were treated by the pirates who took you captive."

"I am unharmed, if that's what you mean. After I was taken from the *Peacock*, I was kept locked in a small cabin until the ship reached an island somewhere to the south of here. We remained there a few days before I was put aboard a merchant vessel and sent to you." .

"I see." Abernathy stepped over to a large desk near one of the windows. With precise movements, he filled a pipe with tobacco, then lit it. Finally, he turned toward her again. He puffed on the pipe while his eyes stared at her thoughtfully.

Cassandra wanted to squirm. She didn't like what she saw in his eyes. There was something about him that made her feel unclean. In an effort to escape his gaze, she turned her head and pretended to study the room.

"Do you know how much I paid for you, Cassandra?"

Her stomach tightened. "I am aware of the terms of the marriage settlement," she replied, reluctantly looking at him again.

"I could have chosen a wife who would not have come so dearly priced."

She felt queasy. "Then why didn't you?"

Abernathy returned to the sofa, this time sitting down. He crossed his legs as he leaned back and smiled at her. "Because, my dear, I never forgot what a beautiful child you were. I knew you would become only more lovely as you grew into a woman. You have not disappointed me. You were worth every pound I paid. You will, no doubt, bear handsome children." He drew on the pipe again.

She knew she should have responded to his compliment about her looks, but it didn't sound like a compliment. His comments left her feeling like a piece of goods one could buy in a shop or a brood mare purchased for his stables.

"Of course, when I sent the marriage settlement, it was with the understanding that my bride would be an innocent, uninitiated into the intimacies shared between a man and a woman."

She stared at him blankly.

"I expected my bride to be a virgin."

She felt her cheeks grow hot. "I assure you, sir, that I am what you expected."

"Come now, my dear. Do you think me a fool? You were the prisoner of those men for nearly a month. Am I to believe that they didn't sample what I paid for in good faith?"

Cassandra rose stiffly from her chair. "Believe what you will, Mr. Abernathy. I have nothing to be ashamed of. If this is how you feel, then I shall return to my parents. We shall see that the marriage settlement is returned to you in full."

His smile broadened as he, too, rose to his feet. "That won't be necessary. If that was what I wanted, I never would have paid the thousand pound ransom which was demanded for your safe return."

"A thousand pounds," she echoed, her eyes widening.

"Yes, a thousand pounds." Abernathy stepped toward her. "You see, Cassandra, I knew you would be worth the price, even if you came to me a trifle sullied."

Her breathing became more rapid as he drew closer. She wanted to dash from the room but was unable to move.

"Of course, we shall have to wait to become more intimately acquainted until after we're certain that you're not carrying some pirate's by-blow. I'm not averse to my mistress giving birth to a bastard child, but I should prefer to know that the child is mine."

"Mistress?" The word was barely audible.

He set down the pipe on a nearby table. "You surely don't expect me to marry you now." His hands closed around her arms. "But neither shall I be without you. I've paid dearly for the pleasure of having you in my bed, and have you I shall."

He bent to kiss her, but she turned her head and his mouth only grazed her cheek.

Abernathy gave her a sharp jerk, his fingers biting into her arms. "Don't fight me, my dear. You shall only regret it."

He did kiss her then, and it was all she could do to keep from gagging as his lips pressed against hers.

The instant he released her, she wiped the back of her hand across her mouth. "I shall not be your whore, sir," she cried in defiance. "You cannot force me to do so."

"Whore is such an ugly term. Would it not be better to think of you as my companion?" He grinned. "Roman!"

The door to the study opened, revealing the servant.

"Take Miss Jamison to the room we prepared for her. I believe she needs time to rest and think about her future."

"No!" Cassandra bolted past the surprised slave and raced from the study. Holding her skirts out of the way, she ran down the hall and through the open doorway. The carriage was just disappearing around the bend, the horses racing at a full gallop. "No," she said again, this time in a whisper. "Please, God, no."

"We shall have to work on your obedience, Cassandra."

She whirled to face Abernathy.

"I expect everyone on Three Oaks—whether wife, mistress, or slave—to obey me or face the consequences." His expression hardened. "You don't wish to know what those consequences are, my dear. I should not like to see a woman as lovely as you bear such punishment."

Her courage had vanished along with Oliver and the carriage. "You cannot do this." Her voice quivered as she fought back tears of fear and despair. "My uncle will not let you get away with this. He will—"

Abernathy laughed. "You don't know the baron as well as I do. He'll not interfere, believe me. In truth, he'll not even know what has happened to you. Perhaps, in a few years, you can return to England. If you're wise, you'll use what you learn here to your advantage. A woman of your beauty could make herself very wealthy, my dear. There are men far richer than I who would pay dearly for what I mean to possess."

She began to shake.

"Take her to her room, Roman, and see that she's not disturbed."

Cassandra felt the servant's hands on her arms just before she was swallowed up by blackness.

Chapter Thirteen

The thundering sound of galloping horses broke the stillness of the night as Damian and ten of his crew followed the road from Charleston to Three Oaks Plantation, their way lit by a full moon. Damian forced himself not to think about what might have happened to Cassandra after Oliver drove away from Abernathy's home, but he couldn't rid his thoughts of what Oliver had told him upon his return.

"I swear 'tis true, captain. He don't mean t'marry her. He means t'keep her as his doxy."

"How do you know this?"

"I stopped to listen outside the window. I thought . . . Well, I wanted to know that she was all right. She'd seemed so unhappy and all. I would've tried to do something myself when I heard the things he said, but I had no weapons

with me. I thought it best that I come for you and the others."

Rage roiled in Damian's chest, driving out the memory. If Abernathy had hurt her, he would gladly draw and quarter him. He would choke the life from the man with his own hands and watch as his eyes bulged and his tongue swelled.

" 'Tis the place up ahead," Oliver called to him.

Damian raised his hand in a signal for the men to slow their mounts. His gaze swept the landscape, stopping on a copse of trees. "We'll leave the animals there. Toby," he said to the *Magic's* powder monkey, "you stay with the horses. Keep alert. We don't know who might be about the place. And stay ready. We'll more than likely return in a hurry."

"Aye, sir," the lad responded. "I'll not be caught by surprise."

In a short while, the crew of the *Magic* had dismounted and were making their way stealthily toward the brick mansion.

Cassandra sat rigidly at one end of the long dining table. Despite the delicious odors and inviting appearance of the food—roast goose, succulent pork, plum pudding, fresh breads, and a variety of fruits and vegetables, many of them unknown to her—she had no appetite.

Earlier, Abernathy had sent a young slave girl to help Cassandra dress for dinner. The girl had stayed to comb her hair, weaving it into an artful design atop her head. Afterward, the servant had pulled a box from the pocket of her dress and held it out to her new mistress.

Cassandra had opened it to discover a glittering necklace of gold, heavily laden with diamonds. She had immediately closed the lid and tried to give it back to the girl.

"Miss Cass'dra, if'n you don't wear it, the master done swore he'd beat me good."

She'd looked at the wan face of the servant—she was little more than a child, really—and had known she couldn't be the cause of her suffering. Silently, she had allowed the girl to fasten the heavy necklace around her throat. It had felt like a hangman's noose. It still did.

"Do you find nothing to your liking, my dear?" Abernathy asked, breaking the tense silence.

She glanced up from her plate. "No, Mr. Abernathy, I do not."

"A shame. My cook worked hard preparing this meal in welcome for you." He motioned for a servant in scarlet livery to pour more wine into his glass. "Perhaps a bit of sherry for Miss Cassandra," he told the man. "It might help her to relax."

"I do not care for any," she said quickly.

"No?" He glanced at the slave. "Pour it, Mando."

Mando carried the decanter down the length of the table and obediently filled her glass. Cassandra ignored it. With her eyes on the man sitting opposite her, she lifted her chin in a

153

continued show of defiance. Her hands were clenched tightly in her lap.

She thought of the way she'd felt when she was first taken prisoner by Damian. How frightened she'd been. How uncertain her future. But it seemed nothing now in comparison to what this man made her feel.

But she had remained unscathed when held captive by a band of cutthroat pirates. She could remain unscathed by this degenerate fop who meant to use her and then toss her aside. She would find some way to send word to her uncle of what had happened here. He would come to her rescue.

"Leave us, Mando. We don't want to be disturbed." Abernathy dropped his napkin beside his plate and rose from his chair. "Not for any reason."

Warily, she watched his approach, flinching when she heard the door close behind the servant, hating the knowledge that she was alone with this man. As he drew near, she dropped her gaze to the table.

Abernathy's fingers fell to the sherry glass. He lightly traced circles around the brim of the crystal, then slowly slid the glass toward her. "I believe I was hasty in the words I spoke to you earlier, my dear."

She glanced up at him.

"I was wrong to say the things I did. I do hope you'll find it in your heart to forgive me."

She searched his face but found no remorse there.

"It was merely because of my concern for you. Imagine what I've been through. Learning that you'd been taken by pirates. Receiving a ransom demand for your safe return. It has been a very trying time for me, not knowing what had been your fate."

"I told you I was unharmed," she stated.

He reached down and took hold of her hand, drawing it up to his lips, then kissing her knuckles. "I have asked for your forgiveness."

"You may have it, sir." Again, she met his gaze. "I shall never tell anyone what words passed between us today. When I return to my family, I shall merely tell them that we didn't suit."

"Return?" He pulled her up from her chair. "I think you mistook my meaning, Cassandra. My haste was in saying we would wait to become more intimately acquainted. I know now that I cannot wait. I shall not wait for you."

His arms were around her before she could react.

"Don't fight me, Cassandra. It's useless. Let's see what your captors taught you. I may find that I'm grateful to them. But I promise, you shall enjoy me more."

The fingers of his right hand twined in her hair, pulling her head back and forcing her to look at him. His left hand slid forward from her back to fondle her breast. She struggled to free herself, but he jerked on her hair so hard it brought tears to her eyes.

"Abominable corsets," he grumbled as his fingers began freeing the buttons of her gown. "I want to see you. I want to feel you."

She kicked him as hard as she could. With a yowl, he stepped back from her. She turned to run but he caught her from behind, knocking her to the floor. As she tried to rise, he flipped her onto her back and then threw himself across her. She struck at him with her fists.

"No!" she screamed.

But he paid her no heed. His face was flushed with anger and something more. She saw the determination in his gray eyes and knew he had no intention of stopping until he had taken from her what she least wanted to give. She felt his hands all over her, tugging and pulling at her clothing. She heard the rending of fabric and felt cool air upon her shoulders. Another rip and a length of her leg was exposed.

"No!" she cried again, closing her eyes, as if it would shut out the reality of the moment. "No!"

His mouth clamped down on hers, wet and vile. She tried to twist away from him, but he held her firmly. He parted his lips and tried to force his tongue into her mouth. She whimpered in protest.

And then his weight was suddenly gone, his mouth no longer covering hers. She heard his yelp of surprise just as she opened her eyes to see him suspended in air above her. A moment later, he was flying across the room and smashing against a wall.

"Damian," she whispered as her eyes focused on the dark visage above her.

He didn't act as if he'd heard her. Long strides carried him across the dining hall toward the crumpled figure of Aldin Abernathy. Damian picked the man up by the cravat, lifting his feet off the floor.

"You worm-infested piece of dung," he growled. "I should feed you to the sharks. They'll eat anything. Even something as foul-tasting as you."

Judging by the expression on Damian's face, Abernathy had reason to fear for his life. Never had she witnessed such fury. She could feel it in the room, like another presence.

But *she* had no reason to fear Damian. Her heart rejoiced at the sight of him. He'd come for her. She'd thought he'd left her to this horrible fate, but he hadn't. He did care. He must. He'd come for her.

"Damian . . ."

His name was a mere whisper on her lips, yet somehow he must have heard her for he turned his head, and their gazes met. Unexpectedly, tears welled in her eyes, blurring his image.

Without looking at Abernathy, Damian gave the man a gruff shake, eliciting a pitiful whine of fear. Then he tossed him into the wall again. "Take care of that scum, Oliver," he ordered.

Quick strides carried him across the room. He knelt on the floor and pulled Cassandra into his arms, cradling her head against his chest. "There now," he said softly as she began to weep in earnest. "I'm here. 'Tis all right now. He can do you no more harm."

"Da . . . Damian, he . . . he was . . . he meant to . . ."

"Hush now." He kissed her forehead and then the tip of her nose. With his free hand, he stroked her hair. " 'Tis over, my lovely. I'm with you."

She looked up at him with tear-glazed eyes. "Ta . . . take me away from here, Damian. Please . . . take me with you."

"I'll not leave you, Cassandra. I promise." He slipped his arm beneath her knees and lifted her from the floor. "I'll not leave you again."

He didn't check to see what Oliver had done with Abernathy or the servants they'd subdued earlier. At the moment, he didn't care. Abernathy was lucky Damian hadn't killed him. It wasn't because he hadn't wanted to. When he'd entered the dining room and seen Abernathy lying atop Cassandra, mauling her as if she were a strumpet in some back-lane brothel, he'd wanted to tear the filthy cur to pieces with his bare hands. He might have if she hadn't whispered his name. He might have if he hadn't seen her tears and felt a need to comfort her, a need greater than his desire to smash Abernathy beneath his fists.

His arms tightened slightly around her, as if to reassure himself that he was truly holding her, that she was all right, that he hadn't just imagined her. Her sobs had quieted, but every so often, she drew in a ragged breath. By the saints, he wished he could make her forget this night. When he thought of what might have happened if he'd arrived only a few minutes later . . .

He felt the fury returning to burn hot in his chest. He forced it aside, making himself think calmly. He had no time for temper now. He had to get Cassandra away from here. He couldn't be sure that one of Abernathy's servants hadn't escaped and run for help.

Holding Cassandra tenderly against him, he strode out of the house and down the drive to where Toby waited with the horses. His men followed silently in his wake.

It wasn't until they were all mounted that he looked around at his crew. In the light of the moon, he could see that Binns had a nasty cut above his right eyebrow and York had a bloody nose, but other than that, everyone seemed to have fared well.

He turned his head toward his lieutenant. "Abernathy?" he asked.

"He'll survive, captain, though his face got a bit bloodied in the scuffle." He shrugged his shoulders. "Don't know how it happened," he finished with a look of feigned innocence.

Damian nodded, then nudged his hired horse into a lope. He wanted to be aboard ship and sailing from the harbor before dawn.

Within the safety of Damian's arms, Cassandra found comfort, and the steady rocking of the horse's gait lulled her into sleep during the ride to Charleston. She stirred when the horses stopped but went back to sleep when Damian whispered softly in her ear, telling her not to worry. All was safe.

She wasn't aware of him carrying her onto the *Magic*. She didn't know when he placed her in the large, soft bed in the captain's quarters or when he removed her damaged gown and replaced it with a simple nightshirt or when he covered her with the soft, down quilt. She never knew when he lay beside her, his body stretched out next to hers, offering her comfort and warmth within the circle of his arms.

Chapter Fourteen

Throughout the night, Cassandra's dreams were filled with a sense of well-being. She saw Damian walking along the beach, leading his fine gray stallion. She saw the sunlight caressing his ebony hair and sparkling across the surface of the turquoise bay. She saw Circe jumping into Damian's arms and heard his laughter. She felt the warmth of his smile as their gazes met and knew a joy in her heart that was nearly unbearable. She wanted it always to be like this. She wanted to stay here in this place, where nothing and no one could ever harm them again, where they would always be together.

Together . . . together . . . together . . .

She sighed as she drifted into wakefulness. She wasn't ready to give up the warmth of her dreams just yet.

Slowly, she became aware of the rolling movement of her bed and realized that she was aboard ship again and they were out to sea. And then she became aware of something else. She wasn't alone in the bed.

She opened her eyes. The pewter light of pre-dawn spilled through the windows that lined the back wall of Damian's cabin and enabled her to see him watching her. He lay on his side, facing her. He was so close that she could see the black lashes that fringed his equally black eyes. So close that she could reach out and touch the dark hairs that curled on his chest, a chest laid bare above the covers on the bed.

He reached forward, laying a calloused hand upon her cheek. She lifted her own hand to cover his. A quiver ran the length of her, and her breathing came hard.

"I won't apologize for bringing you aboard the *Magic* this time," he said in a low voice.

She moistened her lips with the tip of her tongue, then drew in a quick breath before answering, "I ask for no apologies, captain."

His hand slid from her cheek, moving down her neck, over her shoulder, and then around to the small of her back. Once there, he gently pulled her toward him. So close she could feel the warmth of his body, and yet not so close that they touched.

"Cassandra . . ."

She felt another shiver shoot along her spine as the whispered caress brushed across her forehead. She closed her eyes, allowing herself to absorb all these strange, new, wonderful sensations.

His mouth touched her forehead, then spread a trail of kisses down to her temple and over to her ear. As he nibbled on her tender lobe, she let out her breath on a sigh.

Suddenly, his arm tightened, pulling her against him at last. He buried his face in her hair. "I thought I'd lost you," he whispered hoarsely. "When I think what might have happened . . ."

She returned his embrace. "Let's not think of it, Damian. Let's never think of it."

He pulled back for a moment. His hands moved to cup her face, and he stared into her eyes. "You weren't harmed?"

"I'm not harmed."

"I wanted to kill him."

"He wasn't worth killing." Again she covered his hand with her own.

"I feared I wouldn't get there in time."

"But you did."

"Cassandra . . ."

She answered the unspoken question with a kiss. At first it was soft and tender, but within moments, it had deepened, changed. Without prodding, she opened her mouth to accept his tongue. She felt her pulse begin to race. The taste of him excited her. She sucked lightly on his tongue and knew she'd caused him pleasure when she heard the low sound in his throat.

He wrapped her in his arms once more. She felt the rock hardness of his body beneath her hands. She ran her fingers over the sinewy muscles of his back and shoulders. When he moved against her, her hips instinctively pressed forward. An odd frustration built in her loins. She felt an agonizing need to draw closer and closer to him.

His kisses continued even as he drew the nightshirt she wore up to her waist with one hand. She gasped into his mouth when his fingers touched the flat of her stomach. Her eyes flew open, but his remained closed as his touch moved up from her belly, his hand coming to rest on the fullness of her breast.

She felt a flash of panic, but it was quickly replaced with something better as he gently stroked her breast, teasing her nipple between thumb and forefinger. Her eyes fluttered closed again.

"Ah, my lovely," he whispered, his lips lightly brushing against hers as he spoke, "you have been like a fire in my veins from the very first time I saw you."

And I believed you a demon, she thought, unable to say it aloud. The things he was making her feel had stolen the ability to speak. *I thought you were a demon, but I came to love you and knew that it wasn't true. You are magnificent, my pirate captain. Magnificent.*

His mouth plundered hers again.

I love you, Captain Damian.

Conscious thought was driven from her mind as his hands continued to explore her body. There was only room for feeling. And such feelings she'd never known before.

Deftly, he removed her nightshirt and discarded it, tossing it onto the floor of the cabin. She had no idea how he pulled the item over her head without her knowing his lips had left hers nor did she care how he'd done it. She only knew that another new sensation had been added to all the others as her bare breasts were pressed against the hardness of his chest.

Damian . . . oh, Damian . . .

His hands cupped her buttocks and drew her hips toward him. Her eyes flew open as she felt his hardness pressing intimately against her. Once again, panic shot through her. Her body tensed, and she tried to pull back from him. What was she doing? What was she about to do?

"Don't be afraid of me, Cassandra," he said softly. "Never be afraid of me."

No, she wouldn't be afraid of him. Damian wouldn't hurt her. He wouldn't allow anyone to ever hurt her again.

Her body relaxed. *Love me, Damian. Please love me.*

One hand moved from her buttock, sliding slowly to the triangle of pale curls between her thighs even as his mouth returned to hers. His caress was so light, so gentle, so . . .

She should have been horrified. Such an intimate touch had to be wrong; it had to be sinful.

She should have made him stop. Never had she imagined anyone touching her like this. And never had she imagined that a simple touch could cause such feelings as those that surged through her now. She felt herself begin to spin, to spiral upward, to soar. With a sigh of acceptance, she lost herself into a maelstrom of sensations.

Damian's desire was nearly unbearable, but he forced himself to be patient, to wait until she was ready for him. He would not let himself remember that she was an innocent, a virgin, that he was about to take from her that which would be most valued by a husband. He would not let himself think that another man might ever hold her as he was holding her now, that another man might ever touch her and feel her excitement building within. He only knew that he had to possess her, that the thought of being without her was more unbearable than the sweet torture he was experiencing as he waited to bury himself within her softness.

When her head fell back against the pillow and a groan forced its way through clenched lips, he was undone. He whispered her name as he rose above her. Her arms clung around his neck as he nudged her legs apart and slowly entered her. He stopped when he felt the tight resistance.

He looked into her face, saw the questioning fear in her eyes.

"There will be pain, but it will pass," he whispered hoarsely. "I promise you, it will pass."

The fear faded, and he saw only acceptance.

With a feral groan, he pushed himself deeper inside her.

The sudden pain was unexpected, despite Damian's words of warning. Her fingers pressed into his back as she stifled a cry against his shoulder. He stilled a second time, but this time he didn't raise his head to look at her. He waited, she knew not what for, and then began to move ever so slowly.

She was surprised. She had expected to feel the discomfort increase, but it didn't. Although she knew the pain was still there, her awareness of it lessened even as a curious pleasure began to build within her. His movements teased her, enticed her, and before she realized it, she was moving, too, matching his rhythm, seeking something she didn't understand.

He kissed her again, and for a second time she found herself slipping away from reality into a world of sensations, a world without thought. She gave herself up to it, flowing along with the rising of passion's tide, feeling something wild burning inside her, something that made her think she would shatter into a thousand pieces, and finally, crying out when the shattering came at last.

She scarcely heard his own shout of pleasure as she drifted into a place just shy of slumber.

How could he have done this? Damian wondered as he held her against him. Only a few short hours before, he had pulled her from

Abernathy's lusting embrace, saved her from being raped by a man who intended to make her his mistress. He had promised her she had nothing to fear, and then . . .

He was no better than Abernathy.

His gaze caressed her. She looked so peaceful, there in his arms. Her silvery-blond hair spilled over the bedding like a pool of sunlight upon water. Her rose-colored lips were slightly parted. Her golden-brown eyelashes lay against her sun-kissed cheeks.

How could he have taken her this way? It didn't matter that she'd been a willing participant. It didn't matter that she'd given herself to him. She'd been a virgin. She couldn't have known the consequences of what she was doing. He'd seen the surprise, the uncertainty on her face.

He was worse than Abernathy. At least Abernathy had been honest with her. He had told her he meant to make her his mistress. Damian had told her nothing.

How could he have made love to her, taken her innocence, when he knew there was no future for the two of them? He was sworn to destroy her uncle, and when he destroyed her uncle, he would be destroying Cassandra and her parents as well. The squire might be as innocent as his daughter in regard to Farley's machinations, but Henry Jamison would go down with the baron all the same. It couldn't be helped.

If only she weren't related to the baron.

168

No, it would have made no difference. There still would have been no future for the two of them. How could he ask her—or any woman—to risk her life as he plundered his sworn enemy's ships? There was no place in his life, or in his heart, for her. There couldn't be. Not now. Perhaps not ever.

He stared hard at her heart-shaped face, memorizing the turned-up tip of her nose, the stubborn point of her chin, the wisps of pale hair that curled near her temples and across her forehead.

She was like an angel. Would he have people think her a pirate's whore instead?

Condemnation filled his chest and burned his throat like a bitter bile.

That's what she thought him. A pirate. And she was right. That's what he was. It didn't matter that he only took merchandise from Tate ships, ships and merchandise that would have been his if not for the lying schemes of her uncle. But that didn't change what he was or what he'd become. It was only an excuse.

And if she stayed with him, others would think the worst of her.

Damian ran his fingers over her hair, feeling its softness. She was soft, too. She was not made for the life he could give her. He could not ask her to spend months aboard the *Magic*, risking her life in storms or in battles. Nor could he ask her to spend long and lonely months waiting and praying for him to return to Sorcery Bay.

And if he did ask her, he would become soft. He would forget what he'd set out to do. She would change him, and he couldn't allow that.

He closed his eyes as he pulled her closer into his embrace, holding her head in the curve of his shoulder and neck. The ache in his chest was nearly unendurable as he acknowledged again the cold, stark truth.

There was no future for the two of them.

He couldn't give her back what he'd taken from her. He'd told her she needn't be afraid of him, but he'd lied. She should have been afraid, for he'd taken what was not his, by right, to take.

She would hate him now. When he told her the truth, she would hate and despise him. And that was as it must be. She *must* hate and despise him.

He brushed his lips across her forehead, bidding her one last, silent farewell, knowing he would never experience another tender moment such as this and reluctant to have it end.

Cassandra raised her head from his shoulder and opened her eyes to look into his. She saw something within the ebony depths that frightened her. She saw him pulling back, retreating from her, refusing what she had so willingly given him.

"Damian?"

He slipped his arm from beneath her, rolled away, and sat up on the side of the bed. It was then that she saw the scars that crisscrossed his back. The old wounds, faded with time but still agonizingly clear, reminded her of what Professor had told her of Damian's first master in Barbados. She wanted to reach out and touch him, to take away the memories and the pain.

"Damian . . ." she whispered again.

His back stiffened. He ran his fingers through his hair, then lowered his hands to grip the edge of the mattress.

"Damian . . . what's wrong?"

"What's wrong?" he echoed her. "Isn't it obvious what's wrong?" He glanced over his shoulder. "I never meant to let this happen, Cassandra."

Clutching the sheet against her naked breasts, his scars forgotten, she slid toward him, reaching out with one hand to take hold of his arm. "I wanted it as much as you."

He laughed sharply. "You couldn't have known what you wanted. You were a virgin."

"Damian? Look at me."

He turned his head.

"Damian, I . . ." She swallowed the lump in her throat, then moistened her dry lips with the tip of her tongue. "I love you." She had thought—had hoped—that her words would make things right. Instead, they seemed to make everything worse.

He rose abruptly from the bed and grabbed his clothes from the bench where he'd dropped them the previous night. He dressed quickly, keeping his back toward her. Only when he was finished did he turn to look at her again.

"When I've told you the truth, Cassandra Jamison, you'll forget that you ever spoke those words to me."

"The truth?" she whispered. She clutched the sheet more tightly against her chest, all too aware of her nakedness beneath the light covering. She felt exposed, vulnerable, frightened.

"You don't even know who I am." He spoke with an odd combination of anger and disgust.

"You're Captain Damian of the *Magic*. You're the owner of Sorcery Bay Plantation. You're the man I love. What more do I need to know beyond that?"

He stepped toward her. "My name is Sanford Damian Tate. I'm the son of Sanford and Margaret Tate and the rightful owner of Tate Shipping."

Cassandra's eyes widened.

"Your uncle stole Tate Shipping from my father."

"You must be mistaken. Uncle Far would never . . ."

He took another step forward. His hands were closed into fists at his sides, and his face was dark with hate. His eyes seemed not to be looking at her but back in time. "He not only stole my father's business, but he sent my father to prison and me into indentured servitude."

"No . . ." she whispered, shaking her head in denial.

"He accused my father of treason. He planted false evidence. It was the only way he could get his hands on what he wanted. And Dunworthy always gets what he wants." Damian's handsome face twisted into an expression of agony. "Do you know what they do to a man convicted of treason, Cassandra?" he asked hoarsely. "Have you any idea what torment he must endure before he's blessed by the comfort of death?"

She shook her head again, not wanting to know.

"They string him up by the neck. They let him hang there just long enough to wish for death but not quite long enough to die. Then they cut him down and the sport begins. The executioner slices off the convicted man's cock and ballocks." He glared at her. "Do you know what I'm referring to, Cassandra?"

She wasn't sure, but she had a horrible suspicion that she knew what he meant.

"And then, as if the other weren't enough, the executioner carves open the condemned man's belly and tears out his entrails."

"Oh, God," she moaned, wishing he would stop. She let go of the sheet and used her hands to cover her ears. She squeezed her eyes closed to shut out the sight of him.

"Finally, just to make sure there's no chance the man will survive the torture, he's beheaded and his body's cut into quarters."

Cassandra shook her head once again as she choked back a sob.

"There's nothing left to bury." His voice was filled with unmeasurable pain. "There's nothing left of him for his family to claim or to mourn. He's gone. Discarded. 'Tis as if he never even existed."

She opened her eyes and saw him through a blur of tears. "I'm sorry, Damian. I'm so sorry."

He showed her his back once more. For a moment, silence gripped the room. She wiped the tears from her eyes, trying to find something to say to comfort him.

But her comfort wasn't wanted.

Damian turned about. "I have sworn to destroy the man responsible. I won't rest until Dunworthy is ruined. I won't know a moment's real peace until I've repaid him for my father's death. I'll take back what was taken from me. Tate Shipping will be mine again. And if I must, I'll kill him." He spun around and walked to the door. As he opened it, he said, "And if that makes me a barbarous, bloodthirsty pirate, then so be it."

The door closed firmly behind him, leaving Cassandra alone with her shocked anguish. She lay down on the bed and pulled the blankets over her. She stared up at the ceiling of the captain's quarters, trying to make sense of the things she'd heard.

He was mistaken, of course. Her uncle couldn't have had anything to do with Damian's father's death, nor would he have acquired the shipping company through any but legitimate means. Uncle Far was a peer of the realm. He was a respectable and honest man. He loved her and had been good to her. He couldn't have had anything to do with the horror which Damian had just described to her. Damian had been only a boy when he was sent to the Caribbean. Someone had lied to him about what had taken place. Another man was responsible for these terrible things. Another man. Not Uncle Far.

Somehow she would make Damian understand that he was mistaken. Somehow she would help him see the truth.

Unbidden, unwelcome, Professor's words came back to haunt her. *Damian bears more scars than those put on his back by Spotswood. The ones on his soul will be more difficult to heal. It will take more than Jedidiah's kindness to soothe Damian's desire for revenge.*

Her love would heal the wounds on his soul, she told herself. Her love would temper his desire for revenge. Her love would make him forget all the terrible things in his past, and she would show him how to look toward the future.

But even as she told herself that everything would be all right, the Professor's words continued to echo in her memory, filling her with black despair. Turning onto her stomach, she pulled the pillow against her body, curled herself around it, and wept.

Chapter Fifteen

Damian stood at the helm, his hands clenched around the wheel, his gaze set on the horizon. No one had approached him for hours. No one had dared. His crew knew that look. When the captain's eyes reminded a man of a hurricane, 'twas best to leave him be until the internal storm passed.

Oliver shook his head in dismay. It had been a long time since he'd seen Damian in such foul spirits. He could almost feel the rage, clear from where he stood on the main deck.

No one had been more surprised than Damian's lieutenant when the captain had stalked onto the deck that morning. He'd glanced at Oliver and snapped, "We sail for England." Before Oliver could respond, Damian had headed for the helm. He'd been there ever since.

Oliver scratched the stubble on his chin, then

walked to the hatch. He made his way quickly to the captain's cabin. He hesitated only a moment before knocking.

"Enter."

He opened the door.

Cassandra was sitting on the end of the bed. Her hair hung in a single, silvery-gold braid over one shoulder. She was wearing one of Damian's white shirts; the hem of the shirt reached to her knees, and she'd belted the oversized garment with a sash from the window curtains. Her legs were covered with a pair of the captain's black breeches, and she'd rolled the extra length into a cuff at mid-calf. Her feet were bare.

Oliver realized he was gaping and quickly closed his mouth as he whipped his cap from his head. "Beggin' your pardon, miss."

She stood up. " 'Tis all right, Oliver. Come in."

He stepped into the cabin. "I . . . I'm sorry to disturb you, but I was hopin' you might be able to shed some light on what's troublin' the captain."

"I'm afraid *I'm* what's troubling him, Oliver." She offered a wan smile.

"Aye, I'd guessed as much."

"Where is he now?"

"At the helm, miss. 'Tis where he always goes at such times."

"Such times?"

"When he's filled with the devil himself," he replied.

Oliver had seen Damian like this too often in the years they'd sailed together. He knew that the captain was remembering his father and how he'd died. He knew he was recalling every time his own back had felt the lash. He knew he was counting up the debt that Farley Dunworthy owed him and savoring the way he would extract payment.

"Oliver? What can I do to help him be rid of that devil?"

"I ain't sure I know what you mean, miss."

She shook her head, causing her braid to sway back and forth across the front of the captain's white shirt. "Of course you do. You're his friend."

He looked at her in silence.

"Oliver, I know who the captain is. He's Damian Tate and he says his father used to own Tate Shipping. He blames my uncle for his father's death." She looked at him with pleading eyes. "But he's wrong, Oliver. Uncle Far could not have had anything to do with it. My uncle is a fine, caring, giving man. He couldn't have done this."

The scar on the side of his face began to itch, but he resisted the urge to scratch it. "Sometimes we don't know folks the way we think we do," he said sagely, though he longed to say more.

"You must think my uncle guilty, too, or else why would you serve Damian this way? He's made you and the rest of this crew pirates. Why do you all follow him so blindly?"

"It ain't blindness, miss."

"Then tell me what it is you know."

"I can't."

She clenched her fists at her sides. "Why are you all bloody stubborn?"

Another time he would have shown surprise at her swearing, but not now. He was having trouble enough holding his tongue. "The crew of the *Magic* all swore an oath of secrecy. 'Tis to protect us. The captain alone decides what t'tell outsiders."

She drew in a quick breath of air. "I'm not an outsider, Oliver. I love him."

"Aye," he replied, not surprised at this revelation. He'd guessed it long before now.

Cassandra turned and crossed to the gallery windows. "Professor told me about Damian's years as an indentured servant on Barbados. *He* trusted me enough to talk to me."

He shook his head. "I'm sorry, miss. Professor's not held by the same oath. And I reckon he didn't tell you much or you'd not be askin' me."

Cassandra's shoulders lifted and fell as she let out a deep sigh. Then she spun around and walked toward him. "I must go to Damian. I must talk to him."

"Sink me, but I think 'tis best you let be for now, miss," he advised. "The captain's in no mood to talk."

She stood a little straighter. She flipped the braid over her shoulder with her right hand and lifted her chin in a show of courage. "I can't let it be, Oliver. The captain has made a grievous error. I have sat here all morning, trying to think of how I might help him to understand. I must talk to him. And if you won't tell me anything more, then I might as well do it now."

Damian saw her climb the steps to the poop deck. He almost smiled when he saw what she was wearing. Almost. Then he reminded himself that he couldn't let down his guard, even for an instant. Cassandra was Dunworthy's niece. When he'd held her in his arms, he'd forgotten that. He could not let himself forget it again.

"I don't recall requesting your presence at the helm," he said as she drew near. He kept his eyes averted.

She stopped abruptly.

He glanced at her then, purposefully making his gaze a cold one. "If you have something to say, say it and be off with you."

"Damian . . ." She swallowed, and he couldn't help but notice the tiny quiver in her chin. "Damian, we need to talk."

"What about?"

"You know what about."

He set his gaze on the sea once more. "I believe we've said whatever needed to be said."

"No!" She stepped forward. Her hand settled over the top of his.

He shook her free. Turning another icy glare in her direction, he said, "Understand this, Miss Jamison. You are no longer of value to me.

You've been nothing but a thorn in my side from the day I brought you on board, and now I'm saddled with you for another long journey. If I were not already sailing for England, I'd have left you to find your own way back to your parents. Don't cross me or you'll find yourself marooned on the first bit of land I come across. Am I understood?"

Damian's chest felt as if someone had taken a cleaver to it. Every word that had spewed from his lips added another wound; he was condemned by his own speech.

"Damian, don't do this. You're mistaken. Someone has lied to you. Uncle Far could never . . ."

At the sound of his enemy's name, fury exploded in him as it always did, wiping out the remorse he'd felt at his intentional cruelty. He let loose of the wheel and stepped toward Cassandra, drawing close, using his size to intimidate her. "Silence!" he shouted.

Her mouth closed, but she didn't back away; she didn't quake with fright. She simply stared up at him with wide eyes, waiting, as if for him to strike her. She was braced for it; she refused to run.

She should have run, damn it! She should have cowered, gone into hiding. Why didn't she? Why did she refuse to make this easier for both of them?

He tried to stay angry. He tried to stoke his rage with reminders of who her uncle was and what he had done not only to Sanford and

Damian Tate, but to most of the men on this ship—even to his own niece, though she knew it not. But when he looked down into those courageous eyes, it was hard to remember that Farley Dunworthy's blood and hers were the same. It was hard to remember all the reasons that kept him from taking her into his arms and kissing her supple lips and carrying her back to his bed.

She saw the softening in his eyes. Laying her hand on his arm, she said, "Please, Damian. Let us find the truth together. I shall prove to you my uncle's innocence. Come with me to England. Come and speak to him."

He swore violently as he turned and strode back to the helm. When he faced her, she saw that she had lost him again.

This was not the man who had sat on the deck with her in the middle of the night as they sailed toward the Caribbean. This was not the man who had walked with her along the beach at Sorcery Bay. This was not the man who had come to her rescue at Three Oaks nor the man who had made love to her in the pre-dawn light in the captain's quarters.

This man was the demon-captain, the pirate known as Captain Damian, a man filled with hate and a desire for revenge that overwhelmed everything else.

But she had caught—if only for a second— a glimpse of the man she loved, and a glimpse was all she needed to give her hope. It wouldn't be easy, but she wasn't going to give up without a fight. She had found her grand passion. She wasn't going to lose it because of a lie.

And she knew it was a lie. Her uncle was a kind and honest man. He would never have done the things of which Damian accused him. He would never have had a man sent to such an agonizing death so he could steal his business. Neither would he have sent a child to labor as an indentured servant in the cane fields of the Caribbean. That was not the Uncle Far she knew.

I'll find some way to prove it to you, she promised as she stared at Damian. *And when I do, you'll be free to love me as I love you.*

She turned away without a word. She held herself erect, her head high as she walked toward the steps leading down from the poop. She would not give in to tears or despair. As soon as she reached England, she would find some way to make Damian meet with her uncle. She would find some way to put everything to rights.

Damian poured himself another glass of rum. "Keep her away from me," he said again, his gaze lifting to Oliver. "Keep her away from the crew, too. And for pity's sake, find her something decent to wear or I'll have to lock her up again. I can't have her traipsing around the ship dressed in nothing but one of my shirts."

"Aye, captain. I'll do my best, but 'tis not likely any of us have anything that'll do better."

Damian knew his lieutenant was right, but he

183

didn't want to hear logic at the moment. What he wanted was to get drunk so he could lie down on his bed and go to sleep without thinking of Cassandra. He didn't want to remember the way she'd offered herself to him that morning or the way he, foolishly, had taken what she'd offered.

"Are you sure 'tis wise for us to go to England again so soon, Damian?"

"We're going to England." He took a long drink of the rum in his glass, then lifted his eyes to meet Oliver's gaze. "I want to wash my hands of her. The sooner the better."

"Has it occurred t'you that you'd be takin' a risk t'take her back? She knows your name and the name of this ship. She knows about Sorcery Bay. She could lead her uncle or even the Crown t'you if she chose t'do it."

Damian shook his head. He knew in his heart that Cassandra would never betray him. "She won't, Oliver. You know it as well as I."

"Aye, captain." Oliver moved toward the door, opened it, then glanced over his shoulder. His expression was grim. "I've no love for Dunworthy," he said, lifting his hand to touch the scar on his face, "but perhaps the girl is right. Perhaps 'tis time we should forget what—"

"Don't say it." Damian's hand closed tightly around his glass of rum. "We've been friends too long now."

"Aye, that we have."

"Good night, Oliver."

"Good night, captain."

As the door closed, Damian lifted the glass to his lips, draining the contents.

Think of Dunworthy. Remember what he did.

He'd waited eighteen years to destroy the baron. The desire for revenge had kept him alive when nothing else could. He'd savored it when there was no other food or drink to sustain him.

Revenge . . .

He'd thought of it as he'd carried his only shipboard friend up from the stinking, over-crowded, disease-ridden hold and thrown his lifeless body into the sea. He'd thought of it the day he was pulled off the *Seadog* and sold as an indentured servant, sentenced to serve nine years to pay for a passage that had cost the captain no more than a few pounds.

Revenge . . .

He'd thought of it as he'd baked beneath the merciless tropical sun of Barbados, his fingers bleeding as he worked in the cane fields. He'd thought of it the first time William Spotswood had taken a whip to his back because he'd asked for nothing more than another drink of water. He'd thought of it whenever he'd let his eyes stray to the northeast, toward England, his father, and home.

Revenge . . .

He'd thought of it when he returned to England and learned of his father's grisly death, a man falsely accused of treason, his business and home and all he'd possessed sold off. He'd thought of it almost constantly during the years he'd served with Captain George Hendrickson as a privateer during England's war with Spain.

Revenge . . .

He'd realized, sometime during those eighteen years of thinking and planning his day of revenge, that running a sword through Farley's black heart would be too quick, too easy. He wanted the man to suffer as he'd suffered, as his father had suffered.

And he'd been making him suffer. For three years, he had slowly, meticulously brought the baron closer and closer to disaster. He couldn't give up now. He couldn't turn his back on the promise he'd made to himself and to his father's memory. He couldn't let down the men who had joined him, who had their own reasons for wanting their pound of flesh from Farley Dunworthy.

He couldn't stop. Not even for Cassandra.

Damian poured himself more rum. When he'd emptied the glass—and three more besides— he rose from his chair and began to disrobe, dropping his clothes on the floor on his way to the bed.

The drink he'd consumed had softened the edges of his thoughts, but it hadn't driven Cassandra's image from his mind as he'd hoped. He could still see her as she'd looked that morning, her glorious hair spilling across the sheets, her eyes wide pools of indigo staring up at him in wonder. When he pressed his face against the pillow, he could smell her faint lilac cologne.

Her memory was like a siren, calling him to her. Even strong drink couldn't stop the rising tide of desire that her memory stirred in him. Her cabin was so close. Only two doors and a short length of passageway separated them. It would be so easy to go to her, so easy to lose himself in her loving arms.

Damian, I love you.

He'd not known love in many years. He'd known the kindness of Jedidiah Benjamin. He'd known the friendship of Professor and Oliver. He'd known the respect of his crew. He'd known the pleasures to be found in a woman's arms. But he'd not known love since he was a boy. Not since his father was taken to Newgate.

What devilish joke was it that the love offered to him was from a woman whose family he was sworn to destroy? In keeping his oath to his father's memory, he would also be destroying the love Cassandra offered him. There was no way he could escape it. It was far better that he not taste its sweetness again. Far better for them both.

With the cold discipline he'd learned many years before, Damian hardened his heart against the tender feelings Cassandra had stirred to life. And in doing so, he knew he had one more wrong to be laid at Farley Dunworthy's door. He had one more reason to hate him, one more reason to continue his unrelenting acts of revenge against the man who had taken away everything that mattered to Damian.

Everything that had *ever* mattered. Especially Cassandra.

Chapter Sixteen

Cassandra did her best to keep her spirits up, but as days turned into weeks and still Damian refused to speak to her about her uncle—or anything else—it became more and more difficult.

Nights, she lay in the bunk in her tiny, solitary cabin and longed to feel his arms around her, longed to taste his kisses, longed to know again the tumultuous wonder of her body joined with his. It didn't matter that she knew it was wrong to lust after a man in this fashion, a man who not only wasn't her husband but who had never said he loved her, a man who had made it clear that he wanted no part of her in his future.

She spent long hours making plans for the day they would reach England. It would do her no good to be set aground and have Damian sail away without her. She had to find a way to make him accompany her to her home in Northumberland. She had to make him agree to speak with her uncle. Once he did, he would learn that he was wrong about Farley. And once that was done, she knew she could convince him they belonged together. He would believe not only in her love for him, but he would realize he loved her, too.

She held on to that hope with a fierce stubbornness she hadn't known she possessed. When despair tried to raise its ugly head, she knocked it down, refusing to believe things wouldn't work out as she'd planned.

To the crew of the *Magic*, she showed only a smiling, self-assured countenance. And on the infrequent occasions when her eyes met the captain's, she let him see her love.

She hoped that would be enough to save them both.

It was in the last hours of daylight, when the *Magic* was less than two weeks away from England, that another ship was sighted in the distance. Binns shimmied up the mast for a better look with a spyglass.

It was more than a quarter hour before he lowered the glass from his eye and shouted down to the captain, "She's a Tate, all right. 'Tis the *Venture*."

Damian strode to the ship's rail and peered across the water. "The *Venture* . . ." he murmured.

The ship was one of Tate Shipping's East

Indiamen. This wasn't her usual route. She shouldn't have been this far west. What was she doing sailing toward the Americas? Perhaps Farley was sending a new shipment to the colonies, and one of the ships that normally plied this route had been damaged. That could have been the reason.

"She's sailing right for us, captain," Oliver said as he stepped up beside him.

"I know." He glanced down the length of the ship. His crew was watching him, waiting for his orders.

"Do you suppose she hasn't seen us yet?"

"Maybe." Damian turned his gaze back across the water. "Something doesn't feel right, Oliver."

They'd boarded the *Venture* three times before. The captain of the ship had always ceded without much of a fight. He'd had little choice. Farley had been forced to cut corners in many different ways. One was to have fewer cannon on board his ships so that there was more room for cargo. Another way was to reduce the size of his crews. The unlucky men who served aboard one of Tate's ships knew they had to work doubly hard for their miserable wage, and none of them was willing to die for a pittance.

The *Venture* had always been easy prey. Damian shouldn't have given more than a passing thought to taking her.

Only something wasn't right.

"Oliver?"

"Aye, captain."

"See Miss Jamison to my cabin. Tell her to stay there until I send for her."

The lieutenant gave him a questioning glance, then started away.

"Oliver!"

Again the man stopped and turned. "Aye?"

"Tell her I said she's not to leave my quarters until I come for her myself."

"I'll do it, sir."

Damian watched until Oliver had disappeared down the hatch, then he set his gaze on the *Venture* once again. She was moving through the water at great speed—better than ten knots, he guessed. She had an empty hold. She'd seen the *Magic* and knew that she wasn't one of Tate Shipping's fleet. There was only one plausible explanation. Farley was no longer waiting for Captain Damian to find his ships. Now Farley had gone on the attack. He was searching for the *Magic*.

Well, if so, he'd surely found her.

Damian's fingers tightened on the railing. His eyes narrowed as the distance closed between the two ships. The *Magic* was well-armed, and her crew was a seasoned one. His men weren't afraid to fight. Many of them had served on a ship owned by the baron, and of those who had, all had suffered because of it. They would fight if that was Damian's decision, and they would win in the end.

But at what cost? If he was right about the *Venture*—if she wasn't bearing cargo but was, instead, armed for war—it meant even more danger than usual. And while he wasn't afraid for himself or his crew, he couldn't risk Cassandra's life that way. The captain of the *Venture* had no way of knowing that Farley's niece was on board this ship. He would fire upon them before he could learn otherwise. More than likely, his instructions had been to sink the *Magic*—or any other pirate vessel—and leave no survivors.

Damian climbed up to the poop deck. "Bring her about, Mr. Simon," he told his quartermaster. "Wind dead astern."

"Aye, captain. Wind dead astern."

"Mr. Binns, run up our standard. We want them to know for certain 'tis the *Magic* that leaves them in her wake."

"But I don't understand, Oliver," Cassandra said as the man guided her along the passageway toward the great cabin. "What's happening?"

He didn't answer her.

The ship shifted suddenly, and she bumped into the wall with her shoulder. Her pulse quickened. "Why are we changing directions? Why won't you tell me what's going on?"

"I'm sure the captain'll tell you when he's got the time. He said for you t'stay here 'til he comes for you himself."

"He hasn't spoken to me in weeks, Oliver. Why do you think he'll spare the time to explain anything to me now?"

" 'Cause he said he would, miss." The lieutenant opened the door to Damian's cabin.

Cassandra stepped inside. She felt a painful tightening in her chest as her gaze darted quickly around the room, stopping on the large bed beneath the windows. She sucked in a quick breath as she closed her eyes, trying to shut out the memory of the night she'd spent in this cabin with Damian. Before she could open her eyes again, Oliver had backed out of the room and closed the door.

She turned at the sound. "Oliver . . ." But it was too late. He was gone.

With a sigh, she faced the stern again. It was then, in the fading light, that she saw the ship sailing toward them. She stepped toward the windows and stared at the sight of the East Indiaman in full sail. It was an awesome sight— white canvas unfurled to catch the wind, the vessel sliced through the ocean at tremendous speed, bearing down on the *Magic* with the obvious intent of overtaking her.

Cassandra's pulse quickened as her eyes narrowed. She strained her eyes, trying to see the flag the ship was flying. Could it be one of her uncle's ships? Was that the baron's standard upon a field of blue? Had he come to rescue her? If so, she wouldn't have to wait for England before proving the truth to Damian. If she could signal them that she was aboard . . .

The thought was scarcely realized when the pursuing ship tacked suddenly to port. She saw a flash of light and a cloud of black smoke aboard the other ship. A funnel of water shot up from the ocean not far from where she stood just as the sound of an explosion reached her ears.

It was another moment before the realization sank in. They were being fired upon. Before she could back away from the window, another funnel erupted, this one closer to the *Magic* but off to the starboard side. She felt the ship make a sudden correction in course. The next cannonball fell even closer, this time off the port side.

In horrified fascination, she stared at the attacking vessel and knew they meant to sink the *Magic*. She wondered if she would go to a watery grave with Damian still rejecting the love she had to offer.

Farley ended the notation in his journal with a flourish, blotted the ink, then closed the book. He lifted his eyes to stare out the windows of his study. In the gray light of early evening, the hills surrounding Kettering Hall resembled black whales surfacing out of a rolling sea of grasslands. Closer to the house itself, he could see that the grounds of the estate looked somewhat shabby. He'd been forced to let several of the gardeners go a few months before, but as soon as Cyrus Polk, the new captain of the *Venture*, sent word of the *Magic*'s destruction, Farley would hire more men to care for the lawns and gardens. Once that troublesome pirate and his crew were killed or captured—he cared not which—Farley knew he could recoup his losses in a short period of time. He could restore his estate to its rightful beauty.

He glanced at the letter on his desk from Roland Bennett, Farley's "London associate," and his mood once again turned sour. Bennett was trying to renege on their agreement. He was saying there was nothing he could do about the taxes placed upon shipments of goods to the colonies.

Farley sneered. Bennett was wrong. There was always something that could be done. Always.

He refolded the letter. Then, picking up several other items, he rose from his cluttered desk and crossed the study to the fireplace. After moving several books that lay on the mantel, he drew out a small gray stone. Placing his hand into the narrow opening, he closed his fingers around a handle secured in the mortar, then pulled. A section of stones moved, swinging on hidden hinges, revealing a dark hole in the center of the fireplace. Farley added the items he held to those inside the secret compartment, then pushed the stone portal back into place. He returned the loose stone to its place and was setting the books back in order when he heard the knock on the study door.

He turned around. "What is it, Mullins?" he called. "I told you I didn't want to be disturbed."

The butler stepped through the opening.

"Your sister is here, milord. She wishes to speak with you."

Farley rolled his eyes toward the ceiling. "Very well, Mullins. Show her into the drawing room. I shall join her there."

Mullins nodded and withdrew.

Zounds! He wasn't in the mood to put up with one of his sister's fainting spells. She hadn't stopped pestering him about Cassandra since he'd returned with the news of the girl's kidnapping. He had sought help through his government contacts, of course, though it had done him little good. He'd been complaining for three years about the *Magic*, but since no other shipping line had ever seen or heard of the vessel, there were those who thought the owner of Tate Shipping was falsely reporting the attacks in order to excuse losses at sea that had nought to do with piracy.

Farley's jaw clenched, his anger flaring when he thought of his enemies laughing at him. By heaven, he wasn't about to become a laughingstock for a bunch of peacocks. He would crush them as he'd crushed Sanford Tate.

But he would have to deal with those men later. Right now, he had to deal with his sister.

It didn't even cross his mind to wonder what really might have happened to his niece in the weeks she'd been missing.

Damian stared up at the unfurled sails. They were flying everything but the captain's own nightshirt, catching every breath of wind available to them. So far, they had managed to stay ahead of the *Venture*'s cannonballs. In truth, he thought they were beginning to pull away from her.

He glanced at the darkening sky. If they could lose the *Venture* between now and the rising of the moon . . .

"The gunners are all at ready, captain," Oliver said as he stepped up onto the poop deck.

Damian nodded. He hoped the precaution wouldn't be necessary.

"I think we're pulling away from her, sir," the quartermaster reported, echoing the captain's earlier thoughts.

Damian nodded again, then glanced toward his sailing master. "Mr. Davis, chart a course for Capetown. As soon as we shake the *Venture* from our tail—"

"Capetown, captain?" Davis questioned.

"Aye. And Madagascar after that."

Oliver glanced at him in surprise. "I thought we were taking Miss Jamison back to her family in England."

"It seems Dunworthy has changed our plans," Damian replied stiffly.

"We've not got the supplies for such a journey," his lieutenant reminded him.

"Then we'll get them." Damian's gaze shifted from Oliver to the other officers standing near the helm. When he spoke, his words encompassed them all. "Dunworthy's decided to make war on us. If we're lucky enough to outrun the

Venture, I mean to accept his challenge. We'll strike him where he has the most to gain and the most to lose. We'll cripple his trade with the east. We've only toyed with him in the past. Because of Mouse, our risk has been minimal, our success assured. I say we change the rules of the game." Again, he looked at each of them, this time pausing for their answers.

"We're with you, captain," Simon responded in his booming voice.

"Aye, we'll not fail you, captain," Davis said with a confident grin.

Oliver moved his head in agreement, but Damian could tell he was holding something back as he said, "We'll do as you say, captain."

He knew his lieutenant wouldn't speak freely in front of the quarter and sailing masters. Oliver wouldn't gainsay the captain in front of his officers. With an internal sigh, Damian motioned for the other two men to return to their posts, then he looked at his lieutenant. "Say it, my friend, and be done with it."

"We should get Miss Jamison safely away before we return to Madagascar. That den of thieves ain't no place for her. For that matter, this ship ain't no place for her, either. Not now." He glanced behind him, staring at the warship pursuing them as day gave way to night. "We're hunted men, Damian. Dunworthy's out for your blood, and he ain't the sort t'care if his niece is lost when he takes you."

"And how safe do you suppose she'll be back with him in England?" Damian replied gruffly.

199

"He'll sell her to the first man to offer a good price for her hand in marriage. Do you think she'd want that? I've already saved her from such a fate once. I don't want to have to do it again."

Oliver touched Damian's shoulder. "Is it your duty t'save her, sir? Perhaps 'tis not your place at all."

He didn't want to hear this. He didn't want to think about it.

"You're right, Oliver. 'Tis not my place. Neither is it yours." Damian's curt warning caused both men to fall silent. After drawing a deep breath to rid himself of the bitter taste his words had left in his mouth, Damian continued. "I'll see about buying Miss Jamison passage home as soon as I think 'tis safe to do so. Will that satisfy you?"

"Aye, captain."

Damian didn't wait for his lieutenant to move away before he turned and strode aft, his gaze locked on the *Venture*, all the while struggling with his own churning emotions.

Bloody hell! He cursed the day Mouse had told him of Farley's plan to kidnap his niece and hold her for ransom. He cursed the day he'd boarded the *Peacock* and carried her away. He cursed the blue of her eyes, the silver of her hair, the rosy shade of her lips, the smell of lilacs that even now seemed to tease his nostrils. He cursed her courage and her tears.

But most of all, he cursed himself for not wanting to let her go.

Chapter Seventeen

Sunrise was already tinting the eastern horizon before Damian left the deck. During the blackest hours of the night, they had lost the *Venture*, but it had been far from easy to do. Judging by what he'd seen, Farley had hired a new captain for the East Indiaman. This captain wasn't going to give up easily, and Damian had spent much of the night trying to convince his opponent that he was still bound for England. Only after the quarter moon sank in the west did Damian order the ship set on its southerly course.

Now, he wearily made his way toward his cabin. All he wanted was a quick meal and a few hours of much needed sleep. But he knew he would have to deal with Cassandra before he could treat himself to either of those.

Drawing a deep breath, he opened the door to his quarters and stepped inside.

She was lying across the bed, wearing her odd assortment of sailor's attire. She still wore his white linen shirt, belted at the waist, but it was a pair of Toby's breeches that covered her legs now. One of the men had given her a pair of cowhide boots, the toes stuffed with rags, so that she no longer had to go barefoot. She looked quite fetching in this attire. All the men thought so.

He closed the door forcefully behind him.

She started, then sat up, blinking the sleep from her eyes. "Damian . . ." she whispered. "Is it over?"

"Aye, we've outrun her."

"It was one of my uncle's ships, wasn't it?" She slid to the side of the bed and rose to her feet.

"Aye, that it was."

"Why didn't you signal them that we meant no harm? If Uncle Far was on board, we could have resolved the matter. I know if I could just talk to him, everything could be settled between you."

Saint's bones, she was a stubborn wench! It didn't matter to Farley whether or not she was on the *Magic*. He would have sunk Damian's ship without giving Cassandra's safety a second thought. That was the sort of man he was, if she would only open her eyes and see for herself.

"What are you going to do now?" she asked,

brushing back some stray wisps of hair as she spoke.

"I'm afraid you'll be obliged to remain with us awhile longer, Miss Jamison. We won't be going to England. Not for quite some time. But I promise to send you home as soon as I'm able to buy you safe passage."

He saw her lift her chin, watched as she straightened her shoulders. She took two purposeful steps toward him. "I don't want to return to England. I want to stay with you, Damian. I'll gladly go wherever you take me."

God's blood! She was beautiful. If he believed she would go on feeling that way, even as he destroyed her family . . .

"Damian?" She touched his sleeve. "Let me post a letter to my uncle. Let me prove to you his innocence."

He shook off her touch. "No."

"He only pursues you because he thinks you a pirate."

"I *am* a pirate."

Frustration entered her voice. "But you don't *have* to be. You could give this up. You could go back to Sorcery Bay and be a planter. You wouldn't have to be a hunted man. You can trust me, Damian. I'd do nothing to put you in danger." She paused and her voice lowered. "We could be together."

The picture she painted with words was an attractive one, but one he couldn't allow himself to contemplate. He turned his back toward Cassandra and crossed the room. He poured water into a bowl, then splashed his face. When he straightened, he had managed to banish the tempting thoughts from his mind.

"Don't you think your uncle would object to you living with the man who's been pirating his ships?"

"You don't know my uncle. Once it was explained to him, he would forgive you. We could—"

Something snapped inside Damian. His fury was so great he wanted to lash out at anything near him. He didn't care who or what at the moment. "Damn you, Cassandra! I don't want that bloody murderer's forgiveness. I want his head! I want to see him in pain. I want to see him suffer for what he's done." He stepped toward her, grabbing her by the arms. "Do you think I wouldn't make you my whore if I thought it would cause Dunworthy grief? I would, my dear Cassandra. I would. I would flaunt you before him, letting him know that you had chosen me over him."

He let go of her and gave her a tiny shove. The back of her knees bumped against the bed, and she sat abruptly. Her face had faded to a sickly shade of pale.

But Damian took no note of her stricken expression or the tears that were forming in her eyes. If he had, he would only have used them for his benefit. He had to use any method he could to drive this woman from him. She was like a sickness in his blood. He had to be free of her. She would stop him if he let her.

She would make him forget the promises he had made to his father's memory, to himself, to the men of this ship.

He took another threatening step toward her. "You don't understand, do you? You refuse to hear what I'm saying. You say you love me, but you don't believe me, do you, Cassandra? Do you? You still think your uncle is the innocent one."

The pain in her heart was nearly more than she could bear. She fought to swallow the hot tears. She fought to keep the sobs from tearing from her throat.

"Don't," she whispered, her voice quivering. "Please don't."

Damian let out an exasperated sound as he turned away from her and headed for the door. As he opened it, he looked back over his shoulder. "You don't know the man you try to protect. If not for him, you would never have been my prisoner. If you knew the truth about him, you'd shrink back in horror. And if you knew the truth about me, you'd do the same. I'll hurt you, Cassandra. I warn you. I'll only hurt you."

The door closed firmly in his wake.

Cassandra stared after Damian, his angry words replaying time and again in her head, and finally, she couldn't refuse to acknowledge the truth any longer. Damian didn't want her or her love. Hate and vengeance meant far more to him than she did. He would continue his attacks on Uncle Far until one or the other of them was dead.

She lay down on the bed and curled into a ball, her arms hugging her chest as if to keep her heart from breaking. She was certain it *would* break. She couldn't bear to live without Damian. But if he were to kill her uncle, that would destroy her.

She closed her eyes and thought of the man whom Damian had tried to tell her was a fiend, but all she saw was the uncle who had given her a pony when she was seven and who brought her exotic gifts whenever he returned from a journey abroad. All she saw was the uncle who had taken her to London when she was nine, the man who had taken her for a boat ride on the Thames. All she saw was the uncle who had spoiled her with pretty dresses and fancy jewels and who had helped sponsor her first season in London.

And what of Damian? Was he the man he said he was? Was he a ruthless pirate who would take her for his mistress and discard her when he was finished with her? Was he a man possessed by the lust for blood, a man who'd forgotten all the rules of polite society?

No, she refused to believe it. That wasn't the Damian she knew and loved. She had seen too often his kindnesses, both large and small. She'd seen the home he'd made for so many less fortunate souls at Sorcery Bay. She'd seen the respect he'd earned from his men. She had experienced for herself the tender side of this man. He wasn't what he was trying to make her believe he was.

But one thing was true. These two men would destroy each other or themselves if she didn't do something to stop them. She had to find some way to stop them before it was too late.

Cassandra was surprised when she awakened and discovered she was still lying on Damian's bed. The light beaming through the windows announced that it was already midday. The cabin itself had grown warm and stuffy as she slept.

She sat up, then slid her legs off the bed and stood. She stretched and yawned as her gaze moved to the ocean beyond the windows. The sea was dark green today, the foaming caps the color of cream. An azure sky stretched in an unbroken canopy overhead.

She allowed herself an unburdened moment to enjoy the sight before turning her attention to the matter uppermost in her mind. She'd realized something important as she'd drifted off to sleep earlier. She didn't care about her uncle's innocence or guilt or anything else. The only thing that mattered to her was for her to be with Damian. Perhaps, one day, she would find a way to convince him that he was wrong about Uncle Far. Perhaps she could convince him to give up his acts of piracy upon Tate Shipping and to settle down at Sorcery Bay. Perhaps she might even convince him that she loved him.

She knew what she was choosing. He hadn't said he loved her. He'd warned her that he would make her his mistress—his whore—if only to flaunt it before her uncle, but she was willing to take the risk. She *had* to take the risk. She loved him too much to give up her grand passion without a fight.

Cassandra pressed her fingertips against her temples. She didn't want to think of what the future might hold in store for her or for them. There were too many questions, she thought, and not enough answers.

Her stomach growled just then, and she realized that she was famished. She hadn't eaten anything since yesterday's midday meal. Apparently, she'd been forgotten while she slept in the captain's cabin. Or perhaps Damian simply meant to let her starve.

She glanced quickly toward the cabin door, feeling apprehensive. Had he locked her in?

She hurried across the room, grabbing hold of the latch and lifting it with a swift movement. She let out a sigh of relief as the door opened before her.

Without thought for her disheveled appearance, she headed toward the galley, hoping that Duffy would have something left for her to eat.

It was the sound of Cassandra's laughter that made Damian stop in the passageway. He listened for a moment, then followed the sound.

"Truly, Duffy," he heard her say, " 'tis the best meal I've ever eaten."

"Now you're spinnin' a yarn, miss. 'Tis just 'ungry ye are, an' like as not, ye'd've found bis-

cuits an' bilge water a tasty dish if'n 'twas all I
'ad t'set afore ye."

Damian stopped just out of sight, then leaned
forward to peer into the galley.

Cassandra was seated at the cook's table, finishing off a bowl of lobscouse, a dish made of
salt beef, potatoes, peas, and hard tack. Her
hair had a certain wind-swept appearance that
he found attractive, and her face, in profile,
still had a sleepy look that made her seem
vulnerable. He watched as she dabbed dainti-
ly at the corners of her mouth with a cloth.

"I assure you, sir, I am much more discern-
ing than that. Bilge water is only acceptable
when served with pork."

Duffy guffawed as he stirred the ingredients
of a large black kettle, looking over his shoulder to show her a gaping grin.

Cassandra's smile faded. "Where are we
going, Duffy?" she asked softly.

The cook shrugged.

"Are we going back to Sorcery Bay?"

Damian heard something wistful in her voice,
and despite himself, he responded to it. "Is that
where you'd like to go, Cassandra?" he asked,
stepping into the doorway.

She jumped in surprise, and her spoon clattered to the floor.

Damian bent to retrieve it. When he looked
up, his gaze met hers. "I'm afraid it wouldn't be
safe for us there. Not until we're certain we're
not still being followed."

He held the spoon out toward her. Her fingers touched his as she took it from him, and a flare of wanting ignited in his belly.

It exasperated him that he wasn't able to put her from his mind as he wanted. It frustrated him that he couldn't simply forget her. He'd managed to avoid her during the past four weeks at sea, but suddenly, he'd lost the strength his rage had once provided.

She stared at him with a gaze that begged him to believe in her love. But how could *she* still believe it? After the things he'd said to her, she should hate him as he hated himself. Why didn't she scream and rail at him as she should, as he'd meant for her to do?

He straightened and turned so suddenly that he struck his forehead against the lintel. Cursing under his breath, he lifted his hand to touch the broken skin. His fingers came away bloody.

Her touch alighted on his arm, causing him to face her. "Here, let me look at that."

She pulled him back toward the bench, tugging on his arm until he sat down. Then she picked up the cloth beside her plate, turned it to a clean corner, and dipped it in a pan of water.

"There now," she said, drawing the cloth gently across his forehead. " 'Tis only a scratch." Her hand stopped. Her fingertips settled on his hair. She drew in a long, slow breath, and he felt a quiver move through her. "You must take care, captain. The galley ceiling is not high enough for a man such as you."

He, too, sucked in a deep breath, then lifted his eyes to meet her gaze. Her cheeks were flushed. Nervously, her tongue darted between her lips to moisten them.

His resistance stretched to the breaking point. If he lingered a moment longer, he wouldn't be able to control himself.

He stood. "I'll remember that, Miss Jamison." He stepped past her into the doorway.

"Captain?"

He stopped but didn't look back.

"Where are we going, if not to Sorcery Bay?"

It wasn't a captive's right to know where she was being taken. And that's what Cassandra was. She was his captive. He told himself he was only keeping her with him until he could find some way to send her back to her parents. Perhaps he would seek another ransom for her. Yes, that would justify her presence on the *Magic*.

"Captain?"

"We sail for Madagascar."

"Madagascar? But isn't that . . ."

" 'Tis a pirate's haven," he answered quickly, seeking to remind both of them just who and what he was. "Just right for the likes of me and my crew."

He hoped she would remember that. He hoped she would remember and stay the hell away from him before it was too late.

211

Chapter Eighteen

Cassandra had sighted the island about an hour earlier. Now, as they sailed toward the harbor, her gaze studied the sleepy little village that lined the shore. The low, whitewashed buildings reminded her of Sorcery Bay. So did the fields of sugarcane she could see to the east of the village.

" 'Tis the island of Madeira," Oliver said as he stepped up beside her.

"I thought we were going to Madagascar."

"We are. We've stopped here for provisions. When we sailed from America, we didn't lay in supplies for this long a journey. Before we leave here, there won't be room to swing a cat in the cargo hold."

She glanced at the ship's lieutenant, bewildered by his sailor's jargon.

He must have understood her confusion. He

grinned. "Means things'll be too crowded to use a cat-o-nine-tails. Takes plenty of room to wield the whip."

The memory of a scarred back flashed in her mind. "Damian," she said softly, her chest hurting.

Oliver stared at her a moment as he scratched the stubble on his jaw. "Those marks didn't come from no boatswain, miss," he finally answered. " 'Twas the overseer on Barbados that scarred the captain's back that way." He glanced toward the helm, his gaze finding Damian. "Besides, there's not a man aboard who'd ever need the threat of the cat t'follow the captain's orders, and the captain'd never allow it even if one did."

"Why is this crew different from any other?"

A cloud seemed to pass across Oliver's sun-browned face. He looked about to answer, then simply touched his forehead and said, "I'd best be about my duties." Then he walked away.

Cassandra pondered his words as she turned from her view of the island to watch the sailors as they furled the sails, hauled and pulled on rigging, and scurried about the ship in a general buzz of activity. She realized that she'd never really spoken to any of these men, other than an occasional "good morrow" or "good evening." What *did* make them different from any other crew? Why were they—to a man, according to Professor and Oliver—so loyal to Damian Tate?

"Drop anchor, Mr. Davis."

She followed the sound of Damian's voice. As it always did when she looked at him, her stomach somersaulted; her breath caught in her chest.

I would follow him anywhere.

But if he kept up his pirating ways, one day the Crown would catch him, even if her uncle did not. They would hang him, and she would lose him as surely as if he'd left her at Three Oaks with Abernathy. She had to stop him. She didn't know how, but she had to stop him.

She glanced once more at the village, then her gaze shifted to the other ships that were anchored in the harbor. The closest ship was a Spanish galleon. Although England was now at peace with Spain, it made Cassandra nervous to have what looked to be a former warship so close by. While still aboard the *Peacock*, she had heard sailors talking about the Spaniards' atrocities to prisoners of war. She wondered if, even now, there were captives in the galleon's bowels who were forced to serve at one of the oars that propelled the ship when the seas were becalmed.

She shivered and moved her gaze to the next ship.

She knew the vessel was French by the two jibsails at the bow. Her uncle had explained the method of identifying ships at a distance by the jibsails. While Spanish ships had only a small jib or none at all, the French usually had two. English ships, on the other hand, had but one.

There were two English ships in the harbor. The closest, a three-masted square-rigger, had a distinctive figurehead that drew Cassandra's attention first. The carving was of a woman with fiery red hair that flowed and swirled around her, providing only glimpses of what was obviously an otherwise naked body. Her large eyes were the green of emeralds, and she was smiling, as if she knew a special secret. Her right hand was outstretched, and she seemed to beckon those who chanced to look her way to come closer. The name of the ship was carved along the bow—the *Enchantress*. It seemed an appropriate appellation.

The other ship, a frigate, seemed dwarfed between the English merchant ship and the Spanish galleon. After a brief glimpse, her gaze drifted back to the *Enchantress*. She wondered what the ship's destination might be. Was she headed home to England, her hold filled with silks and spices, or was she on her way to the east?

It was much like her own future, she thought. The course she had chosen was equally unknown to her.

Damian stared at Cassandra's profile. He could tell she was mentally chewing on some sort of dilemma, the same way she was chewing on her lip.

Damned attractive lip, too.

He spun away, a scowl drawing his brows close together. He wasn't pleased with that particular turn of thought, but it seemed to be the direction his mind always went of late. No matter where he went on this ship, there seemed to be some reminder of her.

Hell's bells! He'd even allowed her to take over his cabin. When they'd been under attack by the *Venture*, he'd given orders for her to go to his quarters and stay there until he ordered her to leave. But he'd never ordered her to leave. He'd been the one to find a different place to sleep.

He ran his fingers through his long hair, unmindful when the ribbon at his nape slipped free and fell to the deck.

Unable to resist, he allowed his gaze to return to the woman at the ship's rail. The breeze caused wisps of pale hair to flutter around her face and the white of her linen shirt to press close against her feminine curves. Why did it seem that she was even more exposed that she'd been in the last dress she'd worn? He knew it wasn't true, but . . .

He turned his head again, and this time he saw several of the other crewmen doing what he'd been doing—watching Cassandra.

Saint's bones! He had to get her something decent to wear before he had a mutiny on his hands. He would have Oliver buy some dresses for her when he went ashore for supplies. Another week of her looking like this, and she would be leading the men on this ship around by their noses.

But there wouldn't be another week of this,

he reminded himself. The *Enchantress* was one of Sorcery Bay's own ships, and it was his intention to send Cassandra back to England on it. She would most likely be relieved when he told her. After all, he hadn't made the past weeks easy on her. Like the pirate he was, he'd taken her innocence and shown little remorse for it. He'd rejected the affection she offered him. How many times had he spoken cruelly to her, words designed to grieve and offend? How many times had he told her she meant nothing to him?

God forgive him, but he was a great liar. She meant far too much to him. That was his problem. He didn't want to send her away. He wanted her to remain his captive. He wanted to keep her on this ship, in his cabin, in his bed.

He frowned, cursing silently. It didn't matter what he wanted. He knew what was the right thing to do, what was best for Cassandra.

Using the handrails on either side of the steps, Damian vaulted from the poop to the main deck with a smooth, quick motion. The sound of his feet landing on the wood planking caused Cassandra to turn toward him. Her eyes widened as he approached with purposeful steps.

" 'Tis Madeira," he said.

"I know. Oliver told me."

He nodded. He should have known Oliver had told her. Oliver had made it his business to see that she wasn't too lonely, much as Professor had done during the voyage to Sorcery Bay. He wondered if his lieutenant had also told her about the *Enchantress*.

Perhaps she's bewitched us all.

"How long shall we be here?" she asked.

He'd never seen eyes so wide nor so blue. A man could drown in such eyes. They beseeched, beguiled, and bewildered him. When she looked at him like that . . .

She *had* bewitched him. That's all there was to it.

Damian motioned with his head toward the merchant ship. "I mean to speak to the captain of the *Enchantress* about your passage back to England."

"But there's no need, Damian. I'm going to stay with you."

" 'Tis not up to you."

Her mouth thinned and her chin rose. "You are wrong. It *is* up to me."

"I'm sending you back to England."

"I won't go."

"Damn it, woman! Do you know what's ahead of you if you stay?"

Cassandra stared at him, feeling her love swelling in her chest. The first time she'd seen him, she'd thought he had the eyes of a demon. She'd thought they revealed a man without a soul. But she saw things more clearly now. Now she saw that his eyes revealed a tormented heart, and it caused her own heart to ache in response. If only she could reach past the protective shell of anger to the man inside. If only she could make him see that her love was unshakable and forever.

"Aye, captain," she whispered, fighting sudden tears, "I do know what's ahead of me if I stay. 'Tis what I want."

"You're deceiving yourself, Cassandra. You think you can stop me from having my revenge, but you can't. Nor will you stop me from returning to my own cabin, to my own bed. And if you're in it, then you'll not be able to stop me from taking you as I did before." His fingers closed over her upper arms. His dark brows drew together into a frown of warning. "Do you hear what I'm saying? There'll be no pretense between us. I will use you as I would use any woman who offered herself to me as you're doing." He released her and stepped backward. "Go back to England while you have the chance."

Cassandra squared her shoulders. "You cannot bully me out of loving you, captain. No matter what you do, I shall still love you, and somehow, I shall prove it to you."

Chapter Nineteen

You cannot bully me out of loving you, captain. No matter what you do, I shall still love you, and somehow, I shall prove it to you.

God help him. He wanted to believe her. He wanted the love she offered more than he'd ever wanted anything in his life. Even revenge.

Two days after the *Magic* had sailed from Madeira, Damian was still haunted by those words. He remembered the way she'd looked, her pointed chin thrust up stubbornly, her blue eyes meeting his gaze without hesitation.

When he'd remained silent, she had turned and walked into the bedchamber. She'd left the door open, and he'd known he could walk through and join her.

He hadn't.

Damian clenched his hands into fists as he

crossed the poop deck and leaned his forearms on the taffrail. He stared across the water, wondering why he hadn't sent her away on the *Enchantress* as he'd intended. He'd tried to tell himself it was because he'd realized how dangerous that would be. She knew his real identity now. There were many who thought the *Magic* was nothing more than a figment of Farley's imagination. Cassandra had the power to change all that. She could guide the Crown to Sorcery Bay. She could destroy him and all the people he'd sought to help and protect.

But he'd been aware of those dangers long before now. The truth was that he hadn't sent her away because he'd suddenly realized what it would be like without her.

He swung away from the rail, and his gaze went to the opposite end of the ship. He found her standing on the forecastle deck, just as he'd known he would.

She turned toward him, as if sensing that he watched her. The wind blew her hair—worn loose today—into her face, and she had to lift an arm to sweep it back. For some reason, the motion tugged at his heart, and when her eyes met his, he knew he was lost.

He walked the length of the ship, gathered her into his arms, and kissed her.

The wind whipped her hair against their cheeks, but Cassandra paid it no mind. Nothing else mattered now that Damian was holding her, kissing her. Her heart soared as her lips savored his. She was oblivious to the snap and rattle of the sails and rigging overhead. She was oblivious to the salty spray that flew up from the bow. The rest of the world had ceased to exist the moment he'd climbed the steps to the forecastle and folded her into his embrace.

She opened her eyes as his lips withdrew. He stared down at her, his hands sliding up her arms to cradle her face.

"You'll regret this," he said.

"Never."

"I haven't changed my mind about your uncle."

"I know."

"I mean to get Tate Shipping back. I mean to make Dunworthy pay for what he did to my father."

"I know that, too."

"You'll come to hate me with time."

"That day shall never come. I will love you always."

His thumb tenderly rubbed her cheek. She turned her head and pressed the heel of his hand against her lips as her eyes drifted closed.

He hadn't said he loved her. He hadn't offered her marriage. He hadn't promised anything for the future. And yet she had seen hope in his eyes where once she'd seen none. That was enough for now. She would make it a beginning.

She looked up as she folded her hand around his. Wordlessly, she guided him down the steps and toward the foremast. With a gentle tug on his arm, she encouraged him to sit beside her, their backs pressed against the towering spar.

"Tell me," she said as she stared out at the rolling sea.

"Tell you what?"

"Tell me about when you were a boy. Before you went to Barbados. Tell me about your life then."

It wasn't an easy thing to ask of him. He'd purposefully blocked those memories from his mind. Looking back was too painful.

Her hand tightened. He looked down at her long, tapered fingers, her skin so pale against his. Gentle fingers.

"Tell me, Damian."

"I was born on board one of my father's ships, as my parents returned from the Far East." He spoke haltingly at first. He'd suppressed the memories for so many years. It was difficult to put them into words. "Our home was in Plymouth in Devon, and we were often in London. But my earliest memories are of sailing on one of my father's ships."

He smiled to himself, recalling how he used to follow his father about the decks, scrambling to help the other sailors. Now that he commanded his own ships, he knew he'd been more in the way than of help. It was a wonder one of the sailors hadn't tossed him overboard when his father wasn't looking. Come to think of it, it was a wonder his father hadn't tossed him overboard.

"My father's ships sailed all over the world, bringing back to England everything imaginable. Mostly, I remember the way it smelled."

He closed his eyes, speaking softly. "Coffee and spices, tobacco and rice, furs and timber." He stopped, then added, "My father was a brilliant merchant."

Cassandra's fingers stroked his hand. "What of your mother? What was she like?"

"I don't remember her very well," Damian replied with a slow shake of his head. "She had black, curly hair and a pretty smile, and I remember she laughed a lot. She loved to sing, too. There always seemed to be music wherever she was." He paused a moment, listening to some long-forgotten tune in his head. Finally, he continued, "She died in childbirth when I was five. The baby died, too."

"You have no other family?"

He thought of his father's cruel death, and his jaw tensed. "No. I'm all alone."

"No, Damian." Her fingertips cupped his chin and turned his head so that their eyes met. "You're not alone. You have me."

Stubborn wench. Stubborn and beautiful.

"Tell me more," she persisted.

"There's not much else to tell. I spent every school holiday on my father's ships." He stared out across the ocean and drew in a deep breath of salty air. "Sailing was all I wanted to do. I resented having to go to school and spend long, dreary months in England when I could have been sailing to Bombay or Calcutta." He remembered the first time he'd seen the exotic ports of Rangoon and Macao. He recalled the bustling ports in the colonies through a child's eyes—Boston and New York and Jamestown. He grinned. "Life at sea was much more exciting than listening to long lectures by some stodgy old man who'd never been outside of England even once in his life."

"You must have plagued your father constantly."

Damian chuckled. "Aye, that I did, but he said I would be a gentleman some day and he'd have me be an educated one. There was no changing his mind. I was forced to continue my schooling." His lingering smile faded. "It did me little good when I was laboring under the hot sun in the cane fields."

She pointedly ignored his last statement. "Would you care to know about my childhood?"

He brought his eyes back to her. Her pale hair was a tangled mess from blowing in the wind. Her skin had been browned from weeks in the sun, for she was always forgetting to wear one of her bonnets. In fact, he could see a smattering of freckles across the bridge of her nose. In truth, he rather liked them. He could almost imagine what she'd looked like as a child.

"Were you a tomboy, Miss Jamison?"

"Goodness, no, sir!" she exclaimed in mock horror. "I was the most decorous of young ladies. I was tutored in proper etiquette from the time I was very small. 'Twas my duty, after all, to marry well, and how should a young lady do that if she behaved like a hoyden? I'll have you know I can sew a nearly invisible hem, and my embroidery stitches were always remarked upon as nothing but extraordinary. I have a pleasant singing voice, so I'm told, and have a modicum of talent at the harp, though I confess that I detest playing it."

"Sounds quite dull, learning all that." He couldn't suppress another grin.

She sighed dramatically. " 'Twas frightfully so, I'm afraid." Then she smiled, and her whole face lit up. "Truly, Damian, I had a charmed childhood. My parents and . . ."

He knew she'd been about to mention her uncle and had thought better of it.

"My family all spoiled me quite outrageously. Our home in Northumberland is quaint and lovely, and I've many friends there. We used to have picnics and go fox hunting. I always loved autumn the best, for that was when Mother would have grand house parties at Kettering Hall. I far preferred spending time there to my two seasons in London, although I enjoyed those well enough, I suppose."

"And tell me, Miss Jamison, you are not in your first blush of young womanhood. You are what? Twenty years? How is it you're not married if your sole duty was to marry well? You can't tell me that Mr. Abernathy's offer was the only one you'd ever received. You're far too lovely for me to ever believe that falsehood."

The smile left her lips and her eyes. "I am one and twenty, sir, and no, 'twas not my only offer."

Damian felt immediate regret. What a bumbling fool he was. He'd meant only to tease her. He hadn't meant to cause any distress. It had been careless of him to bring up Abernathy.

Her expression was sad when she spoke. "My parents are wonderful people, and I love them dearly, as they love me. But I have seen too well what an arranged marriage can mean." Her eyes took on a faraway look. "I think Mother was in love with another man before she married Papa. She never said so, but I know 'tis true. She always told me that a woman should feel a grand passion for her husband. I suppose I was waiting to fall in love. No one who ever offered for me made me feel the way . . . the way I knew I should feel."

She looked at him then, and he saw what she felt for him shining in her eyes. He wished he had the ability to return her love, but he didn't. That gift had been stolen from him eighteen years ago. It was difficult enough for him to accept her feelings as real or lasting. It was impossible for him to believe he would ever be able to return them in kind.

"Then why did you accept Abernathy's offer?" he asked gently, unable to stop himself.

"Because my un—my family needed the money that the marriage settlement would bring. If I had refused another offer, we might have been ruined. I couldn't let that happen to them. They'd always given me so much. How could I not do my duty by them?"

Damian felt a stab of guilt. His acts of piracy upon Tate Shipping were what had put her family in that precarious position. It was his fault that she'd nearly been forced to marry a man like Aldin Abernathy.

Cassandra knew what he was thinking. For the second time, she cupped his chin with her fingers and drew his gaze to hers. " 'Twas fate, Damian, else how would we have met? I had to be on the *Peacock* or our paths would never have crossed."

"It does seem fate had a hand in it," he replied solemnly, "but are you so sure 'tis a happy fate?"

She tried not to let his words hurt her, but they did. She knew it was going to take time for him to accept that their future lay together, not separately. Still, his continual rejection of all that she offered couldn't help but distress her.

She forced herself to smile and say, "Fate has placed me where I'm meant to be. I shall *make* it a happy one."

She took hold of his hand again, and they sat in companionable silence beneath the white canvas clouds of the *Magic*.

Roland Bennett could think of a dozen things he'd rather be doing than joining Farley Dunworthy for lunch at the other man's town house in fashionable Soho Square. He'd been less than pleased to receive the baron's summons. And that's exactly what it had been. A summons. Dunworthy never *asked* anyone for anything. He demanded it, as if it were his due. The fellow needed a good set-down, and it looked as if he would soon be getting it, too if the rumors about town could be trusted.

Roland's smug grin wasn't brought under control until the carriage rolled to a halt in front of the town house.

When the footman opened the carriage door, Roland poked his head out and frowned at the persistent drizzle. Thank goodness he would be leaving the City for his home near Eastbourne before long. It it weren't for his sister's daughter, who was in town for her first Season, he would be in East Sussex now, but appearances demanded he remain until the London season came to its bloody end.

With a sigh, he stepped out of the conveyance and hurried toward the entrance to the baron's town house. The door opened almost before he'd had time to rap, and he was ushered inside by an aging servant in faded livery.

"Good day, my lord. We haven't seen you in Soho in some time."

"It has been awhile, Prescott. How are you faring?"

"Well enough, my lord," the old man said as he took Roland's hat and walking stick. "Lord Kettering has asked that I show you into the dining hall. He's waiting for you now."

Roland nodded. "No need to show me in. I know the way."

As he walked toward the dining hall, his sharp eyes noted several missing items. There were two paintings gone from the walls, and the large table in the entry hall was empty of the silver candelabrum which had always stood in the center. These things had, no doubt, found their way to a lender in the City. He sincerely doubted they would ever be returned.

Farley looked toward the door as Roland entered the dining hall. "You're late, Bennett."

"I apologize, Kettering, but I had a number of matters which I had to see to before I could join you." He knew his answer would irritate the baron. Farley didn't like to think that anything could take precedence over him.

"Yes, well . . ."His host motioned toward a chair at the table. "Do sit down. Do you care for a glass of champagne?"

"Champagne?" He hid a smile. He knew damned good and well that Farley couldn't afford such extravagances now, but he also knew the man's pride wouldn't let him admit it. "Yes, I believe I would like some."

While he filled two glasses, Farley said, "I was concerned by your last correspondence, Bennett. I cannot believe you were telling me that there is no way around the absurdly high tax we're paying to ship our goods to the colonies."

"I'm afraid I was telling you just that, Kettering."

"I expected better of you."

Roland shrugged. "I've done what I can."

"And what of my plea for help with these blasted acts of piracy? What of this ship, the

Magic? Why hasn't something been done to capture this man?"

"The Royal Navy does its best to stop all acts of piracy. But it can do no more for you than for anyone else. I don't know what you think I can do for you in that regard."

Farley turned from the sideboard and carried the two glasses across the room. He set one in front of Roland, then sipped from the second before walking to his place at the table. "We've worked together for a long time."

"Yes, we have."

Roland recognized what game the baron was about to play and sighed internally. Before he would come to the point, Farley would remind Roland of all the baron had done for him through the years. Which was true, of course. Investing in Farley Dunworthy's enterprises had proven most beneficial to him. As the fifth son of a viscount who was far too fond of the gaming tables, Roland had needed to build his own wealth. But he'd been wise enough to sever most of his financial ties several years before. Perhaps it was because he'd become tired of soiling his hands with Farley's dirty work. Perhaps it was because he was growing older and wanted to take fewer risks. Whatever the reason, he preferred not to be associated with the man any longer. It appeared, however, that the baron wasn't going to let him off the hook so easily.

It took Farley more than a quarter of an hour to finish his speech, detailing a number of matters which Roland had forgotten about completely and several he would have preferred to forget. When he was done, Farley leaned back in his chair, pressed his fingertips together, and leveled a cool gaze on his guest.

"Roland, my friend," he continued after a lengthy pause, "we have worked together for too many years to let anything come between us now. Without your help, Tate Shipping will be ruined and I along with it. And if I'm ruined, so shall you be."

"I? But I have nothing invested in Tate Shipping."

"I don't refer to your finances, although I'm sure those would be forfeit to the Crown should your—shall we say, past indiscretions?—come to light."

Roland straightened in his chair. "Are you threatening me?"

Farley smiled. "Threatening? Good heavens, no. But I would regret terribly if certain documents—bearing your signature, mind you—were to fall into the wrong hands. I don't suppose the Crown looks kindly on those who—well, I'm afraid you know better than most what the Crown does to a traitor."

A fine sheen of sweat broke out across Roland's forehead. "You would be implicated, too," he said. But as he looked at Farley's confident expression, he wasn't certain that his statement was true.

Had the man actually saved those letters and forged documents all these years? He thought of the baron's cluttered office at Kettering Hall. Papers and record books everywhere. The man didn't seem to discard anything. But surely he wouldn't be reckless enough to keep papers which might confirm the part he'd played in sending an innocent man to his death. Would he?

Another glance at the man across from him seemed to answer his question.

Roland rose from his chair. "I'll do my best to see that your taxes are modified, Kettering. In fact, I believe I shall beg off from partaking in the superb luncheon your cook has undoubtedly prepared and get directly to work on the matter."

"I appreciate your help." Farley stood. "And the pirate situation?"

"I'll look into it again." His throat felt dry and scratchy, but he wanted to escape the house far more than he wanted a drink.

"I look forward to your next report, Bennett. I'll send Mouse for it next week."

Roland nodded and hurried out of the dining hall, feeling as if the hounds of hell pursued him.

Chapter Twenty

Cassandra stepped through the hatch just as the sun was slipping into the sea. Her gaze immediately sought and found Damian at the helm.

She'd spent hours down in the great cabin, changing her clothes several times, braiding and rebraiding her hair. It was silly that she was primping so. Damian had seen her in all manner of dress. But silly or not, she'd wanted to look her very best tonight.

It seemed an eternity since he'd risen from the deck where they'd been sitting, their backs resting against the mast. He'd reached for her hand and pulled her up after him. He had work to do, he'd told her, and then he'd kissed her cheek. She would have sworn she could still feel his lips on her skin.

"Give us a song, McGruder," she heard someone call behind her.

She turned just as the musician began to coax a lively tune from his pipe. A moment later, a second man brought out his horn and added the music from his instrument to that of the first. She smiled as her toe began tapping in time with the melody.

"Do you dance, Miss Jamison?"

She felt her heart skip a beat, not really surprised that he'd joined her and glad that he had. "I love to dance, captain."

"And will you dance with me?" He took hold of her hand, not waiting for her reply.

The music changed, slowed. His eyes never left her as they began to move slowly about the deck. She knew others were watching them, but she couldn't have pulled her eyes free from his dark gaze if her life depended upon it. Everything around them became a blur as night fell over the ship. There was only the two of them and the music.

Cassandra had no idea how long they danced. It could have been minutes; it could have been hours. She only knew she didn't want it to end. Never before had she felt so lighthearted and gay. She wanted to go on forever, dancing with Damian, having him look at her as he was now. His eyes sparkled with laughter when they danced to the lively notes of a jig. His gaze was like an intimate caress when they danced slowly. She was sorry when the magical spell was broken by the voice of another.

"Excuse me, captain." Oliver cleared his throat. "But a few of the men . . . Well, they thought, if Miss Jamison would agree . . . They were hoping . . ."

Damian raised an eyebrow as he glanced at her. "Cassandra?"

It took her a moment before she understood what was being asked. When she did, she smiled again. "I'd be pleased to dance with you, Oliver."

"Oh, not me, miss." Color swept up from his neck. "I've no knowledge of those fancy steps you an' the captain have turned about the deck."

"Then you show me how you dance, and I shall follow."

Oliver shook his head. "There's others much better suited than me. Mr. Davis there and Mr. Simon and young Mr. Binns."

"But I wish to dance with you first, Oliver. 'Tis as easy as climbing the ladder down to the skiff. Once you take that first step, 'tis not nearly as bad as you thought it at first."

She heard the men's good-natured joking as they dared the lieutenant to dance with her, and then the music began again. Reluctantly, Oliver took hold of her proffered hand. It wasn't long before he was deporting himself quite admirably, despite his continued protestations to the contrary.

The music changed, and she found herself with another partner—and then another and another and another. She wondered as she

looked at these men—these corsairs and buc-
caneers, these ruthless outlaws of the sea—why
they had all seemed so fearful to her when
she'd first seen them. They were all smiling
and friendly. They made her laugh. Some of
them were old enough to be her father. Many
of them were hardly more than boys. A few *were*
still boys. But none of them seemed fearful to
her any longer.

Yet, they weren't any different than they'd
been two months ago. It was she who was different. She was the one who had changed. And
she had changed because of Damian.

As if he knew she was thinking his name, the
captain claimed her for another dance. When
he stepped close to her, he bent his head forward and said, "I've shared you enough, my
lovely. I'll share you no more."

Her heart tripped, and her feet followed suit.
He drew her against his body as he steadied her
with his arms.

"We've done enough dancing," he said, his
voice low and husky.

Wide-eyed and silent, she nodded.

With nary a word to the crew, Damian swept
her up into his arms and carried her below
deck. She nestled her face against the white
linen of his shirt, her hands locked behind his
neck. Her stomach felt tight, and there was a
strange, gnawing sensation in her loins. She
thought of the things he'd done to her body the
morning after he'd rescued her from Abernathy,
and she knew she wanted him to do it all again.

She wanted him to touch her in all the places he'd touched her then. She wanted him to kiss her in all the places he'd kissed her.

Damian opened the door to the great cabin and carried her inside. He lowered her slowly, letting her body slide against his until her feet touched the floor. She gazed up into obsidian eyes that seemed to glow with a secret fire and felt her own body warm in response.

"Wait here." He bent and kissed her lips, his mouth moving over hers with a feather-light touch that inflamed her senses.

When he moved away, she felt a draft of cool air swirl around her and longed to have him return to hold her. She thought of crossing the cabin to the bed but seemed unable to command her legs to move.

Sounds of men's laughter filtered through the gallery windows along the stern. Up on deck, the pipe and horn continued to play, slowing to a haunting melody that made her yearn all the more for Damian's return. Why, she wondered, had he told her to wait there? She wanted to be with him. She wanted to be with him now.

The door to the connecting cabin opened, and Damian stepped through.

He paused to stare at her. The cabin was illuminated by the rising moon. The light spilled through the windows, not stopping until it was a pool around Cassandra's feet. It reflected off her silvery hair, giving the impression of a halo encircling her head. Truly, she was like an angel. Too lovely to be believed.

Desire came upon him, hot and insistent, but he willed himself to wait. He would not be hurried. Not tonight. Tonight he would teach her untutored body that there was more to making love than just a heated coupling. Much more.

Wordlessly, he walked to her, took her by the hand, and led her into the other room. He saw her questioning eyes move from his face to the long brass tub set in the center of a room lit with a dozen candles.

"I thought you might be tired of washing in a basin."

"A real bath," she said, sounding as if he'd presented her with the moon. "You did this for me?"

He nodded, suddenly *feeling* as if he'd presented her with the moon.

"How . . . when . . . ?"

"While you were dancing."

" 'Tis a wonderful surprise, Damian. Thank you."

"Come . . . while the water is still warm." He reached to slip the first button on her bodice from its catch. "Come and enjoy."

He loved watching her eyes as he undressed her. He could see so many things written in the blue depths. She was nervous but not afraid. She was willing but uncertain. When he pushed her gown from her shoulders, she sucked in a quick breath of air. He felt a tightening in his groin as her tongue darted out to lick her lips.

When at last she stood naked before him, her pale skin aglow in the flickering candlelight, he guided her to the tub. She stepped into it, then sank into the warm liquid.

Water licked at the bottom of her well-rounded breasts. Her nipples were taut, tiny ridges forming on the dark areolas. As Damian knelt beside the tub, he reached out to caress first one breast, then the other.

Again, she moistened her lips, and again, he felt the rising of his desire.

He moved to the end of the tub, lifted a bar of scented soap, and began to bathe her, starting with her back. His hands moved slowly over her body, soaping and rinsing, enjoying the feel of her. Occasionally, he would lean forward and kiss the nape of her neck. She would always respond with a tiny whimper of pleasure.

As he continued his ministrations, he moved from the end of the tub and along one side. With faint strokes, he washed her arms, then glided the soap over her breasts, circling each generous mound before kneading them with gentle fingers.

When he lifted her right leg out of the water and slid his fingers along the tender flesh of her inner thigh, she made a choked sound in her throat. His eyes met hers as his hands slipped down the length of her leg to her foot. Gently, he massaged it with fingers made strong by years aboard a ship. She gave a groan of pleasure. In response, he leaned forward to kiss the arch of her foot, then nibbled his way up her leg, only stopping when water splashed against his chin and nose. Drawing a deep breath to help steady his own passions, he ran the soap along the skin he'd so recently kissed. Moving to the other side of the tub, he repeated the process with her left leg, then soaped and rinsed his way back to her breasts.

The soap slipped to the bottom of the tub as his hands cupped her breasts. He used his thumbs to tease the nipples and watched as her eyes half-closed and her head fell slightly backward.

"The water grows cool," he said.

"Does it?" she asked in a languorous tone.

He smiled, hearing something special in her reply. "Aye, it does."

Strange. She didn't feel cool. In truth, she was over-warm. But she was loath for this to end. She'd never been bathed by another before. At least, not since she was a child and her nurse had seen to her bath. Certainly, she'd never had anyone soap and rinse her the way Damian had just done. She'd never realized how truly delicious water could feel, lapping at her skin.

He moved away from her and began snuffing the candles until they were enveloped in darkness. She heard more than saw him return to her side. With a touch that was still gentle and unhurried, he drew her up from the water and wrapped her in a blanket, then lifted her into his arms and carried her back to his bed-chamber, where he placed her on the edge of the bed.

Once again she felt his hands moving over her, this time drying her skin with the blanket. She closed her eyes completely this time, allowing herself to simply enjoy the feelings he invoked. They were all so foreign, so wonderful.

"You're beautiful, my angel," he said in a voice thick with emotion. "Never before has a woman . . ." His words drifted into silence.

She knew what he was telling her. Her love was special to him. *She* was special to him. A shiver of pleasure moved through her.

And then the blanket was gone, and so was Damian.

Cassandra opened her eyes, for a brief moment afraid that the spell had been broken, that he had gone off to sleep in another chamber as had been his practice since the day of the *Venture's* attack. But he hadn't left her. He was there, standing beside the bed, illuminated by the moonlight, his darkly handsome features seeming even darker and handsomer now.

She watched as he peeled the damp, white linen shirt over his head. Scarcely knowing she did so, she rose onto her knees and reached forward to touch the muscled contours of his chest. She traced the line of black hair that began at the base of his throat, spread wide across the upper portion of his torso, then narrowed as it disappeared beneath his breeches.

His entire body stiffened when her fingers paused at the waistband. She glanced up and was mesmerized by the look she saw in his eyes, a look of wanting that caused her breath to falter and her heart to pound so hard it was almost painful.

She withdrew her hand from his skin but didn't move away. She couldn't have even if she'd wanted to. But she didn't want to. She wanted to draw closer. She felt a need of her own and knew that only he could assuage it.

As he unfastened his breeches, she felt a quick flicker of fear as she remembered the pain of their first joining, but it was replaced by a memory of something much better.

She became aware then that he was as naked as she. She looked at him as she'd never looked at him before, a sound of surprise slipping between slightly parted lips. She hadn't known . . . she'd never imagined . . . He was so different, so . . .

Magnificent.

Her gaze darted back to his face as he reached for her. He drew her up against his chest and knelt on the bed beside her. She felt his hardness pressing against her belly as his lips captured hers in a kiss that left her quaking and feeling that she might explode. Instinctively, she pressed closer to him.

"Damian . . ." she whispered plaintively.

He eased her back onto the bed, his body stretched out beside hers. Like a great musician, his fingers stroked her, drawing out a melody such as she'd never heard before. Her body moved of its own accord, arching closer to his magical hands even as his mouth captured a taut nipple and suckled lightly. His touch elicited a groan from deep within her.

Her fingers wove through his thick, long hair, and she pulled his head up from her breast, her mouth seeking his with a hunger to match his own. She wanted more. As wonderful as the sensations his hands evoked were, she wanted more. She needed more. She thought she might perish if he didn't . . . if he didn't . . .

She didn't understand this great need to become a part of him. She only knew she must do so or surely perish from the wanting.

"Damian, please!" she cried out.

Her eyes flew open as he rose above her, and she felt his hardness pressing for entrance where his fingers had been only moments before. She saw his desire flaring in his eyes as she opened herself to him and felt him drive inside her.

And then there was no room left for thought.

Later, their passion spent, Damian lay on his back, Cassandra's head on his shoulder, her body curled next to his. With a slow, steady rhythm he stroked her hair. Every so often, he kissed her forehead.

"Damian?"

His hand stilled. "I thought you were asleep."

"I don't want to sleep. I want to cherish these feelings a while longer." She lifted herself on her elbow, then leaned forward to kiss him on the mouth. "Is it always like this? Between a man and a woman, I mean?"

"No, my lovely. It isn't always like this."

"We're special," she whispered as she settled back onto his shoulder, her hand moving over him, lightly playing with his chest hair.

"Aye." His heart tightened. He hadn't known real fear in many years, but now he was afraid. Afraid of this slip of a girl who made him feel things he'd never felt before and had never expected to feel. "Aye, my sea sprite, we're special."

" 'Tis because I love you, Damian."

He closed his eyes as another wave of fear washed over him, fear that he could lose what he had found. "Aye, Cassandra. Because you love me."

Chapter Twenty-One

Early the next morning, the weather turned foul. Blackened skies emptied their contents upon the *Magic*. Strong winds whipped the seas into a wild spray. Giant waves battered the vessel. The ship bounced about like a child's toy in a bucket. More than once, the *Magic* seemed on the verge of breaking up.

Cassandra was forced to stay in the great cabin, but Damian spent long days and even longer nights up on deck, battling along with his crew to keep the ship afloat. Helplessly, Cassandra watched the storm-tossed sea through the gallery windows. Often, she wondered if they could survive such a storm. As soon as the doubt popped into her head, she promptly sent up a prayer for the safety of Damian and his crew.

Three days later, Damian entered his bed-chamber at sunrise. Cassandra awakened and sat up the moment she heard his footsteps. She slipped out of bed and hurried toward him. Unmindful of his drenched clothes, she embraced him.

"Is it over?" she asked a long time later.

"Aye."

She could hear his exhaustion in the simple answer. Taking hold of his hand, she led him across the room to a chair near the bed. With her hands on his shoulders, she pushed him down onto the chair, then began to undress him, starting with his boots. When all was removed except his breeches, she urged him back to his feet and removed the sodden trousers before drying him with a blanket. Moments later, he was in bed, the covers drawn up to his shoulders, already fast asleep.

Cassandra stared down at him. She contemplated crawling into the bed and nestling against him, but seeing the weariness in his face, she knew she didn't want to risk disturbing him. There would be time later to snuggle in his embrace. She would let him sleep for now.

She glanced out the windows at the pink and lavender clouds that soared above a dark green sea, a sea that no longer resembled some medieval monster as it had during the worst of the storm. She couldn't help but wonder how it could change so quickly. Everything looked peaceful once again. She was hard pressed to remember how frightened she had been, how certain that they would perish.

Dressing quickly, Cassandra left the captain's quarters and went above deck. As she stepped through the hatch, she drew in a deep breath, relishing her renewed freedom. She was willing to concede that the past three days had not been as terrifying as the time she'd been locked in her windowless cabin during a storm. At least this time she'd been able to see what was happening.

Spying Oliver on the forecastle, she waved at him. He returned the greeting, then dropped down to the main deck and walked over to her.

"Good morrow, Miss Jamison. Seems you've weathered the blow right enough."

"I'm well, thank you, Oliver." She saw the weariness etched in his face. "And you?"

"I'll be right enough when I get me a few more winks."

"What of the others?"

"One of our carpenters broke his leg, and young Toby suffered a sprain, but that was the worst the storm did to our crew."

She frowned. "Will they be all right?"

"Aye. The surgeon set Mr. Bowker's leg. With luck, 'twill heal straight. The boy's in a bit of pain, but he'll be up and about in no time."

"Perhaps I could help care for them until they're well," Cassandra suggested.

Oliver grinned. "Sink me, but I think they'd like that, miss. There's not a man aboard what doesn't think you're . . ." He stopped himself, color rushing into his cheeks. "Well, we know you've made the captain . . . Ah, we're grateful for . . . You see, we all admire the captain, miss, and we know he and you . . ." He stopped again, his face now bright red.

Cassandra wondered that it wasn't she who was blushing. After all, the crew of the *Magic* knew she was sharing the captain's quarters without benefit of clergy. A few short weeks ago, the idea would have horrified her. Now she was merely pleased to know she had the approval of his officers and crew.

Oliver cleared his throat, then continued. "We'll be putting in at Fort James to make a few repairs."

"Fort James? But that's a British port, Oliver. Is it safe for Damian to stop there? What if this ship is recognized? You might all be in danger of discovery."

Oliver laid a comforting hand on her shoulder. " 'Tis no danger, miss. The *Magic* won't be flying her black flag when she sails into port, and that's the only way anyone would know her as other than a Sorcery Bay ship."

Cassandra wasn't convinced, and her expression must have showed it.

"The captain may not like me sayin' this, but I think 'tis time you knew a few things, Miss Jamison. Damian's no pirate, as I've told you before. 'Tis only Tate ships that have ever seen the *Magic*'s black standard. There's nothing else to set her apart from a hundred ships. That's why you see no distinctive figurehead on the bow and no name carved upon her stern."

She felt a spark of hope. "Then Damian Tate isn't being sought by the Crown for piracy?"

"There's fewer than those you could count on your fingers who know Damian's last name. He's not used it since he arrived in Barbados. Most think him a bastard who don't know his father's name. Besides..." Oliver grinned. "Why would the Crown seek one of her own heroes?"

"Hero?"

Oliver wore a pleased expression. "Sink me, but 'tis true, miss. The captain was knighted for his service during the war. Sir Damian is what he's called when we're in England."

Cassandra turned and walked to the port side railing. She tried to sort through her swirling thoughts. Damian wasn't a criminal—at least, not in the eyes of the Crown. In truth, he was a nobleman, a knight. Sir Damian. And not just a knight—a hero of the war. If not for his belief that Uncle Far had stolen Tate Shipping and sent his father to his death, Damian would not be committing any acts of piracy. He would not be placing his life and the lives of these men in danger. If she could convince him of her uncle's innocence, perhaps this could all be put behind them. Perhaps they could return to Sorcery Bay. Perhaps he might even decide he loved her. Perhaps they might marry....

"If I could just find proof for Damian," she said softly, "he could stop all this."

"What proof do you seek?"

She turned around to face Oliver. His expression was stern, his brows drawn together in a frown.

"Proof of my uncle's innocence," she answered, lifting her stubborn chin.

"To hell with the bloody oath," Oliver muttered, as if to himself, but the sea wind carried his words to her ears. He stepped closer. His hand touched the scar on the right side of his face. "Do you know how I got this, miss? 'Twas your uncle himself who carved me this pretty line. I was serving as a fo'c'sle boy on the *Peacock* under Captain Tate, Damian's own father, when he was taken for a traitor. I remember it well, the day Dunworthy came aboard and let us know he was the new master. He sailed as the captain before he got his fancy title, an' there wasn't a man among us who didn't suffer because of it."

Cassandra shook her head as he spoke.

"Aye. 'Tis true. I got this 'cause I did no more than spill his supper into his lap one night. He accused me of doin' it on purpose. He grabbed the knife off the table and swung at me. I didn't duck fast enough."

She flinched inwardly.

"He might have done worse, but another stepped in t'help me. Mouse lost his eye for his troubles."

"Mouse?" she echoed, remembering the weathered-looking, one-eyed sailor who'd served her uncle for so many years. "I know him. He was on the *Peacock* when I was taken."

"Aye, he never left Tate Shipping. Dunworthy had other uses for him because he thinks he's an ignorant fool. But Mouse ain't no fool. He's been helpin' Damian these past few years. If your uncle were to find out, he'd kill Mouse in the blink of an eye."

Cassandra shook her head. She couldn't believe what Oliver said about her uncle. Oh, she'd heard him raise his voice in anger a time or two. Her mother was prone to provoking him into a temper. But she'd never seen Uncle Far show a violent streak.

Or had she? She remembered the time he'd taken his whip to a team of horses after losing a race. But he wouldn't do the same to the men who worked for him. Would he?

"Did Professor ever tell you how he lost his fingers?" Oliver asked, cutting into her thoughts.

She glanced at him, apprehension making her voice quiver. "He said he was caught stealing bread from the ship's galley."

"Aye, and the owner who ordered his punishment was none other than Farley Dunworthy. The same bastard that told Professor there'd be more food for others if his wife died."

Cassandra covered her ears. "No. It can't be true," she whispered.

"Hear me out, miss," the lieutenant said, stepping closer and pulling her hands from the sides of her head. "Your uncle's a hard, ruthless man. He don't care 'bout the suffering of others if it'll fill his pockets with blunt. There's those aboard the *Magic* that have had the cat laid across their backs by Dunworthy himself. An' he's not above misusing his own family. 'Twas he who planned your kidnapping from the *Peacock*. Only Damian heard of it from Mouse an' took you first. 'Twas Dunworthy who collected the ransom from Abernathy, not us." He released her hands and moved back from her. "The captain'll not be pleased for what I've just told you, but 'twas time you knew the truth. Past time."

She continued to shake her head slowly. It couldn't be true. It just couldn't be.

"You've got the power to see that we all hang, if you choose to believe that uncle of yours instead of Damian." His gaze narrowed. "You know the captain, miss. You know him with your heart even if you don't know all the facts. He wouldn't lie t'you."

"No, he wouldn't lie to me," she whispered as she turned around to face the sea.

"I wouldn't lie t'you either," Oliver added.

She listened as Damian's lieutenant walked away. She searched her mind for any plausible reason for her uncle's behavior. She tried to imagine that the man Oliver had described was the same Uncle Far who had always treated her as if she were his own daughter, but she couldn't. It was impossible. Surely there was some mistake. Surely they were wrong.

But how could they *all* be wrong? She thought of Oliver's scarred face. He hadn't imagined who swung the knife at him. And what of Professor's missing fingers? Had he imagined that someone had ordered them cut off?

Leaning her elbows on the rail, she lowered her head into her cupped hands. It was too much. She couldn't think straight. If it were true, if what Oliver had told her about her uncle were true, then everything she'd always believed in could be a lie.

'Twas he who planned your kidnapping from the Peacock . . . *'Twas Dunworthy who collected the ransom from Abernathy. . . .*

Heaven help her, it must be true—and if it was, then she didn't know her uncle at all.

Anger and betrayal washed through her, followed by a terrible sense of loss for the love and affection she had once been so sure of, and finally, she felt the guilt. She thought of all those who had suffered because of her uncle, and she felt somehow responsible for them. She wanted to make it up to them. To all of them.

She closed her eyes as a new emotion took hold. Fear. Fear for Damian. If Uncle Far would actually plan to have her kidnapped, if he would collect a ransom without knowing—or even caring—what had happened to her, his retaliation against Damian would be even worse once he learned his identity. And one day he would learn it. No secret could be kept so well or so long.

"Oh, Damian," she whispered, "how do I keep you safe?"

Chapter Twenty-Two

Fort James was a British colony built at the mouth of the Gambia River along the west coast of Africa. From here—as well as other points to the south—the Royal African Company conducted its business, shipping men, women, and children across the Atlantic to be sold to masters from Jamestown in North America to Rio de Janeiro in South America.

Damian stared at the other ships anchored in the harbor as the *Magic* sailed toward them. If they hadn't suffered damage to their sails and lost some of their food supplies during the storm, he would have by-passed Fort James. He hated seeing the slave ships, hated knowing that once-proud native warriors, their wives, and even little children were being marched into the cargo holds and packed into every spare inch of space. He knew that the owners of the vessels would consider it a successful voyage if better than eighty percent of the slaves shipped were delivered alive. They gave little thought to the conditions the Africans would live in during their six weeks at sea or to those who would die along the way.

"Damian?" Cassandra's fingers touched lightly upon his arm.

He glanced down at her, still frowning.

"Is something amiss?"

"Aye, but there's naught I can do about it." He turned his gaze upon the docks again. " 'Tis an ugly thing, slavery. I wonder that those captains can sleep at night."

"Not all men understand the truth about it as you do."

He nodded, glancing at her once more, distracted for the moment from the slave ships. Something was bothering Cassandra. Damian had felt her agitation for the past two days. When he'd asked her about it, she'd replied that the storm had left her nervous and unsettled. He'd tried to pursue the matter further, not completely satisfied that she was telling him the whole truth, but she'd distracted him with her mouth and her body.

At least, whatever was troubling her had nothing to do with him, he thought, for their nights had been filled with lovemaking and they had slept—their passions spent—wrapped in each other's arms.

"It won't take long to secure the supplies we need," he told her. "We'll leave Fort James before nightfall."

"May I come ashore with you?"

He frowned again. " 'Tis not a place for a lady."

"I promise I'll cause you no trouble." Her eyes were clear of guile as she gazed up at him. "I simply would like to be off the ship for a while."

It was a small enough thing to ask of him. Life at sea could become monotonous, always the same thing to look at, always the same people to talk to. They still had several weeks of sailing ahead of them before reaching Madagascar. He couldn't really blame her for wanting a change of scenery while she had the chance.

"I suppose it would do no harm," he replied finally, reaching out to touch her cheek. It was always like that of late. He was always touching her. And if she wasn't close enough to touch, then he went looking for her. It came to him then that he would have been hard pressed to deny her whatever she asked.

She smiled a soft, tender smile, a look that made him feel warm and content inside. There'd been few enough times in his life that he'd felt like this, and he was still surprised by the unfamiliar sensations.

"Captain!"

He turned away from her, following the sound of his boatswain's voice.

O'Toole—a short, barrel-chested man with

green eyes the color of willow-leaves—crossed the deck toward the captain. "We're ready to go ashore, sir," he said as he stopped before Damian and Cassandra.

"Very well. Let's be off then. The sooner we're away from here the better I'll feel."

Cassandra glanced around her in horror, for the first time really feeling the full impact of what Damian had been telling her. The captured natives were marched toward the ships, scantily clad and yoked together like oxen. Many had been beaten, some were bleeding, all seemed hopeless.

She began to wish that she'd stayed on board the *Magic*. She was relieved to know that their stay in Fort James would be brief. She didn't like being here. It made her long for another bath, as if she could wash away the bad feelings.

She tightened her grip on Damian's arm.

He looked at her, and an understanding smile touched his mouth. "Would you care to take a look about the post? O'Toole can manage without us. There's only a bit of canvas and a new topsail yard to buy, and Duffy knows what the galley needs." He lifted a lock of hair from her shoulder. "Perhaps we can find a hair ribbon for you."

"I don't need any hair ribbons, Damian, but I'd love to walk about."

"Captain?" O'Toole interrupted. "Before you go . . ."

Cassandra listened to the boatswain for a short while, then let her attention wander once again to the busy wharf. The noise was ceaseless and deafening. Men were shouting orders, others were answering. The rhythm of the surf rolling onto the shore, then backing away, droned on. The clip-clop of horses' hooves upon hard-packed earth added to the general din.

It was a minor miracle that she heard the whine amidst all the racket, but she did. At first, she paid it little heed, but when it persisted, she grew curious. She slipped her hand from Damian's arm and stepped toward the crates that were piled nearby. Looking in between two stacks, she found the source of the whimper.

It was probably the most pitiful looking animal she'd ever laid eyes on. The dog's long black and white coat was a mass of knots, burrs, and weeds. It was almost small enough for her to carry in the pocket of one of her gowns. It shook, either from fear or hunger—probably a combination of the two. From the looks of the dog, it had been a long time since it had feasted well.

"Hello," she said softly, crouching down and holding out her hand toward the animal. "Don't be afraid."

"Cassandra!"

She jumped at the sound of Damian's gruff voice. The dog pressed itself against the crates, looking as if it expected the world to end.

"What is it you think you're doing?" Damian demanded as he strode over to her.

"Look, Damian. It's starving, poor thing."

"God's blood, woman. Have a care. It could take your hand off."

"Don't be silly, Damian. It hasn't the strength to bite me. Look at it." She held out her hand again, but Damian grabbed hold of her and hauled her to her feet.

"I said to have a care. Doesn't it occur to you it might be rabid?"

She couldn't stop the laugh from bubbling up from her throat. It seemed so preposterous that such a helpless-looking animal could be cause for alarm. "Look at it, Damian. 'Tis no more rabid than I am. 'Tis simply in need of food."

"Then I'll have one of my crew find some scraps for it."

Her smile vanished. "I won't just throw it some food and leave it there," she replied stubbornly. "What if a larger dog came along and ate the scraps first? Please, Damian. It needs our help."

"*Our* help?" He raised an eyebrow.

She continued to stare up at him, not speaking, just waiting for him to realize that she was right. Here, at least, was something they could do to alleviate a small part of the suffering around them. She could not help the slaves, but she could rescue this defenseless creature.

He muttered another oath under his breath. "All right, Cassandra. As you wish." He knelt down, reached between the crates, and pulled out the sorry-looking mongrel. "But before we do anything else, we see that it's washed. 'Tis no doubt crawling with all sorts of vermin."

She beamed. "Whatever you say, Damian." She'd known he would do the right thing. She'd just known he would.

It wasn't really a dog. It was a long-haired, black and white rat, Damian thought as he looked at the freshly bathed animal.

And he hated rats.

Cassandra, on the other hand, looked as if she'd never seen anything more beautiful in her life. Standing outside a tavern in the midst of Fort James, she cradled the small, wet animal in her arms while it lapped milk from a bowl. She smiled and talked softly to the dog as if it could understand her. Damian couldn't make out her words. It didn't matter. He doubted they made any sense anyway.

" 'Tis time we returned to the ship," he said, causing her to look up at him.

"We're ready," she replied.

"We?" He shook his head. "You aren't planning to take that thing aboard the *Magic*."

"I can't leave him here. He'll starve to death."

"A ship is no place for a dog."

"I'll see that he doesn't get in anyone's way."

He went on shaking his head.

Cassandra's chin punctured the air defiantly and her mouth flattened into a stubborn line. "I won't leave him. He'll die without our help."

Damian glared at the miserable-looking dog. It wasn't that he didn't like dogs. He did. He was quite fond of Circe, for example. But she was back on Sorcery Bay where she belonged. Besides, Circe didn't look like an oversized rat with big ears and matted fur. This miserable beast in Cassandra's arms was beyond a doubt the ugliest thing he'd ever seen in his life. Why would anyone want it around? It would be better off dead. It would be out of its misery.

His gaze moved to Cassandra's eyes, pools of blue pleading for understanding.

Oh, he understood, all right. He understood that he was giving in to her far too often and far too easily. He was the captain of a ship. He owned a whole *fleet* of ships and commanded them all. His word was supposed to be law.

Against his better judgment, he'd taken Cassandra into his arms, into his cabin, into his bed. He'd fallen into a tender trap, letting her beguile him with her eyes, with her lips, with her body. He knew he should have left her on the *Magic* today. He never should have let her set foot in Fort James. But here she was, staring up at him with her wide, wonderful eyes, and he could feel himself weakening.

No! He wasn't going to do it. He didn't need a dog underfoot on his ship, especially that ugly-looking thing in her arms. If he weakened in this regard, he might weaken in others that were of more importance. Was he ready to let that happen?

No! He wouldn't allow it.

But she really did have the most amazing eyes. Come to think of it, she hadn't asked all that much of him today—or any day, for that matter. She'd only wanted to come ashore with him. And whatever had been bothering her the last couple of days seemed to have been forgotten. Maybe she just needed something to take care of while Damian was about his duties.

But this . . . this cur? Did it have to be *this*?

Bloody hell! Why bother to fight it? He could tell her no from now 'til doomsday, but he knew that dog was going to end up on the *Magic*.

"Bring him along then, but keep him the hell out of my way or I'll give him the boot over the rail."

Cassandra's smile mollified him somewhat. "Thank you, Damian. I knew you wouldn't abandon him."

He cursed as he took hold of her arm and guided her toward the docks.

She named him Wizard, and if making food disappear was magic, Wizard deserved his name. Anything Cassandra set before the little dog was quickly devoured. He seemed especially fond of Duffy's special salmagundi, a concoction of marinated meats, pickled vegetables, eggs, and anchovies, seasoned with garlic, pepper, salt, and vinegar.

As the *Magic* sailed away from Fort James, Cassandra sat on the floor of the great cabin, her legs curled beneath her, watching the dog lick the last evidence of food from a bowl. When he was finished, he sat back on his haunches, his tongue darting out to clean his muzzle.

"If you keep eating like this, you'll get fat," she warned him.

"If he keeps eating like that, the rest of us will go hungry before we reach Madagascar."

She looked up, surprised that she hadn't heard Damian enter the cabin. "Wizard thinks Duffy is an excellent cook," she said proudly.

"Wizard?" Damian raised an eyebrow, but there was a hint of a smile in the corners of his mouth.

Cassandra's heart faltered, and her stomach tightened. She swallowed, her throat feeling suddenly dry. "I . . . I thought it might make him feel more at home when . . . when we go back to Sorcery Bay."

Gathering her courage, she rose from the floor. She hadn't been planning to say anything to him just yet. She hadn't really thought things through. Only for some reason it seemed very important to her that she not wait.

"Damian, I've been thinking . . ."

"Have you, my lovely?" He crossed the room, the smile fading from his lips. "And what thoughts have been going through your pretty head these past few days?" He lifted her chin with his forefinger, drawing her gaze up to meet his.

She loved him so, and suddenly she was so afraid. She didn't want to go to Madagascar. It wasn't where they belonged. She had a terrible premonition that the island held nothing but unhappiness for them. She wanted to go home—home to Sorcery Bay. She wanted to live there with Damian, to be his wife, to bear his children. Of course, he'd never mentioned marriage. He'd never spoken of the future, but still she hoped.

"Damian, let's go home to Sorcery Bay. Let's go home now. Today."

"We can't," he answered softly.

She put her palms flat against his chest, then leaned into him, placing her cheek in the space between her hands. "Forget about my uncle, Damian. You have your plantation and your own shipping company. You're successful. You have everything you need." Her voice dropped to a near whisper. "You have me for as long as you want me."

He remained silent.

Her heart began to race as her anxiety increased. She lifted her head from his chest and stared up into his black, enigmatic gaze. "Damian, you must forget this plan for revenge. It will serve nothing. It won't bring back your father or give you back your youth."

She half-expected him to become angry with her, but his voice was mild when he spoke. "I can't forget, and I can't go back to Sorcery Bay. Not yet. This is something I must do, Cassandra." He drew her up in his embrace, taking her mouth with his in a kiss that was both tender and shattering. Afterward, he pressed her head into the curve of his neck and stroked her hair with his hand. "I would do many things for you, my little sea sprite. I would give you many things just for the asking. But I can't forget what your uncle has done. I can't let him go unpunished."

There was a pain in her chest. An almost unbearable pain.

"Let's be grateful for what time we have together," he whispered as his lips brushed the crown of her head.

She blinked back the hot tears that burned her eyes. She tried to think only of the way he called her his lovely, his little sea sprite. She tried to concentrate on the tender tone of his voice and the feel of his hand as he touched her hair. But she couldn't quite stop the tiny voice of doubt from whispering in her ear that he hadn't said he loved her, that he hadn't promised any future with her.

The uncertain dangers of Madagascar loomed even closer on the horizon.

Chapter Twenty-Three

Madagascar

The land erupted, green and jagged, out of the Indian Ocean. High above the coastal plateau was a shelf of land thick with forests and violent rivers, and beyond these, massive mountains running the length of the island jutted against an azure sky.

It took the *Magic* several days, after the island was first sighted, to reach her destination. Before sailing into the deep-water cove on the northeastern coast of the island, Damian ordered his ship's unique pirate standard run up the mast.

From her place on the forecastle, Cassandra stared at the sorcerer against a field of black and again felt a premonition of doom. She hugged Wizard against her chest, seeking comfort from the small animal, but he wasn't much help.

She turned her gaze upon the island and watched as the land grew closer. On the top of a hill, she saw a sprawling white mansion with a red roof and green shutters at the windows. Below it were many smaller buildings that followed a winding path down to the wharf area. Although she saw a number of fishing boats, there were no other merchant ships in sight.

By the time the *Magic* had maneuvered into its place alongside the wooden dock, a carriage pulled by two white horses was rolling down the path from the mansion on the hill. It stopped directly opposite the ship. The driver hopped down from his seat and hurried to open the door.

The first thing to appear was a wooden stump which served for the man's right leg. The rest of him was just as surprising. Above average in height, he was dressed entirely in red velvet. His fingers were burdened with large rings set with precious gems. A curly black wig appeared from beneath a broad-brimmed tricornered hat with an enormous red ostrich feather set against its crown. His face was hidden in shadows.

"Quite the fellow, isn't he?" Damian asked as he stepped up beside Cassandra at the rail.

Her gaze remained upon the man in red. "*Who* is he?"

"Captain Myron Oglethorpe of the *Jezebel*. At one time, he was the terror of the Indian Ocean and the Red Sea. Now he rules his own kingdom, the one you see before you. St. John's Cove, he calls it." He lowered his voice, serious now. "He's a friend of mine, Cassandra, but be careful of him. He has a great fondness for beautiful women, and he's sure to take a liking to you."

Cassandra glanced at Damian to see if he was teasing her, but she saw no humor in his dark eyes.

"Come on. They're putting out the gangway now." He looked at the dog in her arms. "Maybe you should leave Wizard in our cabin."

"Will we be here long?"

"Aye."

"Then I'll keep him. He'll be frightened without me."

Damian's mouth pressed together in a flat line—even after four weeks, he still wasn't any fonder of the friendly mutt than he'd been the day they'd found him—but he said nothing more as he took hold of her arm and guided her down from the forecastle deck.

"Saints be praised!" Oglethorpe exclaimed as the couple descended the gangway. "If it ain't Captain Damian in the flesh. I thought you'd long since sailed off the end of the world, my friend."

Damian stepped forward and the two men clasped hands. " 'Tis good to see you, Myron."

"I see you've got someone better to look at than Oliver these days," the other man said as

269

he leaned to one side to glance around Damian.

Cassandra was surprised to find a handsome, rather refined face beneath the wide brim of the red hat. Oglethorpe had a long, straight nose, a square chin, and a pair of twinkling, light-blue eyes. He wasn't a young man any longer but neither was he old.

"Cassandra, may I introduce you to Myron Oglethorpe, the King of St. John's Cove. Myron, this is Cassandra Jamison."

"A pleasure." He took her right hand and raised it toward his lips. "*Miss* Jamison?"

She felt herself blushing as she nodded. She didn't know how, but she was certain he'd already guessed she was Damian's lover.

"I hope you'll feel free to call me Myron." Oglethorpe reached out and patted the top of Wizard's head. "And who might this be?"

"Wizard," Cassandra answered.

"Lucky dog, this Wizard, being held so close to your heart." That said, Oglethorpe tucked her free hand in the crook of his arm and drew her toward the carriage. "Come. 'Tis too blasted hot to stand about in the sun in the middle of the day. Queenie saw your ship and is waiting to greet you."

When they reached the carriage, Oglethorpe helped her in. Damian's hand on the man's shoulder stopped him before he could follow her inside. They stepped away from the vehicle and talked briefly. Twice, Oglethorpe pointed out to sea.

Finally, both men walked back to the carriage. Oglethorpe waved Damian inside first, and he took his place beside Cassandra. Oglethorpe sat opposite them.

Cassandra turned her gaze out the carriage window as the horses trotted through the village, where houses and taverns clung to the hillside like barnacles to a ship's belly. She saw many faces in the doorways, both men and women. Their expressions were curious, a few suspicious.

"St. John's Cove ain't like it used to be, my friend," Oglethorpe said wistfully. "When I think back not more than fifteen years . . ." He sighed. "Ah, but you were just a lad then. You would not remember those glorious years. But then, you are different, you and your crew." Again he sighed. "There are few of the true brotherhood left in these waters."

"You don't seem to be suffering because of it," Damian countered with a chuckle.

Oglethorpe laughed with him. "Aye, I saw no need to waste my gold on drink and women like these other fools. I knew our days were numbered. Now, while many of those I sailed with lie at the bottom of the sea or live in wretched conditions . . ." He let his voice trail away as the carriage pulled up before the mansion on the hilltop.

A native footman opened the door for them. Their host disembarked first, then turned and offered his hand to Cassandra.

"Come, my dear Miss Jamison. My wife will be anxious to meet you."

He swept her out of the carriage and through the open doors of the house without waiting for Damian. They traversed a lengthy breezeway before he turned aside into a large, high-ceilinged room that faced the cove and the ocean beyond. Through the windows that lined the wall, Cassandra could see for miles in three directions.

"You may put your little dog down, Miss Jamison. Tanan will see that he doesn't get into trouble."

She glanced at the turbaned servant who stood just inside the doorway. The dark-skinned man gave her a brief nod, and she turned Wizard loose to explore. She was just straightening when Damian entered the room, a woman by his side.

Cassandra knew she was staring at her, but she couldn't seem to help herself. The woman's voluptuous figure was clad in a costume almost identical to Myron Oglethorpe's, from her white cravat to her long waistcoat and dress coat to her breeches and black boots. Except, instead of red, her clothes were a brilliant green color. Beneath the tricornered, emerald-colored hat, which hid her face from view, was a cascade of thick red curls.

"Queenie," Oglethorpe said, "come meet Miss Jamison."

The woman removed her hat as she moved from Damian's side. "So," she said in a husky voice, her hazel eyes perusing Cassandra, "our Damian has at last found himself a woman. It is good."

She wasn't a great beauty, as Cassandra had expected. Her eyes were too widely spaced, her mouth a bit too generous, her jaw too large and square. She was exceedingly tall for a woman, a good three inches taller than her husband. And yet there was something very striking about her that made Cassandra feel colorless and plain.

The woman lifted Cassandra's chin with her forefinger. "Have you a given name, my girl, or must I call you Miss Jamison?"

"Cassandra."

"Cassandra? I'll call you Cassie then. You call me Kate, though I can see I'm old enough to be your mama, and you should probably call me Mrs. Oglethorpe." She turned her head. "Tanan, have the cook prepare refreshments for our guests. We'll take them on the veranda."

Cassandra had never met anyone like the Oglethorpes. One moment they spoke and acted like the royalty they were purported to be, and the next their language was so salty her ears burned.

Over the course of the afternoon, she learned that they had sailed together on the pirate ship *Jezebel*, Myron Oglethorpe as its captain and Kate—who was called Queenie by her husband and their former crew—as his lieutenant. They had made their fortune with attacks upon the treasure-filled ships of the Muslim Moguls of India. For more than a decade, they had sallied forth from their pirate's lair at St. John's Cove to plunder cargoes of ivory, drugs, precious stones, and more. Better yet were those ships that had delivered their merchandise and were returning to their home ports with chests filled with gold and silver.

Cassandra learned that Kate could wield a cutlass and pistol as well as any man. She spoke openly of the man she'd killed for trying to take liberties with her when she had not offered him the same. Cassandra was both fascinated and appalled by Kate's revelations.

"But those were different times, exciting times," Kate said, followed by an exaggerated sigh. "The great captains are all either dead or retired. We shall never see the like again. I must be content now with news brought to us from other ships. I suppose it's for the best. I grow older. And, of course, there are the children."

Cassandra's eyes widened. "Children?"

Oglethorpe slapped his knee as he laughed. "You've surprised her now, Queenie. You never have looked the motherly type."

Kate ignored him. "We have six children. You'll meet them at supper." She rose from her chair. With a regal wave of her hand, she said, "Now I shall have Tanan show you and Damian to your room. You'll want to rest and freshen yourselves, I'm sure. We dine at nine."

Cassandra didn't speak again until the servant had shown them to a large bedchamber with a view of the cove. The moment the door closed, she heard Damian's chuckle.

"I guess I should have warned you," he said as she turned toward him. "Myron and Kate aren't your usual king and queen."

"I should say not."

Damian sobered. "Make no mistake, Cassandra. I may be fond of this couple because they've been good to me in the past. But they can be as ruthless as they sound. They may no longer sail on a pirate ship, but their hearts haven't changed. They're pirates still, and they live by a special code."

Cassandra felt a shiver flash up her spine. She leaned down to pick up Wizard from the floor, nervously stroking the dog's coat as she looked at Damian. "Why are we here?"

"This is where you'll be staying."

"Where *I'll* be staying?" Her voice was soft and breathless.

"Aye. I can't take you with me. 'Twould be too dangerous for you. If we were to be fired upon . . ." He stopped, then added, "I must know that you're safe."

She'd known, of course, that they'd come to Madagascar so he could continue his raids upon Tate Shipping, but it hadn't been until this moment that it had become real to her. They'd sailed all these weeks without incident. It had been a beautiful, idyllic time for Damian and Cassandra. It had been easy for her to forget his mission, to forget that revenge was what he lived for.

275

"But *you* shall not be safe, Damian," she whispered. "Not as long as you continue on this course."

He came to her then. He took Wizard from her arms and gently set the dog on the floor, then straightened and pulled Cassandra against him. "I'll come back to you," he said, his lips against her hair.

"You cannot promise me that." She managed to swallow the hot tears that burned her throat, determined he wouldn't guess her heart was breaking.

Damian tilted her chin, forcing her to look up. He wished he could promise her what she asked. He wished he could tell her their future was assured. But he couldn't. "There are no certainties in this life, Cassandra," he said softly.

"But you're looking for danger."

"No, my lovely, I'm looking for justice."

She shook her head, then pressed it against his chest again.

He knew he'd disappointed her. He knew she wanted to argue with him, to try again to change his mind. He was grateful that she hadn't. This was difficult enough. He'd already seen how easy it was for him to give in to her, despite his resolve. If she ever knew what she'd come to mean to him . . .

He loved Cassandra. He loved her with every fiber of his being. It was more than the ecstasy they shared when they made love, more than the way his breath caught in his chest when he saw her on the deck of his ship, more than the way she could make him smile. His feelings went deeper, into the dark, long-forgotten corners of his heart.

He longed to tell her how he felt, but he couldn't—even if he could have found the words. There probably weren't words to express what he was feeling, and even if there were, he couldn't say them, not until he'd kept the promise he'd made to his father's memory. When he'd destroyed Farley and regained ownership of Tate Shipping, then—and only then—would he be able to tell Cassandra he loved her.

He closed his eyes and held her more closely against him as the ache in his chest increased. He would have no tomorrows to share until he'd kept his pledge.

Chapter Twenty-Four

Much to Cassandra's surprise, she found she truly liked the outspoken and highly unusual Kate. It hadn't taken many days for her to discover that beneath the rough, pirate exterior was a woman with a caring heart. It was most clearly seen when she was with her brood of six boisterous children. Certainly, Kate seemed to understand Cassandra's anxiety whenever Damian was away from the mansion on the hill, and she did her best to distract her house guest. Sometimes she even succeeded.

But not today.

Cassandra escaped from the general commotion of the drawing room, where the older children were taking their music lessons, using the excuse of needing to walk Wizard. Once outdoors, she started down the path toward the village and the harbor, the faithful dog trotting at her side.

Damian would be coming back soon, and she wanted to be waiting for him. Though he hadn't actually said so, she was certain he would be sailing on the morrow.

She had watched his preparations for the coming voyage with a growing sense of dread. He'd treated her with great tenderness in the days since they'd arrived at St. John's Cove, and their nights of loving had been glorious, but nothing had shaken her feeling that disaster loomed ever closer.

If only there were some way she could make him see the error of his thinking. Damian couldn't change the past by punishing her uncle. He was only risking his life and the lives of his men. And if Uncle Far wasn't guilty, if he hadn't done the things Damian and Oliver said he'd done, then he was risking his life for nothing.

But how could she reach him? How could she make him see?

Her throat thickened. Even if she could make him see, what good would it do her? He might still sail back to Sorcery Bay without her. She'd given him many opportunities to say they would always be together, but he hadn't done so. He'd never said that he loved her, that he wanted to marry her, that he wanted her with him forever.

Perhaps she didn't mean as much to him as she liked to think she did. Perhaps she would never be more than his mistress. Perhaps he didn't want her at Sorcery Bay.

She felt the frustration building inside her.

Why was he being so stubborn? Damian owned an island and a fleet of ships. What was he trying to prove by pursuing his reckless path of revenge? If he would just listen to reason . . .

"What is it we 'ave 'ere?"

Cassandra stopped suddenly as the voice dragged her attention back to the present. Two men—their faces hidden beneath bushy beards, their bodies clad in traditional and colorful pirate garb—stood in the middle of the road, both of them smiling broadly. The smell of liquor was strong on them, even there on the open road.

"Do ye be lost, mistress?" the one with the red beard asked.

"We'd be glad t'help ye find yer way."

Wizard growled as he moved forward.

"Git," the second man snapped at the dog.

But Wizard ignored the warning and began to bark.

"I said git!" The man's kick caught the dog in the belly, lifting him up from the road and hurling him into the dense underbrush off to one side.

"Wizard!" Cassandra cried. She gathered her skirts in one hand and hurried after the animal. "Wizard!" She found him quickly, sitting beneath a tall frond, wearing a hurt expression. "Poor Wizard," she crooned as she bent to pick him up. When she straightened, she found the two men had followed her into the brush.

"Ain't smart t'wander off the road. The natives 'ave been known t'cause trouble. Sometimes they've carried off womenfolk an' they've never been seen nor 'eard from again."

The other man grinned. "I 'ear tell they be partial t'women with fair hair like yours."

She looked straight into the drink-bleary eyes of the red-bearded man and said, "Thank you for your warning, kind sir." She was glad her voice didn't quiver. "I was waiting for . . . my husband. He should be along any moment now. But perhaps it would be better if I waited for him at the house."

"For 'er 'usband, she says." The man winked at the fellow beside him. "An' just who might 'e be?"

"He might be me." Damian appeared through the dense foliage. His black eyes flicked first to Cassandra, then to the two men. His right hand rested on his left hip, near the handle of his cutlass.

Cassandra held her breath, afraid to move.

Damian's scowl grew even darker. "Well, well. If it isn't Tully."

Tully's skin paled beneath his red beard. "Cap'n Damian." He glanced nervously toward Cassandra, then back at the ship's captain. "We didn't mean 'er no 'arm. Just 'avin' us a bit o' fun is all."

"The lady doesn't look like she was having a good time, Tully." His hand closed on the hilt of his cutlass.

281

Watching him, Cassandra didn't doubt for a moment that he would slit Tully from end to end if the man made a wrong move. His black eyes revealed a cold and calculating fury. This was the demon-captain she'd first seen aboard the *Magic*. She'd almost forgotten how terrifying he could be, and she quivered at the sight of him—not because of what he might do to Tully but because of what he might do to their still fragile love.

The second man swept his cap from his head and bobbed a quick bow in Cassandra's direction. "Beggin' yer pardon, mistress. We didn't mean ye no 'arm."

Tully echoed the apology, then the two men pushed their way through the greenery and scurried back toward the village.

But Cassandra barely heard their words. She was still staring at Damian, still remembering the look of death that had been in his eyes.

"What were you doing out here alone, so far from the house?" he demanded as he stepped toward her.

Reflexively, she stepped backward, her arms tightening around Wizard.

Damian stopped and his eyebrows raised in question. "Cassandra?"

"I . . . I was coming to meet you."

"Well, you shouldn't have done it." His fingers closed around her arm, and he guided her back to the road. "I won't always be here to protect you. From now on, stay close to Oglethorpes'. The men of St. John's Cove may be retired from their pirating days, but they're not in their dotage. They're dangerous men. They're used to *taking* what they want, and they'll do what they must to take it."

"Are they so different from you then?" she whispered, her eyes widening as she looked up at him. She didn't know what had made her ask such a thing. She didn't even know where the thought had come from.

"What?"

Suddenly, she wanted an answer to her question. She wanted to know if he'd simply taken what he wanted from her or if he cared enough to promise something for their future.

He held out his hand. "You're frightened and upset. You don't know what you're saying."

She jerked away from him, her fears and frustrations bursting into anger. Setting Wizard on the ground, she turned on Damian with a fury of her own. "I know exactly what I'm saying. I want to know if those men are so different from you. Don't you take what you want, when you want it? Isn't that what you did with me? Isn't that what you're doing with Uncle Far? You're justifying what you do by calling it an act of justice, but you're really just stealing."

"Cassandra . . ."

She lifted her chin and straightened her spine. "You're a thief, Damian Tate. You're a pirate and you terrorize those who are weaker than you."

She wished she could stop. She wished she could take back the words she'd already said.

She was hurt, and she wanted him to hurt in return. He was planning to go away, leaving her here without him. He was going to go on risking his life when they could be building a life together.

Damn him! Damn him, damn him!

"I don't seem to frighten you," he said slowly, just a hint of a smile in the corners of his mouth.

She could stop now and say no more. They could forget what she'd said. They could be happy as they'd been those last weeks aboard the *Magic*. He was offering her a chance.

She didn't take it.

"Not any longer, you don't. I'm not afraid of you, and I'm not going to sit quietly by while you destroy yourself and me and my family." She took a step forward, her knuckles resting on her hips. Her voice rose. "Maybe my uncle *did* do the terrible things you said he did, but even if he did, you're a fool to think that plundering his ships will change anything. It won't. It only makes you a thief. It only makes you just like him."

"*I ... am ... nothing ... like ... Farley ... Dunworthy.*" He spoke each word with icy precision.

"Aren't you? Then give this up. Give up your crazy scheme for vengeance. Come away with me. I love you. I want to be with you."

"I can't, Cassandra."

"I thought you might learn to love me. I thought you wanted to be with me. If you didn't, why did you bring me here?"

His face was like granite. "I offered to send you back to England. You refused."

Her blood seemed to turn to ice in her veins. A sick weight lay in her stomach. "You said you would make me your whore, and that's what you've done." Her voice rose slightly. "Isn't it, Damian? That's what you've done."

"We each do what we must," he answered darkly. "I must avenge my father."

The last thread of her control broke. She struck out with all her fury and pain, slapping him hard. "Go then! Go and be damned with you! I care not if I never see your face again."

Cassandra grabbed hold of her skirts and whirled away. She ran up the hill, her anger already fading, replaced by a great sorrow, certain that her heart was breaking. She raced up to her bedchamber, threw herself across the bed and, pressing her face into a pillow, sobbed out her anguish.

She heard the rapping on her door through a haze of sleep.

"Cassie? May I come in?"

She rolled over on the bed and sat up. She was surprised to find that the shadows of twilight had invaded the room.

"Cassie?"

She glanced toward the door as it opened and Kate's head appeared.

"May I come in?" the woman asked again.

Cassandra nodded.

Kate crossed the bedchamber and sat on the bed beside her. "Are you not feeling well, my dear?"

"I'm all right," she answered, her gaze locked on her hands in her lap. It wasn't entirely true. Her head ached from weeping. Her nose felt stuffy, and her eyes felt dry and scratchy.

"I'm sorry about Damian."

Cassandra nodded miserably.

"I'd hoped he would tarry a bit longer."

Her heart caught as she raised her eyes to look at Kate.

The woman placed an arm around Cassandra's shoulders. "Don't worry. He'll be back soon enough. A matter of a few weeks at most."

"He's gone?" Her question was almost inaudible.

"You didn't know? But I thought that's why you were crying."

Cassandra jumped up from the bed and ran to the windows overlooking the deep-water cove. The *Magic* was gone.

"Damian . . ." she whispered. "Not this way, Damian. Don't let it end this way."

She didn't hear Kate walk across the room, but suddenly she was there, her arms once again around the younger woman. "Lovers often quarrel, my dear. The fun is in making up."

"But you don't understand. I told him I never wanted to see him again."

Kate sighed as her hand stroked Cassandra's hair. A long silence followed before she lifted

Cassandra's chin, forcing her to meet Kate's gaze. "I said the same thing more than once to Myron. He never believed me, even though I meant it. He kept coming back until I gave up and married him. And look what it got me. Six children." She smiled gently. "He'll be back."

Chapter Twenty-Five

She wished she could die.

Cassandra leaned over the chamber pot and retched. When she was done, she lay back on the bed and closed her eyes while the maid placed a cool cloth on her forehead.

"You're making yourself ill," Kate said in her most authoritative tone. "You spend hours in this room, crying your heart out, and when you're not crying, you're moping. You refuse to eat a decent meal. You are wasting away to nothing. What sort of woman will Damian find when he returns? Do you want him to see you like this?" She leaned slightly forward. "The truth is, you look bloody awful, Cassie."

"He's not coming back," Cassandra replied flatly.

"Of course he's coming back. Now, I will not

put up with any more of this nonsense. You're going to get dressed and take some air. And then you're going to sit down and have breakfast with me on the veranda. You'll feel better when you do."

Cassandra hadn't the strength to argue with her. She would rather just lie there and die, but it seemed Kate wasn't going to let her.

"Mai," Kate said to the maid, "help Miss Jamison dress and then see her downstairs."

The girl curtsied.

"Very well. I'll be waiting, Cassie. Don't be long."

A short while later, wearing a blue gown that was one shade lighter than her eyes, her hair combed and braided, Cassandra walked into the drawing room to endure Kate's inspection. When she was done, the woman pronounced it an enormous improvement.

"Now don't you feel better, my girl?"

Cassandra nodded, not knowing or caring whether or not she felt better. In truth, she was numb. And that's all she wanted to feel. It was better than the pain. It was better than thinking about Damian and remembering the ugly words she'd hurled at him before he left. It was better than knowing how much he must hate her.

"Come on. We're going to walk."

Kate took hold of Cassandra's arm and propelled her out the door. They followed the path all the way to the wharf, then back to the house. Kate chattered the whole way, telling Cassan-

dra about everything and everyone they saw
along the way. She kept the pace brisk, and
by the time they returned, both women were
breathing heavily.

The numbness was beginning to wear off.
Cassandra was beginning to feel just a little
bit angry—with Kate.

"Now we'll sit down and eat," the woman
announced as she guided Cassandra onto the
veranda.

"I'm not hungry," she snapped in return.

Kate raised an eyebrow but didn't respond.
Instead, she forced the younger woman down
onto a chair and summoned the maid. "Bring
our breakfast," she commanded.

Cassandra sighed in resignation, her brief
surge of anger already spent. "Kate," she said
softly, "I'm *really* not hungry."

"Well, *I* think you should eat. Once you do,
you'll see that I'm right. You followed my advice
about a walk and you're feeling better. I know.
There's some color in your cheeks again. When
you've put food in your belly, you'll feel better yet."

It was useless to argue with Kate Oglethorpe.
After all, she was the self-styled queen of this
enclave of retired pirates. When Kate was in this
kind of mood, she demanded—and expected—
to be obeyed. Cassandra would be foolish to
fight her, and she knew it.

She turned her gaze upon the ocean, unconsciously looking for tall masts and white sails.
All she saw was water all the way to the curve

of the world. But he was out there.

*Damian, I love you, and I do want to see you
again. Please come back.*

*Go then! Go and be damned with you! I care
not if I ever see your bloody face again.*

Damian's fingers tightened around the wheel
as his eyes scanned the horizon.

In the past, he'd always found comfort at the
helm of his ship. It was where he'd felt most in
control of his destiny. But he'd found no comfort there of late. Not since they'd sailed from
St. John's Cove.

*Don't you take what you want, when you want
it? Isn't that what you did with me?*

He massaged his forehead with the fingers
of his right hand. But that, too, was useless.
He couldn't rub away the echo of her words.
They were with him, day in and day out.

*You're a fool to think that plundering his ships
will change anything. It won't. It only makes you
a thief. It only makes you just like him.*

No, he wasn't the same as Farley Dunworthy.
Damian only took what was rightfully his.
Farley was the real thief, and he had stolen
more than just Damian's birthright. He had
stolen Sanford Tate's life. It wasn't the same.
It wasn't.

*Then give this up. Give up your crazy scheme
for vengeance. Come away with me. I love you.
I want to be with you.*

How could he give it up? It was all that had
kept him alive for eighteen years. It had been

the soul of his existence for too long. Thoughts of revenge had been his food when he was hungry, his water when he thirsted, his fire when he was cold. He couldn't just walk away from it now. He couldn't.

You said you would make me your whore . . .

He imagined he could still feel the sting of her slap.

Go then! Go and be damned with you!

Cassandra caught a whiff of the salt fish, buttered eggs, and bean porridge and raced to the side of the veranda. She fell to her knees and retched but there was nothing left in her stomach to come up.

"I'll be damned if I'm not three kinds of a bloody fool," Kate said behind her.

She glanced over her shoulder through teary eyes.

"Here." Kate shoved a glass of water into her hands. "See if you can keep this down."

Cassandra sipped sparingly, testing her queasy stomach before trusting herself to turn and sit, her back resting against a pillar.

"Do you have any idea what's wrong with you, girl?" her hostess asked with a smile.

"I'm dying," she whispered, half-hoping it was true. Life would not be worth living without Damian. It would be better if she died now and be done with it.

"Nonsense! You're not dying. You're breeding."

She looked at Kate, not comprehending.

"You're increasing, you foolish chit. You're going to have his babe."

Cassandra shook her head even as her pulse quickened.

Kate grinned. "Don't shake your head at me. I've carried six of them beneath my heart, and I'm telling you, you're going to have Damian's baby."

"But how . . . when . . ."

"When was your last menses?"

Pregnant with Damian's child? Could it be true?

"Cassie, you're starin' at me like I've lost my bloody mind. Now answer me. When did you have your last monthly flow?"

"I . . . I'm not sure. I . . . I guess it was just before we reached Madeira."

"And *when* was that?" Kate persisted.

Cassandra frowned as she tried to think back. "Not yet two months, but near enough."

"I knew it!" Kate clapped her hands together, then knelt down beside her. She placed a hand on Cassandra's flat stomach. Their gazes met. "You've a babe growing in here, my girl, and we'd best be taking care of it for Captain Damian."

"Damian's baby?"

"Unless you've been sharing your favors with another man."

She shook her head as the sense of wonder spread throughout her body. "Damian's baby," she whispered, and her hand covered Kate's.

She smiled. "Damian's baby."

"Aye, love. You'll have a great surprise for the bloody fool when he returns to St. John's Cove. Unless I miss my guess . . ." She paused and stared up at the veranda roof as she counted silently. "As I said, unless I miss my guess, you'll be holding his babe come April." Kate rose to her feet. "Now, I'll see Cook about preparing something a little more to your liking. And don't worry. This sickness will pass." She disappeared into the house, leaving Cassandra alone on the veranda.

"Damian's baby." She closed her eyes, her hand still on her belly, and leaned her head against the pillar at her back. "Come April. Damian's baby."

For the first time in days, she felt hopeful.

When he came back . . .

Oh, surely he would come back. When he knew she was carrying his child . . .

He would be glad. She knew he would be glad. He would look at her and she would see the love in his eyes and everything would be forgiven between them. They would go back to Sorcery Bay.

Damian's baby. Come April . . .

Was it possible Cassandra was right? Was he no better than Farley?

Damian leaned on the taffrail, his gaze turned south, in the direction of Madagascar. A nearly full moon hung in a clear sky, its light bouncing off the rolling ocean below.

"We could turn her about," Oliver said as he crossed the poop deck to stand beside the captain. "Three days of t'gallant breeze would see us to St. John's Cove."

Damian wasn't surprised that his lieutenant had guessed his thoughts. "What about my promise to this crew?" He glanced at the man next to him. "I told them we would make Dunworthy pay for the wrongs he committed."

"Sink me, but you've made us all rich men, captain. We've homes to go to. We've no master who can tell us what we must do or what we must eat or where we must live. How many other men can say the same?" Oliver nodded. "I'd say the crew'd be grateful for what you've done, sir. Fact is, I know it. They'd not fault you for findin' a bit of happiness for yourself. 'Tis time for it, I'd say."

"She was plenty angry with me when we parted," he said softly. "She might not want me."

"Not want you, captain? She wants you more'n she wants the air she breathes, and that's the truth of it."

If only that were true.

"Captain? We could be home to Sorcery Bay in a few weeks time, if the winds were good to us."

Sorcery Bay and Cassandra. He could see her walking along the beach in a free-flowing skirt, her hair flying in the gentle, tropical breeze, her bare feet sinking into the sand as the tide rolled in. He could see her smile. He could hear her laughter. They were a sight and a sound that belonged at Sorcery Bay. They were a sight and a sound he longed to see and hear.

Cassandra . . .

He would ask her to marry him. Why hadn't he done so before now? Why had he allowed her to think even for a moment that she was no more than his doxy? He loved her too much for that. And he knew she loved him. She had told him in more ways than one that she was his and wanted to always be with him. It had long since ceased to matter to him that she was Farley's niece. There was no reason for them not to marry.

Finally he understood. Finally he could see things clearly. He could see what she'd been trying to make him see. He loved Cassandra more than he hated her uncle. If he must choose between having Cassandra forever or destroying Farley, then he must choose Cassandra. Put in those terms, there was no other decision he could make.

"Have Mr. Davis chart a course for St. John's Cove," he said.

"Aye, captain."

Damian could hear the smile in the other man's voice.

"I'll do it at once, sir," Oliver finished, then hurried away.

Except for the sailor at the helm, Damian stood alone on the poop deck for a long time. He listened to the sounds of the sea, to the curling of the waves as the ocean folded in upon itself, to the wind filling the canvas sails, to the sucking of the wash around the hull. He stared at the moonlight upon the water, and slowly, he began to really believe he could have that happiness Oliver seemed to think he deserved.

Cassandra . . . I'm coming for you.

Chapter Twenty-Six

They were less than two days out of St. John's
Cove. It was hot, and the sun was brilliant in
a cloudless sky. The day seemed little different
from the one before. And then they sighted the
Maggie Love, a Tate Shipping East Indiaman.
She was riding low in the water, obviously filled
to capacity with precious cargo.

"We'll send one last message to Dunworthy,"
Damian told his lieutenant, feeling a rush of
excitement. "Run up the *Magic*'s standard."

Oliver didn't argue with him. "Aye, captain."

They gave chase, and it wasn't long before
Damian's sleek, swift vessel closed the space
between the two ships.

The *Magic* had nearly drawn up alongside the
Maggie Love when Damian felt a strange urge
to drop back, to let the ship go, to head on to St.

John's Cove and forget he'd ever seen the ship. But, of course, he couldn't do it. He couldn't let it go. It was the last time. He wanted to strike at Farley one last time, and then he would hurry back to Cassandra.

"Fire a warning shot over her bow," he commanded.

His crew had gathered on deck, wearing their guns and swords. They were ready for whatever resistance the men of the *Maggie Love* might offer.

They offered none.

Never before had Damian taken an enemy ship with more ease than he took this one. Even the men of the *Peacock* had looked as if they would fight once they discovered that the *Magic* was not the ship they'd supposed her to be. This crew didn't even offer that token of resistance. They simply laid down their weapons and allowed the pirate crew of the *Magic* to swing aboard.

Damian pulled his tricornered hat down on his brow, shading his eyes from the sun, then scratched the week's growth of beard on his chin as he surveyed the deck of the *Maggie Love*. He was alert for any kind of trickery, but nothing happened.

Why, he wondered, had they surrendered so quickly?

It didn't take him long to discover why once he'd joined his men on the enemy's ship. The crew was a pitifully small one. There were hardly enough men to sail the ship from the Indian

Ocean around the Cape and on to their final destination, let alone to wage a battle.

As soon as the *Maggie Love*'s crew was secured, Damian sent his men to start unloading the cargo. Moments later, Oliver returned to the main deck, his face set in an ugly scowl.

"You'd best come with me, captain."

Damian didn't question his lieutenant. He knew that whatever had sent Oliver to him in such a foul mood couldn't be good. He followed in silence.

Before they'd stepped through the hatch, he heard a sort of low humming sound. No, it wasn't really a hum. It was more like—like a collective moan. The sound sent a tremor of dread through him. Even as the first glimmer of realization alerted him to the truth, he tried to deny it. Not on a Tate ship. For the love of God, not on a Tate ship!

They were crammed into a specially constructed, shallow deck just below the main deck. Over four hundred Africans, men and women alike, crowded into a space insufficient to allow a person to stand. There was barely room for a man to crawl on his hands and knees. They were packed in, shoulder-to-shoulder, no one able to move without disturbing his neighbor. No matting softened the planks or protected their skin from slivers. No blankets offered warmth when the air turned cold.

Damian's voice shook. "Get them out of here. Get them all out of here."

"Aye, captain."

"Tell the men to leave the rest of the cargo. There'll be no room for it on the *Magic*." He straightened and turned away from the inhuman sight. "Then set this ship afire."

"Burn it, sir?"

"Aye. Burn it." He swallowed the bile that scalded the back of his throat. His fingers clenched and unclenched at his sides. "Tell Mr. Davis to chart a course for Mozambique. 'Tis no doubt where they've come from. We'll set the captives free there."

"And the crew, sir?"

"Other English ships will come to Mozambique eventually. They can sign on with them and work their way home." He moved toward the hatch. "I'm going back to my quarters. See that I'm not disturbed."

"Aye, captain."

His cold fury grew with every step he took. He felt it seeping through his body, hardening his heart, numbing his emotions. Numbing everything except hatred for the man behind the suffering he'd just seen. Farley would pay for this. He would pay.

Damian grabbed hold of a rope and swung across to the deck of the *Magic*. He paused, glancing over his shoulder at the *Maggie Love*. He remembered his father's pride in this East Indiaman. To think Farley had defiled it in this way . . .

Never again would a ship bearing the name of Tate be used to haul slaves. If he must, Damian would sink every one of Farley's ships before he was through. But he would be certain that his enemy never sold another human being for profit.

As he stepped into his cabin, he thought he caught a whiff of lilac cologne. He stopped abruptly and closed his eyes.

Cassandra . . .

For nearly forty-eight hours, he'd been able to believe that he could take Cassandra to Sorcery Bay and put the last eighteen years behind him. What a fool he'd been. He could never forget it. He had to destroy Farley, or he would be haunted forever by the knowledge of what he should have done. He would never forget what he had just seen, and he would never let Farley do something like it again.

Cassandra had weakened him. She had nearly succeeded in turning him away from what he knew must be done. He couldn't let her do it. It would be better if he never saw her again than to break his oath of revenge.

Cassandra leaned over the trunk filled with tiny garments. She reached in and pulled out a lacy cap, placing it over the fingers of one hand and holding it up to the sunlight.

"Are you sure you want to give me these things?" she asked as she looked across the trunk at Kate.

"Aye, that I am. There'll be no more babes for me." A shadow of sorrow passed over her face, then disappeared behind a smile. "Not that I'd

want another, mind you. I've enough as it is."
She reached into the trunk and pulled out a
velvet coat for a toddler. "There's many a fine
thing in here. This was meant for a prince, you
know, but it was my Tom that wore it."

Pirate booty. Cassandra glanced up once
again. It was difficult for her to remember that
Kate was a pirate. Half the time, she didn't even
notice the woman's masculine attire or think
she looked different from anyone else. She was
simply Kate.

"Was it because of Myron that you became a
pirate?" she asked suddenly, then covered her
mouth with her hand, regretting her question.

Kate shook her head, not seeming to mind.
"Not at all. I did it for myself. For the freedom
that could be found at sea. There was little for
me in England. I spoke well enough to have me
a position with an earl and his countess. But the
earl decided he wanted more from me than I
was willing to give. I was let go when I refused.
Turned out without references. 'Tis a long story
how I found my way onto my first ship, and I'll
not bore you with it." She gave a slight shrug,
then smiled. "It was two years after that when I
met Myron. Handsomest bloke I'd ever laid eyes
on. I knew the moment I saw him that he was
the man meant to warm my bed." Kate's hazel
eyes twinkled. "I'd wager you felt the same the
day you saw Damian."

"No," Cassandra replied, remembering. "I
was scared half to death the first time I saw him.
His face was covered with a shaggy black beard,

and his eyes . . ." She shivered. "I thought he was a demon. I didn't think he had a heart."

"He's got a heart, right enough, but e'er since I've known him, it's been as cold as ice. You've melted the ice, Cassie." Kate sat back on her haunches, her arms folded across her generous chest. "Blimey, if you ain't bloody well melted the ice."

Black smoke belched toward a darkening sky as fiery tongues climbed the masts of the *Maggie Love*. Even from the deck of the *Magic*, Damian could feel the heat of the raging fire as it consumed everything aboard the East Indiaman. He watched her burn until she began to sink into the sea, then he ordered the sails unfurled.

"Bring me the *Maggie Love*'s captain," he told Oliver as he turned away from the railing. "I'd like a word with him."

While he waited, Damian strode the length of the ship, from stern to bow, his hands clasped behind his back. His fury hadn't abated since he'd first recognized the moaning of the slaves crowded 'tween decks on the *Maggie Love*. He had hoped that the burning of the ship would ease the black rage that filled him, but it hadn't. He would find no satisfaction with the destruction of only one of Farley's vessels. He wanted more. He wanted them all.

"Captain?"

He turned toward the sound of Oliver's voice.

In the dim light of evening, Damian studied the man standing beside his lieutenant. He was of average height and perhaps fifty years of age. He wore a meticulously trimmed mustache. His hair was short and uncovered by either wig or hat.

Damian stepped down from the forecastle, his eyes continuing to peruse the older man. "Your name, sir," he said at last.

"Elias Howe."

"Do you know who I am, Captain Howe?"

"I've heard of the *Magic*. There's none with Tate Shipping who hasn't."

"Tell me, Captain Howe, what are your personal feelings about your human cargo?"

Howe wore a confused expression. "My feelings?"

"Aye."

"Well, I'd rather not carry them, if that's what you mean. They're a good deal of bother. But 'tis not my ship, so 'tis not my decision."

Damian turned away, his gaze moving to the cloud of black smoke against the darker sky. His voice hardened. "*I* have feelings about it. Definite feelings." He spun about and took a threatening step toward the other captain. "Hear me and hear me well, Elias Howe. I will see that you have safe passage back to England. When you get there, call upon Baron Kettering and tell him what happened to the *Maggie Love*. Tell him that the captain of the *Magic* means to sink every Tate ship he comes across. Tell him that I'm no longer satisfied to merely toy with him. Tell him I'll see him penniless before I'm finished. Better yet, I hope to see him in hell."

He paused a moment as he glared at the man. "Can you remember all that?"

Howe's complexion had turned ashen. He jerked his head in short, abbreviated nods.

"And then I recommend that you make sure I never find you on another slave ship. Because if I do, I shall slit you from end to end and feed your entrails to the sharks."

Damian motioned for Oliver to take the man away, then called for him to stop. "One more thing, Howe," he said as the other captain faced him again. "Are there any other Tate ships in these waters?"

Howe's eyes darted nervously from Damian to Oliver and then out to sea. Finally, he looked down at the deck. "I can't say."

"Can't?"

Howe glanced up, meeting Damian's gaze. "I don't know, captain. The *Venture* was due in Bombay at the same time as we, but she never arrived."

"The *Venture*," Damian echoed softly. "No others?"

"Lord Kettering doesn't discuss his business matters with me, sir."

Damian nodded, satisfied for the moment. "See him back to his quarters, Oliver." He touched the corner of his hat with his index finger. "Thank you for your cooperation, Captain Howe. Remember what I said."

He turned toward the ship's railing and stared out to sea. Unless the *Venture* had followed the *Magic* around the Cape, she was most likely still guarding the seas off England's coast. If Captain Howe was correct, no more Tate ships were in the Indian Ocean. Farley had always used more ships in his trade with the colonies in America, and if Damian wanted to sink the baron's ships, the Atlantic was where he needed to be.

Except for releasing the slaves in Mozambique, there was only one thing keeping Damian in these waters.

Cassandra.

Chapter Twenty-Seven

"There's a ship coming, Mama," little Anthony called to Kate from the veranda.

Cassandra's heartbeat faltered. It had been nearly two weeks since Damian had left St. John's Cove, and she had almost given up hope of his returning.

She dropped her sewing into a nearby basket as she rose from her chair, then hurried toward the doors leading outside. She squinted her eyes against the gray glare of a cloudy day. She felt a rush of excitement when she spied the white sails, followed by a pall of disappointment when she realized that it wasn't the *Magic*.

Kate's hand touched lightly on her shoulder. "He'll come."

Cassandra could only nod as she turned

away, her eyes downcast, her heart aching. Every day he was gone was another day when she couldn't tell him she was sorry, that she hadn't meant the wicked things she'd said, that she loved him, that she wanted to see his handsome face more than anything else in this world.

Oh, Damian . . .

" 'Tis an English merchant ship," Kate said from the veranda. She held the spyglass to one eye. "The *January*."

What cared she if it was an English merchant ship? She cared not if there were a hundred ships crowded into the deep-water cove. Unless it was Damian's *Magic*, she didn't care a fig who came or went.

She sank dejectedly into her chair. She would not cry. No matter what, she would not cry. It was bad enough, this tendency to cast up her accounts in the morning or whenever she smelled certain foods. But she would not give in to the weeping that came on her so easily. Kate had told her these things were normal when a woman was breeding, but Cassandra was determined not to be a wet-goose. Her mother had been given to the vapors and tears on demand, and Cassandra had always loathed Regina's penchant for the dramatic.

"The molly shops will be having a fair time tonight. We see few enough sailors come ashore here these days. Time was when there was at least one ship anchored in our cove on any given day. Now . . ." Kate shrugged her shoulders and returned inside. "Times have changed."

Cassandra picked up her sewing from the basket and began work again on the dress she was making, a dress with ample girth.

"You won't need that gown for many months yet," Kate said as she came to sit nearby. "Why don't you put it aside for now? We could play a game of whist."

"There's only two of us," Cassandra replied as she took another stitch.

"Myron is sure to bring the captain of the merchant vessel home for supper. He always does. That will make four."

"I don't believe I care to see anyone else."

Kate waved a hand in dismissal, and her many rings glittered in the lamplight. "That's how you feel now. By the time the ship comes into port and Myron brings the captain home with him, you'll feel different."

"No, Kate. Really, I . . ."

"Of course, you will. You'll see."

Cassandra knew it was useless to argue with Kate Oglethorpe. The best she could hope for was to make an appearance, then plead weariness and retire to her room while the evening was still young.

If only it had been Damian's ship . . .

Fate had been merciful for a change. That was Damian's thought when he saw the English merchant ship rocking at anchor in the light of the last quarter moon.

"Make the arrangements, Oliver," he told his

lieutenant as he started to descend through the hatch.

"Captain, are you sure . . . ?"

"Do it, Oliver," he snapped harshly. "And don't bother me with details."

"Cassie! Cassie, wake up, girl!"

She sat up in bed, her heart racing in response to the pounding on her door. "What is it, Kate?" she called as she reached for her dressing robe.

Her door flew open. " 'Tis Damian. He's returned. He's sent for you."

"Damian?" She jumped out of bed and raced to the window. Sure enough, there was the *Magic*.

"You're to take everything with you now. We must pack your trunk."

"Damian," she whispered again.

Kate laughed. "God's teeth, girl! Will you stand there whispering his name or will you take yourself down to his ship and see him in person? Bathe yourself and put on your prettiest dress. Be quick about it."

"Yes!" She whirled away from the window. "Oh, yes!" She ran across the room and threw her arms around Kate, giving her a tight hug. "Oh, Kate, he's come back for me. He's really come back for me."

Kate's smile softened as she cradled Cassandra's face in her hands. "Of course he has. Didn't I tell you he would? Now, go to him and tell him your news and be happy." She kissed Cassandra's forehead. "I'll miss you, girl. You write and tell me about the babe when it comes. I'll want to hear how you're getting along."

"I will. I'll write often."

"You'd better." The older woman nodded, then turned and crossed to the door. "Now, take care of your dressing. I'll send Mai to help you pack your trunk."

"Kate?"

"Aye?" She glanced over her shoulder.

"Thank you for everything."

Kate only smiled as she left the bedchamber.

Cassandra ran back to the window, as if afraid the *Magic* might disappear and she'd find it had all been a dream. But it was still there, anchored not far from the *January*, the merchant ship that had arrived the previous afternoon.

Damian was waiting there. He had sent for her.

Quickly, she discarded her dressing robe and nightrail, poured water into a bowl, and began to wash. She mustn't keep him waiting. She must hurry, just as Kate had said.

Thirty minutes later, she was standing outside the front doors to the Oglethorpe mansion, clutching Wizard in her arms. Her trunk had been loaded on the back of Myron's own carriage, and Kate, Myron, and their children had all said their farewells.

Cassandra found herself fighting tears as Myron helped her into the vehicle. As soon as he closed the door, the pair of white horses started forward. Cassandra leaned out the window and waved one last time to the family, then sat back against the cushions and waited anxiously for the carriage to carry her down to the wharf.

Faster. She wished it would go faster.

She glanced out the window again, this time toward the cove. The two ships were both anchored away from the docks. The ebb and flow of the tide rocked them in almost perfect unison. Masts with furled sails swayed like tall trees in a wind.

And Damian was waiting for her on the *Magic*.

The skiff was tied to the dock, and three sailors were there to unload her trunk and help her into the boat. She hardly gave them any notice as she settled onto her seat. Her gaze was locked on the *Magic*. Was he watching her from the deck? Where was he? Surely, since he'd sent for her . . .

Her gaze shifted away from the *Magic* as the skiff veered to the left, taking them closer to the *January*.

"Wait. Where are you going?" She pointed toward Damian's ship. " 'Tis to the *Magic* you should be taking me."

"The cap'n said t'bring you straight-way t' the *January*, miss," answered the man closest to her.

She looked at him closely. She didn't recognize him. Her gaze shifted to the other two. She didn't remember seeing them before either.

Shouldn't she have recognized them?

But there were doubtless many of the *Magic*'s crew whom she hadn't seen. It was a large ship and a large crew. As many hours as she'd spent above deck, never once had there been a moment when all the men were there at the same time.

"The cap'n will explain, miss."

Of course. Damian would explain. She stroked Wizard's coat, unconsciously seeking to reassure herself. Perhaps Damian was good friends with Captain Samuel Eden of the *January*. But if so, why hadn't Captain Eden said something last night when Myron brought him home for supper?

"Are you sure . . ." she began.

"The cap'n will explain, miss," the man repeated.

They must be friends, Captain Eden and Damian. That was the only explanation. Certainly it wouldn't surprise her if that were true. Damian seemed to know someone everywhere they went. Perhaps he'd had her brought to this ship because he was visiting even now with Captain Eden. Perhaps he was watching for her at this very moment.

Damian watched the skiff slice through the water on its way to the *January*. He could see Cassandra, wearing an apple-green dress, sitting in the center of the boat, her head turned toward the merchant ship.

He turned away from the gallery windows,

walked swiftly to the sideboard, and poured himself a glass of rum, caring not that it was not yet mid-day.

He hated drunkenness. He'd seen too much of it in his years at sea. There was always liquor available on board a ship, an easy way for a sailor to spend his earnings and ease the boredom or loneliness that could fill his days. But in Damian's mind, it was a serious weakness of the flesh. It was better a man face the world with a clear head.

He drained the glass and poured another.

Once before—the night after they'd first made love—he'd tried to drive the image of Cassandra from his head with strong drink. It hadn't worked then. It wasn't working now.

Damn her! Damn the way she'd taken root inside him, trying to turn him from the things he had to do.

If only he could have seen her one more time. If only he could have held her in his arms and breathed in her lovely fragrance and seen the wonder in her eyes.

Despite himself, he strode back to the gallery windows, his gaze finding her quickly as she climbed up the ladder to the main deck of the *January*, a sailor following her with Wizard in his arms. He saw another sailor help her over the side. He saw Captain Eden talking to her.

She turned suddenly, her gaze upon the *Magic*. For a heart-stopping moment, he thought she might actually see him there. Then she ran along the rail of the *January*, racing the

Robin Lee Hatcher

length of the ship, her eyes locked on the *Magic*'s stern. He saw her lean forward and shout something. His fingers tightened around the glass in his hand as he turned away from the windows, refusing to hear her cry.

"Damian!"

Chapter Twenty-Eight

Three weeks later, the *Magic* returned to St. John's Cove after scouting the Indian Ocean one final time for any sign of another Tate ship. At least, that was the reason he'd given his crew for remaining in those waters. If he were truthful, he would admit that he hadn't wanted to sail for England at the same time as the *January*. He hadn't wanted to look up and see the merchant ship's sails in the distance and know that Cassandra was there, sailing away from him but still within reach. He'd known that if she was within sight, he would go after her.

As his gaze rested on the Oglethorpe mansion, Damian said, "We'll stay only one night, Oliver. I want to replenish our supplies and be on our way by morning."

"Aye, captain. I'll see to it at once."

He saw the carriage, pulled by the matched white horses, start down the hill. He sighed. He would have to explain why Cassandra wasn't with him. Kate would be furious with him. She'd taken a liking to Cassandra from the first, and she would—rightfully—be angry with Damian for deceiving her. He'd allowed her to assume that Cassandra was being taken to the *Magic*. He hadn't been able to risk telling her his plan. He'd been afraid she would tell Cassandra.

But it had had to be done. He hadn't had any other choice but to send Cassandra back to England on the *January*. He would just have to make Kate understand that.

Wearily, he raked his fingers through his hair. How could he make Kate understand when he wasn't sure he understood himself, when he wasn't convinced that what he'd done was right? He'd questioned his decision a dozen times a day since sailing out of sight of the *January*.

No, it *had* been the right thing to do. He'd had no other choice. He had to stop Farley. He had to have his revenge. He'd been waiting for it too long.

But the taste of revenge was no longer sweet.

Cassandra pulled her cloak tightly around her shoulders as she walked along the deck of the *January*. The autumn wind stung her cheeks and pulled her hair from the chignon at her nape, but she paid it no heed. She had more important matters to consider.

They would be in England in about three weeks. She would have to decide before then what to do.

She raised her head, staring for a moment at the billowing sails against a slate-colored sky, then dropped her gaze to the sailor at the helm. She felt a sharp sting in her breast as she imagined Damian standing there.

"No," she said aloud, turning her eyes toward the white-capped ocean. "No, I won't think of him."

She forced the memory and the pain from her mind, closing herself off from both. She had learned something in the past few weeks. She had learned that her mother was wrong. It wasn't better to have a grand passion. A grand passion only brought with it great sorrow and extreme misery when it was over.

She'd thought she would die those first days aboard the *January*. In truth, she had *wanted* to die. Her heart had been shattered by Damian's cruel rejection. She had blamed herself for the things she'd said to him before he left Madagascar. She had blamed herself for sending him away with words meant to wound.

But after a while, her guilt had faded, and she'd faced a harsher reality. She'd spoken the truth to Damian. He *had* made her his whore, and when he was through with her, he had sent her away. She supposed she was lucky he hadn't simply left her at St. John's Cove with no means to return to England, like something used but no longer wanted.

For a few days, she'd even managed to hate him for what he'd done to her, but that hadn't lasted. She knew she'd loved him. She knew she'd chosen to stay with him. It wasn't all his fault. They'd been star-crossed from the beginning. Their love was never meant to be. She could accept that.

What concerned her now was the child. It mattered little to Cassandra what people might say about her because she'd been a pirate's captive for so many months, but she wouldn't let her innocent child's life be destroyed by the harsh judgment of others. She had to protect him.

Cassandra turned her face into the wind and squared her shoulders. *Never*, she promised herself. *Never will my child hang his head in shame. Never.*

"You did *what*?" Kate shouted.

"I sent her back to England on the *January*." Damian glanced toward Myron, then back to Kate. "It was the best thing to do."

Kate's voice lowered slightly. "Did you talk to her before you sent her away?"

"No. 'Twas better that way. Like a clean cut."

"She loved you."

"We were never meant to be together."

"And you love her, if you'd but open your eyes and see it."

"You don't understand, Kate. I hurt her. She told me she never wanted to see me again. 'Twas better this way," he repeated, wondering just who he was trying to convince this time, Kate or himself.

"Men. What a lot of bloody fools you be." Kate braced her feet apart and placed her hands on her hips. She looked ready for battle.

Damian braced for it.

"She was carryin' your babe, Captain Damian, and loving you the whole while you were gone."

He felt as if she'd just punched him in the stomach. He stepped backward, fighting for breath.

"Aye!" Kate's voice rose again. "You might well look at me in that way. You've sent her back to England with your babe in her belly. 'Tis a life of shame she'll have to face because of you, fool that you are." She snorted derisively. "And her loving you and pining for your return. Aye, she told me you'd had words between you before you sailed. But what man and woman in love don't, I'd like to know."

Cassandra pregnant with his child? Cassandra loving him while he was away? Cassandra pining for his return?

But he'd done it because he'd had to. He'd sent her back to England because it was the only way he could keep his oath to destroy Farley Dunworthy.

A cold shiver passed through him.

Farley . . . If he guessed that Cassandra's child belonged to the captain of the *Magic* . . .

God in heaven, what had he done to the woman he loved?

Chapter Twenty-Nine

The journey from London to Northumberland was a long, uncomfortable one, but at least she'd been able to hire a private conveyance rather than being forced to endure a public coach. The money Captain Eden had given her had also paid for her to stay at the best inns along the way. She would be home before nightfall.

Home. She could lay her head against her mother's breast and cry if she wanted—as if she hadn't cried enough already. She could go walking with her father in the fields and watch the sheep grazing on the hillsides. It would be good to hold his hand and simply pretend that nothing could ever disturb the peace she found there. Yes, it would be good to be home again.

She ran her gloved fingers over the black woolen gown she'd purchased in London before beginning her trip. Nervously moistening her lips with the tip of her tongue, she silently rehearsed the story she'd concocted during her last weeks at sea.

She'd been taken unharmed to Charleston where Mr. Abernathy had paid her ransom. However, they'd both quickly realized that they didn't suit, and so she'd secured passage back to England. On the ship, she had fallen in love with the captain.

She felt the painful tightening in her chest as she envisioned her captain—long hair blowing in the wind, eyes as black as pitch, a handsome face with chiseled features, hands that were strong enough to bend iron, yet gentle enough to caress her into ecstasy.

A tiny moan tore from her throat.

No, I won't think of him. I won't.

Stoically, she forced herself to concentrate once more on the story she would soon tell her family.

She had fallen in love with the captain and they'd wed aboard ship. They had sailed first to Barbados, and it had been there that her husband took ill. They'd remained on the island, and for a time, it had appeared he was getting better. They'd been preparing to sail for England so that he could meet her family when he'd suffered a relapse and died.

When she'd hired the coach and driver in London, Cassandra had given her name as Mrs.

Sanford. It was the name she planned to bear for the rest of her life. Perhaps it was a foolish thing, to take Damian's given first name for her last, but a small voice inside her head kept reminding her that their child should have at least some small link to his father. Though her love for Damian had died tragically, she could still acknowledge that they had shared something special while it lasted.

I'm certain your father would have loved you, little one, she thought as she closed her eyes and leaned back on the coach seat.

She wasn't aware that the rocking of the coach had lulled her to sleep until it rolled to a stop and the driver called to her from his perch.

"We're 'ere, ma'am, 'less I've mistaken your instructions."

Blinking the sleep from her eyes, she sat forward and stared out at the house. It was Jamison Manor, right enough. She was home.

She didn't wait for the driver to climb down and open the carriage door. She opened it herself. Holding her skirts so she wouldn't trip, she stepped quickly out and hurried toward the front of the house.

"Mother! Papa!"

She tried to open the door but found it locked. She rapped.

"Mother! Papa! 'Tis Cassandra. I'm home."

The place seemed too quiet. Where was everyone?

Wizard whined and scratched at her gown

with his paw. She glanced down at the dog, who had followed her out of the carriage. Looking at him, she realized that the sound of dogs was part of what was missing. Her mother's three lap dogs should have been raising a ruckus on the other side of the door by this time. Papa always threatened to get rid of them if they didn't quit yapping every time someone came calling, but Mother and Cassandra had always known it was an idle threat. He wouldn't really destroy them or send them away. He was fond of them, too, though no one told him they'd guessed his secret affection for the animals.

Suddenly, the door opened. The housekeeper's eyes opened wide with surprise. "Saints be praised, it's Miss Cassandra."

"Hattie . . ." She threw her arms around the woman and gave her a tight hug. "Oh, Hattie, 'tis so good to see you."

"Merciful heaven, we'd given up hope of e'er seein' you again, miss."

"Where are Mother and Father?" She glanced beyond the housekeeper, hoping to see her mother coming down the stairs or her father stepping out of his library.

"They're not here, miss." She paused. "They don't live here no more."

Cassandra looked back at the woman. "Don't live here? Hattie, what are you saying?"

" 'Tis true, Miss Cassandra. They've sold the Manor and gone to live with his lordship at the Hall."

"But . . . but that can't be," she whispered.

Hattie patted her shoulder. Her eyes brimmed with tears. "They'll be so glad to see you, miss. Having you back will make everything better. Their hearts have been nigh on to breaking these past months. Hurry and go to them."

"Yes. Yes, I will. I will." She turned and saw the driver beginning to unstrap her trunk. "Wait!" she called to him. "We must go on." She bent and picked up Wizard, then hurried toward the carriage.

As she settled into the coach again, she absently patted the dog's head. "What's happened while I was gone? What's happened?"

Prescott opened the door to Farley's office in his London town house. "Your lordship, Captain Howe has arrived."

"Howe?" Farley echoed, setting down his pen.

"Yes, my lord. I've shown him into the parlor."

"Bring him to me."

"Yes, my lord."

Farley stared at the now empty doorway, feeling tentacles of dread wrapping around his chest. Elias Howe should not be in London. The *Maggie Love* shouldn't return to England for another two months at the earliest. There was only one reason he could be there now. Something had gone wrong.

Unconsciously, he wadded up the writing paper, then swore as he realized what he'd done. Now he would have to begin the letter over again. One did not write to a duke on crinkled paper, especially when one was explaining why a payment on a note would be somewhat delayed.

Damn! He couldn't afford another problem now. The money his brother-in-law had given him from the sale of Jamison Manor was nearly spent. Of course, it was supposed to have been used to help find Cassandra, but Henry would never know the difference. It would have been a waste to use the money in such a manner. Farley was certain his niece would never be seen again, and if she was—well, what kind of life could she hope to have after being held captive by pirates? It was better that they never learn of her fate.

He felt a twinge of guilt but pushed it into a dark corner of his conscience. He'd been fond of his niece, but he had to be practical. There were more important matters demanding his attention. If he wasn't able to come up with funds soon, he could be facing complete ruin.

Farley intentionally kept his eyes on his desk when the ship's captain entered the office. It wasn't until the man nervously cleared his throat that he glanced up.

"Captain Howe, this is a surprise. I didn't expect you in London for some time. I trust there isn't a problem."

Howe held his hat against his chest. "I'm sorry, my lord, but there is."

"Really." His voice didn't reveal the desperate beating of his heart. "And what is it, pray tell?"

"Pirates. 'Twas the *Magic*."

The quill snapped between Farley's fingers.

"We hadn't the crew to fight them, my lord, nor the guns either. As you'll recall, you had most of the cannon removed because of the slave deck. I tried to tell you then—"

Farley rose from his chair. "You needn't remind me of my decisions, sir."

"No, my lord."

"The pirates took everything, I presume? Even the slaves?"

"Aye." The captain's gaze shifted to a spot just above and behind Farley's head. "And then he ordered the ship torched."

"He *burned* my ship?"

"Aye." Howe cleared his throat again. "And he sent me back with a message for you."

The gall. The utter brass of that bloody pirate infuriated Farley, leaving him speechless. He waved his hand for Howe to continue.

"He says he means to sink every Tate ship he comes across and that he'll see you penniless before he's through." He swallowed visibly, his gaze once again flicking away from his employer.

"There's more, Howe. Out with it."

"Well, my lord, he said that he meant to see you in hell."

Farley turned his back on the sea captain. "You've delivered his message. Good day to you."

It was a moment before the captain left his office. Farley knew he'd wanted to ask about being posted to another ship, but it would have done him no good. Farley didn't tolerate failure from those in his employ. Not for any reason.

A moment after the door closed behind Elias Howe, a violent curse erupted from Farley as he swung his arm at a nearby shelf, sweeping everything on it to the floor.

"I'll find you, captain. If it's the last thing I do, I'll find you. I'll not be the one that's seen in hell. You will not beat me at my own game."

Cassandra was just stepping out of the carriage in front of Kettering Hall when she heard her mother cry her name. She looked up and saw Regina standing in the open doorway. Quickly, she set Wizard on the ground, then ran toward her mother, almost hurling herself into the woman's embrace.

"Sweet Lord, 'tis you. My Cassandra . . . my Cassandra." Crying, Regina backed away, her fingers wrapped tightly around her daughter's arms, as if afraid she might disappear if not held there. Her eyes studied the younger woman. "We thought—oh, my dear daughter, we thought you were lost to us forever. We have tried every way possible to find you, but we had almost given up hope." She touched Cassandra's face. "But you're alive. You're all right."

"I'm all right, Mother." Tears ran down Cassandra's cheeks. "I'm all right."

Again, Regina pulled her close. "Thank God," she whispered. "Thank God. Thank God."

It was a long time before the two women broke apart again. Both reached for their handkerchiefs and both dried their eyes. As if sensing his mistress's sadness, Wizard whined and scratched at her skirts.

Cassandra picked up the dog, turning him so her mother could see his face. "This is Wizard. He and I have come a long way together."

"Bring him inside," her mother replied, trying to sound cheerful. "You must tell me how you and your little friend came to meet. You must tell me everything."

"And you have things to tell me, Mother. 'Twas Hattie who sent me here."

Regina sighed. "I will let your father tell you about Jamison Manor. 'Tis still too painful for me to speak of it."

"Where is Papa?"

"He'll be along shortly. He takes a walk every evening about this time. He'll be so happy to see you. You cannot know what he has gone through these many months."

"And Uncle Far?"

"In London. We'll send word to him at once of your safe return."

In the back of Cassandra's mind, she heard Oliver's accusations. *'Twas he who planned your kidnapping . . . 'Twas Dunworthy who collected the ransom from Abernathy . . .*

She shivered, not sure she was ready to see her uncle just yet.

*   *   *

Her father had aged dramatically since she'd sailed for America. She'd never before noticed the lines around his eyes and mouth or the ones carved across his forehead. She hadn't noticed the slight hunch in his shoulders, as if he were carrying a heavy weight upon his back. His movements all seemed slower now, too. Yes, he had aged a great deal since last she'd seen him, and it saddened her to think she'd had a part in it.

Cassandra stared at Henry Jamison as the two of them sat near the fire later that same evening. Before her mother had retired for the night, Cassandra had told the story of her deceased husband, and she had heard how her father had been forced to sell the family estate.

" 'Twas inevitable, my child," her father had said. "My investments had not done well of late."

But she'd guessed, from little things said throughout the evening, that her parents had sold the manor to hire men to find her. She wondered if any of those men would expose her lies later. She prayed not. It was bad enough that her parents had lost their home. It would be even worse should they learn that their grandchild—a grandchild they still didn't know would be born—was the illegitimate off-spring of the pirate who brought ruin to Tate Shipping and, therefore, to them.

"You look tired, my child," Henry said, interrupting her thoughts as he leaned forward in his chair to lay his hand upon her knee. "You should go to bed. We can talk in the morning. When you've gotten your strength back, you can tell me more about your husband. You must have loved him a great deal. I'm sorry I never got to meet him."

Her throat tightened. "I'm sorry, too, Papa," she whispered as the image of Damian at the helm, white shirt blowing in the wind, flashed into her mind. "I'm sorry, too."

Standing by her bedchamber window, Cassandra watched the sun come up the next morning. She'd slept little during the night and now was filled with a restless energy. She'd always loved coming to visit Kettering Hall when she was little, but she felt no joy this morning. Nothing was the way it used to be. Nothing was the way it should be.

She closed her eyes as tears threatened to spill. What she wanted was to feel the roll of the ship's deck beneath her feet. She longed to smell the salty breeze and hear the splash of waves against the hull. She ached to look toward the helm and find Damian standing there.

" 'Twas like that for me, many years ago," her mother said softly from the doorway.

Cassandra turned, quickly dashing away the tears. "I . . . I didn't hear you come in. What are you doing up so early, Mother?"

"Don't try to pretend you're not hurting. I understand."

She swallowed, fighting a new onslaught of tears. She'd thought she was over the pain. She thought she'd gotten past the hurt and confusion. She thought she'd placed Damian's memory away where it could no longer wound her.

Regina crossed the room and put her arm around her daughter's waist, then turned them both toward the window again. She stared at the rolling green hills and the orange ball of sun that hung suspended above them. "I was in love like you once. And he loved me, too, my young man. We wanted to be married, but my father and brothers forbade it. I was only sixteen and not old enough to know my own mind, Farley said. Besides, the man I loved wasn't our social equal, nor did he have sufficient wealth, and that was very important to my family. His mother was our governess when we were children, Gregory and Farley and I." She shook her head. "I should have defied them. I should have run away and married him, but I hadn't the strength. I was never very strong." Regina tightened her arm as she glanced at her daughter. "You were lucky, my child. You took love where you found it. I wish I'd had your courage."

Cassandra wondered if her mother suspected that the story she'd told was a fabrication, that there was no Mr. Sanford, that there had never been a wedding. She wondered if her mother had already guessed that there was a baby on its way.

"What happened to this man you loved?" she asked quietly.

"I never saw him again. He and his mother moved away after my marriage to your father was arranged. I learned years later that he'd married and had a son."

Cassandra watched her mother's face. "Have you been so terribly unhappy with Papa?"

Regina blinked away her own unshed tears, then shook her head. "No, my dear. Your father is a good and kind man. He has cared for me, even when I have not been easy to care for." She touched Cassandra's cheek. "And if not for him, I shouldn't have you. For many years, I feared I should never have a child. You were the blessing we needed." She shook her head again. "No, I've not been terribly unhappy with Henry."

Cassandra had often suspected that there'd been another love in her mother's past, yet it still seemed strange to think of the woman beside her ever being young, ever feeling about a man the way Cassandra had felt about Damian.

Regina pulled on her hand. "Come and sit down, my dear." She went to a sofa and settled onto it, patting the seat beside her. "I should like to hear more about your Mr . . . Sanford."

Cassandra's breath caught in her throat. The way her mother's voice had paused before she spoke the name. She *must* know Cassandra had made it up. Should she tell Regina the truth?

No, she could never tell anyone the whole truth. Not even her mother or father. She had to protect her child from society's scorn, and that meant no one could know the truth about her months at sea.

But she could share bits of the truth, and that was what she did now.

"He was wonderfully handsome, Mother. I'd never seen anyone like him. He was taller than any man I'd ever met, and his shoulders were so broad and strong. When he held me in his arms . . ." She felt herself blushing as the memories assailed her.

"And he loved you, too?" her mother asked.

She hesitated a moment, then said, "Yes, he loved me." She wished she believed the words. She hoped he'd loved her, at least for a short while. Perhaps he had, but now she would never know. "He didn't know how to say it, but he loved me," she whispered sadly.

"I'm glad he loved you, daughter. Even if you only had a short time together, I'm glad you experienced such happiness."

Cassandra went to sit beside her mother. She laid her head upon the older woman's breast. "Does the pain ever go away?" she whispered.

"It will ease," Regina answered as her hand stroked Cassandra's hair. "Given enough time, it will ease."

Chapter Thirty

Farley couldn't believe his good luck. Cassandra was back in England. And not a moment too soon. He would find her a husband closer to home this time. He would have to move quickly. His creditors weren't going to be held off much longer. He would need an old man, someone who prized beauty above anything else. Farley couldn't be sure how much his niece's reputation would be blemished. He'd tried to keep her kidnapping a secret, but his idiot brother-in-law had blabbed it about in his effort to gain aid from the Crown.

Well, he could do nothing about that now. Farley doubted she was a virgin after spending months with a shipload of pirates. But, God willing, her beauty would not have suffered any. She should still bring a tidy sum from an old man eager to sire an heir. Nothing like Abernathy had paid, of course, but tidy nonetheless.

Farley glanced out of the carriage window as it approached Kettering Hall.

He wished his sister's note had given him more information. It had simply read, *Cassandra has returned safely to Kettering Hall. She is well. Regina.*

But how did she escape her captors? How had she survived the past six months since she was taken from the *Peacock*? Did she have any information which would help him find the captain of the *Magic*?

The moment the carriage rolled to a stop in front of the stone mansion, Farley pushed open the door and stepped down. He strode swiftly to the front door, his layered greatcoat billowing in the crisp October breeze.

"Regina! Henry! Cassandra!" he bellowed as he entered the house, deciding that this was not the time for restraint. He turned and headed for the stairs.

Cassandra heard her uncle calling her name. She turned toward the door of her bedchamber, but for some reason, she couldn't seem to make herself move forward. Her heart beat erratically, and her breathing was rapid. She felt suddenly chilled.

"Cassandra!"

Her door flew open, swinging back on its hinges until it struck the wall. She stared at Farley Dunworthy as if he were a stranger.

Tate Shipping was stolen from my father by your uncle . . . He accused my father of treason . . . Dunworthy always gets what he wants . . . 'Twas he who planned your kidnapping . . . 'Twas Dunworthy who collected the ransom from Abernathy. . . .

"My dear . . . thank God you've been returned to us." Her uncle crossed the room and took her into his arms. "I've feared for you all these months, but now you've been restored to us. 'Tis a miracle."

"Hello, Uncle Far," she responded softly.

He stepped back, studying her with his piercing light blue eyes. A frown wrinkled his brow. "What is this dress about?"

"I'm in mourning."

"Mourning? For whom?" His frown became a scowl. "Sit down, girl, and tell me everything. Your mother's note told me nothing. I've been half-crazed during the trip up from London, imagining all sorts of terrible things. I promise you, my dear, that the pirates who took you shall be found. I have my friends in the government. The Crown shall not let those men go unpunished."

Don't tell him anything about Damian, her subconscious warned.

"I'm in mourning for my husband," was what she answered.

"Your husband?" Farley sat down on the edge of the bed. "What are you saying? Did your captors take you to Abernathy, after all? Have you inherited his estates in the colonies?" The

338

crease in his forehead smoothed, and she saw
that he was quite pleased with the idea.

"No, Uncle Far. I didn't marry Mr. Abernathy,
though my captors did indeed return me to him.
The truth is, he was a—a horrible man, and
we would never have suited. I booked passage back to England on another ship. I fell
in love with the ship's captain and we were
married on the way to Barbados. The ship was
to bring a shipment of sugar to England, but
he took ill while there and eventually died."
She saw the unspoken question in her uncle's
eyes. She answered it with a tinge of bitterness
in her voice. "There will be no inheritance. Mr.
Sanford owned nothing to speak of."

"I can see that I've upset you, my dear." He
rose from the edge of the bed. "I shall leave you
to rest. We'll talk more later."

She didn't want to be told to rest. She didn't
want to talk more later. She didn't want to discuss anything with anyone. Talking wouldn't
help. Her heart was broken and her mind was
plagued with suspicions, and all she could tell
anyone was half-truths and lies. She would
rather be left alone.

As if he'd read her mind, Farley said, "We
must talk about what happened on the *Magic*, my dear girl. That devil must be captured.
He must be stopped. We are facing total ruin
because of him." He hugged her again. "I know
I can count on you to help. Your poor mother
has suffered enough, fearing you dead or worse
all these months, losing her home. I know you'll

help me keep even more disaster from befalling the family. You've always been a dependable daughter."

"I'll do what I can, Uncle Far," she replied stiffly.

Mouse met with Damian in a dingy, rented room of a dockside inn. He brought with him several interesting tidbits about Farley's recent London activities.

Farley, it seemed, had been badgering the Crown for months for aid in stopping the *Magic* from attacking his fleet. There were those who had actually accused him of trying to blame his losses from poor investments on a pirate who didn't exist. He'd been forced to sell five more Tate ships. Only the *Peacock* and the *Venture* were left of what had once been a significant fleet of ships, and Farley was looking for a buyer for them now.

" 'E's stranglin', cap'n, that 'e is, an' 'e knows it's ye who's got 'im by the throat."

"Good," Damian answered. "I want him to know it's me."

"You'll be lookin' fer 'is niece. Am I right?"

Damian leaned forward. "What do you know of Cassandra?"

"Only that Dunworthy 'eard from 'is sister that she's returned. 'E's gone north t'be with 'er." Mouse scratched his head, then added, "An' find 'er a rich 'usband quick as 'e can."

It always amazed Damian how careless Farley was around Mouse, trusting him with a great deal of incriminating documents simply because he thought—mistakenly—that Mouse couldn't read or write. Farley also thought the one-eyed sailor was too stupid to understand what was said in front of him. Mouse was always a fountain of information when he met with Damian, and he'd never been wrong in all the year's they'd worked together.

" 'E means t'marry 'er off t'the first bloke who can come up with the blunt. She'll 'ave no say in the matter."

"Maybe not," Damian said as he rose from his chair, "but I will. You can reach Sir Damian at his Northumberland property with any further information."

Oliver spoke from the opposite side of the room. "Are you sure that's wise, Damian? Dunworthy's seen you now. He just might recognize you."

"I was wearing a full beard the only time he saw me. I've not spoken my given name to any of his captains, nor to Dunworthy, and there's fewer than a dozen men who know my last. In England, I'm simply the mysterious Sir Damian, war hero and owner of Sorcery Bay Shipping. 'Tis rumored, I believe, that I'm the bastard son of a duke." Damian shook his head as a cold smile curved his mouth. "He'll not know me. But he'll pay attention to the size of my purse."

"What's your plan?" Oliver queried.

"The most important thing is to get Cassandra safely away from her uncle. After that . . .

well, we'll see what happens."

" 'E's a dangerous man, cap'n." Mouse's single eye peered up at Damian. " 'E'll not 'esitate t'use 'er against ye if 'e discovers who ye are."

"I'll be careful, Mouse. You can be sure of that." Damian turned toward his lieutenant. "Send word to Dunworthy's solicitor that Sir Damian is interested in buying the ships the baron has for sale. Let him know that I'm spending a few weeks at my Northumberland estates. He'll notify Dunworthy. Since we're neighbors now, Dunworthy will feel free to call on me, no doubt to increase the asking price. Notify Fleming that I want the *Enchantress* to remain in London until further notice. We may need her here. I want you to supply the *Magic* for the voyage back to Sorcery Bay, then sail her up the coast. Fly the Sorcery Bay standard and use the blue canvas for the course sails. That should be enough of a disguise should Dunworthy chance to see her."

"I'll see to it, captain."

"If I need to get word to you, I'll send it through old Turk at Blyth."

Oliver nodded.

"Very well, gentlemen. I suggest we depart separately. God speed."

"God speed, captain," the two sailors echoed softly and then were gone.

Damian lifted a prayer that Cassandra would remain safe until he could reach her before he, too, slipped out into the teeming masses that worked the London wharf.

* * *

Farley swirled the wine around in his glass, staring into its burgundy depths. "You have no idea where you were until you reached Charleston?" he repeated, impatient for Cassandra's answer.

"I've told you, Uncle Far. I was kept locked in a cabin with no windows. The only person I saw the entire time I was on the *Magic* was a young boy named Toby. He brought me my meals."

"Surely there must be something you can tell me that would help identify the captain."

Cassandra shook her head. "I'm sorry. There's nothing. I don't know anything about him. Besides, it was months ago now that he sent me to Charleston. Even if I'd heard something inadvertently, it's forgotten by now."

Her dark blue eyes met his straight on. She didn't flinch, didn't blink, yet he was certain she wasn't telling him the truth. He didn't know why he felt that way. Was it the way she looked at him? Was it her guarded smile? Certainly there was something different about her, but he couldn't quite put his finger on it.

"Really, Farley," Regina said from her place at the table, "don't you think you've asked her enough questions? 'Tis plain to see she knows nothing that will help you."

"I suppose you're right, dear sister." Blasted woman. If he had to put up with her much longer . . .

"I believe I'll go to my room," Cassandra said

343

as she placed her napkin beside her plate.

Yes, there was something different about her, about the way she carried herself, about the way she looked at him. Whatever it was, Farley was afraid he wouldn't find the same compliant young woman as the one he'd talked into a betrothal to a virtual stranger. He would have to be careful how he approached her about the matter of another marriage.

He stood and hurried to pull out her chair for her. He placed his left arm around her back as he took hold of her right hand in his own and guided her toward the door. "I'm sorry if I've pressed you too hard, my dear. The weight of all these matters has left me weary and terse." He kissed her temple. He lowered his voice when he spoke again, making certain it contained just the right tone of sympathy. "Your mother is right to chastise me. I've scarcely got used to the notion that you were married and widowed since the last time I saw you. The death of your husband is clearly uppermost in your thoughts, as well it should be." He tightened his fingers on her upper arm. "Don't give a thought to my worries. I'll find some way to see that we aren't thrown out of Kettering Hall and left without a home to call our own. I could not bear to fail my sister that way—nor you and your father either."

Enough, he told himself as he released her at the bottom of the stairs. He had planted the idea tonight. He would water it tomorrow and see what grew.

Chapter Thirty-One

Farley couldn't believe it. His luck really *was* changing, more than he'd hoped to believe when he'd left London three weeks before.

He glanced at the letter in his hand again. Sir Damian of Sorcery Bay Shipping was not only interested in buying out Tate Shipping—or, rather, what was left of it—but rumor had it he'd come to England to find himself a bride. And to put the icing on the cake, he had come to Northumberland to check on his estate here. It couldn't have been more perfect if Farley had arranged it himself.

He leaned back in his chair as he dropped the letter from his solicitor onto his desk. Pressing his fingertips together, he stared into space, wondering just how he should proceed. The loan he'd received from the duke wouldn't hold off his creditors for long, so he couldn't afford to proceed too slowly. Still, these things should be handled delicately, carefully.

Besides, his niece was being less than receptive to the idea of another marriage.

He frowned. He couldn't understand the girl. She'd always been so pliable, so willing to please. She'd always sought his advice and followed his counsel. Now, even though they were living in the same house, he rarely saw her. It wasn't like Cassandra to be so reclusive. It was almost as if she were avoiding him.

Perhaps, once he found out more about this Captain Sanford she claimed to have married. . . . But it would take time, several months at least, to hear back from his solicitor on that matter. For now, he must turn his attentions upon Sir Damian.

Ah, there was an intriguing man.

The owner of a large Caribbean plantation and a shipping business larger than Tate Shipping at its greatest. A man who had distinguished himself during the war with Spain and been knighted by the Crown. A man with no last name—or, at least, one he refused to reveal to anyone. A bastard son of a duke, he'd heard, although no one seemed to know which duke that might be. Sir Damian had invested in several properties in England over the past few years. He owned a place in Plymouth, a house in London, and an estate that bordered Kettering Hall, but as far as Farley knew, this was the first time Sir Damian had ever come to Northumberland.

Farley had learned all this information several years before, when Sorcery Bay Shipping had begun trading in the same ports as Tate Shipping. It was always good business to know your competitors, especially if you could learn something which might be embarrassing to them. But the baron was concerned with only one thing at the present time—Sir Damian was a wealthy man in search of a wife.

He rose from his chair, crossed the room, and opened the door. "Mullins!" he called. "See that my carriage is brought 'round. I'm paying a call on our neighbor at Pointe Cottage."

"Sir?" Damian's butler stepped through the doorway into the parlor. "You have a guest."

Damian hid a grin of satisfaction. He didn't need to ask; he could guess who his visitor was.

"Farley Dunworthy, Baron Kettering," the butler supplied needlessly.

"Show him in, Gyles."

Damian tugged on the sleeve of his black coat and hoped that his cravat was properly tied. His choice of clothing was simple and unadorned. He wore no jewelry, nothing flashy that would declare his wealth, yet he knew he cut an imposing figure. An enigmatic figure, he hoped, wanting to add to the element of mystery that surrounded the owner of Sorcery Bay.

Waiting for Farley to come to Pointe Cottage had been difficult once Damian arrived in Northumberland. He'd wanted to ride directly to Kettering Hall and whisk Cassandra away, but he couldn't be sure what he would find there. He didn't even know if she would welcome him. Most likely, she hated him for sending her away as he'd done. He couldn't blame her if she did. He'd been wrong to treat her so callously, and he was certain he'd have to prove to her how sorry he was.

But there would be time later to beg her forgiveness. There would be time later to explain everything and to tell her that he loved her. Right now, he had to concentrate on her uncle.

He rose from his chair as Farley was ushered into the room. "Lord Kettering, how good of you to call."

"Sir Damian, 'tis a pleasure to meet you at last."

The two men shook hands.

Farley's gaze studied Damian with great care. He was open about his perusal, not trying to hide his curiosity. Thankfully, there was no glimmer of recognition in his eyes.

Damian, for his part, schooled his own expression into one of mild interest as he motioned for the baron to be seated. He didn't dare let the other man see the hatred and contempt he felt.

"I would have come to welcome you sooner," Farley said, "but I only recently learned of your visit to Northumberland. I can tell you I was surprised. I knew, of course, that you owned Pointe Cottage, but after all this time . . ." He shrugged and smiled.

"I regret that I don't get to England more often, but my businesses keep me occupied elsewhere."

"Yes." Farley cleared his throat. "I understand you have a number of interests. Shipping, sugarcane . . ." He paused, as if expecting Damian to add anything he might not know about.

Damian crossed to a sideboard and drew two glasses from the cupboard beneath it. He glanced over his shoulder. "Sherry?" he asked.

"Thank you. I believe I shall."

He filled the two glasses, then carried them back to where the baron was seated. Handing one to Farley, Damian said, "I don't need to tell the owner of Tate Shipping how much such a concern occupies a man's time."

"No. No, indeed."

"Is it true what I hear? Are you selling? Because if you are, I'd be interested to discuss price with you. But perhaps you've already heard from your solicitor about my interest."

"No, I'm afraid I haven't."

Liar.

Farley's feigned calm didn't fool Damian for a moment. The man was nearly breaking out in a sweat, so eager was he to know what Damian would offer him. But Damian wasn't going to tell him quite yet.

He leaned slightly forward in his chair. "Lord Kettering, I know that we are only just met, but may I talk freely with you?"

"Of course, my good man."

"There is something of more importance than the purchase of your ships which has brought me to Northumberland."

The baron's eyes widened. "What is it, sir? Perhaps I can be of help to you."

Damian sipped his sherry, then stared into the transparent liquid. "Indeed, I hope you can."

"Do go on," Farley encouraged him, his tone solicitous.

"Lord Kettering,'tis time that I take a wife. That's the real reason I have come to England. As you may know, despite the knighthood bestowed upon me by the Crown, my ancestry is—shall we say, questionable. It will not be easy for me to find a woman who is willing to settle for such a husband."

The baron nodded. "I see."

"But I must have heirs to inherit all that I've built and acquired when my time comes to leave this earth. I want my children to be able to move among people of quality. I want them to be welcome in the best homes in England. If I can find the proper wife, a lady of gentle birth . . ." He shrugged. "You see my dilemma."

"Yes."

Other men might not have recognized the gleam in Farley's eyes, but Damian did. He knew what the baron was thinking. A nudge and he would have his invitation to Kettering Hall.

"I was wondering, my lord," Damian continued, "if I might prevail upon you to introduce me to some of the gentry in Northumberland. I do not ask for your endorsement, for you know me not."

"I know enough, Sir Damian. A man should not be punished for his father's"—Farley cleared his throat—"er, shall we say, indiscretions. You are a knight, and you've proven yourself in business as well. You should be treated with the respect you've earned. I would be pleased to be of service to you. As a matter of fact, the Earl of Stynford is hosting a small gathering on Friday. I'll prevail upon him to extend you an invitation."

Damian leaned back in his chair. He flashed a smile at his guest. "You don't know what this means to me, Lord Kettering."

"But I do not *want* to attend the earl's house party," Cassandra said again. Not that it would do her any good. She had been saying it for the past four days.

Regina touched the back of her hand to her forehead and closed her eyes. "Please don't argue with me about this, Cassandra. My brother has been quite insistent that you accompany us. He realizes that you are in mourning, but he feels this is something you should do for your own well-being. Please do not disappoint him."

Robin Lee Hatcher

Cassandra wasn't fooled by Farley's show of concern. Her uncle wanted to introduce her to as many potential husbands as possible. There must be a very wealthy man attending the gathering for him to insist so strenuously that she attend.

She opened her mouth to refuse yet again. Then she looked at her mother's strained expression and couldn't do it.

With a hearty sigh, she said, "All right, Mother. I shall go with you."

"Wonderful." Regina's eyes flew open, and she smiled with relief. "Do hurry with your toilet. We should leave within the hour."

"I won't keep you waiting."

Her bedchamber door closed behind Regina. Cassandra stared at it for a moment, then turned toward her wardrobe to look at the black gowns hanging there. She could only hope that any possible suitors would be frightened away by the color of mourning. If necessary, she would make it clear to anyone what a wretched wife she would make.

Finally, with another deep sigh, she shed her gown, then poured water into a bowl and bathed herself. Afterward, she donned a dress of black damask. She had dispensed with her corset two weeks before, depending upon the generous over-dress to disguise any hint of her condition. It also had allowed her an excuse for not needing a maid to help her in dressing. Since the staff was short-handed at Kettering Hall, no one had seemed to notice her unusual

352

behavior. It didn't seem strange to Cassandra any longer. She'd spent so many weeks and months without her own personal maid that she found she preferred it this way.

Turning to the looking glass, she brushed her hair, then pulled it back into a severe bun atop her head, covering the knot with a simple black cap. She wore no jewelry, no hint of color or even a touch of white to break the austerity of her attire. Certainly, no man would give her a second glance, looking as she did. After all, the Earl of Stynford was bound to have any number of young ladies of marriageable age present at his house party, and they were sure to be bedecked in their prettiest and most colorful attire. No one would notice the bland Widow Sanford.

Damian galloped his horse along the road, anxious to arrive at the earl's country estate and even more anxious to see Cassandra. More than once, he'd been tempted to forget all his carefully laid plans—to simply go to Kettering Hall and take her away, by force if necessary—but caution had prevailed. From his interview with her uncle, he'd surmised that Cassandra was in no immediate danger. He suspected the man had not yet learned his niece was expecting a child. It was even possible Kate had been wrong; perhaps Cassandra wasn't pregnant. There seemed no reason to act rashly unless forced to do so. If his plans succeeded, he would have his revenge against

Farley while still protecting Cassandra from any harm.

But revenge wasn't what had brought him to England. Damian had come for reasons beyond Cassandra's safety or because he'd learned she was carrying his child. He'd come simply because he knew he didn't want to live without her. He'd come because he needed to know what her feelings were for him after what he'd done. He needed to know if she might still love him, despite everything. He needed to know if she might be able to forgive him. He'd even realized that, if she asked him to, he would leave Northumberland immediately. He had to let her know that she was more important to him than revenge. Far more important.

Damian's thoughts were brought up short as the Earl of Stynford's country estate came into view. Lacey Park was a two-story stone house set against a rocky hillside. It overlooked a river that flowed toward the sea. Damian had heard that the earl came to his Northumberland estate every spring and fall. He was said to be particularly fond of the hunting season and enjoyed inviting other members of the gentry to join him in such pursuits at Lacey Park.

Damian slowed his horse to a trot as he approached the front of the house. Numerous carriages could be seen off to one side of the stone building, the horses standing with heads lowered, clouds of white frost forming in the air close to their muzzles. He could hear the muffled sounds of barking hounds, probably kenneled some distance from the house.

As soon as he drew near, the front doors opened and a liveried servant came out to take hold of his horse. Damian dismounted, straightened his coat, then climbed the steps to enter the house.

Chapter Thirty-Two

Cassandra stood near a window, her eyes turned upon the hills behind the house, her back to the crowded drawing room. There was a constant pounding in her temples. She longed for a moment of quiet, away from the din of voices and laughter.

Regina stepped up beside her daughter. "You shouldn't be standing off by yourself, my dear."

"I didn't wish to be here at all," she answered without looking away from the window, ashamed of her sharp tone but unwilling to apologize.

"I know that you feel you can't join the other young folk in the ballroom, but you could at least speak to some of your old friends. Please, try to enjoy yourself. It won't help to mope in a corner."

"I'm not moping, Mother."

Before Regina could speak again, the butler's voice boomed out the name of another guest. "Sir Damian of Sorcery Bay Plantation."

Cassandra turned, her gaze flying across the lengthy room to the doorway. She saw him, resplendent in black and white, towering above everyone near him. Unlike all the other gentlemen, he had eschewed the use of a wig. His long, dark hair was caught at the nape with a shiny black ribbon. He looked magnificent, as always.

"Cassandra, what's wrong?" her mother asked anxiously.

"Nothing," she whispered. "Nothing's wrong."

Regina's hand closed around her arm. "But you're as pale as a ghost."

Damian's gaze swept over the room, almost arrogantly. It paused upon her, so briefly she couldn't be certain he'd even seen her, then moved on. Her breath caught in her throat. A strange buzzing in her ears muffled the voices of the people around her.

She saw him move forward, stopping for a momentary introduction here, a quick greeting there. He didn't look at her again, yet she knew he was coming toward her. Damian was here, and he was walking toward her.

"Cassandra?" Regina's hand squeezed lightly.

She turned her head, glancing at her mother.

Regina's face was tight with worry. "Who is that man? Do you know him?"

"No. No, I . . . I don't know him." Her reply was so low, even she wasn't certain she'd spoken the words aloud. "No, I don't know him," she said again, audibly this time.

Regina continued to frown with concern.

"I'm all right, Mother." She turned her back on Damian and the rest of the drawing room. "Really I am."

But she wasn't all right. She was frightened and angry and hurt and . . . hopeful.

This was insane. He should never have come back to England. He should never have come to Northumberland. He should never have come to Lacey Park. Not today of all days. Uncle Far was here. He would see Damian and might recognize him. Damian's very life could be in danger.

She knew why he'd come. He had come to finish what he'd begun. He'd come to destroy her uncle, to crush the baron once and for all. Revenge was all he'd ever wanted.

She knew he hadn't come because of her. He had sent her away. He'd been unable to return the love she'd offered him.

Yet, despite what had brought him here, he'd seen her, and now he was working his way across the room. And despite the fears and anger and pain, her heart leapt with the joy of seeing him again.

Her uncle's voice intruded on her thoughts. "And here's the rest of my family, Sir Damian. Regina, Cassandra, I should like to introduce you to our neighbor. He owns Pointe Cottage."

She turned around.

"Sir Damian," Farley continued, "this is my sister, Regina Jamison, and her daughter, Cassandra Sanford."

"Mistress Jamison, 'tis a pleasure," Damian said as he bowed to Regina. His gaze moved to Cassandra. "Mistress . . . Sanford."

Was there a slight lift to his eyebrow when he said the name? Did she hear a question in his voice over the name she wore? Or was it amusement?

"Would you honor me with a dance?" Damian asked, his black eyes studying her face.

The buzzing sound returned to her ears. Her heart was beating so rapidly in her chest that she feared the entire room would hear it. Her mouth had gone dry.

"As you can see, my daughter is in mourning, sir," Regina interjected. "She is recently widowed and is not dancing."

Farley spoke quickly. "Perhaps a walk in the earl's maze. I understand he's quite proud of it."

" 'Tis too cold outside," his sister stated firmly.

Damian took hold of Cassandra's arm as his gaze flicked to Regina. "I promise not to keep your daughter outside too long, madam." Then his eyes met and held Cassandra's. "We must get your wrap," he said softly.

Regina couldn't have explained the odd sensations she felt as Sir Damian escorted Cassandra across the drawing room. He was extraordinarily handsome, but that wasn't the cause of the uproar in her stomach. Besides, he was young enough to be her own son. No, it was something far different than his dark good looks.

"Who is he?" she asked her brother.

"A very wealthy man."

She glanced at him sharply.

Farley smiled. "I believe he shall prove quite important to us, Regina. I suggest you treat him with the respect he deserves."

She hated her brother's patronizing tone. She should have grown used to it after a lifetime of the same, but she hadn't. At least when she'd lived at Jamison Manor, she hadn't been forced to see him every day, hadn't been forced to listen to him belittle her. For over two decades, she'd managed to escape his iron-handed rule. Now that she and Henry were forced to live at Kettering Hall, Farley was back in control again.

Without another word to him, Regina moved away, walking the length of the drawing room, not stopping until she'd reached the window overlooking the earl's gardens. She glanced out at the tall maze of green shrubbery.

Why had Cassandra reacted so strangely? Or was Regina only imagining that she had? No, Cassandra had been upset.

She saw the couple leave the house and walk slowly toward the maze. They weren't speaking, weren't even looking at one another. Perhaps it was all right. Perhaps she was merely imagining that there was something going on that she didn't understand. And yet . . .

Regina stared at the man. Why was it she felt this strange connection to him, as if she should know him? And what did his presence here mean to her daughter?

The moment they stepped into the protection of the maze, Damian stopped and turned to face Cassandra. His fingers closed around her upper arms. He longed to pull her into his embrace. He longed to kiss her lips. But he couldn't. Not just yet.

"What are you doing here?" she asked stiffly as she drew back from him.

"I came for you."

"For me?"

"Yes."

She was silent while her gaze studied his face. Finished with her perusal, she said, "Kate told you about the baby."

"Yes."

"I see."

He didn't like the strange tone of her voice. "Cassandra . . ."

She pulled free of his hands. "Go away, Damian. Go back to your ship and your crew. Take whatever you can from my uncle, but don't ever think you can take this child away from me."

"I didn't come to take your child from you. I want both you and the baby. I want us to be married."

"So?" Her chin tilted defiantly. "Now that I'm breeding I'm good enough to marry? Does it not still bother you that the baron is my uncle? What of your plans for revenge, Damian?"

"I'll give them up if that's what you ask of me."

"For how long?" She stepped toward him. Her blue eyes sparked with a rekindled rage. "How long before you tell him who you are, that you made his niece your doxy? How long before you cast me off again?"

He grasped her shoulders and pulled her toward him, trying to soothe her fury. But she wouldn't be placated. She began to pummel his chest with her fists. She struck him again and again. He didn't try to deflect the assault or move away. He deserved her wrath. He simply waited for it to play itself out.

"Why?" she asked, her anger blurred behind tears as her fists stilled. "Why did you do that to me? Why wouldn't you let me love you?"

"I just couldn't," he answered honestly. "I didn't know how to be loved." He swallowed the lump in his throat. "Cassandra, I've come to ask you for your forgiveness. I didn't come because of the baby or for revenge. I came for you."

He took a deep breath. He knew how much he'd hurt her. He had much for which to atone. He prayed she'd be able to give him a second chance. It would be hard for her to believe him now. She might never believe him. She might never forgive him.

He placed his finger beneath her chin and lifted her face, forcing her eyes to meet his again. "I love you, Cassandra."

He heard a tiny gasp of air escape her lips as she stepped back from him again. Her eyes rounded. Her face turned pale. Once again, he reached for her, and once again, she pulled away.

"I hated you for what you did, Damian."

"I hated myself."

"I wanted to punish you, to hurt you back."

"I deserve your punishment."

"I thought I should never see you again. 'Twould have been better that way."

"No, Cassandra," he said softly. "I don't deserve that. Give me another chance."

" 'Tis too late," she whispered. "I've mourned you already. I can't let you back in my life again. I . . . I couldn't bear to let you back in." With those words, she spun away and hurried out of the maze.

Damian stared after her, feeling strangely calm in the face of her pronouncement. He knew in that moment that she loved him still, but he would have to win back her trust.

And that was exactly what he meant to do.

Chapter Thirty-Three

Cassandra was in the salon, three days after the earl's house party, when Mullins entered the room with an armful of hothouse flowers. "Miss Cassandra, Sir Damian is without. He asked me to give these to you, along with his regards. He requests that you grant him a moment of your company."

She glanced at the profusion of colorful flowers in the butler's arms as she let out a lengthy sigh. Twice yesterday and twice the day before, she had refused to see Damian. She had also refused his gifts of champagne and chocolates and jewelry, much to her uncle's irritation.

"Please tell Sir Damian that I—" she began.

"Tell Sir Damian that Cassandra is delighted to see him," Farley interrupted as he stepped into the room, "and show him to the salon at once."

Cassandra rose to her feet, angered by her uncle's interference. "I don't wish to see the man."

"But *I* wish you to see him, my dear girl. Isn't that enough?"

Accusations swirled in her head. She wanted to scream them at him, demand that he deny them, but she couldn't.

"Cassandra, please listen to me." He stepped toward her. "Your parents and I need your help. Now more than ever before. We stand to lose everything. Sir Damian has not only expressed interest in buying what is left of Tate Shipping, but he told me he was interested in choosing a wife while in England. 'Tis clear he was taken by your beauty at the earl's party the other night, despite your widow's weeds. At least give the man a chance to win your affection."

She stared at her uncle, realizing for the first time how haggard he looked. She knew he looked that way because of the very man he was championing to her. It would have been amusing were not the circumstances so serious.

"All right, Uncle Far," she said. "I shall see Sir Damian this once. But don't think that means I shall agree to marry him."

She looked past her uncle as the sound of footsteps reached her ears. Her heart skipped crazily in her chest. For a moment, it was as if she were on the *Magic*, listening to him walking down the passageway, hoping he would stop outside her door, wanting him to open it.

A moment later, Damian stepped into the salon. His gaze flicked quickly from Farley to Cassandra.

"Sir Damian," Farley said in a jovial voice, "what a pleasure to see you again."

"Thank you, my lord," Damian replied without taking his eyes off of Cassandra.

"Yes . . . well . . ." Her uncle cleared his throat. "I hope you will forgive me if I don't stay, sir. I have matters of estate to see to in my study. You young folk have a pleasant visit." He closed the salon door on his way out.

Silence hung between them. Cassandra allowed herself to stare at him, to let her gaze linger on the chiseled lines of his face and the breadth of his shoulders. It surprised her that no one else seemed able to see the pirate beneath the gentleman's clothes.

"It must humor you to have Uncle Far welcoming you into his home." She turned her back toward him.

"No, it doesn't humor me."

"It should. My uncle faces ruin. Unless he can marry me off soon—"

"I care not what happens to your uncle."

She turned her head, glancing at him over her shoulder. "Do you expect me to believe that?"

" 'Tis true, Cassandra."

She sighed and turned away again. "You're wasting your time here, Damian. Uncle Far is no more danger to you. He has lost, for I shall not be married off in order to save him. You have had your revenge."

Damian stepped up behind her. His right arm closed around her, pulling her back against the broad expanse of his chest. His cheek lay against her hair. "I didn't come to seek revenge. I came for you and you alone."

She should have pulled away, but she couldn't do it. She wanted to be here. And she wanted to believe him. She wanted to believe him more than anything in the world.

Cassandra closed her eyes and relaxed against him for a moment.

"Listen to me, love," he whispered near her ear. "Hear me out, and if you want to send me away afterward, I shall go and not bother you again."

Her heart tightened at that thought. Once before she had sent him away, saying she never wanted to see his face again. It hadn't been true then. Could she bear to send him away a second time?

"For eighteen years, revenge was all I had. I was filled with bitter hatred for your uncle. It wasn't until our quarrel that I realized revenge wasn't worth the price of losing you." His lips brushed over her hair in a feather-light kiss. "When we were at sea, I thought about all you'd said. You were right about many things. But I never thought of you as my whore. You were much more to me. You *are* much more to me."

His hold tightened. She lifted her hands and closed her fingers over his forearm, turning her head toward his shoulder, her eyes still closed.

"We were only three days, maybe four, out of St. John's Cove when I understood that no amount of revenge against your uncle was worth being without you. I was on my way back to tell you so when we came across the *Maggie Love*. It was the ship my father named for my mother."

Cassandra felt a chill gripping her insides.

"I meant only to send one last message to Farley, and then I was coming back to ask you to marry me and live with me at Sorcery Bay."

"What happened?" she asked in a hoarse whisper.

"The ship was filled with slaves."

"Oh, Damian . . ."

"After she was emptied, I had the *Maggie Love* set afire. I was consumed with rage that he would use my father's ship in such a way. I guess I even blamed you a little. I was angry because you'd made me forget my promise to myself. I thought you were making me weak. And so I had you put aboard the *January*."

He turned her around, forcing her to open her eyes and meet his gaze. "I was wrong about many things," he continued, "but sending you away was the worst mistake of all."

"Can you forget the things my uncle did to you?"

He shook his head. "No, Cassandra, I won't ever forget. Those years are a part of me. I can't erase them. But I should like to put it all behind me and begin to live a new life."

"What of the other men my uncle has harmed? What of Professor and Oliver and Mouse?"

" 'Tis time we all let go of the past. Oliver made me see that. 'Tis time we face the future. You're my future, love."

Cassandra took a deep breath and pulled away from him, then walked across the room and stared out the window. It was easier to think clearly when she wasn't in his arms, yet back in his arms was where she most wanted to be.

He was offering her all the things she'd wanted from him, and now that he was, she was afraid to take them. She was afraid of being hurt again. She would rather die than feel the pain of his rejection another time.

"I believe you." She hugged her arms across her chest. "I believe you about Uncle Far. I wish I didn't. I always loved him so. He was good to me as a child. Honestly." She turned to face him. Tears glittered in her eyes. "I can't find it in my heart to love him any more but he is still my uncle. I don't wish him harmed. I don't want to see him in prison. Can you understand that, Damian?"

"Yes."

"And you would leave here and seek no more revenge upon him?"

"If you asked it of me," he stated, his voice deep, his eyes watchful.

Suddenly, she realized that he felt just as uncertain as she did. He had been hurt, too. Coming here hadn't been easy for him. Offering to give up his plans for revenge had cost him much. But he'd done it because he loved her.

Damian bears more scars than those put on his back . . . The ones on his soul will be more difficult to heal . . .

Professor was right. It would be difficult. But she could do it. With love, she could do it.

"Damian . . ." she began.

Just then, the salon door opened and Regina breezed in. "Cassandra, dear . . ." She stopped. "Oh, I didn't realize we had company." A slight frown drew in her brows. "Good day, Sir Damian."

Cassandra glanced from Damian to her mother, then back again. " 'Tis all right, Mother. Sir Damian was just leaving."

She saw the slight stiffening of his jaw, saw the flicker of sorrow in his eyes before he could conceal it from her.

"But," she continued quickly, "I have invited him for supper tomorrow night. You will come, won't you, sir? My family and I would all like to become better acquainted with you."

"Nothing could keep me away, dear lady," he replied, a new layer of softness in his voice. As he stepped forward to take her hand, his gaze touched her face like a tender caress. "Until tomorrow."

"Until tomorrow, sir," she whispered, her throat suddenly thick with emotion.

Damian repeated his bow over Regina's hand before leaving the room.

Cassandra turned away quickly, not wanting to answer her mother's questions—and Regina was certain to have questions. But she was surprised again.

"I look forward to tomorrow night," was all Regina said before she, too, departed the salon.

For a young widow who had clearly been languishing in despair, yearning for her dead husband, Cassandra's response to Sir Damian struck Regina as highly peculiar. Certainly he was handsome—*dangerously* handsome, one might say—but there was something else that kept niggling at Regina's mind, something she couldn't quite put her finger on.

As she sat across from him at the supper table the next evening, she studied his dark profile. Rarely was she able to see his full face, for his head was constantly turned as he spoke to Cassandra. He never said anything inappropriate, never spoke so that others couldn't hear, and yet Regina felt there was a most private conversation taking place right before her eyes.

These two have met before.

This was no sudden, overwhelming infatuation. This was something deeper. She felt embarrassed to be there, watching them. It was almost as if she were peeking into another's bedchamber.

She glanced away, her gaze moving to the head of the table, where her brother sat. He was wearing a smug, self-satisfied smile. Oh, yes. She had no doubt that he was most pleased with what he was seeing. He hoped for a match between the two. Anyone could see that. But it wasn't for Cassandra's happiness that he wanted it, but because of his own greed. If his eyes weren't clouded by the image of hundreds or thousands of pounds, Farley might have wondered about what he was seeing, too. For Cassandra's sake, Regina was glad he couldn't see beyond his own selfishness.

Quickly, her eyes returned to Cassandra and Damian. If this man could bring a smile back to her daughter's lips, then she could only be glad he was here, she decided, and she would treat him accordingly.

Farley was more than satisfied with the way things were progressing. Not only had Sir Damian been smitten by Cassandra's beauty and quiet demeanor, but earlier this evening, he had again mentioned his interest in buying out the remainder of Tate Shipping. Now it was up to Farley to speed along both processes. He couldn't allow either a long courtship or a prolonged negotiation.

As for the sale of the ships, he had already sent for the *Peacock* so that Damian might examine her without a lengthy trip to London. She should arrive along the coast of Northumberland within a matter of days.

As for his niece . . . He leaned back in his chair, studying her face over his glass of wine. He didn't think she would cause him much trouble. She seemed quite taken with the gallant knight and war hero. Apparently, her sea captain husband was more easily forgotten than she'd led him to believe.

More importantly, he thought as he shifted his gaze, Sir Damian must be hurried into offering for her hand in marriage, and he must want her enough to pay dearly. Farley would have to be careful. He must squeeze every farthing possible from Sir Damian without spoiling the match. There wouldn't be time to find another husband for her.

He frowned, thinking of the way Cassandra had tried to defy him, telling him she had no intention of marrying again. Surely, she'd forgotten her declaration and would be willing now. She had to be. Farley would see to it.

Chapter Thirty-Four

For Damian, the evening seemed interminably long. He answered the squire's and his wife's questions, describing in colorful detail his home in the Caribbean as well as his years as a privateer in Her Majesty's navy. Since he didn't want to lie to Cassandra's parents, he settled for ignoring questions he simply didn't want to answer and asking questions of his own, turning the conversation upon others at the table.

Henry Jamison's interests lay totally in the land and the tenants, the crops and the livestock. Even though he'd sold Jamison Manor, he continued to care about the welfare of those who had worked and lived on Jamison land for many generations. Damian decided that Cassandra's concern for others had been inherited from her father.

Regina Jamison was a puzzle. He sensed that she was wary of him and that she wasn't as easily deceived as her husband. And yet he felt her cautious acceptance and knew it was because Cassandra appeared to care for him. Regina would want whatever or whoever would make Cassandra happy. Damian had no intention of disappointing her. Making Cassandra happy had become his primary goal, replacing a much more sinister one.

His goal might have changed, but it didn't make spending the evening with the baron any easier. Damian hated it every time he was forced to answer one of the man's questions. He hated sitting here at his table and eating his food and making polite conversation with the very man he had sought so long to destroy. Most of all, he hated having Cassandra in this house. Even though she seemed to have accepted his apology, even though she appeared willing to go away with him, he would continue to fear for her safety until he had her beside him on the deck of the *Magic*, England at their backs.

"Sir Damian, I was wondering . . ."

Damian turned his eyes toward Farley, carefully disguising his feelings for the man.

"Do you expect to remain at Pointe Cottage much longer?"

"No, Lord Kettering. I think my business here will be accomplished before long." He glanced at Cassandra again. He saw a blush rise in her cheeks. It was all he could do to refrain from taking her by the hand, dragging her off to some dark chamber, and kissing her until her entire body was flushed with heat.

"Then perhaps we should discuss the matter of the ships I have for sale."

Damian reached for his glass of wine and answered without looking up. "I would rather leave that matter to my solicitor."

"Of course, if that's what you wish." Farley's chair scraped the floor as he pushed it back from the table. "Why don't we all retire to the drawing room? Perhaps we can persuade Cassandra to entertain us with a song. My niece is quite accomplished, Sir Damian."

Damian smiled as his gaze went to Cassandra once more. *I know,* he thought as their eyes met. *Even more than you think, baron.*

It was after midnight before the rest of her family—at her uncle's insistence—finally excused themselves from the drawing room and retired for the night. Cassandra had been afraid her mother would refuse to leave Damian and Cassandra alone, even for a moment. But then Farley had pointed out that Cassandra was a widow, not a girl just out of the nursery. She was entitled to speak privately with a man if she so wished.

"I don't believe your mother cares for me," Damian said softly as the drawing room doors closed behind the others.

Cassandra turned toward him. "She's simply confused. I told her I loved my—my husband. She saw me weeping for him."

"I see." He stepped toward her. "Mr. Sanford was a fortunate man."

She nodded as she drew in a quick breath of air. Her skin prickled at his nearness.

"But he never should have let you go."

"He . . . died."

"He was a careless fool. No intelligent man would die and leave you a widow."

Her throat felt thick. "I loved him."

"And what about me, Cassandra? Can you ever love me?" His hands closed around her upper arms. His eyes searched her face.

"I do love you, Damian," she whispered. "I never stopped loving you."

He wrapped her in a possessive embrace, and she surrendered to it. She lifted her mouth to accept his kiss, thrilling at the feel and taste of him after so many months. She was surprised by how quickly the rest of her body responded to his caresses. She pressed herself against him, seeking to be closer, to be a part of him.

She didn't know how long they stood there, locked in each other's embrace, but it must have been a long time. She was completely without breath by the time they drew apart.

"We'll be married at once," Damian said, his fingers still stroking her face, her hair, her arms.

"I can't."

Damian's expression revealed both surprise and hurt.

She lifted her hand to cup the side of his face. "I don't mean I can't marry you," she assured

377

him. "But we must wait a little while."

"Why?"

"Because I don't want my parents to know that I lied to them about Mr. Sanford. I must give them some time to grow used to the idea that I love you. They lost me once before. 'Twill be hard for them to send me away a second time." She pressed herself against his chest again, rubbing her cheek against the fabric of his black dress coat. " 'Twill be hard for me to say good-bye as well."

He stroked her hair with one hand while the other slipped to the small of her back. "I'm afraid for you, love. 'Tis not safe for you here. Your uncle . . ."

"My uncle doesn't know who you are. You've said so yourself. He wants this match. He shall be my greatest ally with my parents when I announce that we are to be married. Besides . . ." She took a deep breath, then let it out in a sigh. "Uncle Far would never hurt me. Not physically. He's done some terrible things. You've convinced me of that. But he has always been good to me. I can't forget everything he's been to me."

"And what if he should guess the baby belongs to the captain of the *Magic* rather than this deceased Captain Sanford? He might . . ."

"He doesn't know about the baby. No one does."

Damian's hold grew tighter. "One week. I'll wait one week before talking to your father. No more."

"All right," she whispered in agreement, secretly glad that a week was all she would have to wait.

The next morning, Cassandra stared at her reflection in the mirror. If anyone were to see her without her clothes, she wouldn't be able to hide her condition. She turned sideways and ran her hand over the gentle swell of her belly. She was lucky the current fashion included a generous over-dress. It helped disguise the careful letting out she was doing in the waistlines of her black mourning gowns.

She sighed as she turned from the looking glass.

She supposed Damian could be right about the danger if Uncle Far should suspect the truth. But why should he? Besides, she had only a week to wait. A week wasn't so very long, and it would mean a great deal to her and to her parents.

I'm afraid for you, love.

Her uncle wouldn't harm her, she'd assured Damian, and she stubbornly continued to believe her own words. No matter what else was the truth, she wanted—and needed—to believe there was some good in the man who had helped raise her.

Still, it was also true that she could barely stand to have Farley touch her. There were times she wanted to scream at him, to ask him why he'd accused an innocent man of treason simply so he could steal his business.

379

She wanted to demand to know what other terrible things he'd done. She wanted to know what other innocent people had suffered because of his greed. And she wanted to know how he could sell his own niece in order to keep his ill-gotten gains.

Cassandra let out another sigh of frustration as she finished dressing, then left her bedchamber.

The house was quiet today. Her mother had taken her three precious pets and Wizard for a visit to one of their neighbors. It was no secret that Regina's brother despised the dogs, and after Farley had threatened this morning to drown each and every one of them, Cassandra's mother had thought it best to take them away for the day. Henry had accompanied her.

Yes, the house was quiet. Too quiet. It seemed strange not to see Kettering Hall's normally large staff bustling about, cleaning chambers, dusting the entry hall, preparing elaborate meals, but there were fewer servants to do the work now. Evidence of the shortage was everywhere. Dust lay thick on the mantel in the drawing room. The floors were dull and scuffed. The meals were simple affairs.

In the days since Uncle Far had returned from London, he had made no pretense about their precarious financial condition. He had talked about it incessantly. Cassandra knew it had to be true. The baron would never have let members of his staff go unless he was forced to do so. He was too fond of his creature comforts.

Earlier this morning, when Farley had mentioned how advantageous an alliance with Sir Damian would be, she had almost told him his wish was about to be granted. She'd nearly declared her love for Sir Damian of Sorcery Bay, but she had managed to simply nod in agreement, torn between truth and lies, hating the absence of trust that had once been an integral part of her life.

Her thoughts unsettled, Cassandra wandered aimlessly through one room after another and finally went outside. Away from the house, the November breeze was cold, but next to the stone exterior of Kettering Hall, with the late morning sunshine beating down, Cassandra found the bench she settled on quite comfortable.

She closed her eyes, enjoying the feel of the sun on her face. She folded her hands over her stomach, and suddenly she smiled, her troubled thoughts disappearing. Come spring, she would be holding her baby—Damian's son, for she was certain it was a boy. He would have his father's black hair and dark eyes, and one day, he would be just as tall as Damian. He would have his father's love of the sea. He would be intelligent and handsome and brave and honest. He would be . . . like Damian.

Damian . . .

Soon she would be his bride. Soon everything she'd ever wanted would be hers.

A grand passion . . . She smiled softly, thinking of the nights they would share—a lifetime of nights together.

Magnificent . . . She imagined him then, picturing him at his most magnificent—when he was at the helm of the ship. She saw the wind in his hair and smelled the tang of the ocean and felt the roll of the deck beneath her feet.

Soon, Damian . . .

Farley riffled through a stack of old letters. He knew it was here somewhere. He would never have thrown it out. He'd known it could prove very valuable in the future.

Ah . . . there it was.

He plucked the paper from the pile and scanned it quickly with eager eyes. Yes, this was it. It ought to be worth several hundred pounds.

He rose from his desk, feeling impatient. Where was Bennett, anyway? It was almost noon. The man had surely followed Farley's instructions and come to Northumberland to meet with him. He wouldn't try to defy the baron. They had worked together for too many years.

Restlessly, he moved about his study, his mind working constantly, trying to find ways to raise more money. A lot of money. A bloody fortune was what was needed.

Cassandra seemed the only lasting answer. He had to marry her off soon. Luckily, things seemed to be going well with Sir Damian. But marriage settlements took time—something he didn't have an abundance of—and solicitors always took their bloody time. Farley couldn't afford to wait. He had to raise some money to hold him over.

He unlatched a window and started to push it open.

"Excuse me, Lord Kettering," Mullins said behind him.

Farley turned to look at his butler.

"Mr. Bennett has arrived from London, my lord."

"Show him in, Mullins." He tried to keep the eagerness from his voice. "Show him in at once."

Farley returned to his desk and sat in the large chair behind it. He leaned forward, resting his forearms on the desk top, the letter stretched between his hands.

On the stone bench, Cassandra awakened slowly, her mind muddled by the nap and the warm sun on her face. As she stretched and arched her back, working out the kinks, she became aware of the voices drifting to her through an open window in her uncle's study.

"You can't be serious!"

"But I assure you, I am, Bennett."

"You're blackmailing *me*?"

Farley's voice lowered. "Blackmail has such an unpleasant ring. I prefer to think of it as an investment."

"Call it what you will, 'tis extortion by any name."

"Are we agreed on the price? A thousand pounds?"

Cassandra turned her head toward the window, but she didn't dare move. She scarcely dared to breath.

When the man called Bennett spoke again, he sounded more in control. "How do I know you'll destroy the letter once I've paid the thousand pounds?"

"I give you my word," Farley replied smoothly. "We've worked together too many years not to have a certain trust between us."

A lengthy silence followed before Bennett said, "I've told you before that you'd be implicated with me. If the Crown knew of your illegal activities . . ."

"Ah, but do you want to go to prison—or worse—just to see that I'm punished along with you?" Her uncle chuckled. "Besides, I have more letters, other records. You should know me better by this time, Bennett. You should know how meticulous I am about saving things. There are other men in the government who owe me favors. You might find that your accusations were turned against you. I think you would find yourself in prison while I was proved innocent. Do you want your family to suffer because of a thousand pounds?"

"Are you telling me that you've kept records of our . . ." He stopped, then continued, "Simpson, Webb, Tate, Pilkington . . . It's all in writing? You've recorded it?"

Tate. He'd said Tate.

Cassandra closed her eyes and leaned her head back against the stone wall. She felt lightheaded, and her heart pounded like a drum in her ears. She didn't hear what her uncle responded. She didn't hear if Bennett said anything more.

It was true. It was all true what Damian had told her, what Oliver had told her. Uncle Far had confirmed it with his own words. She'd been forced to believe it, of course, after what Oliver had told her, but there'd been a small part of her that had resisted the evidence. Now that last bit of hope was gone.

She felt a sick shiver run through her. The man she'd known as she was growing up didn't even exist. He was a fabrication. The real Farley Dunworthy was someone else, someone she didn't know, someone very treacherous.

What was she to do now? She touched the swell of her stomach. Damian was right. She could be in danger. If her uncle found out, if he even suspected that this child might be the offspring of the *Magic*'s captain, what would he do?

Sanford Tate ... Mrs. Sanford ... She had thought the use of the name inspired, a way to pass on some heritage to her child, but now she realized how foolish it had been. What if it jogged something in his memory? What might he do then?

Slowly, she eased up from the bench and

slipped around the corner, away from the open window. As soon as she knew she was out of sight and hearing, she hurried back to her room, closed the door, and locked it behind her.

She stood there, staring at the locked door for a long time, letting the panic wash over her in agonizing waves. But eventually, she began to conquer her fears. Damian was nearby. Her parents lived in the same house. In a little over a week's time, she would marry and be gone from this place. She had nothing to fear.

But others did. Farley had to be stopped before he ruined more lives. She didn't know this Mr. Bennett or why her uncle was blackmailing him, but whoever he was, Uncle Far was threatening him, too.

And then she thought of something else. This Mr. Bennett knew something about Sanford Tate. Bennett had obviously been involved with Farley's lethal schemes for a long time. He'd mentioned records. Letters . . . records . . . papers . . . There must be proof somewhere in her uncle's study. She had to find the proof. She could clear Sanford Tate of the charge of treason. Damian could use the name of Tate again with the pride it deserved. She could restore it to him, perhaps atoning in some small way for what her family had done to his.

Cassandra backed up until her knees hit the side of the bed. She sat down, her eyes still on the door.

The Magic

The answers were downstairs in the study. She was sure of it. She would find the answers in Farley's study. She only had to wait until her uncle was gone from Kettering Hall, and she could find the proof she needed.

Chapter Thirty-Five

Damian paced restlessly across the drawing room. He was anxious to see Cassandra, but he had hours yet to wait. He'd been invited to dine at Kettering Hall again. The baron was entertaining a number of his neighbors this evening and wanted to introduce Sir Damian to them.

But he cared nothing for meeting a duke, an earl, and several minor lords, let alone their faded wives and vacuous daughters. He wanted only to see Cassandra.

He never should have allowed her to put him off, not even for a week. She didn't believe that Farley would harm her if he should learn the truth, but Damian knew better. Farley wouldn't let a small matter such as family concern him.

Damian should have demanded that she leave with him. He should have carried her away if that was what it would take to make her go. But he'd done that before. He'd taken her against her will once. He wouldn't do it again. He'd failed her. She'd lost faith in him. He had to earn it back. If only this nagging sense of danger would cease . . .

"Sir?"

Damian turned toward the sound of the butler's voice. "What is it, Gyles?"

"Lord Kettering is here to see you, sir."

Damian tensed. "Show him in."

A moment later, the baron walked through the drawing room doors with his hand outstretched and a smile on his face. "Good afternoon, Sir Damian. I hope you don't mind my just dropping in this way."

Damian schooled his features into a neutral expression. "You are welcome any time, my lord," he lied as he shook the man's hand.

"I realize you're having supper with us this evening, but I'd hoped to have a few words with you in private."

Damian motioned toward a couple of chairs near the fireplace. "Shall we sit down then?"

Farley nodded and moved toward the indicated seat.

Instead of joining him immediately, Damian crossed to some crystal decanters on a sideboard. He drew two glasses from a cupboard and placed them on the table, then turned, a decanter in hand. "Some sherry, Lord Kettering?"

"If you please, Sir Damian. I could use a

brace against this weather." The baron rubbed his hands together. " 'Tis bloody cold in these parts in the winter. But nothing like aboard a ship. Isn't that the truth, sir?"

Damian walked toward Farley, a glass in each hand. "Aye," he replied with what he hoped was a pleasant tone. But he wasn't taken in. Farley hadn't come here for just a friendly chat. The man wanted something. Either that, or he'd grown suspicious. Damian wasn't about to let down his guard, even for a moment.

"Did you know I used to captain a ship myself?"

"Really? And why did you give it up?"

Farley turned his gaze toward the fire. "When my brother died, I inherited the barony and was needed here. Perhaps if I'd been able to supervise more closely the running of Tate Shipping . . ." He shrugged. "As you most likely know, we've had a devil of a time with pirates in recent years."

"So I've been told."

"But the *Peacock* and the *Venture* are both fine ships. You'll be glad you added them to your fleet."

"I hope our solicitors are able to come to terms," Damian replied noncommittally, his gaze on the sherry in his glass. He was aware that Farley had stiffened in his chair, but he didn't glance up. He waited in silence.

Finally, the baron seemed to relax. "Yes. Well, I hope so, too." He paused, then continued, "But from what I've seen, we may have other matters to discuss between us."

Damian raised his eyes. "Oh?"

" 'Tis quite apparent that you've taken a liking to my niece. Since it was you yourself who informed me that you are seeking a wife, I could only assume . . ." He let his voice trail off, punctuating the sentence with a shrug. "What else was I to think? Am I mistaken about your interest in Cassandra?"

It was dangerous to toy with a man like Farley. If it weren't for Cassandra, Damian would have enjoyed continuing the game, watching as Farley tried to hide his anxiety. He wasn't afraid for himself, but he had to think about Cassandra. She was still residing under this man's roof, and he would use her against Damian if he ever learned the truth.

"No, Lord Kettering, you are not mistaken. I find the Widow Sanford much to my liking."

Farley grinned. "I thought so. I am pleased, sir. Very pleased indeed."

Cassandra looked around the study, overwhelmed by the task before her. The bookshelves were filled with ledgers. Every available space was stacked high with papers. Empty ink bottles stood beside full ones. Account books from her great-grandfather's days were shelved beside current ones. She remembered how her mother had once complained that Farley never threw out anything. Now she understood Regina's lament.

Where was she to begin?

Drawing a deep breath, she walked over to his desk. She reached for the first stack of papers and began thumbing through them. They seemed to be nothing more than ordinary correspondence, but how could she be sure? She didn't even know what she was looking for.

Settling into the chair behind the desk, she read as quickly as possible, looking for names she might recognize, clues to her uncle's dealings or relationships with any of the men whose names were signed to the bottom of the letters, but she found nothing ominous in any of them, nothing that sounded illegal or questionable.

There were letters from tenants and shopkeepers as well as dukes and earls. There were invitations to hunting parties and house parties and balls, some of them several years old. She found bills of sale for items her uncle had purchased and items he had sold.

She had no idea how much time had passed before she heard her mother's footsteps in the hallway and the clatter of tiny dog claws on the wood floor. Quickly, she dropped the letter she was reading and stood up, trying her best to still the rapid beating of her heart and praying that her face didn't look flushed and guilty.

"Oh, Cassandra," Regina said with surprise as she looked into the room, "I didn't expect to find you in here. Where is your uncle?"

"I don't know. He went out." She hoped she didn't sound as agitated as she felt.

"Oh, dear. I did wish to speak with him about the cook." Regina touched her forefinger to her chin, tapping it several times. She frowned as she considered something silently, her eyes clouded with thought. Finally, she looked at her daughter again. "Well, I suppose it can wait." She started to turn away, then glanced back. "I wouldn't let your uncle find you in here when he returns, my dear. Farley hates for anyone to intrude upon his study. This room is quite sacred to him. I got a most thorough scolding when Franklin ran in here one day. I thought Farley would shoot the poor dear." She leaned over and stroked Franklin's furry head, then petted the other dogs as well.

"I was just looking for something to read," Cassandra explained quickly.

Regina straightened. "In Farley's study? He's not likely to have anything of interest in here, my dear." Her gaze swept over the cluttered room. "Even if he did, it would be impossible to find."

Cassandra skirted the desk and crossed the study. "I did notice things seemed a bit disorganized. Perhaps I could help with straightening up. With fewer servants, it must be impossible for Uncle Far to maintain order. Do you think he would let me help him?"

"Not likely," Regina replied as she hooked her arm through her daughter's and turned so that they could leave the room together. "But I can see you need something to do. You seem so distracted, my child. I do hope you're not letting your recent bereavement color your judgment. About Sir Damian, I mean."

Cassandra shook her head. "I'm not, Mother. I promise."

She wished she could tell her mother the truth—the truth about Damian and their baby and Uncle Far—but Regina had never been a strong woman. Cassandra couldn't burden her with her suspicions and accusations, let alone tell her that she had been a pirate's lover. How could she tell her mother that her own brother was blackmailing people, that he'd accused an innocent man of treason, that he'd even tried to have his niece kidnapped for the ransom it would bring? Regina could never bear to hear such things.

And Cassandra's father? She couldn't tell him either. He had already lost too much. It was bad enough knowing he had been forced to sell Jamison Manor to raise funds to help find her. How could she tell him she was in love with the pirate who'd kidnapped her, the very man who'd brought on the loss of Jamison Manor? And how could she tell him that her uncle—the man who had taken them in when they no longer had a home—was a thief, probably even a murderer?

No, she couldn't tell her parents any of it. Not yet. Perhaps not ever. This she would have to do alone.

Farley leaned back against the cushions as his carriage sped along the country road toward

Kettering Hall. He was feeling quite satisfied. Although Sir Damian had been careful not to commit himself just yet, he had been plain enough about his intentions. He would offer for Cassandra before very long.

He frowned, thinking of his niece. He couldn't quite figure the girl out. She'd been so adamant about not marrying again, about not considering Sir Damian's suit. Then there'd been this sudden about-face. That, in itself, pleased him, of course. But when combined with the odd reserve she'd shown toward him ever since her return . . .

His thoughts drifted back to Sir Damian. The bastard son of a duke, the rumors said. But which duke? Farley felt that he should know. There was something familiar about his neighbor.

Damn! He wished it didn't take so blasted long to get reports from those idiot lackeys in London. And they would have only just begun their investigation, trying to learn more about Sir Damian's mysterious ancestry. Still, if they were able to turn up a wealthy duke in the family closet, all the better for Farley Dunworthy. It would most likely be worth some blunt to keep the nobleman's by-blow's name from being linked with his own.

Sir Damian would offer for Cassandra. Cassandra would accept. Sir Damian would settle a handsome sum upon her and be generous with her family. Farley would discover the name of Damian's father and add to his own treasury after discreet correspondence. Everything was working out beyond his best expectations.

So why was he plagued by a sense of distrust? It had something to do with Sir Damian . . .

Chapter Thirty-Six

In the days that followed, Sir Damian came daily to Kettering Hall. It was obvious to everyone that the war hero was smitten with the lovely young Widow Sanford, and Cassandra had proven to be receptive to his attentions. Farley's feelings were equally obvious. He encouraged the match at every occasion. Even her father seemed pleased, commenting that it was good to see her smiling again.

Only Regina seemed less than satisfied with the appearance of things. As much as she longed for her daughter's happiness, she couldn't shake the sense that all was not right. For a young widow who had clearly been painfully mourning her deceased husband, Cassandra was responding all too quickly to a man she supposedly had never seen or met before. Something was not as it appeared. However, Regina kept her thoughts to herself.

Cassandra had no idea of her mother's concerns. She was enjoying herself too much to care what others thought. Every day, Damian came to see her, bringing her flowers and candy and even a bit of poetry. When they were allowed a few minutes together, they exchanged quick kisses. Perhaps it was silly of her to feel like a green girl, but she did. It was like being sixteen again, going to her first balls, and having the handsomest man there pay special attention to her. Only this was better, because she knew Damian already loved her.

Cassandra had only two more days to enjoy the courting ritual, and then Damian would tell her father that she'd agreed to marry him. It was just as well the time was so short. She was already more than four months gone in her pregnancy. The voluminous over-gowns she wore could only be expected to disguise her condition for so long. She wanted to be married and on her way to Sorcery Bay before anyone guessed about the baby. She didn't want Damian's son to bear a fictitious name when he could, by rights, bear his father's with pride.

Yes, she was eager to be his bride and to return with him to Sorcery Bay. But until she married Damian and left Kettering Hall, she was determined to find the evidence that would prove Sanford Tate innocent of treason. She still believed the proof was somewhere in her uncle's office. Every night, long after the rest of the house was enveloped in slumber, she made her way silently down to the study and continued her laborious search. After five nights, she was growing disheartened, yet she refused to give up. She would find the proof. She *had* to find the proof.

There were shadows beneath Cassandra's eyes that worried Damian. "Are you feeling well?" he asked softly when they were left alone in the drawing room. "You look tired."

She hesitated briefly, then said, "I'm a bit restless, but it will pass."

"You must take extra care of yourself, love." He brushed his lips across her forehead.

She nodded, her eyes not quite meeting his.

"Is something troubling you, Cassandra?"

"No, Damian." She glanced up at him. "I'm quite happy. Nothing's troubling me."

He peered down into her candid expression but wasn't comforted. He took hold of both of her hands with his. "I think 'tis time I told your father that you've agreed to marry me. I want you out of here." He kissed first one hand and then the other. "I want you with me."

Before Cassandra could answer, her mother returned to the room. Regina's eyes took in the scene before her—Damian sitting so close to Cassandra on the sofa, her hands in his—and her lips pressed together in a thin line.

Damian wished he knew why the woman didn't approve of him. It was doubtful that she would like him any more when she learned he planned to marry her daughter.

He rose from the sofa, drawing Cassandra up with him. "I'll go and speak with your father," he said softly, then kissed the back of her hand. "I'll return on the morrow."

He crossed the drawing room, pausing when he reached Regina. "Good day, Mistress Jamison." He offered a bow in her direction.

"Good day, Sir Damian."

It wasn't that she didn't like the man, Regina thought as she watched Sir Damian walk the length of the hall. Actually, she found him quite personable. It was plain that he'd fallen in love with her daughter and would cherish and care for her. That, in itself, was enough to make Regina fond of him.

But there was something else about him. If only she could put her finger on what was bothering her about him.

"Mother?"

She turned to find Cassandra standing beside her.

"I think I'll retire to my room. I'm feeling a bit tired."

"You haven't been looking well these past few days," Regina agreed. "Is it because of Sir Damian?"

Cassandra nodded. "Yes, Mother. It is because of Sir Damian. In truth, I haven't been sleeping well, and he is the cause." She smiled, and a warm glow brightened her face, softened the shadows beneath her eyes. "I love him."

"Your husband has been deceased only a few months," Regina cautioned, even though she could see it was useless. "Are you certain you . . ."

"I feared that I would never feel this way again. Perhaps the rules of mourning say I should not, but I do. Don't deny me the happiness I've found." A glitter of tears appeared in her eyes. "I thought I had lost it forever."

Regina put her arms around Cassandra. "Never would I deny you the happiness of love, my child. Never."

Cassandra kissed Regina's cheek. "Thank you, Mother. Thank you for understanding."

"If Sir Damian can make you happy, if he can bring a smile of joy to your face, if he can give you back laughter, then I shall love him as my own son." She hugged her daughter. "But love or no, I can see you are weary. Go to your room and lie down. We shall talk more of your wedding later."

Cassandra nodded, her mouth still curved in a sweet smile.

Regina watched the young woman cross to the stairs and climb to the second story. She'd meant what she said. If Sir Damian could give her all the love and happiness she wanted for her daughter, if he would cherish and care for her as she suspected he would, if he would be faithful and kind, then Regina had nothing to fear. And yet . . .

Her gaze moved down the hall where moments before Sir Damian had disappeared.

Something was not as it seemed. But what was it?

Cassandra closed her bedchamber door, then leaned against it and shut her eyes. She *was* tired. The nights spent searching her uncle's office were beginning to catch up with her. So was the strain of pretense. She didn't like lying to her parents. She wished she could tell her mother that her love for Damian wasn't new, that she'd always loved Damian, almost from the first moment she'd seen him.

She pushed away from the door and crossed the room to her mirror. She looked at the circles beneath her eyes. Her mother and Damian were right. She didn't look well. But she couldn't give up. Even now Damian was talking to her father, telling him of their plans to marry. As soon as a license could be obtained—a few days, a week at most— she would be Damian's wife and they would be sailing for the Caribbean. She had to find the proof before then.

She turned from the mirror as she began to disrobe, her thoughts still churning. Damian would be furious with her if he knew what she was doing at night, but he would get over it when she found the evidence they needed to clear Sanford Tate's name. He would be grateful. He wouldn't have to feel that he'd failed in keeping his promise to his father's memory.

Damian had given up his quest for revenge because he loved her, because she'd asked it of him. And because she loved him, she had to uncover the proof of his father's innocence while there was still time. She had to make sure that Farley was stopped from hurting others as he had hurt Damian.

But right now she didn't want to think about her uncle and the wicked things he'd done. She would rather think about Damian and their baby and the future.

Stripped to her shift, she ran her hands over her rounded belly, a secret smile lighting her face.

"Dear heaven . . ."

Cassandra turned quickly, her smile disappearing as she stared at her mother, who stood framed in the doorway. Regina's gaze flicked from her daughter's abdomen to her face and back again. Finally, she stepped into the bedchamber and closed the door.

Cassandra expected her mother to swoon or to take to her bed with a sick headache, but she was in for a surprise.

"This baby . . . 'tis Sir Damian's," Regina said as their gazes met once more.

For a moment, she considered denying it. But in the end, she couldn't. "Yes."

"There was no Mr. Sanford?"

"No."

Regina walked toward her daughter, stopping before her. " 'Tis time you told me the truth."

How could she tell her the truth? It was all so ugly, so sordid—the lies, the treachery, the deaths, the slavery. Everything.

No, she couldn't tell her these things. Her mother wasn't strong enough. She'd never been strong.

"I know what you're thinking, daughter, and you're wrong." She reached out and touched Cassandra's cheek. "I can see that you love him and he loves you. I am glad for you, though I would have had you wed before you were with child. But there are other reasons for what goes on here. If not, you would already be married."

Suddenly, she couldn't keep the words to herself any longer. Turning toward the window so she wouldn't have to watch her mother's horrified expression, Cassandra told her the story, from beginning to end. She told her of Farley's plots and schemes. She told her of the first fearful weeks on board the *Magic*. She told her of Aldin Abernathy and Damian's rescue. She told her of the love that had grown between them, of his attempt to bring her back to England, of their journey to Madagascar. Finally, she told her mother of her last quarrel with Damian before he'd sailed and the reason he'd sent her back to England, never knowing she carried his child.

" 'Twas because of me that Damian has delayed asking for my hand," she finished a long while later. "I didn't want you to be ashamed of me. I wanted you to think I'd found a new love. And I didn't want to tell you about Uncle Far. I knew . . . I knew how much it would hurt you." She sighed as she turned around. "Damian agreed to wait one week before speaking to Father. He's talking to him now." She shook her head. "If he knew I was using this time to search Uncle Far's study, he would be furious with me."

Sometime during the discourse, Regina had sat down on the edge of the bed. Now she was shaking her head, her eyes downcast. "Sanford's son . . ." she said softly. "I should have guessed. That's why he seemed so familiar to me."

Cassandra hurried forward. She sat on the bed beside her mother and grasped one of Regina's hands with both of her own. "If you betray him, he could be killed. I beg you, Mother, for my sake—"

"You needn't worry," Regina offered gently. "I would never betray you or Damian." She rose to her feet. "My brother must be punished for what he's done. Tonight I'll help you in your search. Time grows short. If Farley should guess Damian's relationship to Sanford Tate, he would shortly guess the whole truth. You must be safely away from here before that happens, you and your baby."

Cassandra was stunned. Her mother's reaction was so unexpected, so contrary to her usual behavior. It was almost as if this were some other woman entirely.

Regina didn't give her a chance to express any of her confused thoughts. Leaning down, she kissed Cassandra's forehead, then turned and walked to the door. As she reached for the latch, she said, "I'll come to your room tonight after everyone is asleep. We'll search together. You rest now, my dear."

Cassandra nodded, still marveling at her mother's calm resolve but glad that she could talk to someone at last.

She lay down on the bed, hoping that tonight she would find the proof she sought.

Chapter Thirty-Seven

"My brother may be a criminal," Regina said after more than two hours in Farley's study, "but he's not a fool."

Cassandra put down the journal she'd been reading and looked at her mother in the dim candlelight.

"He would not leave evidence which could be used against him where it might be easily found. Perhaps the letters and journals are written in some sort of code." She turned slowly as she surveyed the room, her gaze moving over the many shelves and bookcases, the mantel, the desk. "I know 'tis here somewhere. I'm sure of it. He's always been so protective of this room."

Cassandra mirrored her mother's action, turning her head to view the study. She had already gone through the journals in the book-case next to the desk, and she'd read the stacks of letters piled on the table beneath the window. She'd searched all the drawers in the room.

Regina walked over to the fireplace, staring down into the banked embers. "I always hated this room." Her voice was filled with a bitter anger. "Just as I always resented Farley's inter-ference. But I never guessed he would go to such lengths . . ."

Cassandra quit listening to her mother as she stared at the scene before her. Images of her uncle and the fireplace mantel flitted through her mind. She saw herself as a tiny child, Uncle Far lifting her in his arms, something moving, a dark hole. The memory was dim. She could be wrong. She might be imagining it.

"Mother . . ." She rose to her feet. "Mother, I think I know."

Regina glanced at her, her eyes still glazed with resentment.

"He's hidden it in the mantel," Cassandra went on, feeling excitement taking hold. "He showed me once when I was little."

Her mother stepped back from the fireplace. "Are you certain? Kettering Hall never had secret entrances or hideaways that I know of."

"I'm sure," she replied, a quiver in her voice.

Carrying the candle with her, she moved toward the fireplace, trying to recall exactly what she'd seen so many years before, but the memories remained indistinct. Regina took the candlestick from her, then held it high to cast more light over the area. Cassandra slid her hand along the wood of the mantelpiece, moving her uncle's favorite pipe and a couple of journals and then several books. Her eyes peered through the dim light of the room, trying to see anything unusual.

Frustration grew in her chest as she slid her fingers along the stones and mortar. There was nothing there. Perhaps she'd only imagined the scene because it was what she wanted.

She was about to give up when she felt a small stone jiggle beneath her touch.

"Mother," she whispered breathlessly.

Regina stepped up beside her. The two women exchanged glances. Each knew they shared the other's excitement and trepidation.

Holding her breath, Cassandra took hold of the gray stone and drew it out. She paused, then slipped her hand into the narrow opening. At first, it seemed she'd found nothing more than a loose stone in the fireplace. Again she doubted her childhood memory. And then she touched cool metal. Running her fingers over the object, she discovered that it was a handle.

"You found it," Regina said, apparently seeing the discovery in Cassandra's expression.

She nodded, then closed her fingers around the metal grip and pulled. A segment of stones and mortar moved, swinging outward as easily as a door swung on its hinges. When it was open, they could see that it was, in fact, a door— a door to a secret nook.

Again the two women exchanged a glance.

It was Regina who moved first this time. Setting the candlestick on the mantel, she reached into the dark compartment and pulled out sheaves of papers and two journals.

Cassandra's heart was pounding in her chest, and her mouth had gone dry. Nervously, she licked her lips, but she didn't reach to take the items from her mother as she wanted. The look on the older woman's face stopped her.

" 'Tis true," Regina whispered. "By all that's holy, 'tis true." She sank to the floor, spreading the papers before her and began reading through them.

Once more moving the candlestick, Cassandra joined her mother on the floor and reached for the two journals. In moments, she was engrossed in a tale of deception and greed that sickened her soul.

Damian paced the bedchamber at Pointe Cottage. Sleep had defied him tonight. No matter what he tried, he couldn't shake the feeling that all was not well with Cassandra.

He moved to the window, bracing his hands on either side of the glass, and looked out across the fields bathed in moonlight. The serenity of the scene before him did nothing to calm the worry that continued to gnaw at his gut.

He never should have let her talk him into waiting. She was his woman, the mother of his unborn child. He loved her and she loved him. She would be his wife, no matter what anyone else said or did. He should have refused to play this game.

If she hadn't said how hard it would be to bid her parents farewell, he never would have agreed to postpone talking to her father, not even for a day. But her words had reminded him what it was like to have a family, to have someone who cared for him, and he'd been helpless against her request.

How could he have denied her when she'd looked at him with pleading blue eyes? He had already been guilty of too much hurt. He hadn't had the will to cause any more.

But now he doubted the wisdom of giving in to her. Although she'd continued to assure him that all was well at Kettering Hall, he wasn't convinced. The shadows beneath her eyes alone made him suspicious.

Well, things were going to change. He'd spoken to the squire before leaving Kettering Hall and had promised a healthy settlement, enough to guarantee that his in-laws never were in want again. He planned to arrange the settlement in such a manner that Farley could never get his hands on it. Tomorrow—or rather, today, since the hour was long past midnight—he would tell Cassandra they would be wed at once. He wanted her out of that house. He wanted her in his arms. He wanted her where he could make sure she was safe.

Safe . . . His fingers tightened on the window casing. Why did he have such a strong feeling this night that she wasn't safe?

*　　*　　*

Cassandra looked up from the journal to find her mother quietly weeping. She made no sound as tears slipped down her cheeks and splattered against the papers in her lap.

"Mother?"

Regina glanced up. "I didn't know Farley hated him so much. They were friends once. How could I have known he would do this?"

"You were always a silly twit, dear sister," Farley interjected with a trace of cruel laughter as he stepped into the study. Far from the light of the flickering candle, her uncle's face was cast in eerie shadows.

"Why, Farley?" Regina whispered. "Why would you do such a thing? Sanford never hurt you. He was your childhood friend."

"Why? Because he was an upstart who didn't know his place. Because he had the audacious notion that he was good enough to marry you." He stepped forward. "Because I saw him growing richer while we grew poorer, all because of that damned shipping company. Because I saw an opportunity and I took it. I wasn't a fool like our father or a drunkard like our brother. I was determined not to be penniless when I became the Baron Kettering."

"When you became . . ." Regina's face paled. "Oh my God! Not that, too, Farley. Tell me you didn't."

Farley shrugged his shoulders, tipping his head to one side in a gesture of helplessness.

"You killed Gregory?" Regina whispered.

412

"You killed your own brother for the sake of a title?"

Cassandra let out a tiny gasp of horror.

Farley turned his harsh gaze upon her, ignoring Regina's questions. He grinned. "I don't believe your daughter comprehends everything she's heard, Regina. Shall we tell her? Shall we tell her that you were once in love with your old governess's son and that you wanted to marry him? Shall we tell her how I made sure Sanford Tate and his mother were sent away?"

"Sanford Tate?" Cassandra dropped the journal to the floor. Unconsciously, she placed a protective hand on her abdomen as she felt a faintness sweep over her.

Regina moved to put an arm around Cassandra's shoulders, but her eyes were on her brother. "You've already lost all the wealth you gained, Farley. 'Tis clear you're no better than Father and Gregory at managing the family income. Tate Shipping is gone, and soon you'll have nothing left. When the truth about you is known . . ."

Farley ignored her, waving away her words as he would a pesky fly. He stared at Cassandra, his brows drawn together in a frown. And then his eyes widened. "Bloody hell," he muttered. His gaze moved to Regina. "Damian's not much like his father, is he, my dear sister? But enough so I should have seen it. I guess I did, but I never thought . . . 'Twas the name that fooled me, of course. His brat's given name was Sanford, just like his own. But names can be changed." He laughed harshly, a humorless sound in the emotion-charged room. "Not just Tate's son, but a bloody pirate as well. And I've been entertaining him in my own home."

He moved so quickly that Cassandra was caught totally by surprise. His hand closed roughly around her arm, and he hauled her to her feet.

"You carry his bastard. You've been playing the harlot with the man who's tried to destroy me." He shook her, making her head bob forward and back and her teeth rattle. "I've cared for you like my own daughter, and this is how you betray me. Mrs. Sanford? Could you come up with nothing better? You trollop!"

"Farley, stop!" Jumping up, Regina grabbed at him.

He turned on his sister with fury, catching her alongside the head with the back of his hand. The hard blow knocked her to the floor.

"Mother!" Cassandra hurried to the woman and helped her up. When she turned around, she saw her uncle stuffing the papers and journals back into the hiding place.

" 'Tis no use, Uncle Far. We know the truth now. You can't hide it any longer."

His back stiffened. Then he turned slowly toward her. He was wearing a deadly smile as he leveled a pistol at her. "Make another sound, either of you, and I'll shoot you here and now."

*   *   *

Damian was certain he was going to feel the fool when he arrived at Kettering Hall in the wee hours of the night and tried to explain to Cassandra why he'd had her awakened from a sound sleep. He had never been a man given to premonitions of danger, nor was he a man who gave heed to fear.

But tonight his heart was filled with an apprehension that would not give him rest, and so he found himself galloping his horse through the moonlit countryside on a fool's mission.

The stone walls of Kettering Hall came into view. The sight didn't bring him peace. If anything, he felt an upsurge of dread. He didn't care if he did look like a fool. He would see Cassandra tonight, this very moment.

As soon as the gelding slid to a stop, Damian vaulted from the saddle and strode up the steps to the front entrance. With a heavy fist, he pounded on the door. He waited only seconds before he repeated the action, once, then again and again.

Finally, he heard a voice cry, "All right. All right. Have patience."

The door cracked an inch.

"What do you want, sir?" the servant inquired in a scratchy voice. " 'Tis an ungodly hour."

Damian pressed the palm of his hand against the door and pushed it open. "I will see Cassandra."

"Miss Cassandra . . . But . . . but you can't see milady at this time o' night."

415

"Get her for me or I'll get her myself," Damian threatened.

"Good sir . . ." the old butler tried again.

"God's teeth," he muttered as he shoved the man to one side.

He was halfway up the stairs when Henry Jamison appeared above him, his hair disheveled, a candlestick held in one hand.

"What's this about? What's going on here?" he demanded.

Damian stopped. "I wish to see your daughter, sir."

"At this hour?"

"You may think me mad, but I wish to assure myself that all is well with her."

Henry was, indeed, staring at him as if he were mad.

"Please, Squire Jamison, just go to her room and look in on her. I'll wait here if that's what you want. If you tell me she is sleeping, I'll not disturb her."

"Damn foolishness," Henry muttered as he turned. Louder, he said, "I'll look in on her."

The ensuing minutes were the longest of Damian's life. And one look at the squire's face as he returned was enough to confirm Damian's worst fears.

"She's gone," Henry said, "and so is my wife."

Chapter Thirty-Eight

The careening carriage ride through the night had been terrifying, but wondering what was happening outside the carriage when it had stopped moving was even more frightening. Sitting with their wrists tied behind their backs, their ankles bound, and their mouths gagged, the two women could only communicate with their eyes.

Cassandra knew that her mother was asking herself many of the same questions that were going through Cassandra's mind. Where had Farley taken them? What did he plan to do with them? Would anyone ever know their fate?

She closed her eyes, wondering if she would ever see Damian again, if she would ever hold his baby in her arms.

Cassandra couldn't bear such thoughts. She tried to concentrate on other things. She strained to hear her uncle's voice or any movements beyond the confines of the carriage. It was then that she became aware of the lapping of water, the sounds of surf sweeping up on a beach, and the smell of sea air. But, she thought, perhaps it was only because she'd been thinking of Damian. Damian and the *Magic* and the ocean were so indelibly set in her mind that each was a part of the other.

The carriage door opened suddenly. Farley stood in the opening, a dark figure with the gray light of dawn at his back. He stared at the two women for a moment before he leaned inside and untied their ankles. When he straightened, he said, "Out with you."

As Cassandra stepped to the ground, she saw that she hadn't been wrong. They had come to the ocean. And there, anchored in the harbor, was the *Peacock*. Like an evil omen, a cold wind blew off the water. It clutched at her cloak and whipped her hair against her cheeks.

"Move." Farley gave Regina a shove forward.

Cassandra saw then where he was taking them. A skiff with several oarsmen was waiting alongside the dock. If not for the gag in her mouth, she would have screamed for help. Perhaps someone in the seaside town would have heard her and come to their aid. Then again, perhaps they wouldn't have cared what a baron did with his sister and niece as long as he left them in peace.

Despair clouded her thoughts throughout the short trip from dock to ship. She moved when she was told to move, climbed when she was told to climb. But after a while, the resigned acceptance of her fate began to wear off. She had survived many things these past eight months. Neither pirates nor gales at sea had defeated her. She had endured the pawing hands of Aldin Abernathy, the cannon blasts of the *Venture*, the rejection of the man she loved—and she had come out triumphant. She had even faced the ugly truth about her uncle and sought the proof that would remove the stain from the name of Tate.

She shook her head, as if to shake loose the last vestiges of discouragement. Then she looked around the deck of the *Peacock* as the crew made ready to sail, her uncle calling orders to the men. She didn't need to be a ship's officer to realize that there were too few men trying to do the work.

"Where is Mouse?" Farley shouted at one of the crew.

"Don't know, your lordship. 'E was in the skiff when it went ashore fer you. I ain't seen 'im since."

"Well, get another man up the mizzen mast. I want those sails unfurled. We can't wait for him, the fool." Farley turned away, cursing angrily.

Cassandra felt real hope spring to life in her chest. Mouse. The one-eyed sailor. Mouse was loyal to Damian. If he'd seen or heard what

Farley was about, he would go to Damian. He would tell Damian where she was.

Oh, please God, let Mouse have gone for Damian.

And then Damian would come after them. She knew he would. He would come and rescue them. And until he did, she would not cower before the enemy.

She rose to her feet and walked toward her uncle with determined steps. When he saw her, he glared angrily, but she didn't turn away.

"What do you want?" he demanded.

Garbled words were the best she could do through the gag.

With a sound of frustration, he yanked the cloth from her mouth. "Well?"

She ignored the pain in her jaw and along the back of her head which his action had caused. "I'd like to free Mother's hands and remove her gag. There's nowhere for her to go, and she certainly can't say anything to these men that will do you any harm. Keep me bound if you must, but release her."

He considered her request before hailing one of his officers. "Untie Cassandra, then see her and my sister down to my cabin and lock them in," he commanded. He glanced back at Cassandra. "Cause me a moment of trouble, girl, and the ropes go on again and I'll put you both in the hold."

She had hoped to remain on deck. She'd hoped to learn where her uncle was taking them, though she didn't know what good it would have done her. But at least they would be able to move about in the cabin and talk to each other. They would be able to formulate some sort of plan for escape. They had to be ready for whatever was to come.

Hurry, Damian. I fear there's not much time left, she said in silent prayer as she walked toward her mother, the sailor following right behind them.

Damian had a difficult time convincing Henry that Farley had actually taken the women as his hostages.

"But why? I don't understand any of this," the squire lamented. "My brother-in-law is many things that I don't admire, but he loves my daughter. He wouldn't hurt her. Why would he kidnap her?"

"Because he must have found out about me," Damian answered impatiently. "There's no time to explain more now. We must find them before it's too late. Where would Farley take them? Where would he go to hide? Think, squire."

"He's never had any reason to hide." Henry ran his fingers through his gray hair. "I have no idea."

"Excuse me, sir," Mullins interrupted. "I believe I might know."

Damian whirled toward the butler. "Where?"

"He had the *Peacock* brought up from London. I posted the letter myself. He was hoping you would buy it, I believe, sir. The ship is

421

there now. It's anchored at the mouth of the Wansbeck."

"That's it." Damian glanced at the squire. "Get dressed if you're going with me. I'll explain to you along the way."

"Of course I'm going with you. If there's a chance my wife and daughter are in danger—" He turned without finishing his sentence and took the stairs two at a time.

The sun was a round ball on the eastern horizon as Damian and the squire raced their horses along the road to the sea, the morning sunlight blinding their eyes. Damian explained—as best he could astride a galloping horse—the history between himself and Farley Dunworthy and the truth about his relationship with Cassandra. He had no idea what the squire's thoughts were; he made no comment at any time during Damian's tale.

They were halfway to the coast when they met Mouse.

As soon as the horses were yanked to a stop, Damian asked, "Is she on the *Peacock*?"

"Aye, cap'n. She an' 'er mum."

"How long since they sailed?"

"Not more'n an hour."

Damian glanced at Cassandra's father. "We ride for the *Magic*. Are you coming?"

"I'm coming."

Damian dug his boot heels into his horse's sides. He didn't look back to see if either of the other men followed.

* * *

"I never knew he hated Sanford so much," Regina said softly as she stared out the gallery windows of Farley's cabin. She rubbed her left wrist with the fingers of her right hand. "Not enough to send Sanford to the gallows. Not that much."

Cassandra sensed her mother's need to talk. She left her place by the locked cabin door and went to stand beside Regina. "Tell me about Sanford Tate."

The woman managed to smile, her eyes taking on a faraway look. "He wasn't nearly as tall as his son, but he was as handsome. Their eyes are much the same, I think, though Sanford's were brown instead of black. He had such a commanding way of looking at people, and they were always glad to obey because he was the sort of man who earned respect."

Her mother was right. Damian was like that. It was why his crew was so loyal to him. They trusted him.

"Sanford had a wonderful laugh. He loved to tease me when I was little. We grew up together. His mother was the governess at Kettering Hall. Sanford and Farley and Gregory all played together as boys. They were friends. At least, I always thought they were friends." Sadness replaced her smile. "Then Sanford and I fell in love. Farley was always the most vehemently opposed to a match, though my father and Gregory weren't pleased either."

Cassandra's heart tightened in her chest. She knew what it was like to love a man and know that you must marry another.

Bitter mockery filled Regina's voice as she continued. "The daughter of a baron couldn't stoop so low, Farley said, to marry a commoner. I had to think about my place in society. Besides, the Tates had no money, and it was important that I marry money."

Cassandra swallowed a hot lump in her throat.

Regina sighed, the anger forgotten as quickly as it had come. She turned her gaze upon her daughter. "I didn't want that to happen to you. When I learned what Farley had arranged, I tried my best to stop him. But you seemed willing, and I was powerless. I was always so terribly powerless."

"I *was* willing," Cassandra replied. "You must not blame yourself. I knew that, if I didn't marry Mr. Abernathy, the family would be in grave trouble. But that doesn't matter now. Besides," she squeezed her mother's hand, "if I hadn't gone away, I should never have met Damian."

Their gazes held for a long time, sharing silent understanding.

"Go on with your story," Cassandra whispered at last.

Regina took a deep breath. "Henry wasn't enormously wealthy, but neither was he poor. And he wanted to marry me. I wasn't the beauty you are, Cassandra. There weren't a great many suitors lining up to marry a girl who would have only a small dowry—if my father and brothers didn't gamble it away first." Again she looked out at the North Sea. "Sanford and his mother moved away after my betrothal was announced. I didn't expect to ever hear of them again." She paused, as if lost in thought.

No, Cassandra decided, watching her mother's expression change. Regina wasn't lost in thought. She was lost in the past.

"Many years later, I heard about Tate Shipping and its dashing owner. I learned that Sanford had a beautiful wife named Margaret and a son who bore his own name. He'd become very wealthy, too, rich enough that he was welcomed into the homes of the best families in England. I was very proud of him." A bittersweet smile curved her mouth. "But Farley was furious, for not only had Sanford become a success but our own fortunes had been lost. The Dunworthys and the Jamisons rarely went out in society. We couldn't afford to." She swallowed hard. "A few years later, I learned that Sanford had been executed for treason. I knew then that it couldn't be true. Sanford was an Englishman, through and through. I hated it when Farley told me he'd purchased Tate Shipping, but I never imagined that he . . ." She shook her head. " 'Tis unthinkable even now."

Cassandra blinked away her own tears. She thought of the woman who had hidden from life for so many years because of a love denied her by the selfishness of her brother and the rules of society. She understood so many things now that she'd never understood before. Again, she squeezed her mother's hand.

Regina turned toward her daughter. "And now we've come full circle, and you love his son. I think Sanford would be pleased." Her smile was soft. "Perhaps it was fate. If Sanford and I had married, you and Damian would not have been born. We would have other children, God willing, but they would not have been you and Damian."

The two women embraced then, holding on to each other for a long while, the cabin wrapped in understanding silence.

Finally, Regina said, "We cannot let Farley win again. We must make sure that you and Damian and your child have the happiness he didn't want me to have."

"We will, Mother," Cassandra whispered. "I know we will."

Chapter Thirty-Nine

Damian climbed up the rigging and settled on the *Magic*'s foretop, spyglass in hand. If he'd guessed correctly—that Farley, with only a skeleton crew on board the *Peacock*, had headed south—they should catch up with them soon. If he'd guessed wrong . . .

His fingers tightened around the spyglass. He refused to think about the consequences if he'd guessed wrong.

He put the glass up to his eye and began to sweep the water with his magnified gaze. The brilliant sunshine belied the bitter cold of the November morning, especially high above the choppy waters of the North Sea. But Damian didn't give up his search. Not once in over an hour did he lower the glass from his eye.

Not until he found the *Peacock*.

"There she is!" he shouted before descending from his perch.

The decks of the *Magic* became a blur of activity as the well-trained crew prepared for battle. There was no confusion, no doubt about what each man's duties were. Damian took his place on the poop deck and watched as, slowly but surely, the *Magic* gained on the *Peacock*.

The waiting was agony.

"Mother!" Cassandra hurried toward the gallery windows. "Mother, look!"

Regina joined her.

" 'Tis the *Magic*. Damian's come for us."

Her mother grasped Cassandra's hand. "Farley will see him, too."

Cassandra knew what her mother meant. Farley would protect himself any way he had to. He would stop Damian, and he wouldn't hesitate to use his own sister, Cassandra, or Damian's unborn child to do it.

Not for the first time, she searched the cabin with her gaze, looking for some sort of weapon she could use to protect them, but there was nothing. No knife. No pistol. No cutlass. Not so much as a writing quill. She would have nothing but her wits to keep them all safe until Damian could reach them.

She turned back to the window. Many times she had thought how wonderful the *Magic* looked in full sail, but never had the ship looked as beautiful as she did now.

"Hurry, Damian," she whispered. "Hurry."

*   *   *

As the *Magic* drew closer to its prey, Damian strapped on his weapons. He'd already given orders that the *Peacock* mustn't receive any direct hits. She had to stay afloat. She had to be boarded.

"What if he throws them into the sea?" Henry had asked anxiously some time ago.

"He can't," Damian had replied. "If he does, there'll not even be decent kindling left when we're through with him, and well he knows it."

But there were other things Farley could do to his hostages, and Damian would be helpless to stop him. Not until he was on board the *Peacock*.

His eyes narrowed as he peered ahead. He should have killed Farley years ago. He should have forgotten wanting to make the baron's suffering a prolonged one. He should have captured and butchered him, just as Damian's father had been butchered. He could have done it. He'd had his opportunities.

But now was not the time for self-recriminations. It wasn't even the time to think of Cassandra, with her beautiful wide eyes or her silvery hair that smelled of lilacs. If he thought of her and the baby she carried in her womb, he would be distracted. He couldn't afford that. His every action and reaction must be calculated. Too many lives depended on him. He dared not make even one mistake.

429

The *Magic* sailed on as the sun climbed higher in the sky, the distance between the two ships narrowing. Damian commanded his ship to approach the *Peacock* from her starboard side. He would give Farley no opportunity to sail toward the coast of England. He would force him to remain at sea.

When they were close enough to cause Farley some doubt, Damian ordered the forecastle deck gun to fire a warning shot.

Farley did, indeed, make an attempt to turn his vessel toward shore, but the *Magic* used the maneuver to narrow the gap between the two ships. The *Peacock* angled sharply to port, but she couldn't make up the distance she'd lost.

Damian could see his foe now, standing on the poop deck of the *Peacock*. Neither of the women were in sight. "Oliver, have the men fire a shot across her bow," he ordered.

"Aye, captain."

Minutes later, the *Peacock* returned fire, the cannonballs falling short. But they were closing the distance between them rapidly, and soon they would be in range of Farley's guns. They would be of no use to Cassandra if they allowed themselves to be sunk.

Damian paced back and forth across the deck, his brows drawn tight in a scowl as he pondered a different tactic. It was a risk. There would be falling timbers. There was a good chance of fire. But maybe, if things appeared bad enough, the undersized crew of the *Peacock* would surrender. That might be their only real hope. Farley must have guessed by now that Damian planned to continue to overshoot his target. The baron would have passed that information on to his crew. As long as they believed they were protected from the enemy's assault, they would continue to fight. But if they saw they were losing the battle . . .

"Oliver!" he shouted.

"Aye, captain."

"Aim for her masts. We'll stop her in the water."

"Aye, captain."

If she stood close to the window glass, Cassandra could see the stern of the *Magic*. She knew the two ships were firing upon each other. She also knew that Damian was intentionally missing the *Peacock* while her uncle was doing his best to sink Damian's ship.

And then a volley of cannonfire erupted from the gunports of the *Magic*. The *Peacock* rocked, shuddered as it was struck, not once but several times. Cassandra screamed in surprise as she was knocked to the floor, the shriek echoed by her mother. She heard the sounds of wood splintering. The crashing noises that followed made her fear that the deck above them was about to collapse, bringing everything down upon their heads. The acrid scent of gunpowder filled her nostrils, adding to her terror.

"He means to sink us," Regina cried.

Cassandra feared the same, though she could scarcely believe it. Didn't Damian know they were on board the *Peacock*? She had been so certain . . .

The cabin door crashed open. Both women turned their heads to see Farley standing there. His face was blackened. His coat was torn at his right shoulder.

"Get up," he ordered Cassandra, waving his pistol at her.

She obeyed.

"Above deck. Both of you."

Regina held out a beseeching hand. "Farley, for the love of God, we're your family, your own blood kin."

"Shut up, woman! Can you never just shut up?"

Cassandra took hold of her mother's arm and guided her toward the door. Farley stepped aside to let them pass. She could see how the pistol shook in his hand. She glanced up and saw the fear, the desperation in his eyes. Thinking her uncle had reached the edge of sanity, she was more frightened than ever before.

"Hurry!" Farley shouted. "Get up there."

Cassandra quickened her steps, hauling Regina with her. She could feel her mother's shivering through her arm. "It will be all right," she whispered, hoping to give her the assurance Cassandra no longer felt.

But as she climbed through the hatch, she felt her confidence returning. Amidst the wreckage of splintered masts and tangled rigging, the crew of the *Peacock* had dropped their weapons and stood waiting for the *Magic* to draw close enough for her crew to board the defeated ship.

She felt rough fingers grabbing her arm, then she was jerked backward against her uncle. The cool metal of the pistol's barrel pressed against her throat.

"Would you have her die?" Farley shouted as he sidled to the left, dragging her with him.

Cassandra's gaze frantically sought out Damian.

And then he was there, standing on the deck of her uncle's ship. He, too, was holding a pistol in his hand.

Never had he looked so magnificent, so fearless as he did now. His expression was harsh, cold, even distant. He was like a mountain that would not be moved.

"I'll shoot her," Farley warned.

Damian raised his hands, pointing his weapon toward the sky. "Let's discuss it, Kettering. Let the women go. They've done you no harm."

"No harm?" Her uncle laughed sharply. "They would have joined you in ruining me if I hadn't stopped them. They would have turned against me, even after I've cared for them all these years. An idiot and her harlot daughter. That's what I've been saddled with. Vipers nesting in my own home."

Her father stepped from amidst the crowd of sailors. "Farley, let Cassandra go."

"Papa," she whispered.

433

"Another fool," Farley grumbled near her ear, then shouted, "You're as big a fool as my sister, Henry. Bigger even, for you chose to live with her."

The squire ignored his brother-in-law's taunts. "Look at her, Farley. Cassandra has been like your own daughter. You've loved her as I love her."

"No daughter of mine would be carrying the bastard of a pirate."

Damian moved abruptly forward. "Kettering . . ."

The gun pressed more tightly against her throat. "I'm warning you, not another step closer. Drop your pistol. Unless you give me safe passage from the ship, I'll kill her. Her and your bastard."

Cassandra couldn't stop the whimper that tore from her throat. If Damian put down his pistol, her uncle would shoot him. She was sure of it. If he didn't throw down his weapon, Farley would shoot her. Either way, she was doomed.

Damian's gaze met hers. The look was brief, and yet she understood. He was telling her he loved her. He was telling her to have hope.

He tossed aside the pistol.

Just as Cassandra had feared, she felt Farley turn the gun from her throat toward Damian. She grabbed for her uncle's arm even as she heard a scream—her mother's voice, she thought, although it sounded little like Regina. From the corner of her eye, she saw a blur of movement. Farley's shout of pain rang in her ears, and then there was the explosion of gunfire as Cassandra was shoved to the deck.

Damian had only a moment to react. The piece of timber Regina swung at Farley's head only grazed him, but it caused the baron to fire his pistol before he'd taken aim. Cassandra fell to her knees in front of her uncle seconds before Farley struck Regina and knocked her away from him.

Damian drew his cutlass and rushed forward. A part of him longed to stop where Cassandra lay sprawled on the deck, but he didn't dare. There wasn't time. Farley had already drawn his sword. The best Damian could do was put himself between his enemy and Cassandra, and that was what he did.

"It's over, Kettering," he said in a low voice.

Farley smiled. "Do you think I would let Sanford's brat defeat me? Never. 'Tis not over. One of us shall not survive this meeting."

"If that's what you wish," Damian replied, returning the baron's joyless smile.

He sensed that Cassandra and her mother had both been helped up from the deck by a member of his own crew and pulled back a safe distance, and knowing it, he could now focus all his attention on his enemy.

The two men began to circle, swords glinting in the sunlight. They each tested the other with a quick thrust. They each blocked the other's attack with ease.

Damian had the advantage of size and age, but he knew Farley was skilled with the sword. It would not be a quick or easy victory.

"The brat I sent aboard the *Seadog* was named Sanford Tate," the baron said in a taunting voice. "Like his traitorous father. Were you ashamed of the name, *Sir* Damian?"

"Never," he answered coldly. "I was always called Damian by my parents."

Metal rang against metal as Farley swung his sword and Damian deflected it.

"And I didn't use my last name," Damian continued, as if never interrupted, "because I swore I would have none until the name of Tate had been wiped clean by your death."

A series of thrusts and parries followed. Again and again, one sword would arc in assault and the other would deflect it. Again and again, the clanging sounds of sword upon sword rent the air.

Farley was breathing a bit harder when he said, "I never thought you would survive. The boy I remember was a skinny whelp."

"Hate made me strong." He continued to circle. "Do you remember the day you sold me to the captain of the *Seadog*?"

"I remember."

"You laughed when I swore I'd return. You said it would take a magician to bring me back." His move was sudden and effortless. He nicked Farley's cheek. "As you can see, 'twas the *Magic* that brought me back to you, just as you predicted."

436

His adversary's eyes filled with wrath. Farley made another series of thrusts. The last one made it past Damian's defenses, and the sword tip cut his arm. Damian countered, but he was blocked.

Farley laughed, a sound of triumph.

Damian's smile was grim. Some would have called it deadly. "You haven't won, baron. I've waited for this moment for too many years to spend it quickly. You cannot win, and well you know it."

The older man's laughter vanished, replaced by a half-crazed expression.

The battle began in earnest then. No more words were spoken. None were needed.

Cassandra could scarcely draw a breath for the fear that squeezed her chest. She watched in enthralled horror, not even daring to blink, as if hypnotized by the lethal dance that was being played out upon the deck of the ship.

She lost all track of time. She wasn't aware of her mother holding her arm or Oliver standing close to her other side or anything else that happened around her. For Cassandra, there were only the two men fighting with swords and the blood that slowly began to stain their clothes and spatter the deck of the ship.

She wasn't quite certain when the tide of the battle shifted obviously in Damian's favor. Suddenly she just knew that it had. Sweat beaded on her uncle's forehead, and his face was red from his efforts. The thrusts of his sword became reckless, desperate, and were easily parried by his opponent.

Damian was relentless. With icy precision, he pressed his advantage, driving Farley into a corner, the quarterdeck at his back, the port railing to one side. There was no place for Farley to go. No hope of escape.

For a moment, time seemed to freeze. Neither man moved. They merely stared at each other, their eyes revealing their mutual hatred.

Then, with a vicious swing of his cutlass, Damian knocked Farley's sword from his hand. An instant later, the tip of Damian's weapon was pressed against the baron's throat.

No, Damian, Cassandra cried silently. *No matter what he's done, he's still my uncle.*

It was as if he'd heard her. Damian's head turned slightly, and their gazes met across the width of the ship.

"Damian," she whispered.

The blood lust slowly faded from his eyes, and the cold facade melted away with it. He stepped back from Farley. His sword lowered slightly.

Cassandra took a step forward.

Damian kicked Farley's weapon across the deck toward one of his own crew. "Take care of the prisoner, Oliver," he said, his gaze never moving from Cassandra's face.

He turned and walked toward her. She met him halfway.

Reaching up, she touched a cut near his forehead. There was so much she wanted to say,

438

but all she was able to do was whisper his name again. "Damian."

He closed his eyes a moment, as if savoring the sound.

She leaned forward and rested her forehead against his chest. "We found it," she said, finding her voice at last. "We found the proof that will clear your father's name. He was never a traitor, Damian. The papers are hidden back at Kettering Hall." She lifted her head again, ready to say more.

From the corner of her eye, she caught a near-by movement. She turned toward it, saw Oliver staggering backward, a crimson stain spreading across his shirt. She saw Farley raise a dagger, his eyes locked with hers as he plunged the knife toward her heart.

Later, she would try to recall if she saw or felt Damian move. At that moment, she only knew that her uncle seemed to freeze in place, his hand and the dagger mere inches away from her chest. Then the color drained from his face. The knife clattered to the deck of the ship. Farley blinked once, then twice. He drew in a ragged breath. When he let it out, a rattling sound accompanied it.

Cassandra reeled backward, as if released from some unseen hand that had held her motionless. It was then that she saw the hilt of the sword protruding from Farley's abdomen. Damian's sword.

Another gurgling sound was torn from Farley's throat. He lifted an empty hand toward her, his eyes glossed with pain and surprise. His mouth worked but no words came out. And then he pitched forward onto the deck.

She stared, horrified, at the bloody sword protruding from her uncle's back. He would have killed her. This man who had been like a second father. He would have killed her. She had thought him kind and loving, but he'd been so filled with jealousy, greed, and hate, there'd been no room for real love in his heart. How could she have been so blind to what he was?

" 'Tis over." The tender sound of Damian's voice drew her gaze.

She had been blind to him once as well. She had thought him a demon-captain. She had thought his heart as black as his eyes, as cold as the seas he sailed. But she'd been wrong about him, too. He was good and kind, strong and brave. And he loved her.

"Damian," she whispered, a world of meaning in that one word.

He opened his arms, and with a cry of relief, she fell into the safe harbor of his embrace.

Epilogue

May 1715

Cassandra Tate leaned against the taffrail, her gaze set on the shrinking coast of England. She listened to the wind whistling through the rigging and snapping the clouds of white canvas above her head. She smelled the salty tang of the ocean. She saw the waves break into a flurry of froth against the hull of the ship.

"Are you sorry to leave?" Damian asked as he stepped up beside his wife.

She shook her head. "No. 'Tis time we returned home."

Home. Had it truly been only little more than a year ago when home had meant a simple stone house set amidst the rolling green countryside of Northumberland? Had it only been a year

441

since she'd longed to return there above anything else?

Damian placed his arm around her shoulders. She leaned her head against his chest and closed her eyes.

A year was not such a very long time, she realized. Just a matter of days strung together into months, and suddenly, another year had gone by.

It was hard to believe all that had happened in her life in a year, all that had changed. The past year had brought her moments of great pain and great joy. So much had happened, especially in the months since her uncle's death.

Sanford Tate's name had been cleared of the charges of treason. The papers in Farley's secret compartment had helped convict a number of his associates of varying charges, but there had been none who could—or would—say that Sir Damian Tate had ever participated in illegal activities against the Crown. There had been no one to step forward and call him pirate.

Cassandra and Damian had been married in a small ceremony in November. There might have been those who suspected the child the bride carried beneath her gown was not that of the deceased Mr. Sanford, but no one had ever repeated such suspicions aloud.

Oliver had recovered from the knife wound inflicted by her uncle, but not before he'd won the heart of the young woman who'd helped nurse him. The two had married as soon as Oliver was able to stand up and say his vows.

Damian had purchased Jamison Manor as a gift to his in-laws some months back, and Cassandra had watched as a change occurred in her parents' marriage. Perhaps it was because Farley's interference was no longer a source of friction between them, but whatever its cause, Cassandra was happy to know that her parents would share a new closeness in the years to come. She could even hope that they might be lucky enough to find a real and lasting love.

Sanford Damian Tate III had been born at Pointe Cottage the last week of March in the Year of our Lord Seventeen Hundred and Fifteen. He had his father's black hair and ebony eyes, and Cassandra knew he would be as devilishly handsome as his namesake. At this very moment, he was asleep in his cradle in the captain's cabin, watched over by his vigilant nurse.

Yes, much had happened in the past year, but now they were going home. Home to Sorcery Bay Plantation and the turquoise waters of the Caribbean and the warm tropical breezes.

Cassandra glanced up at Damian, a secret smile curving her mouth. She wondered if he knew that home was wherever he took her, as long as he was by her side. She would have been just as happy to live aboard the *Magic*, sailing to different ports around the world, if that had been what he wanted. Being with him was the only home she would ever need.

Damian knew what she was thinking. He had always—well, almost always—been able to read the thoughts in the indigo depths of her eyes. It was even easier these days. Her gaze held a contentment, a happiness, such as he'd never seen before. He felt the emotions of her heart as if they were his own.

Damian had been many things in his thirty-one years. He'd been an orphan. He'd been an indentured servant. He'd been a privateer and a knight of the realm and a planter of sugarcane and a ship's captain. He'd even been a pirate. But not until he'd found the woman beside him had he ever been truly happy.

He turned Cassandra in his arms and kissed her. When he lifted his mouth from hers and looked into her upturned face, he discovered yet another truth.

The magic in his life was not the ship that carried them to Sorcery Bay. The magic was the woman who had taught him to love . . . and who loved him in return.

Watch for Robin Lee Hatcher's heartwarming new Americana Series, beginning in November 1993, and share in the joys and sorrows, loves and losses of the struggling frontier town of Homestead, U.S.A.